The Greek Boxer

A Debt of Honor and the Ludlow Massacre

i

The Greek Boxer

A Debt of Honor and the Ludlow Massacre

by

Steven James Hantzis

Alinet, LLC

Alexandria, Virginia USA

2025

Alinet, LLC
P.O. Box 7353
Alexandria, VA 22307

ISBN: 979-8-9986067-2-4 (paperback)

Content

Preface

The Greek Boxer is mystery in history. I made up the part that is mystery. Let me clue you in without preempting the narrative.

My grandfather, Harry Hantzis, is real. He came to America in 1904 from Chómori, Greece. He went back to Greece in 1912 to fight in the Balkan Wars, earned four commendations for valor, then returned to America in 1914. He boxed under the management of Leo P. Flynn and toured with Jack Dempsey. Harry was the son of a prominent man in Chómori whom you will meet early in the narrative. Harry did not, however, go to Colorado. Therefore, everything he does in that state is fictional. The things he did in Indiana were real.

The Great Colorado Coal War of 1913–1914 is the backdrop for *The Greek Boxer*. Twenty thousand coal miners and their families evicted from company housing survived for two years in tent colonies in the Colorado foothills. Most were immigrants. The Ludlow Massacre, the strike's historical calling card, claimed thirteen women and children. They burned and suffocated, seeking safety in a tent cellar while militia torched their camp.

The miners mobilized against the Rockefeller-owned Colorado Coal and Iron Company and their strikebreakers. The miners' walkout and the mine owners' reaction prompted the most violent domestic clash since the Civil War. The strike was the bloodiest labor dispute in American history. I have annotated historical events thanks to work by scholars and authors who populate the Bibliography.

A word about Eleni or Helen. You will meet her in Chapter 5. She and her predicament are fictional. Tragedy amid the strike, however, was real. Crimes against the strikers went unresolved and unaddressed. Eleni is a composite of these historical atrocities and loose ends.

I've tipped my hand as far as I can. I hope you enjoy *The Greek Boxer* and the history in which I set it. Finally, I exercise authorial license throughout, but I tilt toward the factual. With that said, Chapter 1 is all true.

1

Chapter 1

The road was dangerous and the mountains beautiful. Rockslides blocked all but a narrow passage, and washouts beckoned to the abyss. Serene hillsides specked with tile-roofed homes drew spellbound eyes to the rocky defile, a siren song for the inattentive. We rounded turn after tight turn as deep valleys and mountain passes framed V-shaped vistas of the Gulf of Corinth, miles away and far below.

Our search had begun the day before, but our German roadmap and our limited Greek worked against us. Late in the day, on a slender section of road and with our fuel running low, we flagged a passing driver for directions. We'd made a wrong turn. He pushed his palms together to show that the road narrowed ahead and warned it was dirt, not asphalt, *homus, oxi asphalto*. So, we retreated to Nafpaktos. Then, with a full tank of gas and an early start, we set off again the following morning.

An American Hantzis had not visited Greece in eighty-nine years. My grandfather, Harry, came to America with his older brother in 1904. He returned to Greece in 1912 to fight in the Balkan Wars, then came back to America in 1914. No American Hantzis had been to Greece since. But now, my wife and I were in Greece and close to . . . what? A reunion? A disappointment? A goose chase? It didn't matter. We were in motion. Whatever had inspired our trip and my earlier visit to the Greek Embassy for a translation of my grandfather's military commendations, none of it mattered now. What mattered now was deciphering a German roadmap and finding the tiny village of Chómori (Χόμορη) tucked away in a no-name valley high in the Navpaktian Mountains.

The late September weather was splendid. The air was dry and clear, and the temperature fell into the sixties as we gained altitude. The grape harvest was underway. Trucks and trailers chugged by packed with crates of purple produce. We later found out that the pickups we passed with armed men in camo were wild boar teams. My uncle Alex described their tactics during a laugh-riot dinner that night at the taverna.

We arrived in Platanos in early afternoon and checked our directions with a coffee-drinking smoker fingering *komboloi* on the *plateia*, the town square. He said to turn right at the Chómori sign a mile up the main road. Just like he said, after winding north from Platanos through free-range goats and road rebuilding, we saw the sign and began a corkscrew descent.

The dirt road was narrow and garnished with rockslide boulders bigger than our Korean rental. Just before the village, we came to a widened bend big enough for a vehicle to turn around, currently in use as a bus stop. We'd hit the weekly jackpot.

The bus unloading before us late that Wednesday afternoon ran once a week from Chómori to Nafpaktos. A dozen passengers descended its steps with shopping bags. Most were women, many in their black village dresses. When a young man stepped out, I motioned to him from our car window, and as he approached, I asked, "*Katalavaíneis Angliká?*"

He said, "Speak English? I'm from New York." That's how we met Johnny. And the ball started rolling.

I told Johnny that I believed my grandfather was from Chómori and that my last name was Hantzis, which, in Greek, is pronounced "Ha-gees." I showed Johnny the photo from 1913 of my grandfather in Greek Army uniform. In it, a handsome, clean-shaven Greek soldier wears an olive drab tunic without insignia and stands at the ready. His build is not menacing, but his stare is resolute. An épée bayonet crowns the barrel of his M1903/14 Mannlicher-Schoenauer carbine. His cartridge belt seems curiously ceremonial. Its five-round Mauser charger packs dangle like brass and lead ornamentation. He's holding the weapon at his hips, feet apart. The four fingers of his right hand grip the stock behind the trigger guard, and he's thumbing a fresh ammo pack into the rotary magazine.

Johnny said, "Looks like he means business." Then he stared hard at the photo. "Park the car here and walk down to the plateia and make yourselves comfortable. I'll round up some men, but it might take a while. It's the middle of the day, and these old guys sleep like horses."

Yes, siesta is a Greek word.

Kathy, my lovely tall and trim, blond-haired, blue-eyed Irish wife wore a long skirt and a modest top. I wore cargo pants and a blue work shirt. We looked politely American. We walked past the taverna and to the plateia along the one-lane road through the village, our thoughts suspended in dreamlike anticipation. The view from the plateia overlooking valleys and ravines and the peaks of mountains reaching high into the faultless sky left us speechless. Metal tables and chairs dotted the plateia, and across the cobble road was a fountain dug into the rock face with three spouts gushing spring water. The water of Chómori was a blessing and a curse. During times of peace, it revived the villagers, and during times of war, it was an attractant for enemy forces, the most recent being the Germans.

An obelisk memorial rose on a corner of the plateia. I read down the seventeen engraved names that started in 1912 and ended in 1943. Near the top was *κον. z χαντζησ 1912* or Konstantinos Z Hantzis 1912, a cousin of my grandfather who died early in the Balkan Wars. This was the conflict that my grandfather volunteered for and received four commendations signed by Eleftherios Venizelos, the esteemed founder of modern Greece. So, as the older men arrived on the plateia in ones and twos, my hopes were high that we traveled well.

My grandfather took the name Harry. I knew him as Harry or Grandpa Greek. I believe he took Harry because it sounded good with Hantzis, a lyrical *nom de combattre* for an aspiring boxer, as in "Harry Hantzis, the Greek Boxer." His proper name was Epamenondas Demetriou Hantzis, as I learned from the eldest man in the village, Gus, then ninety. Epamenondas was a fourth-century BCE Theban general with no Greek transliteration. Demetriou is the Greek equivalent of Jimmy or James, my father's first name, and my middle name.

Gus arrived later. By the time he joined the group, the other men had reached a consensus that I was family, but they couldn't put their finger on it. The last name fit, but Hantzis is not an uncommon name in Greece. It means pilgrim, someone who has traveled to the River Jordan and been baptized there in the Orthodox tradition. Gus pulled all the pieces together when I showed him an advertisement from the November 7, 1914, *Indianapolis Recorder*. Over a picture of a young man in sashed boxing trunks read:

> *Home From the Balkan War.*
> *Will Meet Any Middleweight Boxer.*

4

Harry Hantzis, the Greek boxer of this city who left in 1912 to fight in the Balkan Wars, is home again and willing to meet any local middleweight boxer.

Gus squinted at first, then got up from his chair with the help of his cane. There on the plateia, still clutching his cane, he put up his dukes, just as Harry had posed in the photo. That's when everything came together. Epamenondas, also known as Harry, was the second son of Demitris Konstantinos Hantzis, my great-grandfather. Gus, the son of Harry's father's brother, Michael, was my first cousin twice removed. Gus knew Harry Hantzis the Greek Boxer. Gus said that Harry had toured with Jack Dempsey, and when Gus met Harry in New York in the early 1920s, Harry's grip was like a vice.

Demitris, my great-grandfather, built a home that stood just yards away down a path beyond the lamb spit. So, with no further ceremony, Kathy and I were swept along in a warm and welcoming entourage. Our royal treatment would last through the day and night and into the next morning. That's when we packed our rental car with gifts of fruit and baked goods, spanakopita and boiled chestnuts, and trundled back down the mountains to Nafpaktos.

The home was beautiful. It was a simple two-level rectangle set into the hillside, with a well-tended stone courtyard and ancient grape trellises flourishing alongside. Its taupe stonework was intricate and well-preserved and topped with a terracotta roof. Above its green front door, a Greek Orthodox cross and *1881 Σεπτεμβρ 18* were etched into the arched keystone. We arrived two weeks past its 122nd birthday.

My uncle Alex produced a key, and we went inside, followed by our entourage. Alex Theofanis was my uncle Dimitri's best friend. And, as the Greeks would say, a kissing cousin related through marriage. Uncle Dimitri had just returned to Athens after spending the summer in the family home, and we would meet him later. But for now, Alex was our guide, sponsor, host, and a pure pleasure to be around.

Here's a note about Greek family nomenclature. Everybody you're related to, no matter how distant, is an uncle or aunt or cousin. Dimitri, for instance, was my father's cousin, the son of my grandfather's brother, but by Greek standards, he is my uncle.

The interior of the family home was modest. On the courtyard level were two small bedrooms and a larger kitchen and dining room. Family photos hung above the fireplace on the wall in the dining area. The most prominent picture was of a Greek man in his seventies, seated in a simple straight-backed wooden chair. He wore a dark cape, white stockings, shoes tipped with pom-poms, and a square lamb's wool hat. He held a shepherd's crook in one hand and a curved pipe in the other. I stepped closer to the picture, and women in the entourage began kneeling and crossing themselves. The men didn't kneel, but many crossed themselves. Kathy did a double-take and whispered, "That's you."

The reverent murmuring grew to chatter, mostly in Greek, and mostly about giving us the grand tour and setting in motion that night's celebration at the taverna. The women began organizing with practiced efficiency and palpable excitement. They promoted us to Guests of Honor, and all reservations vanished.

For the rest of the afternoon, Kathy and I toured the village with eager escorts. We marveled at the immaculate church with its chestnut woodworking and gold leaf accents. We walked to an overlook where herds of goats and sheep grazed in the valley. As twilight neared, we passed a widow dressed in black on her way down the steep slope with her crook and a pale. She would spend the night tending the livestock. She was descending to ward off wolves. She personified vulnerability.

We walked past a school where the Albanian laborers lived. Since there were no children among the seventy residents of Chómori, the school was now a dormitory. In the fall of 2003, the Greeks didn't trust the Albanians. They made the laborers promise to not say their Muslim prayers inside the school. The Albanians prayed anyway, and the Greeks knew it, but everybody maintained the fiction. Trust grew when the Albanians saved the Greeks from worldwide embarrassment by completing construction of the stalled Olympic venues in time for the 2004 games.

Across from the school, the basketball court, unused and in disrepair, made me sad. In the ancestral village of George Theofanis, a coach who won two Indiana State Basketball Championships at

Indianapolis Shortridge High School, a plaque might have been in order.

Along our walk, Betsy, our tour guide, pointed out vegetation. From a distance, the herbs and fruits—pomegranates, bay trees, apple trees, cherry trees, tomato plants, and grapevines—could be mistaken for scrub. The terrain was rugged, but the Greeks tended it to full potential. What appeared rocky and crude to the lazy eye was fruitful and succulent to the discerning.

Back at the plateia, the sun was setting beyond the mountains, and the air was chilling. A group of men smoked and drank muddy coffee from small cups, Gus among them. Kathy and I told the men we were grateful for their hospitality. They shrugged with the attitude of, what else did you expect? You're in Greece. This is how we treat travelers. This we have done since the days of Zeus, when a humble visitor might transform into a notable deity.

I asked if anyone could confirm a story that had circulated in the American Hantzis family, one that I never heard from Harry: Before Nick and Harry came to America, they traveled to Romania to work on a relative's farm to get the money for passage.

After a bit of translation and murmuring, Gus spoke for the consensus. Rubbing his thumb and forefinger together, he said, "*Oxi*," then something else in Greek that went right past me. Alex translated, "No. Your great-grandfather had money. He was the village assassin."

We all laughed when Alex told the dinner table about hunting wild boar. I asked if he hunted with a side-by-side, double-barrel shotgun, something was lost in translation. Alex said, "My gun has only one."

Stunned, I asked, "You hunt wild boar with a single-shot slug gun?"

Alex clarified his response in Greek, and someone translated. Alex meant his gun had only one barrel, but it was a five-shot, semiautomatic, and the table erupted into laughter. He said he had switched from his trusty double-barrel because he was getting old. Everyone laughed more.

Alex Theofanis was seventy-eight and had already bagged a four-hundred-pound boar by the time Kathy and I arrived. After a fantastic dinner and lots of local table wine, and after the Albanian laborers and village women had danced to lilting clarinet folk music, we spent the night at Alex's house. The road back to Nafpaktos was too dangerous to drive after dark, and we would never insult the hospitality of our relatives and the entire village with an early departure. It was hard enough getting away the next morning.

Our visit had been singular with time collapsed. We arrived at three in the afternoon and left at eleven the next morning, twenty hours dissipating in ether. Events unfolded in exquisite perfection, neither ruffling the temporal fabric nor rippling the still waters of our awareness. I tried to sleep, but through the bedroom window, the stars, proximate and tangible in the velvet void, kindled a restive myth in a distant but familiar cosmos.

Chapter 2

Cordite seared his nostrils, and his ears clanged from the pounding artillery. The report of his rifle and those of his squad punctuated the cacophony. Prone on his belly on the muddy hillside, Harry sighted a target through the pall, fired, and chose another. Then it was his squad's turn. The sergeant, a grizzled veteran, fearless and tall, stood and waved his arm. The squad rose from cover and ran with their shoulders forward in a crouch. He heard a cry to his right, and his comrade stumbled to the ground with a bullet in his thigh. A Greek had shot him from the rear. Harry charged up the rocky slope twenty yards, then dropped for cover with his squad. His cover was a bloated corpse of a horse the Turks used to pull artillery. The reek of the decaying animal subsumed the cordite.

Harry sighted another target, exhaled a deep breath, and squeezed the Mannlicher's trigger. His aim, aided by resting his rifle on the dead horse, was true. The Turk, forty yards up the hill, rolled away from the bolder formerly his cover. The Turk lay still, face to the October sky. Harry watched the advancing Greek squad drop for cover, and then it was again his turn at the deadly game of leapfrog. The game persisted as the Turks fell back.

The Turks retreated until they could no longer. The Greeks were on their flanks. Another Greek unit advancing on the other side of the mountain blocked their escape. Harry knew they'd fight. Even outnumbered and disorganized, they would fight. He'd seen it before. The Turks were fighters, just like the Greeks. The Greeks would have to kill half of them before the others surrendered.

The Greeks fixed bayonets for the coup de grâce. The blades had crowned many Mannlichers before this order. The hand-to-hand fighting up the mountain had seen to that. A Greek officer raised his sword, then brought it down with a powerful slash. All the Greeks rose and ran at the defenders, screaming at the top of their lungs. Harry met his target, a young Turk, a teenager. Harry was a twenty-three-year-old, well-fed, American Greek trained as a boxer. Harry had the physical advantage, but the Turk held the high ground. The Turk deflected Harry's first thrust with the breech of his Mauser, but Harry was fast and pulled his razor-sharp blade back and across the young man's abdomen. When the Turk grabbed his side, Harry bashed his temple with the steel butt plate of the Mannlicher. The Turk fell to the ground, and Harry drove the bayonet into the center of his chest. The Turk looked stunned and, for an instant, surprised. Then the young soldier went slack, his eyes wide open, his pupils dilated, and his orbs filled with blackness. Harry saw in them the shadow of death. Harry withdrew and moved to the next defender. The bloody engagement was over in minutes. The outnumbered Turks were fighting far from home for a decaying empire. The Greeks were fighting for Greece.

As night fell, the fortunate Turks retreated under cover of darkness and pelting rain. As they did, the 11th Infantry Regiment of the 4th Infantry Division completed its mission, secured its objective, and made camp awaiting further orders. The Greeks tended to their wounded and dead, then the Turkish wounded and dead. They encamped under the shelter of rock ledges. They boiled water for coffee, ate some crusty bread and cheese, and later, they tried to sleep on soggy bedrolls spelling one another on guard duty.

While the soldiers were building small fires under rock outcrops to make their coffee, a runner from 5th Infantry arrived at the rear and sought the commanding officer's tent. There, he briefed the officers and staff, and the word quickly spread to the enlisted men.

Harry and his surviving squad were boiling coffee in a small circle around a cooking fire when their sergeant walked up. The man was from the south, Harry thought Tripoli, and his dialect and idioms were sometimes hard to follow. The lanky, mustached soldier said, "The Turks have gone. They retreat as we speak, and the pass will be ours tomorrow. The 5th Division lost a lot of men from the shelling before they got into the mountains. They are stalled on the right flank. But the Turks are running like rabbits back to their holes."

Harry asked, "What of the Evzones to the west?" Harry was thinking about his cousin, Konstantinos, who was a sergeant in the elite unit. The Evzones were far to the west to flank the Turks at Aliakmon.

The tall soldier shrugged, "It is far away, and there is no word. The Evzones will be victorious, or they will die with honor."

To this, Harry and the others in the circle nodded and raised their metal mugs.

The Battle of Sarantaporo Pass was the first significant engagement for the Greek Army in the Balkan Wars of 1912–13. Not only did the Greeks secure the gateway to western and central Macedonia, but they expelled the demons of defeat that lingered from the Thirty Days' War of 1897.[1] Harry Hantzis received a commendation for his bravery in this battle, and he would win three more for fighting at Katerini, Sorovits, and Korytsa.

Harry and his older brother, Nick, had been part of the epic emigration from Greece at the turn of the twentieth century. During these years, roughly one-sixth of all Greeks, mostly men, came to America.[2] Harry and Nick arrived in Indianapolis in 1904, joining a succession of Navpaktian Greeks already settled there. In 1912, Harry and forty-five thousand other American Greeks returned to fight in the Balkan Wars.[3] After his service in the Greek Army, after the liberation of Thrace, Epirus, the Aegean Islands, and Crete, Harry briefly returned to Indianapolis.

Chapter 3

The two men leaned on the starboard railing and shook their heads. Dimitri said, "Do you think that is their bait? Surely, they are not throwing back their catch?"

Harry said, "I don't know. I have never seen this before. Not even the Greek fishermen behave this way. And I have seen them fight with knives at the harbor in Nafpaktos because another sailed across their nets. They never drew blood, but they made a show of it."

Dimitri responded, "These are Spaniards, so anything is possible. Is it a Catholic holiday?"

Harry leaned farther over the railing to get a better view as the sun sank into the sea off the ship's bow. "I don't think so. They don't look angry. Some tradition perhaps? Maybe an offering to Poseidon to attract the fish? Perhaps they are drunk!"

Both men laughed.

The two young Greeks watched the spectacle as the oblivious RMS *Carpathia* made a steady fifteen knots through the Straits of Gibraltar. Dozens of small fishing boats east of Isla de Tarifa maneuvered close to each other, and their crews tossed fish back and forth. The moment perplexed the Greeks. As the light dimmed, and the ship sailed away, the scene became foggy and dreamlike. Its humor and oddity were relief from their months in the mountains fighting Turks.

Dimitri asked, "What do you plan to do when you get back to America?"

Harry looked at the slender veteran from Crete who he met boarding in Patra, "My brother, Nick, is in Indianapolis. I will go there and work as a butcher at Kingan. Do you know that name? It is a big slaughterhouse started by Irishmen. We are saving to open a business, a restaurant. And you, Dimitri, where will a son of Crete be found in America?"

Dimitri looked away and paused before answering, "I will return to Colorado. There we work in the mines, but it is not good. There are other men from Samaria there. Better I am a butcher in, how do you say . . . Indian-o-polis? I believe we pass through the city on the train from New York to Denver."

Harry asked, "What does your father do in Crete?"

Dimitri answered, "He tends orange trees, some lemon trees, some olives, and he has a small herd of goats. His goats are distinctive because he breeds them with the wild *kri-kri*. Young, they are the best tasting in Crete. You and I are alike, Harry, are we not? We both come from places where we cannot smell the sea, and the hills make our legs ache."

Harry chuckled.

Dimitri continued, "My father is a strong man and well respected in Samaria, but you are the son of an assassin, are you not? I heard that from another man from Nafpaktos, an Evzone, his father was the kapetánios of the city."

Harry shrugged, "Yes, my father is an assassin, but he tends grapes and goats. He sells a small amount of wine, and people pay him to right wrongs. He, too, is a strong man, and it breaks my heart to return to America and leave him and the family behind. But my brother and I will return someday with all the money America can provide, and we will live out our lives hunting and talking of old times."

Dimitri said softly, "I'm sorry for gossiping like a village widow, but the man from Nafpaktos said you received four commendations signed by Prime Minister Venizelos. Is it true?"

"Yes, but I was not the bravest, only the luckiest."

Dimitri pried further, "Can I see them? Venizelos freed Crete. He is himself a son of Crete. He was born in Mournies, near Chania. He is a great man and a man for history."

Harry asked, "Can you read the old language?"

Dimitri assured him he had learned ancient Greek in Samaria, where he went to school through the tenth grade.

Harry said his papers were in his second-class cabin, and Dimitri was welcome to see them there. On the walk to Harry's cabin, Dimitri, a few years younger than Harry, asked many questions about Harry's father and the duties of a Nafpaktian assassin. Harry was circumspect and talked about it reluctantly, but Dimitri's curiosity was unbounded.

Dimitri asked, "In the villages of Crete, we have headmen who right wrongs and see to the–he searched for the right word–*eiréné*."

Dimitri had chosen a biblical word that meant not only peace or peace of mind, but wholeness.

Harry nodded, "A Nafpaktian assassin is the same man. It is a great honor and a burden, but a village needs such a man. Before, when the Turks ruled Greece, the pasha set Greek against Greek by awarding someone property or rights that belonged to another. The Turks were clumsy but good at dividing Greeks, especially the ones with little or no education and the ones who thought they could court favor with the pasha. If a Turk disrupted the eiréné, then it was the honor-bound duty of the assassin to put things in order. Turkish law was no law at all. The Turks hated the assassin because he was the man the Greeks looked up to."

Dimitri asked in a guarded tone, "Has your father ever killed anyone?"

Harry stopped and turned in the ship's wood-paneled hallway, looking straight at Dimitri. "These are matters no one discusses. All there is to know is that to kill another Greek, that man must also have killed a Greek. Turks, it's another matter. When the assassin accepts the honor of his position, he accepts an oath, a blood oath. Do you remember studying the Ephebic Oath?"

Harry was referring to the ancient oath sworn by sons of Athenian citizens upon induction into the military academy, the Ephebic College.

Dimitri nodded. "*Naí.*"

Harry continued, "Then the oath of an assassin is much the same. It can never be broken, must always be honored, and the shame that falls on a failed assassin is unspeakable. It is a fate worse than death."

As they approached Harry's cabin, Dimitri asked, "Will you continue as your father? Will you return to Greece and take his honor?"

"Only time will tell. For now, I will return to Indianapolis and be a butcher and start boxing again. This time I'll make the 160-pound middleweight class thanks to the hills of Albania."

Both men laughed as they entered the cabin.

Later that evening, by a dim light, Harry started a letter to a family he did not know. As he wrote, the words came from his heart, simple and strong.

Chapter 4

The *Carpathia* rocked in the Atlantic swells, first bow to stern, then side to side. In the dark of night and the absence of time, Harry dreamed of things the purgative Atlantic could never wash away; things he would take to his grave.

The Greeks captured Korytsa on the Albanian frontier on December 7, 1912. Korytsa was to be the Turkish bulwark in the western front defending northeast Ioannina, the urban center of Epirus, and Turkish access to the Ionian Sea. The Turks concentrated twenty-four thousand retreating troops around Korytsa, and it was, for them, a last stand.[4]

The village of Dvoran six miles south of Korytsa set astride the Qare Pass, a route ten thousand retreating Turks had to control so they wouldn't be flanked and surrounded. Defense of the narrow defile was a matter of survival. A detachment of Greek Division V advanced on the front, and 4th Battalion Evzones moved east to flank the Turks and attack their rear.

Fighting was fierce. The Turks shelled the frontal attack, and many Greeks fell. As Harry advanced with Division V, his unit attacked the left flank of the Turks in the ravine. The Turks were dug in, and the Greeks fought uphill. As the fight wore on, Harry's platoon was again ordered to advance. Bloody as the fighting was, the Turks were giving ground and securing the pass was paramount.

Harry crouched with four infantrymen and climbed the stony slope into a hail of bullets. Suddenly, the machine gun fell silent, and the nest of Turks began yelling at each other. The Greeks thought the gun had jammed. It was a trap.

The Greeks rose to charge, and the Turks leveled the 7.65mm Maxim.[5] The two soldiers on Harry's right fell like stones, and as the gun swept its deadly field toward Harry, Harry aimed his Mannlicher. But before he could fire, a towering Greek from the Evzone battalion shoved him to the ground. The bullets went over Harry's body, missing by only inches. The Evzone took the bullets meant for Harry. It was the soldier's face that Harry saw in his dreams. His face and the line of cerise rosettes stitched across his chest.

16

Six more Evzones from the flanking force arrived at the rear of the machine gun and charged with bayonets. They killed all four of the Turks in the nest, even the officer who tried to surrender. When they finished, they came to Harry and his comrades, and to their dead brother. Harry was shaken. He couldn't talk. One Evzone grabbed him by the shoulders. The tall soldier looked Harry in the eyes and asked if he was injured. Harry shook his head. When the Evzone left him to tend a wounded Greek, Harry asked, "What is his name? Where is he from?" as he stared at his lifeless savior.

The Evzone returned to Harry, "Why do you want to know his name? He was an Evzone. This is all that matters."

"He saved my life, and I am in debt to his family. This is the way of my family."

The Evzone said, "Our comrade's name is Vasilios Pendagiotis. He is from Crete, and his family is from the village of Loutra in Rethymno."

Chapter 5

The slaughterhouse smelled of copper and the sweat of men toiling close together on the crowded floor. Hundreds of men lunged and slashed in quick and determined moves with impossibly sharp knives as they set on an equal number of hog carcasses. A muddled cacophony of Greek and German and Polish and Old Country Irish filled the brick plant reverberating through the steel girders and off the metal roofing. The men talked but never took their eyes off their work. To do so was to carve oneself.

Harry was a butcher who had worked his way into the best paying craft of his industry, moving up from slaughterer and trimmer. Harry prepared the choice cuts of meat from the trimmed carcass. From his wooden bench where he worked shoulder-to-shoulder with others of his craft, the meat moved to packaging. From there it was sold fresh, smoked, salted, pickled, and canned. Harry no longer cut, trimmed, skinned, sorted, washed viscera, and rendered edible from the offal. He was now at the top of his craft. Although most of the blood spilled earlier in the disassembly, the butchering floor was slick with it and the smell of copper.

Harry worked the noon-to-midnight shift, and when he returned home, his brother, Nick, was waiting for him. Harry thought it was unusual for Nick to be awake since Nick's shift started at six the next morning. The brothers lived in a one-bedroom rented apartment on the near west side of Indianapolis and walked to the Kingan plant.

Nick handed Harry an unopened letter. "Father Hatzimarkou wanted me to give this to you."

Nick was bigger and older than Harry, and while both men were tall, Nick beat Harry by an inch. Nick, who had stayed in America during the war, was heavier and he looked askance at his brother when he handed over the envelope. Nick didn't recognize the village or family name.

Nick went on, "I went to church this afternoon for the funeral of Yorgo's wife, and the priest handed it to me then. He said it arrived two days ago. I'm surprised he didn't bring it by and mooch some coffee and sweets."

Harry nodded as he took the letter and read it out loud.

18

11 January 1914
Dear Mr. Harry Hantzis,

My name is Eydokia Pendagiotis, and I am the sister of Vasilios. I am writing to you to thank you for your warm and comforting letter to our family upon his death in battle. Vasilios was always a brave man, and now that he is with God, he can enjoy his reward.

The faith of our family has been tested much in recent days. Only last week we learned of another family member taken from us. Our sister Eleni was murdered in the state of Colorado in America. She was a young mother with her first son and only married for one year. Many of the Greeks from Crete have gone to Colorado in America to work as miners. Eleni was there with her husband, Alex, and the work there is dangerous.

The Greek miners and others started a protest this past fall and have refused to work. They are living in tents in the mountains. We don't know what happened to Eleni, but Alex wrote she died defending their baby. That is all I know. Alex said that the Colorado officials have not raised a hand to find who is responsible for this cowardly act. I know that you and your family are givers of justice. I understand your father was a lawgiver. I know this because we have a dear friend of the family, Dimitri, who is in Colorado and speaks of you.

If it is God's will, Harry Hantzis, could you please go to Colorado and find who killed my sister and bring justice? I know this is much to ask, but your family and our family are now joined by God's will. I pray you can help and allow Eleni's soul to rest in peace for eternity and lift a curse from the family.

Please find Father Paschopoulos at the church on 37th Avenue and Lafayette Street in Denver. He is in touch with Alex and your shipmate, Dimitri Papas. Father Paschopoulos married Alex and Eleni, and he is a good friend of the Greeks in Colorado. He will arrange for you to travel to the camp at Segundo.

In the bond of Christ,
Eydokia Pendagioti

Harry lifted his eyes from the page toward Nick. Nick looked puzzled and shrugged his shoulders. The brothers remained silent for a moment; then Nick said to Harry, "It is a debt, is it not? Her brother saved your life?"

Harry spoke softly, "I would be rotting in the hills of Epirus if not for Vasilios. I dream of that time more often than I dream of home. It may be his spirit reminding me we are joined."

Nick nodded, "It is an urgent matter, brother. You should go soon. If you need to find a killer, it's better to leave tomorrow than to wait for memories to fade.

"Do you know anything about this protest? I know the syndicalists are strong in America, just like at Kingan. Do you know anything about mining? There will be much you do not know and things you have never seen before, will there not?"

Harry nodded.

Nick went on with his questions. "What will you do about your boxing matches? And your job?"

"The boxing can wait. I will telegraph Leo Flynn in New York and tell him my trip is urgent. He is my manager, let him manage. Nick, you can tell Jerry Murphy that I cannot spar with him or Jack Dillon until we finish this matter. As for Kingan, they will pack hogs with or without me."

"I have read about this demonstration, this labor strike. On my return trip to America, another Greek soldier told me that the mines in Colorado are not good. The company does not respect the miners. But of Colorado . . . I only know it has mountains bigger than Macedonia and Epirus.

"I will go to the station tomorrow and buy a ticket. When I return, we will once again have two to save for our business. I am sorry to leave you, brother, but this is a debt I must pay. The honor of our family is our reward."

20

Chapter 6

Harry took a bus to Indianapolis Union Station at nine the next morning and bought a one-way ticket to Denver, Colorado. His first leg was on the New York Central's Big Four line to Kansas City. Then on to Denver aboard the Santa Fe Railroad's Chicago Fast Mail. As he settled into his berth, he unfolded a copy of the *Indianapolis News*, and on page three, he read:

More Regulations of Labor Disputes Urged

Secy. Wilson Would Limit Use of Guards

Submits Annual Report

Washington, February 4–The recommendation that Congress enact laws to regulate the use of firearms and the employment of armed guards and private detectives in labor disputes, so far as they enter into interstate relations and are under control of federal authorities, is made in the annual report of William R. Wilson, Secretary of Labor, submitted to President Wilson today.

The secretary declares that the use of firearms in this "species of private warfare in connection with labor troubles calls for serious consideration."

"Groups of men," says the report, "on both sides, without military or police authority for it, have used firearms with fatal effect in the coal strike in southern Colorado. These arms and the ammunition have doubtless been procured through interstate commerce, and many of the armed men are said to have been imported into Colorado from other states through a business concern engaged commercially across state lines in supplying corporations with an armed and trained private soldiery of police in numbers running into hundreds and even thousands."[6]

Chapter 7

Harry followed the sun to an unknown land and an unknown history. America was not Greece with its ancient longings and set-in-marble identity. America was in flux, defining itself, something the Greeks had achieved millennia before. In Colorado, an American character forged as owners and workers defended their classes and discovered their power. Harry would find the conflict familiar in form if foreign in contemplation.

In 1913, the torrent of change in Eastern Colorado mixed mighty currents: the United Mine Workers of America, the Greeks, ambitious politicians, and John D. Rockefeller Jr. In history, as in a river, opposing currents give rise to turbulence. For Greeks, the inventors of history, the surge sweeps all before it.

In 1913, history was in motion and harkening. Had the Greeks not risen against the Turks in 1821, would national identity and love of honor, *philotimo*, lead the Colorado Greeks to be so clannish, brave, and impulsive? Had the Balkan Wars, the Turkomachia, not seared the myth of an invincible Greek Army in the minds of Colorado's young warriors, would they have pushed unwise tactics?[7]

Greeks brought to America a passion for history and little trade unionism.[8] Many militant Greeks of 1913 arrived in Colorado as scabs during the 1903 strike.[9] They dreamed a common ambition of returning to the Old Country with money and stories, finding a bride, and starting a business.[10]

Commercial interests, Colorado mining companies foremost among them, used slick advertising, charming photographs, and hollow promises to recruit cheap labor. Lonely Greeks reinforced this pitch by writing to families, exaggerating their accomplishments in America. The Greeks of Colorado were mostly bachelors and young. They knew Suleiman, Orkhan, and Murad. They knew nothing of Eugene Debs, Mother Jones, or Bill Haywood. Their notion of trade unionism was avenger and avenged. Their political outlook was not progressive, but typically that of village conservatism with disdain for modern ideas.

The English and Welsh were the first to reach Colorado, leaving British mines during the economic depression of the 1870s.

Most were experienced miners and used their knowledge to develop the western properties. They soon became foremen and bosses.[11] The English-speaking miners brought a social order and a rich oral history gained from mining coal for hundreds of years. These workers defined industrial culture by bringing class identity, myriad superstitions, and the dream of a union.[12]

To the first wave of Greeks arriving in 1903, striking an employer was unheard of.[13] By taking the jobs of militant Italians and Englishmen, Greeks joined the dissonant succession in the Colorado coalfields. Divide and conquer worked well for the owners. The Greeks kept to themselves as much by choice as by manipulation. They called non-Greeks *xeni,* foreigners.

On September 17, 1912, the Western Federation of Miners (WFM) struck the Utah Copper Company in the mines around Bingham. Militant Cretans were at the heart of the struggle. They demanded the removal of a notorious labor agent. The Greeks communicated news of the strike from their coffeehouse in Bingham. But in October 1912, the talk in Greek coffeehouses was not of the Bingham strike but of war with Turkey.

The Turkish war united and excited the Greeks as no event since the War of Liberation in 1821. In it rang the opportunity to consummate the *Great Idea*, the resurrection of Byzantine glory. Two hundred and thirty-two Greeks left Colorado to serve in the Balkan Wars. Forty-five-thousand American Greeks would return to fight.[14]

The Greeks and their allies—Montenegro, Serbia, and Bulgaria—advanced rapidly. By November 8, Thessaloniki was in Greek hands. By November 17, the Turks were in full retreat, abandoning fifty thousand soldiers in their fortress at Monastir. On the same day, Greek, Italian and Slav miners in Fredrick, Colorado refused to work. The leader of the Greeks was a lean young Cretan, Ilias Anastasios Spantidakis, Louis Tikas.

Colorado once claimed the nation's largest bituminous coal reserves, over twenty-five thousand square miles, with half buried too deep for profitable extraction. By the turn of the twentieth century, the southern fields of Colorado was the biggest concentration of coking coal production west of the Mississippi.

The WFM ignited the union movement in Colorado and throughout the western United States. Although the United Mine Workers of America (UMWA) would lead and finance the 1913–14 Colorado Coal Strike, much of its temper came from the militant WFM. Campaigns like Coeur d'Alene in 1892, Leadville in 1896, Cripple Creek in 1894 and 1903, and the Telluride strike of 1903 set the tone. The WFM organized immigrant and American workers equally, and in 1905, the WFM was the driving force behind the founding convention of the Industrial Workers of the World (IWW).

The WFM's membership base was in the hard rock, precious mineral industry of the Rocky Mountains, while the mines of Eastern Colorado were predominately coal. As the UMWA organized westward, they bumped into the WFM in Colorado, and relations between the unions proved fractious. Unity between the organizations proved elusive but possible. During the second Cripple Creek strike of 1903, the UMWA actively supported the WFM.

In 1903, local UMWA delegates voted to strike the state's largest coal company, the Rockefeller-owned Colorado Fuel and Iron (CF&I). WFM's metalliferous laborers, already engaged in a bitter struggle, welcomed the UMWA coal miners' support. Although many UMWA demands were already law, CF&I smashed the strike. The company immediately evicted union supporters and their families, hauled in scabs, arrested organizers, and terrorized all who fought back.

General John Chase commanded the Colorado National Guard and declared military law. Chase rounded up four to five hundred strikers, loaded them into cattle cars, and deported them to the prairies of Kansas and the deserts of New Mexico. The union abandoned the strike in October 1904, leaving bitter memories and smoldering resentment. The episode saddled the citizens of Colorado with a debt of $950,000 for military services rendered.[15]

In early 1907, the UMWA International Board voted to organize the Colorado coalfields. In the spring of that year, the imposing John Lawson arrived in Walsenburg in the heart of the southern fields to begin the campaign.[16]

Lawson was thirty years old and had grown up laboring in mines near Mount Carmel, Pennsylvania. He was over six feet tall, with broad shoulders and a commanding presence. Lawson began working as a breaker boy when he was eight years old, and his father was a member of the Knights of Labor. Lawson's first strike was a walkout of mine boys, slate-pickers. They quit work to attend a traveling circus.[17]

Colorado coal mining concentrated in two areas: the northern fields located north and west of Denver, and the southern fields in the state's southeastern quarter. In 1913, there were roughly fourteen thousand coal miners in Colorado, 70 percent speaking a first language other than English.[18] The southern fields were the largest in production and employment and made up the strategic aim of the UMWA.

In June 1908, Lawson diverted the attention of coal operators from the southern fields by demanding and winning a contract for the northern mines. There the miners were mostly English speaking, and many owned homes.[19] In 1908, the northern mine owners signed an agreement that provided for a union shop, pay raises, tool expense improvements, and the eight-hour day.

In 1910, the union voted to demand a 5.5 percent wage increase, improved working conditions, and a half-holiday on Saturdays for the northern fields of Colorado. The operators, under pressure from CF&I, resisted the union's proposals and three thousand northern miners threw aside their tools and began a strike that lasted through 1914.

Colorado's majestic landscape was an ironic backdrop for the poverty, abuse, and hardship facing miners and their families. In 1902, John D. Rockefeller Sr. bought control of the Colorado Fuel and Iron Company and the Victor Fuel Company, the primary producers in the southern fields. While political power was essential to the Rockefellers, it was more than merely a matter of paying off sheriffs and judges. In fact, they frowned upon blatant graft. As Lamont Bowers, Chairman of the CF&I board, explained in a letter to Rockefeller Jr. about why CF&I kept large deposits in Colorado banks when higher interest applied elsewhere:

*Without our direct solicitation, we are able to secure
the cordial cooperation of the wealthy officers and
stockholders of several influential banks who, for self-interest
or for the common good, or both, will give us their support.
The four largest banks in Denver had twelve or fifteen
directors who play a mighty important part in this state in
dictating its laws, notwithstanding the enormous majority of
the laboring class.* [20]

There were two types of towns in the coalfields of Colorado:
hub cities and coal camps. Lafayette, Louisville, Walsenburg,
Trinidad, Crested Butte, Oak Creek, and Paonia were all incorporated
hub cities. [21] These cities experienced rapid growth as coal production
mounted. In 1913, CF&I operated twenty-seven coal towns, governing
the lives of roughly twelve thousand miners and their families. The
company owned these isolated camps lock, stock, and barrel. They
owned the land, schools, churches, saloons, cemeteries, the supply and
grocery stores, and the miners' homes.

Coal sales boomed around 1900, and companies began looking
for ways to increase productivity. The owners replaced the most
ramshackle camps with "model" towns, hoping that "clean living"
would make for healthier workers who worked harder. Conditions
were far from progressive, despite the picture painted by the
company's public relations department. [22] Miners paid exorbitant rents
and usually shared quarters with other families. A miner and his family
faced eviction with only three days' notice. Most miners and their
families lived in austere housing. [23] Constructed with clapboard walls
and thin-planked floors with leaking roofs and broken windows, "hut"
was a charitable description. The better, wood-framed structures went
to American-born, German, and Welsh miners, while new immigrants
fared worse.

Coke ovens, power plants, mine tipples, and breaker houses
spewed a pall of pollution over the camps. The smog was so toxic that
flowers and vegetables could not grow. Contaminated drinking water
led to 157 cases of company-reported typhoid fever on CF&I
properties in 1912. [24] Miners' children grew conditioned to their

environment and often went to work in the mines as soon as they could shoulder tools.

In 1912, the average wage per worker in Colorado coal mines came to $640.70 a year, paid in company scrip. A Greek or other Southern European worker was worth $1.75 a day, while they paid a German or Welshman $2.50 to $2.75.[25] Wages of $1.60 a day in company scrip equaled $1.00 a day in US currency.[26] With scrip, miners purchased overpriced groceries at "pluck me" stores, paid for doctors and medicine, and bought mining tools and supplies. Most company stores operated at a 20 percent rate of return.[27]

In the depth of the mines, there was fierce competition for cars that carried coal to the surface. Each new immigrant group received the worst work locations and the least access to the mule-drawn hampers.[28] The coal car drivers called "muleskinners" were among the first mineworkers paid by the hour. They often supplemented their low wages with mandatory tips.[29]

Owners regarded miners as independent contractors with pay based on the amount of coal mined. After a miner bribed a foreman for a good dig and tipped a muleskinner for his hamper, he was still at the mercy of the company's checkweighman. The scales were notoriously incorrect. Miners struggled for fifty years to gain the right to monitor the weigh boss and standardize the scales.[30]

Explosions and fires killed hundreds of workers, but most fatalities were solitary events. Coal cars, roof falls, machinery, or electrocution killed most mineworkers.[31] Coroners' juries, composed of superintendents, engineers, local shopkeepers, and other company dependents, investigated mine accidents and assigned blame. All 1,663 miners killed in Colorado between 1884 and 1912 were judged to have died of personal negligence or that of their coworkers, regardless of the actual causes.[32] Burial societies were rare, and the owners provided neither death benefits nor insurance policies. The dead returned to the surface with their shift, and their bodies went by cart to their widows. Cremation of unmarried men's bodies in coke ovens was legend.[33]

On April 1, 1913, Turkey abandoned claims to Crete and Greek national aspirations soared. On that day, before heading to the Pike

View mine on union business, Louis Tikas took out citizenship papers in Denver. Tikas stayed in touch with the UMWA following his leadership of the Fredrick strike. He would go to work for the union again in the fall. In August, while surveying Greeks in the southern fields, Tikas sent this report to district headquarters:

> *They are ready at any time unless conditions improve to engage in an industrial war and to fight, just as their fathers and brothers in the fatherland have fought the Turks until their freedom has been obtained, so these men are ready even at the sacrifice of their lives to fight until their industrial freedom has been obtained.*[34]

And fight they would. To forestall the union's momentum, CF&I raised wages by 10 percent in April 1912. In early 1913, the company abolished the scrip system, instituted an eight-hour day, and adopted a semimonthly pay schedule.[35] The concessions proved too little, too late. The fall of 1913 brought frosty night air and a sobering sense of the impending showdown. Suspicious mine guards broke up meetings of fraternal societies, church groups, and social events.[36] To the miners, the issue was not would there be a strike but when. The issue was not will there be bloodshed, but whose blood would spill. As a last-ditch attempt to avert a strike, United States Secretary of Labor, William B. Wilson, sought a conference with Rockefeller Jr. The secretary was rebuffed.

Surging political rivalries, the miners' rising expectations, and pressure from socialists roiled internal UMWA politics. In December 1912, the union's executive board ordered the campaign forward at full dispatch and committed funding. In the mining camps, John Lawson worked to restrain his fervent troops until it was time for battle.

Chapter 8

Harry walked out of Denver's Union Station to a line of taxis. The morning was chilly but sunny, and the air was thin and dry. He needed to meet the priest, but it was too early. Father Paschopoulos would be busy with morning service. As Harry climbed into the cab, he asked the driver to take him to a Greek café. The driver, a stocky Englishman wearing a flat tweed cap, thought for a moment. He said he knew a small coffee shop in the Greek neighborhood. Harry said that would do. They pulled away from Union Station, driving southeast on 17th Street, and the cab passed under a massive steel arch with the word WELCOME in electric lights.

It was a quick ride to upper Curtis Street. There, the driver stopped at a small storefront with a painted sign hung over the doorway, KAFENEION. The driver said, "This is the Greek neighborhood. In the summer, I see men sitting outside drinking coffee and talking. Will this do, gov?"

Harry thanked the man, paid his fare, and walked into the business carrying his travel bag. Harry wore a long gray cloth coat, a black Borsalino Alessandria fedora, polished dress shoes, and a gray wool suit and matching vest over a white shirt and a black necktie. He looked Midwestern. Harry thought men on the streets of Denver resembled cowboys in their wide-brimmed hats, loose pants, boots, and ponchos.

Harry entered the kafeneion and saw two men. A big man behind the counter was polishing cups. An older man sat at one of the six tables drinking coffee and reading a newspaper. On the left wall were a tattered map of Greece and a German clock. On the back wall hung photographs of, Harry presumed, the owner and his family. On the right wall hung a large mirror behind the countertop above the coffee brikis and a four-burner stove. The faded walls were brown stucco, and the front of the business was all windows and a door.

Harry sat his bag at a table and approached the counter. He addressed the man he presumed was the owner. *"Ti kanete?"*

The owner smiled. "I'm fine. And you? What can I get for you, brother?"

Harry asked for a Greek coffee, *metrios*, and a ham and cheese sandwich. The owner said, "Coming right up. Mama Fofo made the kataifi fresh this morning." As he spoke, he plated a portion and slid it toward Harry, saying, "You should try one."

Harry smelled the honey and cinnamon, caught a whiff of orange, and nodded.

The owner introduced himself, "I'm George, George Stergiopolous."

Harry didn't recognize the family name, but he knew from the kataifi that the family was from the Peloponnese.

George went on, "My family is from Perigiali, just west of Corinth. And you, brother, what's your name and where are you from?"

Harry introduced himself and said his family was from the village of Chómori in the Nafpaktian Mountains.

George, an animated host, threw up his enormous arms, "Polý kalá! A hillbilly Greek! Well, you're welcome here, Harry Hantzis. What brings you to Denver? A town of many hillbillies and not all Greeks!"

Harry told George that he lived in Indianapolis with his brother.

George pressed his friendly interrogation. "What brings you to the Wild West, Harry? Are you looking for work?"

Harry shook his head and paused for a moment before answering. He didn't want to lie. But he didn't know who to trust with the delicate information about his purpose. "I'm meeting a friend. We have business."

With the use of the term business, George sensed he reached the limit of his inquiry. He tacked, "Where are you staying?"

Harry said, "I hope to travel on after I speak with Father Paschopoulos."

George said, "Now, there is a good man, the father. He's been here long enough. He knows everyone and everything about the Greeks. He's not stuck up or full of himself like some priests. He's been a proper friend. When do you plan to talk to him?"

Harry said he hoped to talk to him later in the morning. George cautioned, "He's preparing for a funeral. They're burying one of those

30

miners the goons shot south of here. The Greeks are fighting another Turkomachia down there."

Harry said, "I have read about the strike, but I know little."

George, continuing to boil coffee and polish cups, spoke to Harry over his shoulder. "It started on September twenty-third. I remember because that was my cousin Xantippe's name day. Twenty thousand miners and their families said to hell with Rockefeller. They moved out of company houses and into fourteen tent towns spread all over southeastern Colorado. It was a mess, twenty-some nationalities, they couldn't speak a common language. They should all learn Greek, no? It's a foundation language!" He laughed.

"Well, the first night of the strike it snowed, and the bachelor Greeks slept outside with the horses. Then things got heated. The miners in Segundo tried to retrieve their belongings from company houses, and the mine guards blocked them with guns. They went back a second time and got pushed and shoved and threatened. Then five Greeks got their guns and took over a company footbridge. They told the guards they'd blow up the bridge if they didn't allow the miners to get their things. So, this guard, Bob Lee, a guy they hated . . . he'd forced himself on miner's wives while the men were working . . . he tried to ride his horse against them. The Greeks surrounded him and when Lee drew his rifle, a Greek shot him through the neck with a 12-gauge. Those boys are now hiding in New Mexico with a bounty on their heads. Things went downhill from there and it's probably going to get worse."

George racked the cups on a shelf above the stove, then summarized, "The miners are mad. They're disrespected, and the company thinks they can push them around with thugs and guards.

"But it won't work because the miners have a secret weapon . . . the Greeks! A lot of these boys just came back from the Old Country and they ain't afraid of goons with guns. They ain't afraid of nothing. Rockefeller and his goons think they're tough. They ain't nothing compared to the Turks.

"Did you go back to fight?"

Harry nodded.

31

George said, "I could tell. You look like you can handle yourself. I would have gone back, but I had to take care of my mother, Fofo. I sent money."

Harry nodded again.

George went on, "Well, then you know what I'm talking about. The Greeks have seen a lot worse than this."

Then George leaned closer to Harry. "Like that old boy over there." And he nodded his head toward the well-dressed older man at the corner table, the only other customer in the kafeneion.

George went on in hushed tones, "He's an 1897 veteran, a kapetánios, and he lost his son in Epirus just last year."

Harry slowly looked over at the man and said to George, *"Me synchoreíte."* Pardon me.

Harry walked from the counter to the table where the older man was reading a Greek newspaper. When the man looked up with deeply set eyes, Harry again said, "Me synchoreíte."

The older man nodded, and Harry went on, "I'm Harry Hantzis from Chómori. The owner told me you are a kapetánios, and that you lost your son in the war."

Again, the man only nodded, his stare steady.

"Sir. I, too, was in Epirus and I can tell you that the Greeks fought bravely. They honored their families and villages. I am sorry that your son gave his life."

The older man took a deep breath. *"Efcharistó."* Thank you.

The older man paused before going on in the softest voice. "My son was a brave and beautiful man. He was my only son, and my wife still walks with his spirit. It is the fate of the Greeks to fight wars bravely. Sometimes we win, and sometimes we don't. But we fight, and that is our legacy. It is a fate that God and history cannot deny. Thank you for your kind words, Harry Hantzis, and may God be with you as your fate commands."

Harry replied, *"Eonia i mnimi."* Memory eternal.

Harry nodded to the older man and returned to the serving counter. George, stirring a briki, leaned toward Harry, "He's still mourning and sad that they buried his son unsung."

Harry took the plate with his ham and cheese and kataifi to the table where he left his travel bag. A moment later, George brought him

32

a small cup of muddy, gritty coffee. A pleasant layer of crema floated atop the bitter remains.

Chapter 9

As Harry finished his breakfast, more Greeks arrived. George hailed each by name. Harry thought about attending the funeral George mentioned, but decided against it. There was no reason to pique the interest of strangers before he talked to the priest. Spies, informers, and gossipers would not make his quest easier. Still, Harry harbored an outsider's curiosity about Colorado and the people living—and dying—there.

He overheard the table talk in the kafeneion as he finished his second coffee. The shop was small, and the Greeks animated. The arriving men talked of many things, but first on their minds was the strike in the coalfields. They debated whether the strikers should shoot guards.

One Greek said, "What choice do the miners have? The goons and militia are shooting them! And defiling their women! They even shoot their children. Goons killed the Slav child, Verhornik, a bullet through his head. They shot him from the Iron Car!"

To this, a second Greek replied, "Yes, yes, but the newspapers make it seem like the miners are bloodthirsty. Then the public, who knows nothing, turns against the strike. The public elects the politicians, and the politicians are the ones who will solve this problem, are they not?"

A third Greek weighed in, "The politicians solve nothing. They have their hands out only for themselves. They care nothing about how men earn a living, how men are treated on their jobs. Better that the Greeks show the miners how a man gains respect, and that means blood until enough has spilled. This is the way Greeks have always fought. We have the same problem on the railroad. But there we have a union that is not afraid to show the boss who's boss. We spilled blood for that union, too."

Others listened and nodded as speakers made points. The debate went back and forth for ten minutes. Then, the table quieted and was off to another topic, this one political, the developing rift between Prime Minister Eleftherios Venizelos and King Constantine.

During the First Balkan War, following the victory at Sarantaporo, Constantine wanted to take Monastir to the north.

Venizelos wanted the Greek Army to march east and take strategic Thessaloniki and its deepwater port. Venizelos prevailed and captured the city only hours before the Bulgarian forces arrived. Venizelos, a democrat and charismatic young leader, was on the rise. The power struggle would last for years and finally give birth to the modern Greek state. As it ran its course, the battle would split Greeks worldwide, and even rend the church. Harry supported Venizelos.

By midmorning, Harry was ready to move on. He would stay the night and talk to the priest the next day. When he went to the counter to pay George, he asked the big man where he should stay. George pointed to his left, "Walked down Curtis Street and you'll see a Greek boardinghouse. It's clean, safe, and cheap. It'll be fine for overnight."

George offered Harry his change, but Harry waved it off. George said, "Come back anytime, Harry Hantzis, don't be a stranger. This place is like a Greek telegraph. All the news comes here first. And, if we're lucky, we solve the world's problems before noon."

Chapter 10

The Transfiguration of Christ Church was modest. Built of wood, brick, and stucco, it beckoned the faithful through a bell tower. High-arched windows added the only exterior drama, a treatment extended to the double-door entranceway.

Harry arrived the next morning at 9:30. It was Friday, and the church was empty except for a woman in black, deep in prayer, seated behind the iconostasis. Harry made the sign of the cross twice as the priest approached through the nave to greet him at the royal doors.

Father Paschopoulos was a tall, trim man of fifty. His full gray beard, long black cassock, and black skufia made him look even taller. He wore a silver Greek cross on a simple chain around his neck, and his eyes were steady and dark as night. He motioned Harry close and spoke low to not disturb the widow in prayer. The priest said, "We buried her husband yesterday, and she is praying for his deliverance."

Harry nodded, "Father, I am Harry Hantzis. I've traveled from Indianapolis. Eydokia Pendagiotis wrote to me. She said I should talk with you about her sister Eleni."

Father Paschopoulos lifted his eyes and squinted. "Stay here, my son. I'll be right back. We can talk in private."

With that admonition, Father Paschopoulos walked to the grieving widow and knelt to speak. Harry couldn't hear their conversation, but when it ended, the priest crossed himself twice, and the widow nodded.

The priest returned to Harry and motioned to the door, "Let's go to the residence."

Harry stepped out of the church and the two men walked to the small home next door. Inside, the priest offered Harry a chair next to a fireplace stoked with coal. The priest asked Harry if he could make him coffee and Harry declined, not wanting to impose. The priest asked, "Do you mind if I make some for myself?"

Harry shook his head and thought, *This is a switch. The priest in Indianapolis is usually the one asking for coffee.*

Father Paschopoulos went to the small stove top next to the sink. "I don't have pastries, but I can offer you some bread with cheese or butter, if you prefer?"

Again, Harry noted the switch, "No thank you, Father. I don't want to take more of your time than I must."

The priest went on making the coffee and talking back over his shoulder. "Time is a luxury and a curse, is it not? When you want something to happen, it toys and stumbles, but when you fear what is approaching, it runs with the wind."

Harry nodded.

Father Paschopoulos said, "Eydokia wrote to me to say that she hoped you would be coming. This matter, the death of her sister, is evil and ugly. As a priest, I believe all lives are in God's hands. The Bible says that we must forgive our trespassers, but it also says we pay an eye for an eye, does it not?"

Again, Harry only nodded.

"I cannot tell you what you must do, Harry Hantzis. But I will tell you what I know to be true. Are you sure you wouldn't like some coffee, son?"

This time Harry relented, "*Nai, parakaló.*"

The priest finished boiling the coffee and asked if Harry wanted sugar. Harry held up one finger and said, "Metrios, parakaló." The priest brought both cups to a small table between the two armchairs. The men sat facing the fire, and Father Paschopoulos began talking.

"The young family, Alex and Eleni, were a beautiful couple. I married them two years ago, and they were blessed with a son a year later. Alex worked in the mine at Segundo, and they lived in the company town.

"It's hard work. Seven days a week, twelve hours a day, digging coal from the bowels of the earth. The miners spend their lives in a dank, dark pit with the devil on their shoulder.

"The miners had many grievances, and they went on strike last September. Alex, Eleni, and their young son, Stavros, moved into a tent. The union has tent colonies throughout the coalfields. There, life was hard, but at least the miners controlled their fate. The union gave everyone a small amount of money, and the miners organized to stop the coal from leaving the mines. But the guards hired by the company ran roughshod over the miners and tormented their families. The guards killed men and children, and now, women.

37

"The question I cannot answer, Harry Hantzis, is who killed Eleni. For this you will need to talk to Alex. Alex is in the coalfields with the Greeks. He left his son with a family in Pueblo. Stavros is well cared for."

Harry asked, "Father, can you tell me how to reach Alex?"

"Of course, my son. But you will need to change before you travel."

Harry looked puzzled, "You'll need some clothes that fit in. You're much too well-dressed for the coalfields. But don't worry, the church has a basement full of charity clothing, and we'll get you outfitted."

At this, Harry took umbrage and protested, "I will not take charity from the church. I will pay for anything I need. Please, Father, use your clothing for people who have fallen on hard luck. I can pay my own way."

The priest apologized for provoking the proud young Greek and assured Harry that the church would accept his donation for anything he needed.

As the men finished their coffees, the priest said, "I must warn you, Harry Hantzis, the coalfields are a battleground. The guards, what the miners call goons, will kill a Greek without hesitation. And the Greeks repay them in kind. Be careful, my son, for I know you are a veteran. Eydokia wrote to me about your family's responsibility in your village. But don't let your guard down. You are a boxer, too? Watch your toe and heel, toe the line, and keep your elbows in, never open. Do you understand, my son?"

Chapter 11

The priest told Harry the truth. Even before the strike, the coalfields were a battleground where casualties fell heavy on the miners. But that changed on September 23, 1913, when twenty-four nationalities came together, strived to communicate, and began settling scores.

The UMWA sent seven demands to the coal operators. Most were already a matter of law. The union said mining would resume when the owners agreed to wage increases, the eight-hour day, and pay for all narrow or dead work, time on the job not digging coal. The miners demanded to elect checkweighmen, and to trade and board anywhere they pleased. They wanted mining laws enforced and demanded the owners abolished the mine guard system. The mine owners refused to meet and ignored the union's overtures.

In a surprising show of solidarity, nonunion miners in the fields set aside tools and joined the UMWA. The strike brought Colorado coal mining to a standstill. Then a shotgun blast at Segundo Camp echoed down the arroyos, heralding the bloodiest episode in American civil history since the War Between the States. The 1913–14 Colorado Coal Strike was the deadliest labor conflict in American history.

The UMWA tent colonies commanded the entrances to the southern fields' most valuable properties. UMWA positioned the camps to stop the shipment of coal and block strikebreakers. Ludlow Camp, the largest of the fourteen, was near a vital crossroads and a railroad depot.

By the first week in October 1913, the tent colonies were functioning with a semblance of order. Ludlow was home to over one thousand, and a union bastion.[37] Twenty-four languages articulated the hopes and fears of Ludlow's youthful colonists. The Stars and Stripes fluttered alongside proud flags of national identity in tidy rows of canvas tents. Bicolor banners embossed with LUDLOW punctuated the dusty colony. A wooden platform and meeting area dominated the common ground with bulletin boards and privies. Across the road from the camp, the residents cleared a baseball diamond.[38] Camp carpenters reinforced the frail tents with wooden floors and half walls. Before long, the miners had excavated cellars under the wood flooring for protection from gunfire. On April 20, 1914, the cellar under Tent Number 58 became a crematorium for thirteen women and children.

While the strikers settled into new routines and learned to endure, the mine owners, led by CF&I, implemented their strategy. CF&I hired fifty gun thugs at $3.50 a day and promised to employ an additional two hundred.[39] The *Denver Express* said this about the recruits:

> *Most of the enlisted guards were scarred veterans of industrial wars in Chicago, Kansas City and St. Louis, plus barrel house bums from Denver's own saloon and red-light district.*

A tell of Rockefeller's mindset arrived on October 5, when the Baldwin-Felts Detective Agency imported four machine guns. Two of these 120-rounds-per-minute weapons were mounted on a reinforced automobile the gloating guards called the "Death Special."

The guards' arsenal included eighteen and thirty-two-inch electric searchlights. Operators shined their powerful beams over the camps at night from up to six miles away. The light played on tent walls, terrifying children, and putting everyone on edge.[40] Miners retaliated by dousing the lights with high-powered rifles.

Following the death of Bob Lee, Trinidad businessmen circulated a petition calling for Governor Ammons to send state troops. In response, the union organized a peaceful parade of over one thousand in Denver to dissuade the governor. Ammons released a manifesto declaring that violence from any quarter would be punished. The owners prepared public opinion to support the National Guard's mobilization.

On October 17, the Death Special rolled into the Forbes colony. A dozen horsemen escorted the lumbering vehicle. The horsemen rode to within a few yards of surprised strikers playing cards. One guard dismounted and approached, waving a white flag. As he walked toward the twenty-five armed miners, he reassured them he was a union man, offered whiskey, and the miners lowered their weapons.

In the next instant, he dropped to the ground and rolled as a volley from the horsemen and the armored car tore through the strikers. A boy, Luke Verhornik, pitched forward with a bullet through his brain. As women and children scrambled to escape, another boy running between tents collapsed screaming with nine rounds in his leg. A young girl, the daughter of a neighboring farmer on her way home from school, took a bullet to her face. Firing on the camp continued into the night.

Following the Forbes incident, Lawson organized the large Ludlow colony along military lines. Tikas became the leader of the Greeks as well as the camp leader. Lawson selected a captain from each nationality and posted twenty-four-hour sentries. He tasked the strikers with maintenance details to keep up morale. He made sure the men were busy.

Lawson organized dances where the Italians played music for all. Worn miners, after spending years in a routine of toil and sleep, now danced. On peaceful nights, strains of music floated from scattered tents as the cultures of Bulgaria, Mexico, Greece, Italy, and America soothed the children and strikers.[41]

As clashes continued to escalate, CF&I appointed K.E. Linderfelt commander of mine guards. Linderfelt would direct the Ludlow Massacre and the murder of Tikas. Linderfelt believed the old Alien and Sedition Acts applied to these rebel immigrants. He smugly stated, "You can't go at it with kid gloves. You've got to get results."

On October 24, mine guards wearing deputy sheriff badges opened fire on a group of pickets harassing scabs in Walsenburg. Four strikers died, but the sheriff refused to intervene. The strikers at Ludlow began demanding the union arm them. When the union refused, the miners went door-to-door in Trinidad, fifteen miles south of camp, soliciting weapons. Trinidad was a hub city and the coal capital of Colorado. Its population of ten thousand proved supportive. With reluctance, the union ordered three hundred rifles, but the deal fell through, perhaps derailed by internal sabotage.[42]

Ludlow secured seventy-one Winchester 94 rifles and five thousand rounds of ammunition from UMWA organizer Charles Snyder. These weapons with the miners' arms brought the camp's total to roughly two hundred guns.

On the afternoon of October 25, while Lawson and Tikas were distributing strike benefits in the main tent at Ludlow, firing erupted from the hills.[43] The long line of strikers scattered, and women and children evacuated to a shallow arroyo. The shooting lasted all day, enraging the miners and killing a guard named Nimmo. As Linderfelt directed the provocation, he knew well the next step. He telephoned the commander of the state militia, General John Chase, and reported a rebellion. Then he wired compelling telegrams to public officials in Trinidad and Denver.

Thirty-six guards, attempting to relieve Linderfelt, tried to take a train to Ludlow from Trinidad, but the train crew refused passage. The next morning, frustrated guards commandeered a train. A telegram alerted Lawson at Ludlow and cautioned him about the train's two machine guns mounted on coal cars.

Five hundred miners assembled in half an hour. Tikas led the vanguard detachment of Greeks. The Greeks moved with military precision, a product of training received in the Greek Army. These young strike leaders, many combat veterans, knew survival and victory came with discipline under command. Ignoring fire from the hills, they fanned out to take up position for attack. The train rumbled near, and when it rounded a curve, exposing its broadside, the miners opened fire. In a hail of bullets, the engine crew reversed to Forbes Junction in full retreat. Linderfelt watched the rout from the hills. He cursed, then wired General Chase, reporting the situation hopeless.

The miners sought retribution for the provocation. They cut telephone and telegraph wires, blew up the railroad tracks and carried sorties to Berwind, Hastings, and Tabasco. Pent-up anger produced ten dead mine guards before Lawson could stop the attack. Governor Ammons mobilized the Colorado National Guard after Denver banks agreed to issue $150,000 in certificates of indebtedness at 4 percent interest to cover the first month's expenses.[44]

On October 28, Ammons ordered General John Chase to muster a force and restore peace to the state. Chase, a refined and fastidious gentleman physician, shared Linderfelt's view of the strikers. Chase's confidants were Edward Boughton, an attorney for the Cripple Creek mine owners' association, and Major Pat Hamrock, a Denver saloon owner. Hamrock had battled Sitting Bull and the Ghost Dancers at Wounded Knee twenty-three years earlier.[45]

On October 31, troops arrived at Ludlow, and Chase wrote in his report:

> *The parade of the troops of the Ludlow tent colony was memorable. Men, women, and children lined the road for a half mile or more between the point of detraining and the entrance to the colony on either side. Many of the men were in the strange costume of the Greek, Montenegrin, Serbian, and Bulgarian armies; for the colony numbered among its inhabitants, many returned veterans of the Balkan Wars.[46]*

Lawson told the strikers the troops would not interfere with picketing, as Governor Ammons assured him. In the early days, the strikers and soldiers had fraternized, eaten together, played baseball and gotten along. Within a few weeks, the welcome had worn thin.

Chapter 12

Father Paschopoulos sorted through a stack of clothing and pulled from it a heavy, gray, button-up wool jacket. The garment was the last layer of serviceable attire, and it rendered Harry indistinguishable from the thousands of miners and supporters in the coalfields. His baggy pants and worn work boots would not betray him as an outsider. He left his Indianapolis clothes with the priest. As he climbed the stairs out of the church basement, the priest handed him a red bandanna. He said, "Wear this around your neck when you get to Segundo. This will tell the strikers you are with them. But it also tells the guards you are their enemy."

Harry nodded and thanked the priest before walking out. Just as he reached the top step, the priest called out, "You are welcome here anytime, Harry Hantzis. May God be with you and guide your journey."

Harry looked at the priest and again nodded.

The train to Trinidad, two hundred miles south, took most of the day. Harry arrived just as the winter sun was setting. As he stepped from his coach to the station platform, the last rays of daylight shone on Fishers Peak five miles south. Rising ninety-six hundred feet, it was the height of Mount Olympus and reminded Harry of the deadly peaks of Macedonia.

Trinidad rested on the eastern edge of the Sangre de Cristo Mountains, the southern foothills of the Rockies. Farther east lay the Apishapa and Las Animas Arches, and beyond, vast plains stretched seven hundred miles across Kansas to the Ozarks of Missouri. At six thousand feet, Trinidad avoided the extreme heat of summer, but winter was brutal, often below zero.

Spanish and Mexican traders had settled Trinidad in the 1840s. They'd valued its proximity to the Santa Fe Trail and the El Rio de Las Animas Perdidas en Purgatorio, or *The River of Lost Souls in Purgatory*.[47] With the discovery of coal in the early 1860s, Trinidad had grown into a commercial center. Thousands of immigrants came to work in the pits and processing plants and in 1878, the Atchison, Topeka and Santa Fe Railway connected Trinidad to points north and south. By 1914, when Harry arrived, the town had a bustling population of ten thousand.

Harry walked from the train station to North Commercial Street. He turned right and crossed the Purgatoire River Bridge to the Trinidad Hotel. The three-story Italianate brick building featured a cut stone front, ironwork on the upper porches, and glass-globe electric lamps on the street. Inside the sparse lobby, he approached the front desk and booked a room. The man tending the hotel's reception was a friendly Italian. He suggested to Harry that there were two places to the left of the hotel entrance where Harry might get a meal, the Niccoli Brothers Bar, and Ottavio's Place. To the right of the hotel, he'd find the Banca Meridionale Italiana. Harry nodded and thanked him.

Harry was hungry, and after settling into his room, he walked to Ottavio's Place. He thought Niccoli's Bar might be trouble. There he might have to deal with drunk Italians who, he presumed lived in this part of town. He had nothing against Italians, and he liked the ones he matched up with. They boxed with heart and fortitude, even if they could be flashy. No, bars and liquor meant trouble, something Harry could do without in a strange town.

Ottavio's was a small place, filled with families. Harry knew a bit of Italian from boxing and caught snippets of their conversations. He ordered spaghetti and meatballs and enjoyed a pleasant meal.

Harry sat in the corner near the kitchen doorway. From there, he overheard an argument or a heated discussion. With Italians as with Greeks, it was hard to tell the difference. The exchange went, "*Non andare lì, Segundo! Molto pericoloso!*" Don't go there, Segundo! Extremely dangerous!

Harry finished dinner and walked through the hotel lobby to his room, past men smoking and drinking in high-backed leather chairs. He passed a tall, mustached man facing the entranceway reading a newspaper, and the man asked in Greek, "*Esý eísai,* Hantzis?"

Harry backed up a step, looked at the stranger, then recognized his friend Dimitri from the *Carpathia*. Dimitri's sunken eyes, mustache, and stubble beard masked the man Harry knew earlier.

"Dimitri, is that you, my friend? I did not expect to see you ever again."

Dimitri said only one word, "*Eydokia.*"

Harry nodded, "We should go to my room to talk."

Dimitri rose from his chair and Harry saw the butt of a French-built Ruby M1914 pistol protruding from an inside pocket of Dimitri's jacket. It was the sidearm issued to Greek soldiers near the end of the Balkan Wars. As the two men walked to Harry's room on the second floor, Dimitri swiveled his head like a soldier on patrol.

Dimitri and Harry had parted in New York City after disembarking the *Carpathia*. The two men discussed traveling together to Chicago. But the plan changed when Harry got a telegram from his boxing manager, Leo P. Flynn, headquartered in New York. Flynn insisted on meeting with the young Greek to discuss his reentry to the professional circuit. He wanted to talk about opponents, touring partners, and training. Harry took the meeting and said goodbye to Dimitri the day of their arrival.

Dimitri had changed. Gone was his relaxed, jovial nature, quick to point out humor in his observations. Now, Dimitri was severe and careful as he told Harry what he knew of the strike and the murder of Eleni. Dimitri said that he was fast friends with Eleni and Alex. Dimitri and Alex met when Dimitri started working at the Segundo coke ovens two years before. Then their conversation took on the tone of a military briefing, and Harry recalled Dimitri's service in a special unit of long-range sharpshooters in the Greek Army.

Dimitri said, "Our area of operation, the Raton Basin, is a hundred seventy-five miles long and sixty-five miles wide. The Sangre de Cristo Mountains mark the basin to the west. To the north, the Wet Mountains, and the Apishapa Arch, and to the southeast, the Sierra Grande Arch."

As he talked, Dimitri sketched on a sheet of hotel letterhead and drew in his points of reference. Harry nodded, but the landmarks were unknown to him.

Dimitri went on, "The miners call the coal area within the Raton Basin, the southern fields.[48] The coal is sorted and processed before they sell it to industrial concerns. The coke ovens at Segundo, where I worked, bake the coal at two

46

thousand Celsius to burn off impurities. They use the coke to make steel.

"This operation runs around the clock. The smoke from the twelve ovens where I work is poison that kills every living thing it touches. Still, I was happy for my job at the ovens because I hate going underground. I worked underground since coming to America in 1910. At the ovens, I loaded the rail cars with the coke. It is hard work, but God abide, I am not trapped with Hades."

Dimitri's was the chthonic nightmare haunting many Greeks.

Dimitri told Harry, "The union camp is near the company town. The tents have reinforced wooden sidewalls and small stoves. The bachelor Greeks bunk six men to a shelter, but the families have tents to themselves. Alex and Eleni's tent was one of the last constructed, on the far west of the camp."

The story of Eleni's murder was hard for Dimitri to tell. He hesitated from sentence to sentence.

"I know only what Alex has told me. It was ugly. And I know Alex is not saying everything out of respect for his wife.

"Eleni was beautiful. Her dark hair and lively eyes could charm the devil. She was young and smart, and the Greeks loved to talk to her because of her spirit. She reminded them of the Old Country, of innocence. She got along with all the miners' families, the Italians, the Irish, and even the Slavs.

"Their son, Stavros, was the joy of her life. She told everyone that Stavros would be an owner of ships and someday rule the port of Piraeus. That is where she and Alex met."

Then Dimitri's eyes dropped to the floor. He quivered, "The women found her in her tent. They came to look after her because Stavros was crying. Eleni was without her clothes, her eyes staring wide. She had bruises all over her body with a deep stab wound to the center of her chest. Stavros lay in her blood.

"It was after dark when they found her, and Alex was in the hills with the men. The women keened and wailed, and many were still crying the next morning when Alex returned."

Dimitri looked up from the floor and away from Harry. Then took a deep breath. "I was with Alex when he was told. Alex is bold and brave, and a man not easily aggrieved, but he folded like a doll when he saw her body. Thankfully, the women had cleaned and dressed her. They handed him Stavros, but he held the child like a bundle of wood. He was cold as stone.

"I asked the women if anyone saw anything, anyone coming or going that they did not recognize. But they all looked down and shook their heads, many still crying. The goons were around camp all day, but not near the tent, so far as anyone knew. The two tents nearby were empty because the Greeks were in the hills. There were union men at the camp, mostly married men with families, but no one saw or heard anything.

"Later, after the men returned and Alex was told, an Italian woman, Marta, came to me. She is the one who found Eleni. She handed me this."

Dimitri withdrew a red bandanna half covered in dried blood from his right jacket pocket.

"Marta said that Eleni was clutching it in her right hand and that she feared telling anyone because she didn't know what it meant. She didn't know if Eleni pulled it from the neck of her killer or used one she found in the tent to stop the bleeding. She didn't know, and I made her promise not to tell anyone. She promised and crossed herself. When Alex returned from the hills, I saw he was wearing his bandanna, like all the men.

"This is all I know, Harry. This is all I can offer for your pursuit. We will go to Segundo tomorrow, and you can talk to the Greeks and others in the camp. We have talked about you coming, and we want you to give justice. But the goons will know you are here. They have spies everywhere. And if the killer is one of them, they will not hesitate to kill you before you can find him.

"The Greeks believe it was a goon that did this terrible thing. I agree, but I am uncertain. We must talk to more people, look at all sides before we assign guilt. This is the way your father would seek the truth, is it not?"

Harry nodded. "Thank you for telling me these troubling things, Dimitri. Get some sleep, my friend, you look worn down. Are we to go to Segundo tomorrow?"

Dimitri nodded.

Harry went on, "Good. Will we buy train tickets in the morning?"

Dimitri shook his head. "We will go by train, but we will not need tickets."

Chapter 13

The caboose was sparse. A small stove warmed the cabin, and the railroaders removed their outer jackets. The smells of roasting coffee and venison stew mingled with coal smoke. Rear brakemen sat high in the cupolas on either side watching the train round bends, looking for axle fires or dragging equipment.

The conductor sat in a booth across from the stove, working his bills on the table and talking to his unauthorized passengers. The six-man crew of the Number 13 Atchison, Topeka and Santa Fe local freight handled a consist of thirty empty coke cars. They were all union men, two brakemen and the conductor in the caboose, and the engineer, fireman, and head brakeman in the locomotive.

Gustav Graf, second-generation German, wore a bushy mustache, bib overalls, and a hickory-striped denim cap. He was in charge. In a sparse Frisian accent, he informed his guests, "We will take a siding just before we get to the ovens. Union rules say that we don't have to cross a picket line. The bosses they will tell us to cross. They say the strike is not authorized. Ha! We tell them to go to hell.

"We will leave the train in the siding, dismount, then play cards in the crew shanty. The bosses can do with the train what they want. I do not know why they ordered empty cokers for the ovens. The scabs are not cooking enough coke to fill a bucket, let alone a coker.

"The bosses will take the train to the ovens if they can get it past the strikers. We leave a little surprise to slow them down. A leaky steam gauge . . . maybe a missing brake handle . . . those things happen on a railroad."

Gustav knew Harry was an outsider. Dimitri had told him that the strikers needed to get an important person to Segundo. Gustav assumed Harry was a union organizer, and he talked about strikebreakers.

"Back in early November, the bosses began rounding up scabs. They promised the poor sons-of-bitches a deed to farmland, respectable jobs, and never mentioned the strike. I know this . . . I talked to them . . . they showed me pamphlets.

"What do they say? If it is too good to be true. . . ?" He shrugged.

"They brought the scabs down on the railroad. Most came from Missouri . . . Joplin. They promised them three dollars and eight cents a day and land rent for a dollar a month per acre.[49] And they were dumb enough to fall for it.

"November thirteenth, when the scabs got off at Ludlow, the women set on them with ball bats and studded clubs.[50] The scabs got the devil beat out of them. The women were fierce, mad as hell. Most of the scabs ran back to the train or hid on the platform behind freight.

"You can't blame the women. They were hellcats. Before the strike, goons cornered them in the daytime when their men were working. Some goons . . . I'm not saying all . . . slapped the women around and forced them to lie with them. The women had no privacy, no respect. Goons and sheriffs busted into their homes anytime . . . waving pistols and shotguns . . . cursing. They treated the women like. . ."

Gustav shook his head and looked away.

After a moment, he went on, "The women would not report the rapes and robberies because the company would evict them.[51] Hell, they knew the sheriffs would do nothing, and most had kids to look after. The bosses knew what was going on, but they never raised a hand. Now, the women have raised it for them, and it serves them right. There are goons in that bunch that deserve the noose."

The women maintained the strike, and the strike became theirs. As they mixed, they educated each other. The Southern Europeans, the most subjugated, learned from Welsh and Irish and American women. Together, they swelled into a rousing current in the roiling river of change. The organizing campaign changed their lives. The need to win the union battle spawned feminism that taught assertiveness as a by-product.

On December 16, 1913, the Colorado State Federation of Labor met in Denver. The gathering of five hundred delegates expected to debate a motion to recall Governor Ammons, but that morning a headline from Garfield County took precedence. The Vulcan Mine, a subsidiary of Colorado Fuel and Iron, operating with scab labor, had exploded, killing thirty-seven miners.[52]

On the convention floor, support for the UMWA was overwhelming. The next day, Mother Jones and Louis Tikas, marching under a Ludlow banner, led two thousand supporters to confront Governor Ammons. The crowd swelled to five thousand by the time they reached the Statehouse. Ammons grudgingly received a delegation but hedged against the Federation's demand that he decommission the troops. Instead, he offered to allow a Federation-sponsored investigating committee that the union endorsed.

As the year ended, the UMWA books showed 19,300 men, women, and children on strike relief.[53] But the strike was dragging, and the only organizers with press appeal were socialists. Reports from the southern fields read like battlefield communiqués, and the UMWA Executive Council reacted warily to the Greek and Southern European leadership.

Mary Harris Jones had been active in the strike from the beginning, but she proved an unreliable team player. But Mother Jones, an independent actor in search of a stage, found a devoted audience in the southern fields. To the union, she was a loose cannon, but they refrained from public criticism. More than once, her emotional appeal for unity salvaged bitter and divisive UMWA conventions, attesting to her rank-and-file support.

Early in the strike, she held rallies riling the masses. Then she went to Washington, DC, to lobby for a congressional investigation. The eighty-two-year-old firebrand returned to Colorado on January 4, the day Eydokia wrote to Harry Hantzis. General Chase, commander of the Colorado National Guard, threw her in jail for twenty days and posted two armed guards as sentries.[54]

On January 22, 1914, the women of the southern fields organized a march to free Mother Jones. They gathered in Trinidad a thousand strong and started down Commercial

Street.[55] As they turned the corner at Main on their way to General Chase's headquarters, they confronted a detachment of mounted troops led by Chase.

Defying his order to halt, the women marched ahead, singing and chanting, weaving between the troops' horses. When Chase rode up to a sixteen-year-old girl, Sarah Slator, and kicked her with his studded cavalry stirrup, his horse spooked and threw him to the ground. As spectators and marchers laughed with derision, the rotund general struggled to his feet, remounted, and waved his service revolver over his head, shouting, "Ride down the women!"[56]

The soldiers obeyed. One woman's ear was nearly severed, another received a gash on her forehead, and they slashed another across both hands as she tried to protect her face. A rifle butt crushed a fifteen-year-old girl's instep. Chase's men ripped down signs and banners, then dragged women and children off to holding pens.

Chase's attack on the Women's March lit a fuse. The miners demanded arms. The union rejected this escalation, but the Greeks planned an attack.

Under cover of darkness, squads of miners from Segundo, Tercio, and Sopris infiltrated Trinidad and took up positions on rooftops. One hundred sharpshooters trained rifles on Chase's headquarters. Mop-up detachments hid with sympathizers awaiting the signal at dawn.

In the hills surrounding Trinidad, behind pinyon pines overlooking the tents of the militia camp, Tikas commanded the Greek contingent waiting to annihilate the guard reinforcements.[57] With the approach of dawn, Lawson learned of the attack and pleaded with Tikas to call off the assault. Lawson explained that the United States Congress had agreed to send an investigating committee, and the attack would hurt, not help, their cause. Tikas ordered withdrawal, tortured by his decision. Deference to politics in matters of honor is not the Greek way.

Chapter 14

"Come in, trooper, and close the door."

"Yes, sir."

"What do you have for me?"

"The Greeks brought in somebody new yesterday, Lieutenant. We spotted him in Trinidad, and we think he's headed to Segundo."

"Another union man?"

"I don't think so. We've been watching Lawson, and we've got men close to him. We intercept his telegrams and tap the union phone. He's not mentioned anything about bringing in another Greek. He's got his hands full with Tikas. No, this may be about something else. He might be a relative of one of the Greeks. We don't know."

"Do we know his name?"

"Not yet, we're working on it."

"Soldier, you go back to Trinidad or Segundo or wherever-the-hell-ever this dago is and tell whoever needs to hear it that K.E. Linderfelt expects some answers. Pronto. You got that?"

"Yes, sir."

Chapter 15

The train slowed to a crawl, preparing to stop for the switch that would line it into the Segundo siding. Harry and Dimitri stepped off the caboose's rear platform as it came to a stop. Both men tipped their hats to Gustav and began their walk to the union camp two miles away. It was late afternoon, the weather fair, and the sky clear. It would be dusk soon. There was a well-traveled dirt road that snaked its way north to the camp. But on the road, they would be in the open, exposed to the guards and goons who roamed the hills. Dimitri said, "Let's take to the arroyo. It will be harder, but we will have cover."

A small creek that fed into the Purgatoire River ran alongside the road. Dimitri and Harry shuffled down its rocky bank twenty feet to the streambed hidden from view. They had hiked only ten minutes when Dimitri, in the lead, held his right hand high in a clenched fist, the signal to freeze. He stood still in his tracks and cocked his ear to the roadway. Then he looked back at Harry and whispered, "Take cover!"

As Harry scrambled a short distance up the slope to lie prone behind a ledge, he heard it, too. The heavy note of the engine sounded like a truck. As it grew closer, he heard men shouting over its noise. He heard laughing.

Then it stopped. Although Harry couldn't see it, his hearing told him it was twenty yards down the road, just over the ridge of the arroyo. Harry was unarmed except for a three-inch Case-Bradford pocketknife, and Dimitri had only his Ruby with nine rounds. They would be no match for what Harry estimated to be five men, well-armed with rifles. And Harry had underestimated their weaponry.

With the engine at idle, the men's voices became clear. Harry heard one say to another, "If you hadn't drunk so much, you wouldn't piss so much!"

The other man said, "Screw you, or I'll piss right here."

The first man said, "If you piss in the car, we'll make you target practice."

Then Harry heard at least three other men laugh and curse.

Harry saw movement to his right about twenty yards up the arroyo at the road's edge. Raising his head, Harry saw a big man dressed in a fedora and topcoat cradling a pump shotgun in the crook of his right arm. He wobbled a bit as he clumsily fingered the buttons on his trousers. He unfastened his pants and began urinating, and Harry saw he was unaware of his predicament and an easy target for a Greek scout. Harry could take the big man with his knife, and he eased it from his right front pocket, unfolding the blade. But Harry knew an attack would be suicidal with the other men holding the high ground.

Then Harry stiffened, an electric current jolting his nerves. He couldn't believe his ears. Harry knew the deadly cadence from Macedonia and Epirus. For an instant, he was there, in Epirus. His squad shredding before his eyes. This rhythm had a distinct note, but he knew well the instrument, the unmistakable staccato of a machine gun.

The man urinating pitched forward, almost tumbling into the arroyo. Harry thought they had shot the man. Then, he heard laughter from the roadway and the tottering man yelled, "You sons-of-bitches! You'll pay you sons-of-whores!"

Then from the roadway, Harry heard, "Get your ass back here! We need to get going! We've got tents to burn!"

Then more laughter.

A minute later, Harry heard the engine roar back to life. Then the vehicle passed above him on its way down the road. When it was out of earshot, and they were sure it was gone, the two Greeks broke cover and returned to the riverbed. Harry said to Dimitri, "What in the devil was that?"

Dimitri answered in a low tone, "That was the Iron Car."

Dimitri called the Death Special the Iron Car. It was a converted open touring car reinforced with steel plating from the Colorado Fuel and Iron works in Pueblo. Aboard were Baldwin-Felts Detective Agency goons armed with shotguns, rifles, and two Colt-Browning M1895 "potato digger" machine guns. These belt-fed weapons fired 450 rounds per minute, fewer than the Maschinengewehr 08s of the Turks, but just as deadly.

Chapter 16

A full moon rose over the eastern peaks as Dimitri and Harry approached Segundo Camp. With the sun's retreat, the thin air bore a biting chill. Harry heard singing as they neared. Then both men froze in their tracks at a resolute challenge, "Stop! Who goes there?"

Two men wearing red bandannas and wielding shotguns stepped from behind rock ledges on either side of the path ten yards ahead. Dimitri raised his hands halfway, and Harry followed his lead. Then Dimitri called, "Donkeys deserve better than this. It is Dimitri. I have with me my friend Harry."

The camp guards lowered their weapons at the mention of donkeys, the current pass phrase, and walked forward to greet the travelers. They exchanged introductions and handshakes, and Dimitri asked, "How are things in camp? Did you get a visit from the Iron Car this afternoon?"

Both men shrugged and shook their heads. The tall guard with the deep voice told Dimitri that things had been quiet. He said the biggest commotion was when three Greeks returned with a feisty lamb. The guards told Harry and Dimitri that the Greeks had bought the lamb from a local farmer and were now stewing it for the camp.

Stewed lamb was a compromise, stretching the meat when mixed with potatoes and vegetables. It was a welcome dish. But every Greek in Segundo would rather roast the meat over an open spit and make tidy skewers of its intestines and organs. Roast lamb was a meal of reverence. Another compromise in the minds of the Greeks was that the cook was Italian, Marta, the woman who had found Eleni. And, to further test Greek acceptance of xénos, the farmer who'd sold them the lamb was Bulgarian.

Segundo was a smaller union camp. Its forty tents stood in rows and columns around a communal area. Harry and Dimitri approached fluttering American, Greek, Italian, and Bulgarian flags. An embossed bicolored banner announcing SEGUNDO flapped at the entrance of the main tent. The twenty-four-foot square canvas stood reinforced with wooden half walls and a framed doorway. Tonight, the strikers buoyed it with hearty voices. Pinyon pine smoke and the

57

aroma of savoring lamb, starchy potatoes, and sweet onions wafted from its metal chimney.

Dimitri entered first. A dozen men and women were clustered together at the far wall, singing. One musician played the concertina, one a guitar, and one a lyre. The rutted rhythm reminded Harry of nights in the Old Country. But the song was different. The strikers sang in English, and the chorus was to the tune of an American Civil War anthem, *The Battle Cry of Freedom*.

> *The union forever, hurrah, boys, hurrah!*
> *Down with the Baldwins, up with the law;*
> *For we're coming, Colorado, we're coming all the way,*
> *Shouting the battle cry of union.*[58]

Dimitri raised his hand like a concert conductor as the two men approached the group. His prominent tenor joined in for the last line. As the chorus concluded on a dramatic chord and practiced vocal harmony, the woman tending the lamb stew raised her wooden spoon, making small circles in the air. When she brought it down, the harmony stopped, and the tent was quiet. A second later, the group erupted with, "Bravo!" and "Polý kalá!"

Marta wore a navy-blue apron over her long gray skirt and white blouse, her hair gathered in a blue scarf that matched her apron. She stood before an ornate cast-iron stove with nickel trim that heated the tent as it simmered her stew and warmed a large pot of coffee. She wrapped her apron around her hand, opened the firebox, arranged the coals, and added another split log from a stack to the right of the stove. She looked up at Harry while Dimitri introduced him to that evening's chorus of strikers. Harry observed her dark, wide eyes and the raven-black hair tumbling below her scarf. She was tall and slender, graceful and poised, even while stirring a pot of stew. Harry guessed she was in her early twenties. She didn't smile, but Harry noted a look of confidence and inquiry in her eyes, not the deference of young women in the Old Country.

After Harry's introduction, Marta sipped from her wooden spoon, looked away, and announced that the stew was ready. The strikers insisted that Harry, as a guest, be the first in line. Harry said he

58

was grateful for their hospitality, but he would only serve himself after the cook, and he nodded to Marta. Marta, untying her apron, looked up and gave the polite Greek a nod of approval.

The stew was delicious, everyone agreed. Still, the Greeks commented on its niceties, and a robust discussion arose over the inferiority of Bulgarian-raised lamb to its Greek counterpart. The Greeks ignored the fact that the nearest Greek-raised lamb was six thousand miles away. They couldn't help themselves and meant no disrespect. Greek discourse over food and its preparation was baked into their culture.

As the dinner broke up, Dimitri and Harry excused themselves and walked to the table where the women were finishing their meals. Dimitri pardoned their interruption. "We would like to thank you for tonight's wonderful stew. It was delightful, a true blessing. We know that much work went into its preparation."

Five of the six women at the table smiled and kept their heads lowered, avoiding eye contact with Dimitri. But Marta looked at the young Greek. "Thank you. But your countrymen wouldn't let us carve the lamb. So, they deserve credit, too. They said that Greeks have a *special* way of cutting the meat that makes it more tender. Is that true?"

Dimitri laughed. "Perhaps a real butcher could give us his thoughts," he said, looking at Harry.

Harry smiled and replied, "I know Greeks *believe* they know best, whatever the problem. As for butchering, I know that a dull knife will cut you quicker than a sharp one."

Marta smiled and rose from the table. She motioned Dimitri and Harry to a corner of the tent and spoke in hushed tones. Looking at Harry, she said, "Dimitri told me you were coming. He told me of your obligation."

Harry nodded. "I am here as an obligation of honor."

Marta looked away. Then her gaze returned to Harry. "Italians know of honor and obligation, too."

Harry nodded.

Marta went on, "Whoever killed our friend should die, and I will help in any way I can, Harry Hantzis."

Then Marta suggested, "We should talk tomorrow. I am sure that Dimitri told you what I saw, but other matters might be important, too. Tonight, you rest, and we will talk in the morning, *va bene*?"

Harry replied, "*Entáxei.*"

Marta knew of honor and obligation. She was in the coalfields to help her brother raise his two children. Their mother had died following the second child's birth. Her brother, Antonio, had traveled to Colorado five years earlier with his wife and first child. He left behind his younger sister, Marta, and his mother and father in St. Louis, where the family sold fruits and vegetables from a horse-drawn cart to the other Lombardy Italians in The Hill neighborhood.

Antonio went west with his wife and young son for the promise of steady work, higher wages, and cheap land. His dream was to own a farm and raise livestock. He took a job at the Segundo mine and soon realized that his pay in company script would never allow him to save enough to buy a farm. Then, when his wife went into labor and died giving birth to their daughter, there was nowhere to turn except to his family. The miner's wives helped during this sad time, but they could not raise the children to adulthood. So, he wrote to Marta and asked her to come to Colorado. Marta had been in Segundo for a year when the strike started, and now, she, like all the women in camp, shared child-raising duties, domestic chores, and schooling the children. Since the strike, women's work had been cooperative, and many found it liberating.

Marta knew of honor. Honor and obligation and family were the unbreakable strands that bound life in America. The Italians, just like the Greeks, survived on its strength.

That night, in the small tent with the other Greeks, Harry rolled on his cot. Earlier that day, the hammering of the machine gun had driven dark memories of cerise rosettes and shredded comrades into Harry's unwanted thoughts. In his restless mind, he struggled to raise his Mannlicher, but his arms would not move. With the late hours slipping past, his weariness overtook his haunting. Sleep came at last with thoughts of the woman, Marta.

Chapter 17

A blast rocked his lingering dream. In Harry's muzzy mind, thunder shook the *Carpathia* on a quiet sea. A quivering whistle rose in heaven. He jolted awake, recoiling from the sequence. A rumbling discharge, a shriek from high pitch to low, and then the impact. By the time he was upright on his cot, the entire tent of six Greeks was awake and scrambling for boots and guns. Harry looked at Dimitri pulling on his boots, "Artillery?"

Dimitri nodded.

Harry put on his boots and scrambled with Dimitri and the other Greeks. Outside, Greeks were rushing from tents, running toward the thunder. All were carrying rifles or shotguns, except for Dimitri and Harry. The men ran past a row of tents, and Marta stepped into her entranceway. Dimitri and Harry approached. She held up her hand to them, then ducked back inside the tent. A few seconds later, she poked through the opening with a Model 94 lever-action Winchester rifle in each hand. Harry and Dimitri looked at each other for a second, thankful for the unexpected gifts. They took the weapons, nodded to Marta, and ran to catch the other Greeks.

In the hills to the west of Segundo Camp, the Greeks climbed rugged pathways toward the sound. Harry and Dimitri knew from their combat in Macedonia that the discharge was from two artillery pieces firing quick volleys of five shells each. But the ordinance was not landing near the camp.

About a half mile up the path, the group of fifteen Greeks reached a ridge overlooking a snow-covered mesa. There, five hundred yards away, uniformed troopers of the Colorado National Guard were conducting target practice with two cannons and an ammo cart. They were shooting at a tree line eight hundred yards away. The impact of the shelling was no threat to Segundo. But the terrifying message to strikers and their families landed all the same.

The Greeks watched for a few minutes, then retreated to a covered area twenty yards down the slope. The senior Greek addressed the group: "I don't believe this is an attack. They are trying to frighten us. We will leave a lookout in case this is a diversion. The rest will return to camp."

Most of the Greeks nodded. But one did not. He wore traditional Cretan *vráka* pants tucked into his stivania boots, and a black sariki headscarf around his neck. He said, "Look at the way they have secured their horses and guns."

The troopers had stacked their rifles forty yards from the artillery pieces and left their horses on a line farther away.

"They have only one trooper for each. We can circle to the north and take the sentries before they know what hit them. Then, they will only have sidearms to defend themselves, and we can capture the artillery before they reposition."

Harry agreed the plan was workable but doubted the wisdom of its goal, capturing the artillery pieces. He kept his counsel and didn't speak because he was new to the group. He could tell that Dimitri shared his concern.

The older Greek, the kapetánios, nodded. "Alex, you are a brave man and an honorable comrade, and your plan has merit. But I ask, what would we do with the cannons? We have no training as artillerymen. The five veterans in this group were all infantry, and I don't believe we have an artilleryman in Segundo. Perhaps, Harry Hantzis, are you trained?"

Harry shook his head, "*Oxi . . . gia pezikoú.*" No . . . infantry.

The kapetánios continued, "If we bring the weapons back to Segundo, the troopers will attack us to take them back. Even if we could fire the weapons, we would have no more ammunition, just what is on the cart. The troopers will have a trainload if they need it. I can't agree with your bold plan."

The kapetánios looked around the group and saw that his insight carried the day. He said to the young man, "Alex, will you stay and watch the troopers for a couple of hours, then we'll send someone up to spell you?"

Alex nodded.

Then, Harry glanced at Dimitri and suggested to the kapetánios that he and Dimitri stay behind with Alex to spell one another and save someone a trip up the ridge. The kapetánios agreed, and the rest of the men began their trip back to the camp down the same path.

As the others left, Harry walked to Alex, held out his hand, and introduced himself. "I am Harry Hantzis. I am here to find who killed your wife. I am sorry I never met Eleni. I am told she was a lovely woman, a devoted wife and mother. *Eonia i mnimi*." Memory eternal.

Alex absorbed the introduction with no reaction.

Harry went on, "Mine is a debt of honor. Eleni's brother saved my life in Epirus. He died, so I could live.

"Eydokia wrote to me and said I should find you. I am sorry I could not be here sooner, but I came as soon as I received her letter."

Alex took Harry's measure. He recognized Harry's substantial continence. Alex knew from talking with Dimitri that Harry had earned commendations for bravery in the war. Alex did not return to fight in the war because, at its outbreak, he just learned of Eleni's pregnancy.

Alex offered his hand, "I am honored to meet you, Harry Hantzis. Dimitri told me about you and your family. I am pleased you are here to help. But this I must tell you . . . *I* . . . will be the man who kills her killer. This, too, is honor. You agree, no?"

Harry understood the younger Greek's insistence and emotion. Not wanting to anger Alex, he replied, "To deliver justice is most important."

The two men nodded, each recognizing a point needing clarification, but each knowing that now was not the time.

Alex asked, "How will you find who killed Eleni?"

"I will talk to people and listen. I would like to see your tent, where they took Eleni's life. In time, we will know the truth. Then we will give justice.

"Alex, you grieve, and you worry about your son's well-being. This is a bitter time for you. But we must talk. My questions will be difficult. I do not mean to dishonor anyone, least of all Eleni. Do you understand?"

Alex looked at Harry, "What are these questions you think I might answer?"

Harry and Dimitri looked at each other. Then Dimitri said, "I'm going to the ridge to keep an eye on the trooper boys and their noisemakers."

When Harry and Alex were alone, Harry went on, "I'm sorry for these painful memories. But when you saw your wife in the tent, did you find anything missing or disturbed? Could it be a thief who killed Eleni?"

Alex shook his head and looked away. Then, his eyes came back to meet Harry's, and he said, "I only remember seeing her lying there and hearing Stavros whimpering in Marta's arms. The women cleaned most of the blood . . . and dressed her. The killer left her naked . . . barren . . . cold and dead."

Alex sobbed. Harry rested his right hand on Alex's left shoulder and looked the younger man in the eye. Then Alex continued, "I saw nothing missing, nothing I can remember. I remember seeing Eleni . . . then someone handed me Stavros. I held him for a few moments. Then a woman took him. I was tired. I just returned from the hills where we had watched for troops and goons all night. I just wanted to see Eleni and get some sleep. I didn't sleep for a week. I still find it difficult."

"Alex," Harry continued, "Did Eleni ever tell you of someone tormenting her and wishing to do her harm?"

Alex shook his head. "In the company houses, sheriffs and guards strutted through in the daytime when the men were in the mine. They bullied the women. Eleni told me of those men. She told me they forced some women to. . . ."

Alex looked away.

"They forced women to lie with men who were not their husbands. The women did not report these crimes. They feared being thrown out of camp, out of their homes. Some feared their husband's reaction to their disgrace."

"Eleni never complained to me. Her spirit scared away these types of men. The swine. They feared she'd put a knife into them and gut them like pigs."

Dimitri came back from the ridge, "They've stopped firing, and they're hitching the horses to the cannons and cart. I think they're finished."

Alex was spent. Harry said to the young man, "Let's return to the camp. We will talk later."

Alex nodded, but didn't look up from the ground.

As the men walked down the pathway, Dimitri and Harry in the lead heard muffled sobs behind.

64

Chapter 18

Marta served the men American coffee, crusty bread, and soft cheese with a dipping bowl of olive oil. She apologized that she couldn't offer Harry and Dimitri a cappuccino. Then she looked at a wooden clock hanging on the tent wall. Correcting herself, she said, "Look at that. It's past eleven o'clock. No Italian would drink frothy milk this late in the morning. It is bad for the digestion. I must withdraw my apology for the cappuccino."

Harry and Dimitri chuckled.

Dimitri retorted, "Our Greek coffee is a simple affair. We drink it day and night so long as we have sugar."

Marta retorted, "I have had your Greek coffee. It tastes like mud mixed with sand. Better you are refined, like Italians."

Dimitri replied, "Signorina Marta, an Italian would not understand."

"Who cannot understand mud?" Marta shot back.

All three laughed aloud.

When the laughter faded, Harry said, "Marta, I spoke with Alex in the hills before we came here. He still walks with Eleni's spirit. He shoulders terrible pain and anger, and we spoke only of simple matters. I hope you can tell us more."

Marta took a deep breath, "What is to know? Some beast raped and murdered her. He deserves to die!"

Harry nodded.

"Eleni was nice. She was funny. She was smart. She was a powerful spirit, and I doubt Alex will ever rid himself of her ghost. She deserved much better than this camp and much better than what happened to her."

Harry nodded, "Dimitri told me you found a bandanna."

Marta looked away, then back at Harry, "She was clutching a red bandanna like the one that all the men wear, soaked with her blood. She used it to stop the bleeding. The poor child, Stavros, was wailing in the tent's corner. Eleni was a wonderful mother, and never did I hear the child cry that way. That is why I looked inside, and what I saw was the devil's work."

Then Marta crossed herself in the Catholic manner.

65

Harry said, "You are a brave woman, Marta. But now I must ask you to tell me what you saw. It could help us find her killer."

Marta stiffened and straightened in her chair. She nodded, then began. "It was near ten o'clock and pitch dark. I lit a lantern, and when I entered the tent. Eleni was lying on the wooden floor, her face to God. She was naked as the day she was born with her eyes open. There was blood in the middle of her chest. From a wound. It flowed to her right side and pooled on the floor. The child lay in a blanket just to the edge of the pool of blood, and Eleni was clutching the bandanna in her right hand. The chairs and table were out of place, a chair toppled, and a cutting board and pan lay on the floor. They threw her dress and shawl and other clothing across the tent. They threw her shoes onto a cot.

"This is all I remember. I ran to get a camp guard, and when we came back, other women arrived and cleaned her body and dressed her. One woman took Stavros and nursed him. That is all I can remember. It was a nightmare. A bloody nightmare. The devil's work."

She crossed herself again, and Harry saw she was crying. Harry pulled a handkerchief from his coat pocket and offered it. She looked up and thanked him.

"Marta, do you want to rest? We can talk later."

Marta shook her head.

"Did Eleni say anything to you about a tormentor? Did she say she was afraid of anyone?"

Marta searched for an answer, "All the women feared the company guards. They were horrible men. They leered at us and said things, filthy things. They broke into homes, waving guns and shouting. They forced some women . . . especially those with children . . . to. . . ."

Harry broke in, "We know, Marta."

Marta sniffled, "One time, Eleni mentioned she was in Trinidad, soon after the strike began. A lout of a man dressed in a trooper uniform with an officer's rank stopped her on the street. He said vile things to her. She said there were three other troopers with him, and they all laughed at her embarrassment. He taunted her, saying, 'I'll see you soon, missy.'

66

"Eleni feared the look in his eye, and she told me when she came back to camp. I told her to tell Alex, but she said it was just a taunt and there was no reason to alarm Alex. She said Alex would go looking for the man and get himself shot by the troopers."

Harry asked, "Did she tell you anything about his uniform or any way to identify him?"

"She said he was an officer and that one man in the group called him by a woman's name . . . *Linda*."

Chapter 19

The troopers with their noisemakers were not troopers. January 1914 saw most of Governor Ammons's National Guard troops return home for business or personal reasons. Their replacements were mine guards. These troops-in-name-only bivouacked in company buildings and were paid by the mine owners for strikebreaking services.

In late November 2013, Ammons lifted his ban on importing scabs from other states. Wholesale arrests started soon after. The militia, without a declaration of martial law and with civil courts standing, incarcerated hundreds of strikers and ignored habeas corpus. The militia blockaded public roads and declared US Post Offices off-limits to strikers. Camp searches became frequent. Interrogations became ugly, and there were reports of thievery and rape.

General Chase, commander of the guards, condoned fake executions, requiring condemned prisoners to dig their own graves. Ordered to write last letters to families, fated miners' forlorn sentiments brought resounding amusement to their militia captors. From the Columbian Hotel in Trinidad, Chase named himself commanding general of the Military District of Colorado and issued orders that all prisoners were under his direct control.

For Christmas, General Chase accepted a silver-mounted saddle from coal operators, from which he would topple a month later in idiotic embarrassment. The union bought presents for the children of strikers. The boys got writing slates, and the girls dolls. The *Denver Express* commented, "It's going to be the happiest Christmas ever for some of these kiddies, for many of them, born in the dingy coal mining towns, have never had a single Christmas present."[59]

On December 30, 1913, Linderfelt provoked Louis Tikas at the Ludlow train depot. Linderfelt pistol-whipped the Greek, then put him under arrest. Tikas had just gotten out of jail after being arrested in a sweep following the shooting of George Belcher. Belcher, a despised Baldwin-Felts goon, had provoked and gunned down union organizer Charles Lippiatt in August before the strike began.[60] On November 20, 1913, a sniper put a bullet through Belcher's head as he stood lighting a cigar in Trinidad with General Chase looking on.[61] The marksman

68

had know Belcher would be at the intersection of Main and Commercial under the town clock. It was the goon's hubristic routine. He was there every evening to berate "goddamn rednecks" and their families. The shot was well-placed and the shooter well-informed. Belcher wore armor plating front and back beneath his suit, with chain mail under it all.[62] Miners from West Virginia, where Belcher earned his reputation for violence, had clued in their brothers in Colorado.

The enraged general ordered the arrest of the striker Louis Zancanelli, and later union organizer Ed Doyle as a coconspirator. Tikas, too, was arrested and held until mid-December.

Tikas gained release from Linderfelt by Chase's orders thanks to a sympathetic officer. Linderfelt fumed. When Professor Brewster, an academician serving on the governor's investigating committee, arrived at the militia camp, a raging Linderfelt showed his machine gun's ability to strafe the defenseless tent city.[63] A dumbfounded Brewster testified, "Linderfelt seemed to rejoice in the handling of that instrument of death."[64]

In early 2014, the United States House of Representatives authorized its Committee on Mines and Mining to investigate conditions in Colorado. John Lawson, the union's lead organizer, endorsed the committee and believed the facts substantiating brutality against the miners would vindicate the union's cause. The owners fell quiet. Nervous over the approaching investigation, several large operators began dumping scabs and attempting to improve their image.[65] By January 31, they'd dismissed a hundred strikebreakers from the Sunnyside and Gresham mines.

On February 1, twelve hundred strikers and supporters marched through the uneasy streets of Trinidad. Marchers sang union songs in front of General Chase's hotel but, as Lawson instructed, remained peaceful. The militia did likewise.

The committee moved from Denver to Trinidad to Walsenburg, hearing testimony for a month. They interviewed miners and operators, owners and union officials, sheriffs and guards. When the committee reconvened in Washington, DC, they talked to the Rockefellers, Senior and Junior. With few notable exceptions, violence subsided during in-state hearings.

On February 27, 1914, Governor Ammons withdrew all but two hundred troops from the strike zone. The militia was bankrupting the state. In six months, the state had provided guard service costing $685,000 for properties yielding an aggregate return of $12,378.67 in annual taxes.[66]

The union was also aware of its financial burden as the March 1914 audit reported 20,508 men, women and children drawing strike relief.[67] UMWA dues were fifty cents per month for non-striking members, with a reported membership of 420,000. Striking miners received weekly benefits of $3.00 per man, $2.00 per wife, and $.75 for children.[68] The UMWA maintained a reserve fund reported to be around one million dollars. The outlay for the strike was threatening financial stability, and uneasiness was growing among the conservative leadership in Indianapolis.[69]

In early February 1914, Louis Tikas became embroiled in a union power struggle. His nemesis was an organizer named Diamond who worked out of the Trinidad office.[70] Tikas wrote UMWA headquarters on February 10, criticizing "certain people known as national organizers" and charging selfish motives. Perhaps the union sought to rid itself of the militant young Greeks, who proved so hard to control. Whatever the motivation, Tikas lost his paid position and took his grievance to the top.

Tikas's struggle played against the bigger picture of immigrant politics within the UMWA. Greeks occupied the bottom rung of the immigrant ladder, receiving meager wages, the most dangerous jobs, and social contempt. Other nationalities received one representative for every two hundred men. Tikas was the only organizer among 547 Greek miners in Colorado, three thousand Greeks in the unorganized mines of Alabama, New Mexico, and Utah, and thirteen thousand Greeks in the union fields.[71] Paid or not, Tikas remained the de facto leader of Ludlow.

Chapter 20

For the next three days, Harry and Dimitri talked with the camp guards, the kapetános, and women who knew Eleni. Most blamed the goons, a term that included troopers, mine guards, and Baldwin-Felts detectives. Some thought her murderer among the riffraff that orbited the strike, looking for opportunities to pilfer or batter strikers for laughs. No one knew who committed the crime. Harry was tight-lipped. He knew Eleni had been clutching a red bandanna that didn't belong to Alex. He knew an officer in Trinidad who troopers called Linda had accosted and threatened Eleni. And he also knew from Marta's description of Eleni's wounds that she fought with her murderer, and the knife used to kill her had a large blade.

Dimitri joined the rotation of strikers serving as camp guards and scouts. Harry spent most evenings with Marta, helping in the common tent or in her shelter where she cared for her niece and nephew. Harry was fond of Marta. She was smart and sure of herself and moved with flowing grace. He talked with her about the murder, and she gave details about camp life and personalities.

At night, in the tent with the other Greeks, Harry listened more than he talked. All the Greeks were unmarried and young. Harry, at twenty-four, was older than most. As a war veteran, he elicited deference. He and Dimitri were the only two veterans in the tent. The other Greeks asked about the war and bragged about their Evzone cousins or uncles. Greek overstatement had these relatives routing entire Turkish companies with only a rifle and a bayonet. Greeks are unequaled mythologizers. Harry and Dimitri smiled and nodded.

Dimitri told Harry that they should travel to Ludlow and talk to Tikas. He said, "Ilias will know about the Colorado authorities and their investigation. He's from Crete and a good man. He's been with the union a few years. He knows the ways of the politicians and the union, and he may know something more than we can learn in Segundo."

Harry agreed. They needed more information and insight. Segundo was a dead end. The two men set out for Ludlow the next day.

Chapter 21

Ludlow was a large camp, larger than most Greek villages. Its fifteen hundred citizens were well-organized and practiced at living in tents in the harsh winter. Tikas was the leader of Ludlow. Although he no longer worked for the UMWA, he was John Lawson's key contact and dutiful lieutenant.

Tikas had joined the union movement in 1910, and he knew the political and institutional landscape like the terrain of the Raton Basin. For this, Tikas earned the hatred of the guards, detectives, and troops who harassed, beat, and jailed him. Regardless, Tikas continually stepped forward into the maelstrom and spoke for the strikers. He was a brave man. Bravery would be his legacy and undoing.

When Harry and Dimitri reached Ludlow, they learned Tikas was in Trinidad and would return that evening. For the rest of the afternoon, the two men talked with strikers and Dimitri's acquaintances. No one discussed the murder. As far as anyone knew, Harry was a friend of Dimitri's and a war veteran.

Later that evening, Dimitri introduced Harry to Tikas, and the three men drank coffee in his tent. Tikas, a tall, medium-built, clean-shaven man, knew what he was doing with coffee. He had owned a café in Denver's Greek town on Market Street in 1910, the year he took American citizenship. The café was next to the local office of the IWW. It was there that he first grew interested in the labor movement.[72]

Harry began by thanking Tikas for meeting with them and asked about his family in Greece. The answer stunned Harry.

Tikas was three years older than Harry, born in Loutra of Rethymno, Crete, and his given name was Ilias Athanasios Spantidakis.

At the mention of Loutra, Harry cocked his head. Vasilios Pendagiotis, Harry's Evzone savior and brother of Eleni, was also from the village. Harry was uncertain about bringing it into the conversation but, if Tikas knew as much as Dimitri said, he was aware of the connection.

Harry asked, "Ilias, do you know why I came to Colorado?"

Tikas smiled and nodded. "I believe you are here to find Eleni's killer, are you not? *Eonia i mnimi.* I am from her village in Crete. I did not know her family, but they are of high reputation and honor."

Harry added, "Eleni's brother, Vasilios, saved my life in Epirus. He gave his for mine. I am here to find her killer and give justice. I'm here to honor my debt to her brother."

Tikas nodded, "I will tell you what I know, Harry Hantzis, and it is not much. The day after Eleni's murder, the union alerted the Las Animas County sheriff. We sent two riders to the office in Trinidad. The sheriff in the office asked if anyone saw anything, and our riders told him no. Then, he asked if the strikers could prove who did this? Again, the riders said no. That was the last we heard from the sheriff.

"Harry, do you know how I learned of your arrival?"

Harry shook his head, a bit puzzled by the question.

"I learned of it from a spy. A spy who spies on other spies.

"The troopers knew you are here, but they did not know your name or intention. By now, they may know both. I am telling you this so you will be careful in all your travels and mindful about who you speak to. These hills and canyons are alive with eyes and ears. When the goons learn you are here to find Eleni's murderer, they will not hesitate to kill you. If one of their own killed the sweet child, they will declare a bounty on you. They will not hesitate to kill a Greek, regardless of purpose. Do you understand?"

Harry nodded. "*Naí.*"

The tent fell silent, and then Dimitri said, "Ilias, we are grateful for your time and your information. Do you have any suggestions how we can unravel this knot?"

Tikas shrugged. "I will tell my spies to learn what they can. I will not tell them you are here. But it is only a matter of time before everyone knows. The only secret in Greece is why Greeks can't keep a secret. Will you be staying in Segundo?"

Harry looked at Dimitri, who nodded.

"If I send a contact, he will identify himself with the phrase, 'spring is near upon us.' Do you understand?" asked Tikas.

Harry nodded.

The men stood to shake hands, and Tikas said, "I am sorry to leave, but the Greeks are planning the Pascha feast. This is good because it takes their minds off the strike. I need to make certain they don't get carried away. The Catholics have their Easter the week before, and the Greeks intend to go them one better. They are talking about roasting thirty lambs and arguing about where they will get their raki. In Nafpaktos, they may call it *tsipouro*? I do not know. It all tastes like kerosene. Oh, and please be my guests."

Harry and Dimitri chuckled. Then, before the men separated, Harry asked, "Ilias, do you know an officer of the guards who answers to the name Linda?"

Chapter 22

Harry and Dimitri spent three days at Ludlow talking to strikers and their families. The citizens of Ludlow thought much the same about Eleni's death as their brothers and sisters in Segundo. Most ventured that a goon had done it, but no one knew who it was or could add pieces to the puzzle. It was all speculation.

On Saturday, March 1, Harry and Dimitri boarded a Colorado and Southern passenger train at Ludlow Station with twenty other Greeks and traveled to Pueblo seventy miles north. They spent the night with the Georgallas family, the family caring for Alex's young son. The following morning, they walked the short distance to Saint John's Greek Orthodox Church for the Great Lent service.

Consecrated in 1907, Saint John's was one of the oldest Greek churches west of the Mississippi. A simple brick building in the classical revival style, the full pediment of its two-story portico rose on four Ionic columns. The building projected presence and permanence, and the columns were familiar and pleasing to its Greek worshippers.

Harry was not a religious man. Dimitri was more so. Like all Greeks, regardless of their religious rigor, Harry respected the church as a spiritual constant, and a social hub in the Greek community. Father Mardikes read from the Lenten Triodion, and Harry looked over the attendees. A few families mingled among single men. Many of the Greeks toiled at the Colorado Fuel and Iron works on the city's south side. The massive complex with its labyrinthine rail yards, towering chimneys and belching furnaces was CF&I's headquarters for steel and mining. Lamont Bowers, chairman of the board, managed the strike from Pueblo. He oversaw infiltrations, propaganda, and recruiting scabs. He was at the center of the war against the union. The mill wasn't part of the UMWA strike, but it suffered layoffs because of the lack of coke.

CF&I was the first vertically integrated steel mill west of the Mississippi River, marshaling all necessary natural resources. The company owned coal, iron ore, limestone, and dolomite reserves, and sixty mines and quarries spread across Colorado, Utah, Oklahoma, Wyoming, and New Mexico. CF&I was the largest private landowner in Colorado and claimed vital water rights along the Arkansas River.

Thousands of immigrants working in mills and mines—Italians, Croatians, Slovenians, Mexicans, Germans, Greeks, Japanese, Hispanics, African Americans, and more—made CF&I Colorado's largest employer. [73]

Other Pueblo Greeks worked for the Denver and Rio Grande Western Railroad, the Atchison, Topeka and Santa Fe Railway, or the Colorado and Southern Railway. In all but a few cases, the Greeks toiled at the bottom of the industrial pecking order as unskilled laborers in jobs that were dangerous, repetitive, and underpaid. Saint John's was a refuge, a place where they reconnected with the Old Country, healed their battered souls, and reclaimed their national identity and pride.

The early spring day was sunny, and after the service, the worshippers stood outside the church's entrance talking and visiting. Harry and Dimitri stood with Peter and Domna Georgallas. Domna held the baby Stavros to her shoulder, bouncing him. They talked of the beautiful weather and how well-behaved the child had been during the service. Then a smartly suited, mustached Greek a little older than Harry approached with his hat in hand. He excused himself for interrupting. Harry didn't recognize him as one of the Ludlow Greeks. He didn't work with his hands.

The stranger spoke formal Greek with a neutral inflection, "Please pardon my interruption." Then, looking at Harry, he continued, "Spring is nearly upon us, no? Ilias said I should talk with you. I can meet you later if that is your wish. You may have a feast before Kathara Deftera in your plans? I do not want to interfere. Today is a special day, no?"

Domna and Peter had a meal planned, but not until the evening.

Harry looked at Dimitri and then at his hosts. Dimitri said, "Why don't I walk back with Domna and Peter? Harry, you can meet us there later, entáxei?"

Domna and Peter nodded.

As the others left, Harry said, "I am Harry Hantzis. What is your name?"

"Yiorgos Vedros. My family is from Paros in the Peloponnese. I work in the office of the steel mill, in the corporation's headquarters.

I hold a university degree from Athens. Pardon my boast, but this is important, as I will explain.

"I came to America in 1910 and found work in Pueblo on the railroad. The CF&I Sociology Department needed a Greek translator and someone to write their newsletter. I bought a new suit, applied for the position, attached my transcript from the university, and they hired me.[74] That was three years ago. Now, CF&I management comes to me for advice on how to placate the Greeks.

"I have cultivated CF&I's trust over the years. They think I am like them, more civilized than the other Greeks. They trust me with information, not all, but some, and I circulate among the bosses in the office. Since the strike, they're careful what they tell me. Even so, I learn things and see things.

"We should go somewhere out of the public eye," suggested Yiorgos. He nodded to a small kafeneion across Spruce Street. "You go there now. I will meet you in a few minutes. Let's shake hands like we're saying goodbye . . . in case someone is watching."

Harry nodded, shook hands, and walked to the kafeneion.

The kafeneion was a small business, much like the one in Denver, with a few more tables. The owner tending the counter was a short, mustached man who wore a white apron and a red bandanna around his neck. Harry ordered a Greek coffee metrios, and the owner answered with the stiff Ionic inflection of a Pontic Greek.

Harry sat at a corner table on the wall, away from the windows. As he waited for his coffee and Yiorgos, he looked at the photographs behind the counter. The women in the photos wore *tapla*, the disk-shaped caps of Pontic women. The dessert case on the serving counter contained the Pontic specialty, *otía*, fried dough rolled in sugar and shaped like an ear. Harry knew Pontic countrymen from Macedonia, and he found their dialect of Byzantine Greek, Turkish, and Persian words hard to understand.

The Pontic Greeks in Macedonia and Thessaloniki were recent exiles from Pontus on the shores of the Black Sea and the Pontic Mountains of northeastern Anatolia. The Greeks had lived there since five hundred years before Alexander the Great.[75] In 1912–13, when Harry was in Macedonia, the Turks were in the early days of ethnically cleansing their Greek populations. Pontic Greeks were prime targets.

Turkish policy would grow deadly and brutal and culminate in 1923 with a population exchange under the terms of the Treaty of Lausanne.[76] The transfer uprooted two million people, 400,000 Turks and 1,600,000 Greeks. Thousands died in the wake.[77]

Harry waited at the small table. It surprised him to see Yiorgos enter from behind the counter. He must have used a rear door. Yiorgos nodded to the owner and walked to the corner table and sat down with Harry.

Harry said, "Your entrance was unexpected."

Yiorgos smiled. Then he motioned to the owner to bring him a coffee like Harry's.

Harry asked, "What is this department where you work, *koinoniología*? I have heard of this before, but only at universities."

Yiorgos smiled, "In 1901, the company needed labor stability. With many strikes and walkouts, it was difficult to predict work. That is when they created the Sociology Department to improve the company towns and control the workers. They built schools, developed a curriculum, and hired teachers.[78] The Sociology Department imparts CF&I's way of thinking to the workers. It *educates* the workers. It tells them how to raise their families and live their lives. It teaches them not to drink and to take care of themselves and not to be sloven. The department tries to mold model Americans out of forty different nationalities working for the company. I tell them about the Greeks. I tell them what the Greeks should read and hear, things that will keep them working, not drinking. And . . . keep them away from the union.

"We instruct wives on cleaning their homes and children on obeying their parents. We are teachers who try to make their students behave as the company would have them. And we report to the company about what the Greeks and Slavs and Italians and Mexicans and dozens of other nationalities are thinking and what has them upset. That way, the company can make gestures that seem like they care. That way, it looks like the company is trying to solve their problems. The company uses the Sociology Department to keep the union at bay. That is its real purpose. Do you understand?"

Harry nodded, but he had no personal experience. His employer, Kingan, was not as sophisticated as CF&I.

78

Yiorgos went on, "We do some good things. We watch out for health problems—flu, measles, tuberculosis, pox. We take precautions if we see a disease spreading. And some nationalities need education about proper personal cleanliness and hygiene and alcohol. But the actual disease the company is trying to keep from spreading is the union.

"For this, they have another department called Security. This department is secretive and not discussed in the open. All their communication is internal, and they guard their letters and documents. But they are not perfect.

"The Security Department spies on workers. They distribute anti-union pamphlets and propaganda. They divide the workers by telling the Greeks that the Slavs are raping their women back home. This department sends guards to beat union workers and evicts families from their homes. There are no Greeks in this department except for the Greek spies in the camps. Every camp has them.

"The Security Department holds meetings in my building. Since the strike, these meetings include Colorado National Guard officers and Baldwin-Felts detectives. These men are boastful, hubristic, and say things in the halls as if employees have no ears. Women work in the office. But these men have no respect and talk about women as they pass. They frighten the women with their crude and vulgar intentions. I often smell alcohol as they pass."

Yiorgos stopped talking when the owner arrived with his coffee. He engaged the owner in the jagged Pontic dialect without hesitation. Harry made out snippets of what they discussed. From what Harry could tell, the conversation was about families and how Great Lent might affect the kafeneion business. When the owner left, Yiorgos returned to a smooth, formal Attic tongue.

"Ilias told me you are here to render justice for Eleni. Is that right?"

Harry nodded. "That is right. But finding the person who killed her is still to come. My father is the giver of justice in our village. But there, everybody knows everything, and few secrets stay secret for long. Here, it is confusing and people. . . ." Harry searched for the words, "People float like driftwood on the sea."

Yiorgos nodded. "You say you are looking for Eleni's killer? What if there were two?"

Harry considered the proposition for only a second. He said, "They will both die. That is justice."

"Even if one is Greek?"

Harry only took a second, "Yes, they will both die if they killed her. If a Greek is guilty, he is worse because he has no honor. They will both die."

Yiorgos nodded and sipped his coffee, "Harry Hantzis, I hope you will excuse my university ways, but they trained me in the method of Socrates. I ask many questions. My purpose is to find truth, not to nose into your business.

"What would you do if the Greek is well respected in the camps but a spy and traitor to the union cause? Would you hesitate to kill someone well-regarded and have the other Greeks think less of you?"

Harry considered the proposition. "If it is true what you say, and the Greek killed Eleni, the only justice is for the Greek to die. What others think is not important. It may be difficult for them to understand, but a lawgiver is a man of honor and obligation."

Yiorgos continued his *diálogos*, "Then, what is guilt? Say one person killed Eleni while the other only molested her and watched while the other drove a knife into her?"

"Again, these are acts of guilty men, and both will die. That is the only way, would you not agree?" Harry turned the tables on Yiorgos.

"I think there is a distinction. In a perfect world, thought, dialogue, and debate might address this subtlety. But we live not in a perfect world. I agree that now, in Colorado, in the middle of another Turkomachia, actions should be direct. Yes, I think both should pay the price of their crime and die."

Yiorgos motioned the owner for another coffee and gestured to Harry to see if he wanted one. Harry nodded.

Both men were quiet while the owner prepared their drinks and brought them to their table. Each man took a sip. Yiorgos returned his cup to its saucer, "How long will you pursue the killers if they are hard to catch?"

Harry thought for a moment. Then he shifted the conversation. He asked Yiorgos, "Why is this your concern? It is my duty and obligation. These have no limits in time, no end."

"I ask because the people I believe are guilty are well-protected for now." Yiorgos took a deep breath, exhaled, and leaned over the table on his elbows, his words hushed. "This is what I know by my own ears and eyes." Yiorgos, his questioning over, began a story that started the week following Eleni's murder.

Yiorgos had been at CF&I headquarters while the Security Department met behind closed doors. During a break, guards, detectives, and company management came into the hallway, smoked, and used the bathroom. By chance, Yiorgos was in a storage room next to the bathroom, out of sight. An air vent connected the two spaces. Yiorgos overheard one man say to the other, "He didn't need to kill her. That crippled Greek was knife happy, and she didn't need to die. If he weren't one of our snitches, I would have killed him. Big deal if she recognized him. I would have told her we'd kill her husband and her baby if she told anyone. That would have kept her quiet. I went there for a little fun and that Greek turned it into a slaughter, blood everywhere. She was a fighter. She got me good on the neck."

Yiorgos waited in the supply room until the Security Department meeting resumed. Then he returned to his office. Later in the afternoon, when the guards and detectives were leaving, he watched from his desk as they filed down the hallway. Two guards stopped in front of his doorway to talk. A broad-shouldered, heavy guard wore a black scarf around his neck. Just above the scarf, on the left side, were four deep marks, like a bear or a desperate woman attacked him.

Harry interrupted: "Would you recognize this man if you saw him again?"

Yiorgos said, "Yes. He looked into my office while he talked to the other man. Our eyes met for only a second. I saw no life in his stare. Only emptiness. He saw me, and he pulled his scarf higher on his neck. When the two finished talking, the second guard saluted the man with the gashes.

"Yes. I would recognize him as I would any *psychopompós*."

81

Chapter 23

Dimitri wondered where Alex had gotten the Mannlicher. A veteran must have brought it from Greece. It was a unique weapon in the mountains of Colorado, equal to if not better than the Springfield rifles of the National Guard. Most strikers carried Winchester carbines or shotguns, potent but not military weapons. A 6.5mm Mannlicher-Schönauer M1903 with a Greek cross stamped on the receiver, Dimitri knew it well. He was an expert marksman, a sniper in the Greek Army. He'd picked off concealed Turks with open sites at two hundred yards. Tonight, his target was unconcealed and glaring.

The guards used eighteen-inch and thirty-two-inch electric searchlights to unnerve strikers in the pitch of night. They played the powerful beams up to six miles across the prairies and hills.[79] The guards hid the lights during the daytime, and the strikers never knew where they would stalk. Alex and Dimitri were lucky. Tonight, the bothersome blaze emanated from a hillside two miles north of Segundo Camp.

The guards played the beam across the translucent tents. Inside, children cried and shivered with fear. Alex and Dimitri were on a low ridge about a mile from camp in a lookout position when the searchlight fired. From their outpost, they worked their way up an arroyo to within two hundred yards.

A 32-inch spotlight is big, but at two hundred yards, it is not an easy target. The two Greeks could advance no farther. Dimitri lay on his back just below a ridge out of sight and took the Mannlicher from Alex. He adjusted the rear ramp sight for the estimated distance. He added an extra notch to compensate for shooting uphill. Then Dimitri rolled onto his stomach and crawled on his elbows to just above the ridge. He rested the Mannlicher on an exposed pinyon pine root and steadied the stock with his left hand. He whispered to Alex, "Get ready to move."

Dimitri took a breath and metered his exhale. He had to extinguish the light with the first shot because the Mannlicher's muzzle flash would give away their position. Halfway through his exhale, he added slight pressure to the trigger until the weapon fired, expelling a 139-grain round at 2,520 feet per second.[80] The searchlight went black, and Dimitri cycled the bolt to charge another round. The two men ran in a crouch back down the arroyo as a machine gun sprayed from where they fired. They kept running and ducking as the machine gun's field of fire widened. Then, the smaller searchlight blazed and began scouring the hillsides opposite their retreat. Gunfire followed the light as Alex and Dimitri continued running in the opposite direction. When they were safely away, they took cover behind a boulder outcrop to catch their breaths. Other than a few scratches from thorn bushes and Alex's sprained ankle, they were unscathed.

Dimitri returned the Mannlicher to Alex and took back the Winchester Marta gave him earlier. Alex said to Dimitri, "You should keep the Mannlicher. You are better with it than me. It is a fine weapon, no?"

Dimitri smiled in the light of the new moon, "You keep it, for now, Alex. This carbine belongs to Marta. I have nothing to trade for it."

In the distance, they heard sporadic firing from the guards operating the searchlight. Dimitri said, "We better keep moving. They might send scouts or a squad to hunt us."

Alex shook his head. "No. They are afraid of the dark without their light. But you are right, we should keep moving just in case."

As the men entered open terrain, they walked side by side, their pace slowed by Alex's ankle. Shooting out the searchlight cheered Alex, lifting his depression. He asked Dimitri, "How was Stavros?"

Dimitri and Harry returned from Pueblo via Ludlow that afternoon. Alex and Dimitri had yet to discuss their trip, "Your son is in loving hands, my friend. He is as round as a pumpkin and strong as an ox. The Georgallas family is wonderful. They treat him like a prince. You are lucky to have them as friends. Do you know them from the Old Country?"

Alex shook his head. "Peter Georgallas was an old friend of Father Paschopoulos in Denver. He was a *laikos* in the church until he moved to Pueblo. You remember Father Paschopoulos, the priest who married us?"

Dimitri nodded. "Yes, he is a good man. And the Georgallas family is a wonderful family. Peter owns a flower shop. He makes a steady living selling flowers to the rich women of Pueblo and arrangements for funerals and weddings. They seem happy. I've heard of other Greeks in this business. When I traveled through New York, I saw many Greeks with flower shops."

Alex said, "Maybe that is the life for me after this strike."

Dimitri gave a considered nod, appreciating the notion.

Then Alex added, "After I have killed the man that murdered Eleni."

Alex limped more noticeably now. Dimitri shifted his Winchester to his left arm and put his right arm around Alex for support. The two men walked together over the open path and continued to talk.

Dimitri said, "Alex, my friend, we have been through much together. You know I want only what is best for you and Stavros. You helped me find work in Segundo. You and Eleni were my best friends.

"But, Alex, think about this. Does it matter who kills the murderer so long as he dies? What if someone kills him by accident or he dies of a fall? Or his horse throws him, and he breaks his neck? Is he not dead?"

Alex, limping but still under his own power, replied in a reasoned tone, "It matters to me because I owe Eleni the honor. I must honor her. Killing her murderer is the only way."

"But you honor her every day, Alex, with your love and determination and with your concern for Stavros, do you not?"

"Yes, but it is not the same, Dimitri. Her murderer must die, and it will be by my hand," answered Alex.

Dimitri shook his head, "Ah, Alex. You are as stubborn as a donkey and as wild as a kri-kri. You belong in the hills of Crete, with the pig-headed beasts."

Both men chuckled.

Dimitri did not tell Alex what he and Harry knew about Eleni's killer or killers. Both men thought Alex too rash and impulsive and unpredictable.

After Harry's meeting with Yiorgos in Pueblo, he returned to the Georgallas household, where he delighted in a Great Lent dinner. Domna served a leavened bread, *lagana*, a steamy bean, tomato, and onion casserole called *yigandes plaki*, and *lahanodolmathes orphana*, cabbage leaves stuffed with rice, tomatoes, zucchini, onions, and herbs. Nowhere to be found were blood or dairy. It was delicious.

The men rode the train back to Ludlow, and two days later, they traveled on to Segundo. In Ludlow, they talked to Tikas, who confirmed that Yiorgos was trustworthy. As they sat in Tikas's tent, they recounted what they knew. Eleni had been murdered and raped on December 27. She clutched a red bandanna in her right hand. A large knife to her heart killed her. An officer of the guards accosted her in Trinidad in early December, someone who answered to the name Linda.

With Harry's mention of the name Linda, Tikas interrupted, "It is Lindy, not Linda. Lindy is what the troopers call Linderfelt, the leader of the guards. He is evil. He is dangerous and knows no bounds. A brute. He terrorizes strikers, demeans women. He hates Greeks most of all.

"He beat me with his revolver," Tikas added, pointing to a scar above his left eye. "It was the last day of the year. I went to him under a white flag of truce, and he beat me with his gun, then arrested me. I didn't see any marks on his neck because he wore a black scarf.

"He is never alone. He cannot be trusted. Since the start of the strike, I have told Lawson and the union that he must go. He is a poison in the air, and if you are close enough to breathe it, you will die."

Harry and Dimitri knew of the man. The Greeks despised Linderfelt. They nodded at Tikas's warning. Still, they did not know if Linderfelt was Eleni's murderer. Yiorgos couldn't identify him at CF&I headquarters as the man with the gashes on his neck. Tikas said he would contact Yiorgos to see if he could get more information and confirm Linderfelt's identity.

Then, there was the matter of the Greek spy, the second murderer. Dimitri and Harry were clueless. Was the Greek from Segundo or some other camp? They only knew, according to Yiorgos, he was a Greek. Did he have a disability? They didn't know if Eleni had recognized him. Was he known around camp? Tikas knew most of the Greek spies. But he couldn't venture who killed Eleni.

Dimitri and Harry left Tikas's tent and walked to the Ludlow train station. Harry said, "We know more than before, but little of the killers. How do we find a Greek spy? He is among us, no? The guard, Lindy, will be more difficult. He is protected. The Greek? Perhaps a trap?"

Chapter 24

The congressional investigating committee returned to Washington on March 10, 1914. No longer under public scrutiny, mine guards resumed operating without restraint. Company goons in militia uniforms leveled the Forbes colony with the discovery of a scab's body on the railroad tracks. They arrested sixteen men and manhandled a striker's wife, who had just given birth to twins. Goons pitched the pleading woman from her tent into the sleet and snow where she fell to her knees.[81] The atmosphere in the coalfields grew tense and foreboding. The militia mused about burning the colonies while pocketing money from mine owners.[82]

By mid-April, Governor Ammons was staring bankruptcy in the face and recalled the remaining militia. The men who went north were among the last bona fide Colorado National Guard troops.

On April 17, General Chase entrained for Denver, and Linderfelt traveled north to recruit, soon to return. The residual force, Troop A cavalry and Company B, were under the command of Major Hamrock. Troop A was a rabble of pit bosses, foremen, guards, and engineers. They were stopgap, recruited to prevent the strikers from overrunning the smaller Company B. Captain Edwin F. Carson, an Englishman, headed Troop A. Carson had served sixteen years in the British Army fighting the Dutch Boers in South Africa and the Dervishes in Sudan.

In his account of the strike, Barron Beshoar, son of the union doctor, wrote:

> *Every pretense of fairness and impartiality disappeared with the troops that went north as the soldiers who remained behind were nothing more than gunmen who economically depended on the coal companies and were subservient to the wishes of the operators.*[83]

Hamrock's testimony later divulged that of the 130 enlisted men at Ludlow; 122 were coal company employees.[84]

87

Chapter 25

"He's here because of the dead woman at Segundo, the one they found in her tent back in December. His name is Harry Hantzis, and he's a Greek war veteran from Indianapolis. He has no connection to the strike or the union or socialist politics. He's here to find her killer. The report from Ludlow is that it's an obligation. He's met with Tikas and talked to the Greeks in camp. He has a friend, Dimitri Papas from Segundo, and that's where he's staying. Papas knew the woman. That's all I've got for now, sir."

Linderfelt sneered, "Obligation? What the hell does that mean? If he's from Indianapolis, he's probably with the union. I don't believe in coincidences. Keep your eye on this man, trooper. I want to know more. And I want to know it the minute you find anything. Understand?"

"Yes, sir. Immediately, sir."

"Dismissed."

Chapter 26

Yiorgos knew Anne well. They had worked together at CF&I headquarters for three years. Anne was a typist–secretary, and the attractive young woman was fond of Yiorgos because of his refined manner, politeness, and respectful disposition. Not all the men at headquarters treated her with respect.

Anne was a staunch Methodist, and Yiorgos's description of the Greek Orthodox faith fascinated her. Yiorgos told her that if it weren't for the Greeks, she couldn't be a Methodist because all the Christian religions were born of the Eastern Church. He told her that the first translation of the Hebrew Bible was into Greek and that he had studied the old language at university. Yiorgos said that it was a challenging course because most others in his class were theology majors, a bookish group. He said theology majors wanted to read the Bible in its *original* Greek, neglecting to mention the earlier Hebrew and Aramaic texts.

Yiorgos pursued an ulterior motive in his conversation with Anne. He didn't want to involve her in his intrigue or give away his sympathy for the strikers. Still, he had to confirm, as Tikas asked, whether Linderfelt was the officer with the gashes on his neck.

Yiorgos knew that since the first of the year, Anne had worked for Lamont Bowers, Chairman of the Board of CF&I in his secretarial pool. It was a promotion, and Anne deserved it. She was bright and ambitious and talked to Yiorgos about applying to the University of Denver, a Methodist school founded in 1864 as the Colorado Seminary. Anne wanted to teach history.

Yiorgos started the conversation elliptically, regretting he couldn't ask outright what he wanted to know. He knew the women in the office despised the guards and the ruffians frequenting CF&I headquarters since the start of the strike.

"How do you like your new job?" Yiorgos prodded.

"The other women seem nice, and some are helpful. The work is not hard, sometimes tedious, and sometimes it requires a bit of patience," Anne answered.

"How do you like working for Mr. Bowers?"

"He seems distant. But then again, he's the boss. I think he's got a lot on his mind with the strike and everything," answered Anne.

"Indeed," prompted Yiorgos. "I imagine he's got his hands full now that's he's dealing with the governor and the Colorado Guard and the detectives."

Anne gave Yiorgos an exasperated look and rolled her eyes.

Yiorgos went on, "Some of these men are foul-mannered, and it can't be pleasant for the women who work here. I have heard them in the hallways and watched how they look at the women. They are not gentlemen."

Anne looked over her shoulder to make certain no one could overhear, "They are vile. And the worst is their leader. Three women went together to talk to Mr. Bowers about their behavior, and he told them they would have to put up with it until this strike is over.

"He said, 'These men . . . the guards, and detectives . . . are here to save the company and we all must sacrifice for that goal.' He said, 'The union is a criminal organization, and the violence comes from troublemakers who aren't miners.' He said, 'They are outsiders, anarchists, and saboteurs.' He said, 'Sometimes you have to fight fire with fire.' Is he right?"

Yiorgos indicated tempered agreement. Then he asked, "But why should they disrespect women in this office? That has nothing to do with battling anarchists. Their leader should exercise his authority and make them act like gentlemen."

"Yes, but their leader is the worst among them. He is a brute and ill-tempered and walks first among them, making lewd comments and leering. The women all try to hide before he sees us."

Yiorgos asked, "Do you mean Linderfelt? I have heard his name before, but I don't know that I would recognize him."

Anne nodded. "He is broad and square jawed. He's clean-shaven and his eyes . . . his eyes are dead like he has no soul. He's glared at me many times, and every time it freezes my heart. I would hate to meet him on the street. At least here in the office, I feel like he can't do anything."

Yiorgos wanted to comfort Anne and change the subject. She was growing agitated. Still, he needed to know it was Linderfelt in the hallway, "Yes, I think I've seen him before, back in January at their big meeting. Was he wearing a black scarf?"

Anne nodded. "Yes, and it's funny you remember. I brought them coffee in the conference room, and I thought it was unusual that he wore it inside. The room was warm, and there was no need for it. You have an excellent memory, Yiorgos."

Yiorgos nodded, relieved that he could change the subject. He joked, "When you take your degree in history, you can write about your experience during these calamitous times. History professors love firsthand accounts. They use them when they publish. You do the work, and they take the credit."

Anne said, "Well, *that* sounds familiar."

Chapter 27

Harry, Marta, and Dimitri sat at a small table in Marta's tent. Harry told Marta what they knew about Eleni's murder over steamy coffee and lemony anginetti cookies drizzled with honey. He told her Linderfelt was a suspect, and he likely had an accomplice. The accomplice was a Greek spy, someone among the strikers. They would set a trap to find the Greek. Harry and Dimitri did not tell Marta the source of their information. They trusted Marta, but there was no need to expose Yiorgos.

Marta, like most of the women in camp, had been the object of Linderfelt's vulgar comments and those of his guards. At the mention of his name and the distinction between Lindy and Linda, she erupted with, "Of course! This is a pig of a man, a devil!" Then she pretended to spit on the floor. "He is without redemption, and *I* will cut out his heart and feed it in pieces to the dogs!"

Dimitri and Harry looked at each other, both thinking Marta might have the same emotional charge as Alex. Her motivation was pure, but the situation, the entrapment of Eleni's killers, required reason, logic, patience, and a plan.

Dimitri tried to lighten the moment with a chuckle, "Marta, you may have to wait in line behind Alex."

Marta didn't like his joke. Her dark eyes glared at the Greek with lethal intensity.

Dimitri thought he'd calm her with another joke, something about making a dog sick. But as he opened his mouth to speak, he thought better. He relaxed back in his chair and looked over at Harry.

Harry returned a glance at Dimitri, "Marta, you are a resourceful woman. There is not a man in this camp who can match wits with you. How do you think we might trap the Greek spy?"

Harry's thoughts about a trap were still forming. In simple terms, it would involve placing bait to draw the killer. He wanted Marta to engage in a plan, one that she devised. That way, she would be less likely to act impulsively.

Marta thought for a moment. "If it is a Greek spy, his biggest fear will be that someone knows he killed Eleni. We must let him know we have someone who saw the crime, and that person is soon to talk to the authorities. He will come to kill the person who saw the crime, and then we will kill him. That is when I will cut out his heart!"

Harry thought, *Better the spy be captured, questioned, then turned over to Marta.* He asked, "Who can we say saw the murder?"

The trio sat in silence, conjuring who might be the best bait. Dimitri said, "It must be someone who was here that night, someone who knew Eleni. It must be someone that we can trust, and someone who can defend themselves when the killer comes for them."

Marta spoke without hesitation. "Then that is me. I was here. I knew Eleni. You can trust me, and I can cut his heart out when he comes for me!"

Harry looked at Dimitri, perplexed, both men thinking the same thing. "Marta, this man has killed women before. He will not hesitate to kill you and do it like a coward. You will be in constant danger once we set the trap. You have your brother's children to think of and. . . ." Harry didn't finish because Marta was waving her arms over her head.

"It is dangerous. The children will miss me. He has killed before," she repeated. "These are true, yet they mean nothing! If we are to find Eleni's killers, we must take risks. This is my decision, no one else. I am the perfect bait, basta! It is over and settled." She crossed her arms.

Again, the two men looked at each other, exasperated. Dimitri said, "Maybe there is another way, so the bait is an object, not a person."

Another silence fell on the group. Then Harry spoke. "The only item we have that might incriminate is the bandanna. The bandanna is of a common sort without marks or distinction. Either way, the bandanna would have to be in someone's possession and whoever that is will be in danger. And we do not know for certain that the bandanna was the killer's. I don't believe this is good bait."

There followed a resigned solemnity. Then Marta said in a calmer tone, "I am the bait. You two Greek gods are my protectors. But if you don't stop the killer, I will cut out his heart and feed it to the dogs."

Chapter 28

The trap required a messenger and a message. Getting the message to the messenger was easy. The strike was rife with rumormongers and spies. Tikas knew their network. The message was the bigger problem.

The conspirators had a premise: Marta is a threat. The killer would reveal himself to remove the threat. But the killer would ask, why did Marta wait to come forward? How could she have witnessed the murder? If she goes to the authorities, are they a threat? The sheriff in Trinidad totally ignored the crime.

The conspirators discussed Marta threatening to talk to a newspaper, instead of law enforcement. Some Denver newspapers supported the strikers. But that route seemed to be not enough of a threat. Then Dimitri suggested a ploy. Marta would meet a representative of the government commission investigating the strike to give sworn testimony. The government commission was the only force the goons and mine bosses seemed to respect. That sounded good.

Then they discussed how the killer would come after Marta. Amid the tumult of the strike, with violence commonplace, would the killer or killers stalk Marta? Or would they cut her down in a machine-gun strafe? With Linderfelt involved, he could order an attack. Segundo wasn't safe.

Where to sequester Marta? Segundo was vulnerable to attacks. Goons could kill Marta and the episode made to look unintended. The only good thing about Segundo was the terrain. In the hills and ravines, fighting would be in conditions that Harry and Dimitri had trained for and lived through in Greece. But Segundo was too vulnerable, too open. The tents offered no protection. No, Marta would have to move, and someone would have to look after her niece and nephew. The children couldn't be part of the bait.

They talked about moving Marta to Ludlow. It was a bigger camp, with more strikers and better defended than Segundo. But Ludlow too was vulnerable. Many of the Ludlow colonists dug cellars under their tents and laid wooden floors. These cellars protected against gunfire, to some extent, but they were emergency structures, and Marta could not live in one.

94

Ludlow, though it was bigger, was still open to attack. The largest deployment of guards loomed only yards away on high ground. Time after time, the guards threatened to machine-gun the hapless tents and burn them to the ground. Strikers knew the talk was not just bluster. Detectives and guards had machine-gunned and razed the Forbes camp back in October.[85]

Then there was Trinidad. The town was headquarters for the guard and the Baldwin-Felts detectives. But Trinidad was governed territory, unlike the camps and surrounding hills. Harry and Dimitri discussed logistics. They would need a hotel or apartment for Marta. A place where they could observe comings and goings.

Then, there was the matter of what to do with the spy once captured. How would they move him to somewhere for questioning? Where would that be?

Alex must be told of the plan. If Alex got word that Marta knew something, he would insert himself and confuse the situation. No, Alex would have to be told and perhaps recruited for security. Harry hoped Alex would see the value of capturing the killer for information before administering justice.

The trap was not simple. Still, it was the only way to draw out the Greek spy and, through him, confirm Linderfelt as an accomplice. Time was not on their side.

Chapter 29

"No! We've discussed this since October, and we are not buying guns! The press is making us out to be bloodthirsty anarchists, and the Executive Council is nervous as hell. They don't need guns in Indianapolis, so why do we need guns in Colorado?"

Lawson slapped a brown booklet onto the conference table. The assembled staff straightened to attention. Then, picking it up, he said, "This fairytale is titled *The Western Federation of Miners from Coeur d'Alene to Cripple Creek 1894–1904*. This is the bosses' proof we are violent. Listen up,

> "*Every union should have a rifle club. I strongly advise you to provide every member with the latest improved rifle, which can be obtained from the factory at a nominal price. I entreat you to take action on this important question so that in two years we can hear the martial tread of twenty-five thousand armed men in the ranks of labor. — President Western Federation of Miners.*"[86]

Then he threw the booklet across the room and growled, "We are not the Western Federation of Miners, damn it! CF&I knows this, but it doesn't matter. To the public, we're all radicals.

"This is a strike, not a revolution. Snyder, you got the guns in November, right?[87] How many did we buy then? Seventy, a hundred? The strikers already had a thousand. Hell, they went door-to-door in Trinidad begging weapons. And they got them! Why did we spend the money? I know it was a show of support, but damn, the Council is nervous. The Council says, stop spending money! Wrap this thing up! Take the governor's offer, arbitrate! We'll strike CF&I later for recognition when the economy is better.[88]

"Gentlemen and brothers, we have got to get this thing under control, or we risk having the rug pulled out from under us. It's that simple. You are organizers. The union pays you to battle for the members. When you're not making progress, retreat is the order of battle. We can't shoot all the guards and expect to win. That's not how this works. We need public opinion on our side. We need politicians on our side. We need the president of the United States on our side. We need the secretary of labor on our side. And we can't shoot enough goons to make that happen.

"Until the Executive Council says otherwise, I'm in charge of this campaign. And anybody with a problem, you come to me. Diamond, do I make myself clear? No runaround or back channels.

"Okay, let's go camp by camp and give our assessments. Start with Ludlow and make it sharp, I've got to go to Denver and meet with the governor's staff. The train leaves Trinidad in forty minutes."

John Lawson was a torn man. His instincts were to support the strikers and take the battle to the guards. But the orders from UMWA headquarters in Indianapolis were to wrap things up. The strike was a loser. CF&I would never agree to union recognition. This message passed through the highest levels of government to the UMWA Executive Council. Looking at upcoming strikes in the eastern coalfields, the union needed to conserve resources.

Lawson was a team player, and he would implement the instructions of the elected officers of his union. But he didn't like it. He knew the plight of the strikers and was proud of their resolve. Now, in March, with spring around the corner, the demand for coal would diminish in an already slow economy. The bargaining power of the strikers would decrease with demand. But violence and retribution have an economy all their own.

Chapter 30

"There is a rooming house in Trinidad. That is where Marta will stay, Alex. We will watch her closely. When the spy comes for her, we will capture him. Then we will question him before we kill him."

Harry and Alex sat together, leaning forward with their knees nearly touching. The kerosene lamp in Alex's tent cast a conspirative drama on the canvas walls.

"When you have finished with questions, will you hand him to me?" asked Alex.

"We will deliver justice. If it is to be by your hand, then that is his fate. It is too soon to know everything. First, we must catch him. You must know the plan so you can help. When we send the message, set the trap, and the spy finds out, the plan will quicken. You need to stay in Segundo until the time is right. Do you understand, Alex?"

Alex nodded hesitantly.

Harry didn't tell Alex about Linderfelt. Harry knew the young man would try to kill Linderfelt, and the commander of the guards was untouchable. If Alex went for Linderfelt, Stavros would grow up an orphan.

Dimitri added, "Alex, this is the time we all work as one. If we don't, the plan will fail, and the killer will go free. Just like hunting the boar, no? Some men chase the boar, and other men kill the boar. At the end of the day, we all eat together.

"Harry and I are chasers. We will run the boar toward the trap. First the trap, then the kill."

Alex again nodded, this time positively, "But I will get to kill him. This is my contribution, is it not?"

Harry repeated, "If it is to be by your hand, then that is his fate. It is too soon to know everything."

Alex settled in. He calmed. He respected the two war veterans and felt a bond with Dimitri. He knew Harry was here as a friend, but the steely Greek was on a pursuit of his own. Alex knew Harry spoke the truth, but the son of the assassin kept much to himself. Alex thought Harry was driven by something unseen, something deep within. Alex doubted Harry would ever be a close friend. But trusting the plan was all that mattered for now.

98

Alex was right. Something deep inside drove Harry. His wartime debt of honor filled his waking mind, and often his sleep. But there was more. Allowing Marta to be the bait unsettled him. Putting her life on the line stirred his mind like the dissonance of a cracked church bell. Using Marta was logical. She was a capable woman, fearless and brave. But the killer was a coward and ruthless, not someone who would fight fair. The killer would strike without warning or mercy. Harry was fond of Marta. He respected her independence and confidence, and her dark eyes were deep pools, both mysterious and familiar.

Dimitri asked Alex, "Can you talk with the Georgallas family about looking after Marta's niece and nephew for a week, maybe two? Their father is with the strikers in the hills. The children will be safest in Pueblo."

Alex nodded and said he would call. If the Georgallas family agreed, he would take the train to Pueblo. He would bring the children on Sunday to attend services and see Stavros. At the mention of his son, Alex smiled for the first time.

Chapter 31

"If we are to be her protectors, we need guns, sidearms. I have the Ruby. We can get you a pistol from the Greek baker at Ludlow depot. No, wait. I remember. Goons raided him in November. Better we use another friend.[89] We will defend at close range, so pistols and knives and maybe a shotgun, no?"

Harry nodded as Dimitri outlined their tactical configuration.

"Marta needs a weapon. She needs a pistol. She already has a knife, no?"

Harry smiled.

"We will take her somewhere to practice with the weapon. Best she carries a revolver. Less complicated, don't you think?"

Harry again nodded.

"The knives are no problem. These, we find anywhere." Dimitri reached down to his boot and withdrew a six-inch hunting knife. The honed blade gleamed in the kerosene lamplight. "But the pistols are more difficult. Rifles and shotguns, no problem. But pistols, good reliable pistols, are rare. I will ask our friend, the Bulgarian, the one who sold us the lamb."

Harry raised his head and interjected, "You trust a Bulgarian with weapons? I'm surprised he will even speak to a Greek. Greece punished his motherland in Thrace at Thessaloniki. The Bulgarians ran home like scared rabbits. He must harbor ill will, no?"

Dimitri shook his head. "No, he is more American than Bulgarian. With him, money speaks loudest. He can buy pistols for us, and no one will know. I think an American Colt forty-five for you, Harry? Perhaps a small thirty-eight revolver for Marta? Are these acceptable?"

Harry nodded. He looked forward to firing the Colt, a semiautomatic with a reputation for reliability and lethality. Marta would be happy with the smaller gun.

Chapter 32

"What is this, a baby gun? I want a gun like yours! Do you think I can't lift a big gun? Are you afraid it will be too heavy for poor Marta? You two have the bodies of Greek gods and the brains of dull donkeys. You think *me* a weakling? Give me that big gun!"

A mile from Segundo Camp, in an opening off a pathway used by bighorn sheep, Marta critiqued Dimitri's choice of firearms. Dimitri explained, "But Marta, yours *is* a big gun. Look, the bullets are almost as large as Harry's. . . ."

"The little gun shoots five, his shoots eight. After I shoot five, am I to find another three bullets, stick them into the tiny cylinders and fire some more? Should I implore the killer, 'Please, sir, wait just a moment while I reinvigorate my little gun?'"

"But Marta, your gun is simple. It is foolproof, a revolver. There is nothing to go wrong when it fires. With the Colt come greater risks."

Marta lifted the Colt from the wooden case, still holding her smaller US Revolver Top Break .38. She weighed both like a scale and put down the revolver. She gripped the Colt in her left hand and drove the loaded magazine into the butt of the grip with the heel of her right hand. Then she moved the weapon to her right hand and cycled the action to charge the first round. She put the gun to safe, and handed it butt-first back to Dimitri. With dripping sarcasm, she swooned, "Here is your big gun. I could scarcely lift it. Now I need a siesta. I am worn to the bone."

Harry couldn't help himself. He laughed, "Marta, take the Colt. It is yours. I will use the revolver. Still, I am curious. The Colt is a respected weapon. If it is not too much to ask, may I fire it? With your instruction, of course."

Marta thought for a moment and answered in a measured tone, "Yes, this we can arrange. You seem. . . ." She searched for the right word. "You seem . . . manly enough."

All three laughed.

Chapter 33

Harry and Dimitri took the train from Segundo to Ludlow. There they hoped to meet Tikas, tell him of their plans, and discuss the best way to insert their message into the spy network. At the Ludlow depot, they detrained and began walking the quarter mile to the camp.

Dimitri asked Harry, "It is best that we have a deadline in the message, no? Three days, maybe? Marta will meet the investigator in three days. Then the killer will need to rush into action. He will be more likely to make a mistake if we rush him, no? Do you agree?"

Harry thought for a moment. "Yes. I think two days is too soon. Three is better. We don't know how long it will take for the message to get through, and we don't know where the spy is. We will talk to Ilias. He will know best what to do."

As they stepped off the raised wooden platform at Ludlow Station, two guards with Springfield rifles stepped around the corner. The first guard, a lanky, wall-eyed man with a slouching posture, ordered, "That's far enough, boys. Where do you think you're going?"

Dimitri looked at Harry. The second guard, a shorter, stocky man with the same slouching posture, grunted, "Answer the man, you damn dagos."

The guards were armed, but not intimidating. Their uniforms were sloven, their appearance rough, and their fighting stance wasn't. Standing with their feet close together and their hips square, they would topple in a rush. Dimitri saw the same thing. Their ill-kept Springfields were of little use in close quarters. Harry saw markings and dirt on their receivers. The guns had been mishandled. And the guards could not bring them to bear in a fight. They would serve as little more than clubs. Without bayonets, clubs would be of little advantage. Harry saw the Springfields lacked the steel butt-plates of the Mannlichers. He doubted these men were trained in hand-to-hand fighting. Neither guard carried a sidearm. The veterans gathered these impressions in a blink.

Dimitri, whose English was excellent, feigned a broken response, "My friend, he do not talk the English. And me? Not so good. Sirs, we travel in Ludlow. It is the name day of Saint Agapios! A holy day! We bear tidings from the church in Pueblo." Then Dimitri offered the guards the sweet bread he carried in a sack prepared for him and Harry earlier that morning by Marta.

"Are you boys carrying any arms?" asked the lanky guard.

"Sirs, we have four arms. I have two and he has two," answered Dimitri, waving his hands before the guards. Harry almost chuckled.

"Guns, dagos! Guns!" the guard shot back.

"Oh . . . no sir. We carry no guns. Only bread." Both Greeks had hunting knives hidden in their high boots.

Just then, two Greeks wearing red bandannas walked up behind Harry and Dimitri. The first striker inquired in Greek, "Is everything okay?"

Dimitri wheeled toward the man and in Greek said in a cheery voice, "I have told these *malakas* it is a holiday. Play along and take some of this bread. *Yassou!*"

The two Greeks played the part, took some bread, and crossed themselves. Then Dimitri turned back to the guards and again offered the bread. Neither guard accepted. The stocky, shorter guard said, "You dagos watch yourselves and don't make any trouble. Understand?"

Dimitri smiled. Harry did not. He watched the hips and feet of the guards. These would be the first to move if they attacked. Outnumbered, the guards cursed and grumbled and retreated around the corner of the station.

With the guards gone, Harry and Dimitri turned to the two strikers and thanked them. The strikers said they were scouts who watched the station for just such encounters. If needed, they could summon other strikers waiting nearby. The tall striker produced a metal whistle, "Just like a New York cop."

Harry said, "Those men did not look like soldiers. Their carriage was craven, and they did not act like trained troops."

The tall striker replied, "They are no more soldiers than I am Rockefeller. They wear the uniforms of soldiers, but they are pretenders, drunks, and simpletons. They think it grand sport to shoot at strikers and bully families and children and leer at women. Give them no respect because they have earned none. They are cowards;

face-to-face they run like rabbits. But they shoot from the hills into tents with children, then laugh loud enough that I hear them in camp.

"They are brazen of late. They talk of burning the tents, bombing the camp, machine-gunning the strikers. They have grown bolder since the government commission left the coalfields. They were afraid of the government people and kept to themselves. Now, they think they have won, and they intend to finish us. They have sent their boss north to recruit more pretenders."[90]

Harry asked, "Who is the boss?"

With disgust on his face, the tall striker answered, "Linderfelt, the devil."

Chapter 34

Tikas was happy to see Harry and Dimitri but leaden with fear for Ludlow's safety. Harry and Dimitri agreed he should worry. Ludlow was too open. There was no way to defend the colony. The tents were tinder. The guards occupied the high ground. There was no defense, and women and children would receive no quarter. Tikas hoped that with the holidays coming, first Catholic Easter, then Greek Easter a week later, the mood would lighten. Perhaps the guards would withdraw and honor the de facto ceasefire that was the subject of endless negotiations.

Tikas's countrymen were as likely to break the ceasefire as the guards. Tikas was the leader of the Greeks and Ludlow's head man. But the impulsive, untamed Greeks were a constant source of worry and volatility. They troubled Tikas as much as the guards.

Harry explained the plan for trapping the Greek spy. Tikas agreed it was wise to move Marta to Trinidad, away from Segundo or any camp. He questioned how Harry and Dimitri could watch Marta at the rooming house. Harry explained they would take a room nearby and take shifts in the lobby or street. Someone would stay in Marta's room. Harry said they would enlist Alex to help protect Marta.

Harry asked Tikas, "Do you have any idea who the Greek spy is? Is there anyone we might watch for?"

Tikas shook his head, "No. It is hard to tell. I would not put it past Linderfelt to lie, even to one of his own. He may try to cover his crime. Yiorgos may have overheard the conversation correctly. But Linderfelt would lie to his own men, to put the blame off on a Greek."

Harry agreed. But the bandanna Eleni clutched suggested her attacker was someone posing as a striker, an impostor. Someone she ripped the neckerchief from in her frantic defense.

Earlier, Harry and Dimitri had discussed the possibility that Linderfelt had lied. If no one pursued Marta, they would fashion another trap. For now, Marta was bait, and they would guard her with their lives.

Harry asked, "What is the best way to set the trap in motion? Should we start a rumor among the spies? We need Eleni's killer to believe that Marta saw the crime and will talk with someone from the government commission in Trinidad."

Tikas thought for a moment, "The guards tap the phone lines. They know everything when we make a call from Ludlow." What Tikas didn't say was that the union tapped the phones from the guards' headquarters in Trinidad, tit for tat.[91]

"You should make a call to someone about your plans. The guards will know about it the instant you speak."

Harry asked, "Is that too obvious?"

"No, they will think they have fooled us. To them, we are dumb dagos. Hubris engulfs them."

With the details set, the only question was when. Harry and Dimitri thought Alex should phone the flower shop in Pueblo in three days. On the call, Alex would talk with Peter Georgallas about bringing Marta's nephew and niece to stay with them. He would ask about his son. He would let it slip that Marta was planning to talk to someone from the government commission about the murder she witnessed. They would meet in Trinidad in three days with a representative's arrival from Washington, DC. When Alex arrived in Pueblo, he would tell Peter of the ploy.

Chapter 35

"Hello, Peter, this is Alex."

"Hello, Alex, so good to hear a from you."

Peter, how are your family and my son?"

"Everyone in the family is well, Alex, and your son is a treat. He is strong and hungry and growing every day like zucchini in summer."

"Peter, I have a favor to ask. This one for our friend, Marta."

"Certainly, Alex, for you and Marta, we are happy to help."

"Marta's niece and nephew need a place to stay for a week, maybe two. They are wonderful children and will not be a problem. Their father is with the strikers in the hills. Marta is to talk to an investigator from the government commission in Trinidad. She will stay at a rooming house in El Corazon until then."

"This is no problem for us, Alex. We will be happy to take the children. Is Marta well?"

"Yes, she is well, but she has delicate business before her. Marta witnessed Eleni's killing, and she must describe what she saw to the government. The local sheriff is not interested."

"Indeed, that is delicate business, Alex."

"She was afraid to talk before now, fearing for her brother's children. But Eleni's spirit haunts her. Eleni told her to speak up and not be afraid."

"Indeed, you and the children are welcome here, Alex."

"If it pleases you and Domna, I will bring the children with me on Saturday, and we can attend the church service on Sunday. Then I will return to Segundo to help the strikers."

"Yes, yes. Come to Pueblo on Saturday, and we will have a fine dinner before church."

"Thank you, Peter. You and Domna are true friends. I am in your debt forever."

"Nonsense. We are friends, and that is all. We will see you this Saturday. You and the children go with God."

Chapter 36

"Sir, you said you wanted to know about the Greek from Indianapolis the minute we knew something. I think this is important."

"Go ahead, soldier. What do you have?"

"The man we have listening to the phone line out of Ludlow sent a report. He said the husband of the dead woman from Segundo called a friend in Pueblo. The husband said a woman named Marta is going to talk to an investigator from the government commission. He said she saw the murder.

"Hantzis, the Greek from Indianapolis, has been palling around with the husband of the dead woman. We think it's all tied together. The woman, Marta, is moving from Segundo to a rooming house in Trinidad. The investigator from Washington is supposed to be here in a couple of days to take her statement."

"Has she left Segundo?"

"We're not sure."

"Then find out and get back to me as soon as you know her whereabouts. Understand? This sounds like the union trying to stir trouble with the government. Dismissed."

"Yes, sir."

It didn't take long for the guards to discover Marta had left Segundo. Harry, Dimitri, and Marta made a show of her going. Everyone in the small camp, including the company spies, knew she had left. The misinformation percolated up the chain of command to Linderfelt. The commander of the guards had a simple plan to make sure Marta never uttered a word to the government, or anyone else.

Chapter 37

Alex took the children to Pueblo. The train was teaming with Catholic strikers and families traveling north for Palm Sunday services at the new Sacred Heart Church. Its Gothic Revival style was grander than the Greek Church. The Catholics had been in Pueblo longer and raised more money. Fathers Machebeuf and Raverdy trekked there in 1860 from Santa Fe.[92] The French missionaries found an adobe hamlet home to trappers, traders, miners, and Mexicans. They stopped long enough to say Mass, bless a few marriages, and baptize children. Then they traveled on to Denver. The two religions shared much, but not a calendar. Palm Sunday for the Greeks would come a week later, on Catholic Easter.

Twenty-five miles north of Walsenburg, the train continued its gradual descent to Pueblo. Entering a greening ravine, it crossed the Huerfano River, filling with the spring melt. The snow thaw sought lower lands and fed the Arkansas River fifty miles north. The Mexican family seated in front of Alex noted the crossing. The father said to his son, "Huerfano means orphan. Learn the word. It is important that you speak English for your education." The boy nodded and repeated the words for his father.

Alex looked over at Marta's niece and nephew bundled in their simple wool coats, asleep, leaning against each other. He had a disquieting thought about Stavros raised an orphan. Alex fought to ignore the notion, but his mind ranged mulish and lucid.

Alex would die to honor Eleni. But what of his son? How would the child's life upend upon Alex's death? Untamable rage burned in Alex, but his depression was lifting. He saw his world now in a widening frame. The flow of the Huerfano was Ananias at baptism. Alex was Saul, with the scales falling from his eyes.[93]

Chapter 38

After three hours, Marta was bored with being bait. She lingered at the view from her second-floor, one-window room. She gazed at two prominent landmarks, Simson's Rest to the northwest and Prospect Point farther to the west. There was little else to occupy her.

The Purgatoire Rooming House was in Trinidad's oldest neighborhood. El Corazon de Trinidad was founded in the 1860s as a waypoint on the Santa Fe Trail. James Williams, a Union major in the Civil War, built the faded red adobe rooming house in 1880. It rose to three levels with seven guest rooms. Harry and Dimitri took rooms on the third level with views of the 1st Street entrance and the rear entrance off Beech Street. That entrance was locked except for deliveries. Marta's two guardians planned to spell one another, one with Marta and the other on overwatch. It had been three days since Alex called Peter and the guards overheard their conversation. Now, theirs was a waiting game.

Harry and Dimitri arrived in Trinidad the night before Marta. They traveled by local freight, avoiding passenger service. They dismounted as the train slowed for a switch to enter the Trinidad yards. Alex went with Marta, helping her with her bags and booking her into the rooming house. Then, Alex returned to Segundo, leaving the appearance to anyone watching that she was alone.

Someone *was* watching.

A short, stocky figure in a tattered cowboy duster and floppy pinch-front felt hat followed the couple from Cimino Park, a short distance from the Trinidad train station. He kept his distance and watched as Marta and Alex entered the rooming house. He watched Alex leave toward the train station and sensed that Marta was alone. He waited for her to come out for a walk or for a meal or any reason. Then he would pick a suitable spot. The crime would look like a robbery or, perhaps, like Marta was soliciting as a prostitute. He hadn't decided. The prostitution ploy was attractive because he could have his way with the tempting young woman before he killed her.

But the watcher was himself being watched. Harry noted the man from behind the drawn curtains in his third-floor room. The stranger followed a block behind Alex and Marta as they approached on South Convent Street, then turned onto 1st Street to enter the rooming house. The stranger saw them enter the rooming house, then he retreated to a livery stable catty-corner from the rooming house where he watched the entrance. Harry couldn't see his face, but he noted a limp.

Harry watched the watcher for a few minutes and then rapped on the wall separating his room and Dimitri's. In less than a minute, Dimitri knocked at Harry's door, and Harry let him in. Both men crossed to the curtained window and through a narrow slit, Harry pointed out the suspect. Dimitri asked, "Should we go down and confront him?"

Harry answered, "It is best if we both go to Marta's room and plan. You go first. You should be able to see him from her window. Then I'll come in a minute. That way, we don't lose sight of him.

"Is the rear door locked?"

Dimitri nodded. "Yes, but I will check it again to make sure. Give me three minutes before you leave for Marta."

Harry nodded, and Dimitri left the room.

Only seconds after Dimitri left, a Case delivery truck carrying a steam-powered tractor chugged down 1st Street headed southwest. It stopped in front of the livery. The driver got out and went inside the business. He parked the rig, blocking Harry's view of the stranger. Harry watched for a few seconds. The stranger stepped around the front of the delivery truck and took up another position with an unrestricted view of the rooming house's entrance, this time on a sidewalk bench. The stranger didn't hide. He thought no one was watching him. Harry waited the three minutes, then went to Marta's room.

Dimitri and Marta saw the same thing, the stranger now seated on the bench. Marta answered Harry's knock, "He is watching. No doubt that is what he is doing."

Harry nodded, then turned to Dimitri. "Can you get out through the back door?"

Dimitri shook his head. "It is locked. But I can open a rear window and climb out."

Harry said, "He won't be able to see you if you go through the backyard and cross over to Commercial Street, then come around behind him. Walk all the way to Animas Street, then back down to 1st Street. I'll go up to your room, and when I see you're in position on Animas Street, I'll come for Marta, and we will go to the front door. I'll stay out of sight. When she leaves the rooming house, she will stay on the opposite side of 1st Street and walk toward the river. That will cause the stranger to cross over 1st Street to follow her. When he does, and his back is to me, I'll follow Marta. You, Dimitri, must try to stay in front of Marta, but not let the stranger know you are watching. Can you do that?"

"I am sly as a marten," Dimitri said with a smile.[94]

"And Marta, you must act as though you are unaware but still wary. We don't want him to think anything is different, that anything is. . . ."

"Yes, yes. I will be the perfect bait. You two just make sure that you can join me when he comes for me. If you are late, he will be of no use to anyone but the devil," Marta flashed.

Dimitri left by the rear window and circled like Harry suggested. Harry went to Dimitri's room with a view of Animas Street. When he saw Dimitri peek around the corner of a dry goods store, he chuckled. Dimitri held an oversized arrangement of flowers and looked as harmless as a love-smitten schoolboy. Dimitri gave a quick wave, then retreated around the corner.

As the sun set behind Spanish Peaks, the waning light cast false serenity. Harry returned to Marta's room, "Are you ready?"

Marta nodded, put on her long beige coat, a matching scarf, and shouldered her brown leather purse large enough for the Colt.

"Your gun. Is it ready?"

Marta stared at the Greek with a blast of indignation and hardened her eyes in cold confidence.

Harry nodded and opened the room's door. She walked past him into the hallway, as poised and unruffled as royalty.

At the front entrance, Harry stayed out of sight. Marta opened the door, and as she did, she said to Harry under her breath, "I know that limp." Then she stepped onto the 1st Street sidewalk, turned left, and began trolling for a killer.

Chapter 39

The dark soul tracking Marta lived a life of deceit. Nikolaos Michaloliakos was the son of a Greek prostitute and a Turkish spy posing as a rug merchant. The couple never married, and villagers shunned the disfigured Nick Michaels his entire childhood. He neither excelled in studies nor could he play sports. He was born with a congenital abnormality that bowed his right leg. The affliction rendered the leg shorter than his left and induced chronic back pain.

Spying for CF&I was his second career in espionage. His first was informing on the Greek Navy from his village of Perama near the Port of Keratsini and its shipyard. He reported to a Turkish intelligence officer and received a few drachmas every month with which he bought ouzo, cigarettes, hashish, and women.

Nick had begun spying for the Turks at fourteen under his father's supervision. He carried a shoeshine box to Keratsini. There he set up his business at the main gate, shining boots, listening, and watching. He developed a keen memory. He honed the skill of allowing people to talk unprompted. He presented himself as a sympathetic figure, focused on the other person, then steered conversations toward the information for which the Turks paid him.

In 1908, with Sultan Abdul Hamid II's rule coming to a chaotic end, Nick left for America. He made his way to Colorado, where he found work in Denver as a bootblack and a petty thief. Nick was shining shoes outside of Denver's Union Station when a well-dressed customer asked about his nationality. Nick said he was from Greece, and he was saving to open his own business. He told the stranger that he hoped to find a better job than shining shoes.

The customer asked if Nick wanted to earn two dollars for attending and reporting on a meeting, a meeting to be conducted in Greek. The meeting was an organizing rally led by the Industrial Workers of the World, the Wobblies. The union was agitating in the Denver area, trying to get a foothold in the hard rock mining camps to the west. The customer was a Baldwin-Felts detective.

Nick accepted the offer, attended the meeting, reported back the next day, and received two dollars. Detailed and informative, Nick's report gave the names of the organizers and key workers. He listed dates and gave a rendition of the militant rhetoric. When the detective asked if he wanted more work, Nick jumped at the opportunity.

By the fall of 1913, at the start of the strike, Nick was posing as a pro-union weighboss at the big Number One Mine in Cokedale. That operation produced fifteen hundred tons of coal a day. The 350 nearby ovens operating around the clock reduced the coal to eight hundred tons of coke.[95] Cokedale was halfway between Trinidad and Segundo, about seven miles in either direction.

Nick was free to range through the company towns. Early in his spying career, he worked at the Victor Mine, and there he used his prominent position to have his way with miners' wives. He told them, "Sleep with me, or I'll short your husband when he weighs out."

Nick's wanton abuse led to a flare-up involving a Slovenian family and an irate, homicidal husband. A big Croat battered Nick to the doorsteps of hell. Nick was spared and Eleni doomed when a company guard rounded a toolshed to urinate, saw the beating, and pulled a pistol on the Croat. The company fired the miner and evicted his family. Afterword, Nick's Baldwin-Felts handlers warned him, "We're paying you enough you can buy sex like a normal man. Stop forcing yourself on women, or you'll be of no use to us. You can go back to shining shoes."

Baldwin-Felts reassigned Nick to Cokedale in 1911. His handlers' admonition stuck until the strike began and all rules were off. Nick was a dark man with a black soul. But whatever the cause, whatever his background, he alone bore responsibility for his traitorous, deviant, and now murderous actions. Pity not Nick Michaels.

Eleni's last words were, "*Na pas sto diaolo sakatévo!*" (Go to hell, cripple!)

Chapter 40

Alex did not return to Segundo. He walked to the train station and waited for the next passenger service to come and go. There was nothing for Alex to do in Segundo, so he reasoned he should stay in Trinidad, keep out of sight, and there he might help. In Trinidad, he might exact the revenge his heart burned for.

Alex knew that Harry and Dimitri would watch the rooming house, and he thought Marta was in expert hands and well-protected. So, he waited in the saloon of the Columbian Hotel, the requisitioned headquarters of CF&I's guard force, three blocks from the rooming house.

Alex was not wearing his Cretan garb or his red handkerchief. He looked much like the other workingmen in Trinidad on a Wednesday evening. The only giveaway was his boots. He wore the tall leather riders that the Greeks preferred, a better design for secreting knives.

Alex stepped to the bar and ordered a beer. The bartender, an older Italian man, took little notice of Alex and delivered a foaming mug without remark. Alex took a couple of sips and looked around for a table. He spotted one in the corner opposite the entrance with a vantage of the room and no approach from behind. He left the bar and headed toward it, but two mine guards cut him off with the same destination in mind. For a second, Alex boiled. But, before he could say anything, a voice from a nearby table called, "Here, friend, sit down and we'll tell each other lies until the rooster crows!" It was Ivan Todorov, the Bulgarian farmer, the seller of lambs and pistols, and a somewhat unlikely friend of the Greeks. Alex knew Ivan, but remained curious about the Bulgarian. It was as Dimitri said, Ivan was more American than Bulgarian. With him, money talked loudest.

Ivan was older than Alex, already in his twenties in 1896 when he arrived in America with a dog-eared copy of Aleko Konstantinov's *To Chicago and Back*. Ivan made his way to the city and worked at Union Stock Yards. The massive complex on the south side was a 375-acre maze of fetid livestock pens, rendering stations, and railroad yards. The operation employed twenty-five thousand people, mostly immigrants, producing 82 percent of the meat consumed in America. Ivan left for Colorado two years later.[96]

He worked as a gandy dancer, a section hand, for the Colorado and Southern Railway in Pueblo. He met and married a lovely and strong-willed Irish woman, and together they marked off a section of land west of Trinidad for homesteading.

By 1904 they had built a comfortable adobe-and-log home and improved the land as required by law. Colorado rewarded the couple with a deed to two hundred acres, property that many shunned as unworkable. But the swelling hills and rough terrain reminded Ivan of his family's farm near Presa de Zhrebchevo in the southern foothills of the Balkan Mountains. First introducing goats, then sheep, and investing all the blood, sweat, and tears two people could, Ivan and Blathnaid made their dream a reality. The tractor being delivered to the livery that day was for his farm, and Ivan was in Trinidad to sign for it.

As the two drank their beers and then two more, Ivan explained his plan for the tractor to Alex. The forty horsepower steam vehicle was a self-propelled power station. Not only could it pull an assortment of farm implements and wagons, but it came with a power takeoff. This belt drive could run machinery from sawmills to wool carders to machines not yet imagined. Ivan's and Blathnaid's lives were about to get more comfortable and more productive.

After the second beer and just before they ordered another round, a young man came into the saloon, stepped up to the bar, and asked for Ivan. The bartender nodded toward the table, and the young man approached. He was the driver of the delivery truck and was there to tell Ivan that the paperwork was ready for his signature.

Ivan said to Alex, "Please come with me to see this amazing machine. You must excuse me if I gloat with pride. There are only a few in the county."

Alex, unaware that the livery was the one near the rooming house, said, "It would be an honor to see such an engine. Is it nearby?"

"Just two blocks. We'll be there in no time," Ivan shot back.

The men paid their tab and left the bar, and their timing could not have been better.

116

Chapter 41

Sometimes luck runs out. It ran out for Nick Michaels that warm spring evening in Trinidad. Marta left the rooming house just as Alex and Ivan left the saloon. Marta walked south down 1st Street toward the river. The street was empty save for a few automobiles and riders on horseback. The only other pedestrians were on the opposite side of the street, including Dimitri. When Marta was a half block past the stranger, Nick Michaels rose from the bench, crossed 1st Street, and began following.

Dimitri saw Marta leave the rooming house and began sauntering on the opposite side of the street, holding his arrangement of flowers and whistling to himself. He was ten yards in front of Marta. Using his peripheral vision and the reflective glass of storefront windows, he kept a subtle watch.

Harry left the rooming house when he saw Nick Michaels cross the street to follow Marta. Michaels was unconcerned about anyone behind him. He didn't look back one time.

Two blocks into her walk, Marta came alongside a vacant lot next to an old storefront. Nick was twenty yards behind her, and just before he began his sprint, he looked around. But Harry saw his intention and ducked behind an automobile parked on the street.

Alex rounded the corner onto 1st Street, on their way to the livery with Ivan. He saw the action two blocks away and knew at once what was happening. He didn't want to rush in and spoil the trap. He said to Ivan, "My friend, I will explain later, but now I need to leave you." He dashed across 1st Street, up Beech Street to 2nd Street. Then, as fast as he could run, he covered the three blocks. His sprint put Alex ahead of Nick Michaels at the opposite end of the vacant lot.

As Marta walked past the lot, she tensed. In that instant, Nick Michaels pulled a hunting knife from his duster and began sprinting toward her. Even with his deformity, he covered the distance with impressive speed. Marta heard the running footsteps, pulled the Colt from her purse and, gripping the weapon with both hands, wheeled in Nick's direction. He had another five yards to finish his attack, but the dark bore of the semiautomatic leveled at his chest stunned him. Nick froze in midstride with the knife at his side. Marta pronounced, "You have met your death, swine."

In the next instant, Nick's world went black. He never heard Harry arrive behind him, nor did he see the revolver butt Harry slammed into the back of his neck. His knife thudded on the sidewalk, and he fell to his knees, then his face. Dimitri tossed his flower arrangement and arrived a second after Harry, his Ruby in hand. Then Alex appeared from the back of the vacant lot with his knife at the ready. For a moment, Harry, Marta, and Dimitri looked puzzled. As he approached, Alex shrugged and said, "I thought I might help."

Harry searched and disarmed Nick. Dimitri tied Nick's hands and elbows behind his back, and Harry motioned to an entrance to the abandoned building. With the prisoner bound, Marta put the Colt back into her purse.

Nick was down for a ten count. Then, in his dizzy world, he sensed two men picking him off the sidewalk and carrying him by his armpits into the abandoned building. Once in the building, Dimitri gagged Nick with a red bandanna and bound it at the back of his neck. They sat the prisoner down on a wall and bound his feet.

The four huddled a few feet away, and Dimitri kept his Ruby pointed at the prisoner. Alex preempted, "This is the best time to kill him. I'll do it now."

Marta put her hands on her hips and started to lay down a marker. Harry cut her off. "We will not kill him here. We need to question him first. This location is not secure. If we kill him here, what will become of his body? It is not a good place. We must move him before daylight. Any ideas?"

There was silence. Then Alex recounted his run-in with Ivan, the tractor delivery, and an idea formed in his mind.

Chapter 42

Dimitri was right. With Ivan, money talked.

Alex and Dimitri walked to the livery, where Ivan was signing papers for his new steam-powered tractor. After marveling over the machine as if nothing was out of the ordinary, Dimitri inquired, "Ivan, how did you get to Trinidad?"

Ivan told him he drove his farm truck.

Nonchalant, Dimitri asked, "Ivan, would you rent your truck to Alex and me for the evening? We will return it in the morning to your farm. You can ride with your new tractor to your home. We will be cautious with your pride and joy. This we promise."

Ivan offered, "Brothers, if you have a need for a ride back to Segundo, I'll be happy to drive you."

Dimitri answered, "No, no. We have a small business matter to attend to before morning. That is all."

"Nothing illegal, I trust?"

"No, no. Nothing like that. No, we need to move a spit for the Easter celebration next weekend. Oh, and we invite you and Blathnaid," Dimitri assured.

Ivan was skeptical. He knew the two Greeks were up to something cagy related to the strike. He supported the strikers and found the Greeks among them regular customers for his lambs, eggs, milk, and especially his *kiselo mlyako*, sour, unstrained yogurt.

Dimitri continued, "Would two dollars make your trouble worthwhile?"

"Gentlemen, it is not the money that concerns me. No. It is the well-being of my truck. Do either of you know how to drive?"

By drive, Ivan meant start, steer, and stop, none of which were intuitive activities with a Ford Model T.

Alex and Dimitri looked at each other, then back at Ivan, nodding and murmuring, "Why, of course."

"Two dollars has bought you a truck for the night. Should I come with you to show you how it starts?" asked the Bulgarian. He knew the Greeks didn't have the slightest notion of what to do.

The two Greeks looked at each other. Alex said, "Please, if you have the time."

119

"Yes. I parked the truck at the hotel. We will walk there when I finish with the papers, okay?"

The Greeks nodded.

When Ivan returned to the livery office to sign the papers, Dimitri asked Alex, "Do you know about this truck? Have you ever driven one?"

Alex shook his head, disconnected from the universe they were about to enter.

While Ivan was signing the papers, Alex ran up the street, collected the flowers that Dimitri tossed, and told Harry and Marta what was afoot. Alex asked if either of them knew how to drive. In the dim light of the abandoned building, Harry remained motionless and mute, and Marta rolled her eyes.

Ivan and Blathnaid's 1910 Model T was a custom, of sorts, setting it apart from the fifteen million Ford Motor Company would build between 1908 and 1927. For their farm needs, the couple bought a mail-order pickup bed kit from Sears Roebuck that replaced the back seat. Given air in the tires and fuel in the tank, a Model T was a rugged little beast as reliable as any machine in its day. But it was tricky to operate, and the most dangerous part was starting.

When they arrived at the truck, Ivan lifted the right engine cowling. He reached into the engine bay and lined a fuel cut-off valve. Ivan installed this valve, so he didn't have to crawl under the truck to turn off the gravity-fed fuel system when he parked it. He didn't need to check the coolant or the oil because he checked these earlier in the day.

Ivan closed the cowling, then went to the front right of the radiator and pulled the choke next to the right fender. Then, he engaged the crank under the radiator, turning it a quarter-turn clockwise to prime the carburetor with fuel.

After priming, Ivan went to the driver's side interior and checked the parking brake lever to make sure it was still in the park-start position. He inserted the key into the coil-box switch and set the switch to battery. Then he did something that every Model T owner knew by heart or painful experience. He adjusted the timing stalk on the left side of the steering wheel upward to retard the timing. Many inexperienced or careless owners shattered their arms when cranking because of backfires from not-retarded engines. Doctors called these injuries "Ford Fractures." Then Ivan reached to the right of the steering wheel and moved the throttle stalk downward for an idle setting.

Ivan walked to the front of the truck, his two students in tow. Before grabbing the crank handle, he cautioned Alex and Dimitri. He told them to use their left arms with their thumbs tucked under the handle. He explained that if the engine backfires the crank will rotate counterclockwise, and it was less likely to break their left arms. Ivan gave the handle a vigorous half-crank, and the engine fired to life.

"We should drive around the block to see how she operates," insisted Ivan.

Both Greeks nodded and climbed aboard. The three men sat on the bench seat under its canvas folding top.

A trip around the block allowed Ivan to show the steering and throttle. These were obvious enough, but the workings of the three foot-pedals and handbrake were confounding. The left foot pedal, when depressed, selected first gear, when halfway depressed, put the truck into neutral, and when released, set the transmission to second gear. The middle pedal was used to engage reverse gear, and the right pedal was the brake. The handbrake, when moved all the way forward, allowed normal driving. In its middle position, it put the truck into neutral. And pulled all the way to the rear, it was for parking and starting.

This overwhelmed the Greeks. But that would not stop them, and each took a turn at driving with predictable results.

After a few trips around the block, Ivan felt the motivated Greeks knew what they were doing. He wagered his investment would be safe. As mentioned before, a 1910 Model T is a rugged little beast, akin to the bighorn sheep stalking the hills above Trinidad. So, with a wave to the Greeks and two dollars richer, Ivan bid them adieu, wished them luck, and joined the delivery driver for the trip to his farm.

Chapter 43

Cokedale was an outlier. Halfway between Trinidad and Segundo, its mines and coke ovens, owned by the American Smelting and Refining Company (AS&R), remained working during the strike. It was a tough place for the union to gain purchase. AS&R housed and paid their workforce better than CF&I. The Guggenheim family owned AS&R and believed their workers should be well-paid and enjoy a taste of comfort and luxury.[97] In 1907, they invested one million dollars in a model camp.[98] It was the same benevolent paternalism that CF&I strove for, but AS&R implemented.

By 1914, the company camp was home to over five hundred miners and their families. A twenty-two-room boardinghouse lodged bachelors with a clubhouse providing billiards, bowling, swimming, and card playing. There was a soda fountain and a library. Miners rented sturdy homes of cinderblocks made of coke, cement, and quarried sandstone, finished in unpainted heavy pebble dash stucco. With a front porch thrown in for good measure, the company charged two dollars a room.[99] The camp provided electricity, water service, telephones, and a school with five teachers. An icehouse, a Catholic church, and a resident doctor added to Cokedale's appeal. The camp even had a saloon, but with the rise of the temperance movement, they converted it to a dry dance hall. The Town of Cokedale included a post office, hotel, restaurants, and the Gottlieb Mercantile Company, whose grand stone building was well-stocked.

For those seeking to avenge Eleni's murder, Cokedale offered transportation to Trinidad by stage and railroad. A trolley operated by the Trinidad Gas and Electric Company Railroad made twelve trips a day for twenty-five cents.[100] But it was an abandoned Denver and Rio Grande Western Railroad spur that drew the conspirators to Cokedale. The rusty track bed ran to an out-of-service switching yard two miles south of the coke ovens. The abandoned yard serviced a mine closed in 1911 when a blasting powder explosion killed seventeen men.

At the north end of the rail yard stood a switchman's shanty, a simple wooden shed with two rooms and a head. It was far from prying eyes, and sounds from the shanty would go nowhere in the sparse pinyon pines of the Sangre de Cristo Mountains.

Dimitri and Alex, still perfecting their driving, collected Michaels from the abandoned building on 1st Street. They wrapped him in a tarp that Ivan carried in the bed of his Model T and tied his feet to the side rail. It was dark now, and as soon as they were out of Trinidad, no one would notice their cargo.

Harry stayed with Marta. As they walked back to the rooming house, both were rebounding from adrenaline. There was no doubt about their captive's guilt. He had information that could complete the picture of Eleni's murder. They would spare him until he proved of no further use. Then he would pay for breaking the human bond.

Harry had reservations about leaving Michaels with Alex. They needed Michaels alive. Harry told Dimitri to remove the gag from Michaels when they got to the shanty. He wanted Dimitri to listen to Michaels, but to wait for Harry before they questioned him. Harry said, "Don't let him provoke Alex. If he does, gag him and let Alex hit him. But don't let Alex get carried away."

Dimitri was in complete agreement.

The young couple walked in silence for the first block on their return to the rooming house. Harry, with the tattered flowers at his side, turned to Marta. "Thank you for not shooting Michaels." Marta had recognized the man from his limp.

Marta looked at Harry, "No, you are right. It is better he is alive and talking. It would have given me pleasure, but. . . ."

Harry cut her off. "No, no. I mean, thank you for not shooting him, because the bullet from your Colt would have gone through him and hit me."

Marta burst into laughter, "Preposterous!"

"No, no," repeated Harry, "That weapon is powerful, and I might be as dead as him."

Again, Marta laughed and put her hand into the crook of Harry's arm.

Back at the rooming house, Harry walked her to her room, and Marta keyed her door. As it swung open, she looked at Harry. "You should come in. Maybe we can sit together and talk. This will let our blood cool and our minds calm. Please join me."

Harry wanted to. Marta was attractive. She was strong, smart, good-looking, and self-assured. But it was not the time for romance.

123

Harry had a debt of honor, and the capture of Nick Michaels was only the first order of a complicated business.

Harry countered Marta, "Let us sit for a few minutes. I will catch the first trolley to Cokedale tomorrow morning. I will spell Alex so he can return Ivan's truck. You should stay in Trinidad for now. You will be safer here. It would be best for you to move to another rooming house or a hotel. But, yes, we can sit for a moment. I . . . I would enjoy that."

And with that, Marta smiled, offered both hands, and Harry crossed the threshold into her room. Without closing her door, Marta rose on her toes and kissed Harry on the mouth. It was a shock and a welcome, long repressed sensation. He put his arms to her waist and drew her close and they kissed again. Harry's willpower shrank and his desire grew.

Then they both heard the sound. A door opened, and another roomer started down the hall, each footfall closer. With their door still open, the couple separated to a respectable distance. The roomer passed and kept his eyes forward. He wore a preacher's frock.

Harry took a deep breath. "I should go to my room."

"No, no. Stay here . . . please. You can sleep on the floor or on the sofa. I will trouble you no more."

Harry shook his head. Marta insisted. And a palette of blankets at the foot of Marta's bed became Harry's resignation for the night.

Chapter 44

Coal dust layered the shanty. Years of laden rail hoppers rolling and coupling on rough track gifted the fine powder to every surface. The shanty's doors and windows were intact, and a small stove stood in the larger room. The smaller room, where railroad conductors worked their bills, was the current cell of Nick Michaels. His captors ignored his acerbic ramblings and pitiful pleas as they built a fire.

Dimitri said to Alex, "When Harry gets here, take the truck to Ivan. Then take the train back to Trinidad from Segundo. Find Marta and stay with her until we finish. Is this agreeable?"

Alex hesitated, then nodded, "But you must promise not to kill him until I am here. I will do it."

"Yes, yes," Dimitri agreed. "But we must make sure Marta is safe. I think Harry and I are best to question him. Listen to him in there. He makes no sense babbling about the sheriff turning him loose.

"Alex, you stay with Marta and make sure she is safe. Anything can happen. Someone else may try to harm her. Anything can happen, my friend."

Alex knew Dimitri was right.

Harry and Marta decided she should check into the Trinidad Hotel the next day. Harry stayed there on his trip from Denver and knew the layout. Her advertised whereabouts in the rooming house had served its purpose. Now it was a liability.

They agreed Marta should use the name Sophia Abella. It was a compromise. Marta suggested she go by the name Yvette Lebeau and pretend to be French. Harry laughed. Looking at Marta and seeing she was serious, Harry explained, "I have stayed in this hotel. There are many Italians there. You, dear Marta, are Italian to any other Italian and you could never hide it."

She argued, but saw Harry's wisdom. "Sophia, it is. This was my grandmother's sister's name, so I take it with pride."

Harry caught the first trolley to Cokedale at six the next morning. He walked the two miles to the shanty before sunrise with thoughts of Marta invading the task at hand. Alex and Dimitri took turns sleeping and keeping watch. Dimitri was awake with his Ruby in hand when Harry approached. Dimitri stepped out of the doorway to greet Harry, and Harry presented him with a sack of bread, cheese, salami, and ground coffee from Trinidad. Dimitri said, "You are my salvation, brother. I did not know a man could work up such hunger from listening to an idiot babble."

Harry said, "It was driving Ivan's truck that wore you down."

"No, no. Alex drove. He's getting good at it. I only hope we can remember how to start the machine this morning," offered Dimitri.

"How is Alex?"

"He's been good. No arguments. He still wants to be the one who kills Michaels, and I have no reason to deny him this. What do you say, friend?"

Harry thought for a moment. "It matters not by whose hand he dies. He will pay the debt. What matters now is finding out if there were others involved so they can pay."

Dimitri nodded and the two men went inside where the coal stove smoked, and the abandoned coffee pot steamed. With the smell of coffee, Alex woke, and Dimitri chided, "The sleep of a horse, my friend?"

Alex did not register the humor. A moment later, Michaels stirred, and his three captors heard him mumbling through his gag. Alex asked, "Should I remove his muzzle?"

Harry answered, "No, he can wait. Let us eat first. Then we offer him some water and see what he has to say.

"Alex, this morning, take the truck to Ivan and see if he has a horse and a buckboard we can rent. Bring the buckboard here. Then take the trolley to Trinidad and stay with Marta. She will wait at the rooming house for you. She is moving to the Trinidad Hotel and will register under an unfamiliar name. We must be careful. If there is a second killer, there is still a threat."

Chapter 45

"Sergeant, did you receive any messages for me last night?"

"No, Lieutenant."

"Nothing from our Baldwin-Felts snitch in Cokedale?"

"No, sir."

"Let me know the minute he checks in, Sergeant."

"Yes, sir."

Chapter 46

Harry pressed his knife to the prisoner's cheek. Michaels's eyes bulged, and he stopped squirming. Harry pushed the razor-sharp tip under the bandanna and, with a butcher's deftness, sliced the gag, the blade whisking an inch from the captive's ear. Michaels was bound to a wooden chair with his arms tied behind his back and his feet tied to the chair legs. He had urinated on himself overnight, and the revolting smell filled the small room. Harry fought a reaction to the stench as he spoke to the murderer. "I will ask you questions. If you provide the truth, you may leave Colorado and never return. If you do not. . . .

"Do you understand?"

Michaels nodded and licked his lips. Harry motioned to Dimitri, who put a canteen to Michaels's mouth. The prisoner drank, water spilling from his mouth and down his chest.

When Dimitri pulled the canteen away, Michaels began stammering and blurted out, "The sheriff and the guards will tell you. I am innocent! I have done nothing. I have committed no crime. No transgression. None!"

Harry turned the knife blade and placed the tip just below Michaels's Adam's apple, silencing the prisoner. Harry stared at Michaels, tension building. Then he flipped the blade upward, drawing blood from a shallow cut. Michaels grimaced and stretched his neck. His veins throbbed and bulged. Harry asked sotto voce, "Who was with you the night you killed Eleni?"

"Who is Eleni? I do not know this woman. I . . . I have never heard of her. My word of honor!" Michaels pleaded.

Harry returned the knife to his Adam's apple. Michaels whimpered and mouthed, "Wait, wait. . . ."

Harry sheathed his knife, still staring at Michaels. Michaels hesitated. Looking down and away from both men, he pleaded, "It was not my idea. I did not want to go there that night. I held no intention of harming the woman or the child. The child . . . the child . . . nothing happened to the child! You understand? I spared the child! What I . . . ."

Dimitri slammed the canteen into the left side of Michaels's face, knocking him and the chair to the floor. Harry looked at his friend with eyes that said, *not yet*.

Both men returned Michaels and the chair upright and Harry asked again, "Who was with you that night?"

"They ordered me to go. You understand? Ordered! They paid me to spy on the union, and they ordered me to go," Michaels pleaded through tears.

"Who was with you?" repeated Harry, unsheathing his blade.

"I can go free, yes? I will tell you if I go free," bargained Michaels.

Harry stared through the sniveling wretch and brought his knife closer to the prisoner's pulsing veins.

"The boss of the guards, Linderfelt. He will kill me if he finds out I told. He ordered me to come with him. He said we would have some fun. I told him they would recognize me in Segundo. He said it did not matter since I would be with him. If anyone saw us, we would kill them and Sheriff Grisham would look away," sobbed the broken coward.

Harry looked at Dimitri and motioned to Michaels. Dimitri withdrew another bandanna from his pocket, gagged the prisoner, and knotted it around Michaels's neck. Then he and Harry walked outside into the morning air and the welcome tang of pinyon pine.

Chapter 47

Harry was right, things were complicated. How much should they tell Alex? Should they tell him Linderfelt was, if not the killer, a partner to the crime and defiler of Eleni? Alex would hunt Linderfelt and die seeking revenge. Still, Alex deserved to know the truth. Could Alex hear reason and caution? Could he wait, embrace patience, then exact revenge when the time was right? Alex would have to be told because Dimitri and Marta would know the truth. They couldn't lie to Eleni's husband.

Then there was Michaels's body. Where would they dispose of it? Dimitri suggested they leave it in the derelict mine. Between scavengers and decay, there would be little left in a few days. Harry didn't like that idea. The body needed to disappear, be gone. In the mine, his bones would remain. When Harry expressed his concern to Dimitri, Dimitri said, "There is one place he can disappear. I might know a way."

As the two stood outside of the shanty, they heard the crunch of gravel and a sputtering motor. Not expecting anyone but Alex and a buckboard, they retreated into the shanty, out of sight. Moments later, Alex pulled to a stop in Ivan's Model T. Harry and Dimitri stepped outside. Alex offered, "Ivan said he would be busy on his new tractor and that we could use his truck. He said he needed it back by Easter so he and Blathnaid could drive to church."

Harry asked, "Which Easter?"

Alex thought for a moment. He knew Ivan was Orthodox and Blathnaid was Catholic, then he reasoned, "He must mean Catholic Easter. In two days."

Harry told Alex everything. As the three stood outside the shanty in the quiet midmorning, Alex absorbed the information. He listened to Harry's warning about going after the well-protected Linderfelt. Harry ended with, "The three of us must agree. When Linderfelt is least expecting retribution, even years from now, we will one, if not all, make him pay for what he did to Eleni. This will be Eleni's revenge."

Dimitri and Alex looked at each other, confirming Harry's reasoning. Alex was the first to put his hand over his heart, then Dimitri, and finally Harry, who pronounced, "The bond is made."

Alex drew his knife and stepped toward the shanty. With his first step, Harry touched his arm and Alex paused. Harry whispered, "Quickly."

Chapter 48

Alex and Dimitri's driving skills and their knowledge of coke ovens well-suited them for the task ahead. Meanwhile, Alex drove Harry to Cokedale. There Alex posted a letter to Greece, then dropped Harry at the Cokedale trolley before noon. Harry boarded for Trinidad.

Harry walked from the trolley stop to the rooming house and knocked on Marta's door. She asked, "Who is it, please?"

Harry answered in a reassuring voice.

Marta opened the door with a big smile and the Colt in her right hand. Harry was solemn. She asked, "Is it done?"

Harry nodded.

Marta sat on the corner of her bed, looking up at the tall Greek, "Tell me, what happened?"

Harry said, "He confessed. He said they ordered him to go along with Linderfelt and that Linderfelt assured him the sheriffs would protect him, no matter what he did."

Marta winced, "Who?"

"Alex," answered Harry. "It is done."

Silence followed. Then Marta patted the bed beside her. Harry joined her and put his arm around her. He told her of the pact and his hope that Alex would leave the unfinished business to another time.

Marta nodded. Then, with blind certainty, she announced, "I too, am in this pact!"

Marta, head hung low, could not see Harry's reluctance, but she felt his breath and exasperated exhale.

Chapter 49

Industrial coke is a refined product. It is purified by baking coal at eleven hundred degrees centigrade for twelve to fourteen hours. The ovens at Cokedale, two miles north of the switchman's shanty, operated twenty-four hours a day. A skeleton crew worked between midnight and eight in the morning.

The Guggenheim family were enlightened employers. The heavy loading and unloading of the ovens took place in daylight, when it was safer. The midnight maintenance crew took their thirty-minute breakfast break at four in the morning. While the workers bolted their sausage, bread, and cheese and drank bitter coffee, the ovens went untended. It was then that the top of the ovens, where the electric engine delivered coal cars to be dumped, was unoccupied.

Dimitri and Alex both worked in the coke operation at Segundo and knew well the loading of ovens.

Chapter 50

"Sir?"

"Yes, soldier."

"Sir. Lamont Bowers's office said they wired the government commission about sending a representative to Trinidad, like you asked. The commission said there were no plans to send anyone to Trinidad or Colorado."

"Are you sure? Did they mention anything about an investigator? Anything about Segundo?"

"No, sir."

"Did you hear anything from our rat at Cokedale?"

"No. He has not reported in."

The cat was out of the bag. Linderfelt smelled a trap. He assumed the snitch Michaels was dead after giving up his secrets, or on the run to safer ground. But the rat's demise changed little in Linderfelt's life. His absolute authority and power over the riffraff under his command and his contempt for the strikers deluded him. In his ego-mad mind, he was untouchable. Linderfelt had the sheriff, the company, and an army of goons on his side, and this was war. People die in war all the time. He would watch for Hantzis and the other Greeks and put them in the ground when the chance came. The woman, the Italian who played along in the ruse, was a new target, and she gained a place on his list of expendables. But for now, there were other plans to make, plans for Ludlow.

Ludlow was the largest camp and the viper's den of hothead Greeks. Tikas was a problem. He was respected and exercised authority. But even Tikas couldn't control his countrymen. The Greeks pestered the guards, foreseeing their movements, divining Linderfelt's tactics. Linderfelt's guards feared the wily, undaunted Greeks, especially the Balkan War veterans. These men had been to war, a bloody, unrestrained conflict. A war they had won. The guards were pretenders. The guards would not fight them man-to-man.

Linderfelt fumed over the loss of Michaels, but he had a bigger worry. He prepared a plan, a coup de grâce, to put the Greeks and the no-nameovichs on their heels. He would open the mines in a matter of days. He would be a celebrated strike-breaker in the councils of American business. He would be the man who saved Rockefeller. Businesses would bury him in service contracts for years to come. It all came down to Ludlow.

Chapter 51

Harry checked Marta, now Sophia Abella, into the Trinidad Hotel on Thursday afternoon. That evening, they ate a pleasant meal at Ottavio's Place. Marta spoke Italian with the waiter and enjoyed a healthy plate of elk medallions and pasta. A measure of Chianti loosened her tongue, rendering her garrulous. Harry drank his share but remained reserved and wary.

She chided Harry: "You are a specter. I know nothing of what you think. I know little of you or your family. You . . . you know everything there is to know about poor Marta. Oh, *scusami* . . . I mean, Sophia. You must tell me more, entertain me, keep me awake. It is our night to rejoice. Let us toast Eleni! To her spirit, to her beauty! And no thoughts of the swine." She pretended to spit on the floor, rousing the diners seated at the next table.

Harry put his finger to his lips. Marta stroked her long black hair away from her face. Then they both raised their wine glasses, clinking. Harry avowed, "*Eonia i mnimi.*" (Memory eternal.)

Marta went on in a hushed, over-articulated voice, "My specter and savior, you are right. We are invisible, we make no scene. Boring little people tonight enjoying our alce and formaggio. You are right. You are right." She threw up her hands as if surrendering.

The waiter approached their table and asked if they needed anything, thinking Marta was signaling him with her gesture.

Harry shook his head, and a smile came to his lips.

The waiter caught Harry's message and excused himself. "*Prego, prego.*"

Marta pried at Harry's defenses. "What is Indianapolis like? I've never been. Can you tell me? Is it a secret place where specters go to haunt the living? Is that why you are so. . . ?" She let the sentence trail.

Harry said, "It is a bigger city than Denver. There are a few Greeks, more Italians, many Germans. My brother and I settled there because others from Nafpaktos were there. It is fine. We both have good jobs. In a few years, we will have our own business. Perhaps a restaurant like this one, only we will serve more refined Greek preparations."

136

Marta retorted, "Oh! I hope our humble Italian cuisine does not grate on your sensitive Greek palate!"

Harry chuckled, "You Italians are touchy. Long ago, it was the Greeks who taught you how to cook."

Marta shot back, "And it took us all these years to correct your mistakes!"

Harry laughed and realized that getting the better of Marta was not in the cards.

They ordered espressos, and Harry paid the bill. The couple entered the hotel lobby arm-and-arm with Marta persisting, "And, Dimitri, how did you meet him? Do all Greeks know all other Greeks?"

"I met Dmitri on the ship returning from the war. We talked many times. We played cards, drank coffee, and. . . ." Harry shrugged. "Then, when we arrived in New York, we went our separate ways. He went to Colorado and me to Indiana. I did not see him again until I came to Trinidad. He met me in this lobby. His family is from Crete, and he knew Eleni's family. Dimitri is a good man. I am lucky I count him as a friend."

"But how did you know Eleni?" Marta prodded.

"It is late. I think we should talk about a plan for you and Alex."

Marta cocked her head, recognizing that Harry didn't want to answer her question.

Harry continued, "Tomorrow is Catholic Good Friday."

"Yes?" answered Marta.

"It is best you and Alex travel to Pueblo and be with your families. Go to church, spend Easter there. Get away from the strike, for now. You will be safe there, and your families will be happy to see you. Alex should be here early. Take a morning train."

Harry's shift in persona took Marta aback. He was all business just when she thought she was piercing his armored personality.

"I'll stay with you tonight. Then you'll be with Alex until we see each other again. Dimitri and I have business here. I will sleep on the floor, nothing improper," he insisted.

Marta toyed with thoughts of impropriety. But the glow of the wine was fading, and she sensed Harry had only her safety in mind.

"Yes, yes. That is sensible," she agreed.

Then the young couple continued across the lobby and up the stairs, Harry reading the eyes of every man in sight.

Chapter 52

Alex arrived in Trinidad early on Catholic Good Friday. Dimitri returned the truck to Ivan. Marta and Alex boarded the first passenger train to Pueblo. Harry returned to the hotel where Dimitri met him two hours later. The two men sat in secluded, high-back leather chairs in the lobby and talked about their next move.

Dimitri began, "We should tell Ilias what has happened. He will need to know. I'm sure we can trust him."

Harry nodded. "Yes, but let us not mention our pact. This, he need not know."

Dimitri asked, "Did you tell Marta?"

"Yes. She must know so she can temper Alex. She is strong-willed. She, too, took the pledge," Harry confided.

Dimitri sensed his friend's exasperation.

"Indeed," said Dimitri, "When she sets her mind to something, she gets it. And, my friend, unless I am mistaken, she has set her mind on you."

Harry looked away, embarrassed, "Now is not the time for such things. We still have business before us."

Dimitri shrugged. "What is a man to do?"

The two men left the hotel, walked to the train station, and waited for the next passenger service to take them to Ludlow, fourteen miles north. When they arrived in late afternoon, they noticed the mine guards were gone. This was unusual but welcome. Harry and Dimitri thought that maybe the Catholic holiday was the cause. It was a wishful notion.

The world around Ludlow was in motion as much as the strikers in the hills. The day before Alex and Marta left for Pueblo, Mexican soldiers detained nine American sailors in the Port of Tampico. This inflamed the already hot political situation between the two countries. A clamor for war rose in the American public and press. Mexico released the sailors within the hour. But United States Rear Admiral Henry Mayo, the commander of naval forces in the area, demanded an apology and a twenty-one-gun salute from Victoriano Huerta's government. Huerta, under attack from Emiliano Zapata's revolutionaries, refused. In two weeks, with negotiations at a deadlock, President Wilson would ask the United States Congress for permission for an armed invasion, the first prior request for war powers by any American president. The Congress agreed two days later, after the United States already occupied Veracruz.

An attempt to defuse another explosive arena failed. Frank Hayes, Vice President of the United Mine Workers, sent a note to John D. Rockefeller seeking a private meeting. Hayes, unmentioned in his letter but known to all, was looking for a face-saving way to end the strike.

Rockefeller didn't respond to Hayes. Instead, he sent a copy to Chairman Lamont Bowers, saying in part, "In conformity with the policy adopted by Welborn (CF&I Vice President) and yourself, I will make no reply."[101]

The policy was no union recognition.

The wealthiest man in America made himself clear before a congressional committee on April 6, 1914.

Rockefeller: *These men [the strikers] have not expressed any dissatisfaction with their conditions. The records show that the conditions have been admirable . . . A strike has been imposed upon the company from the outside . . . There is just one thing that can be done to settle this strike, and that is to unionize the camps, and our interest in labor is so profound, and we believe so sincerely that that interest demands that the camps shall be open camps, that we expect to stand by the officers at any cost.*

Committee: *And you will do that if it costs all your property and kills all your employees?*

Rockefeller: *It is a great principle.*[102]

Chapter 53

Tikas listened to Harry and Dimitri's account. Michaels had made his list of suspected spies years before when Tikas learned of Michaels's transgressions at the Victor Mine. Harry and Dimitri spared Tikas the details and reported that Michaels had killed Eleni and Linderfelt had been with him. It went unsaid, but Tikas understood Michaels had paid the price.

Dimitri asked Tikas, "What has become of the guards? We did not see any at the station and none on our way to camp."

"Governor Ammons ordered the guards to withdraw. Linderfelt was relieved of his command last Wednesday. But he has returned from his efforts to recruit more goons. He is up to no good, of this we are certain. The guards are lying low and out of sight. But they are snakes under rocks waiting to strike."

Tikas was right. The guards were gone. By the following Friday, Greek Good Friday, only thirty-four guards in Company B remained in the strike zone. These men, known to the strikers as "yellow bands," were the worst, most feared strikebreakers, handpicked by Linderfelt, their de facto commander. Their mission was to assault Ludlow.

Troubled by the governor's order to withdraw, an anti-union Trinidad newspaper reported that for the first time in five months, southern Colorado was defenseless. On the night of April 14, 130 men gathered at the Trinidad Armory. After being sworn by Linderfelt, who was uncommissioned, and without National Guard authority, they named themselves Troop A. Of the 130 men, 121 were mine guards, pit bosses, clerks, engineers, and foremen employed by CF&I and Victor American. The rest were sheriff's deputies and local vigilantes.

Troop A formed without training, officers, discipline, or uniforms. The next day, commanded by Edwin F. Carson, Troop A joined Company B on the high ground above Ludlow.[103] The stage was set. As the curtain rose, fearful owners, a legacy of class exploitation, and an unmoored governor, were poised for historic tragedy.

The gunslingers in the hills, with state issued Springfields, high-powered rifles, searchlights, and machine guns, were not the sons of the ruling class. They were not capitalists by birthright. They were mercenaries who regarded the men and women and children in the hapless tents below as no-nameovichs, dagos, wops, spics, and dirty sons-of-bitches.

The guards called miners rednecks, and they were right. The strikers flaunted crimson bandannas. They dubbed the union automobile the "Red Special." The strikers were radical trade unionists before collective bargaining was an accepted social convention. They threatened authority more than profit. Rockefeller recoiled at recognizing their union, his uncrossable Rubicon. The miners hated the guards with as much personal passion as class-consciousness. They were workers at war. While the union cause propelled them to battle, hatred of the enemy erased all bounds. Strikers were the worthy antithesis of the guards. The guards fought for pay and bragging rights and the strikers to save their families and right historical wrongs.

In the tragedy of Ludlow, the manifest atrocity of the mine guards transcended hatred. They shot children, dogs, chickens—anything that moved. They plundered tents before soaking them with coal oil and putting them to the torch. Mine guards were the dark force of history, vainly ordered to staunch the arc of progress. A role they relished under the command of the blackest soul.

Chapter 54

"No, no. The *ovelos* is best made of pine. Metal is not so good. The pine gives the resin flavor. Pine imparts our history into the meat. It is the way of the ancients. Pine is the best." Dimitri intoned his uninvited wisdom to a group of Greeks debating the merits of how to impale the Easter lamb.

A young Greek retorted, "But the metal is much easier. We have it ready at hand. We have it fashioned with a firm handle for spinning the lamb. That is the best way to cook, no?"

"Brothers, if we are to cook a lamb for Easter, we must cook it the best way possible. It must be the best *ovelias* ever made, no? I will go for the pine. Use the metal for the *kokoretsi*. The organ meats are not so delicate," Dimitri assured.

"But, Dimitri, here we only have the pinyon. In Greece, the Aleppo grows tall and straight. Pinyon is crooked and knotted. You will never find one long enough or straight enough. We already have the metal. Relax and enjoy the holiday. The guards have left. There is nothing to do but play baseball and tell lies," the young Greek reasoned.

"Give me until the end of the day. I will have our ovelos, the best you have ever seen. Our lamb will taste of the Old Country. We will eat and drink until we are full as wolf pups at their mother's breasts.

"Today we get the lamb from Ivan. Tomorrow, Good Friday, we slaughter and prepare the ovelos and clean the guts for the kokoretsi. Saturday the ovelias will rest in its spices. Then Sunday . . . Sunday, we will rejoice for our savior and feast like heathens."

With a honed hatchet in hand and his Ruby in his pocket, Dimitri began walking west on the wagon road just south of the Ludlow colony. On his way, he spotted Harry leaving Tikas's tent and encouraged Harry to join him on his mission of culinary importance. It was early afternoon on a beautiful spring day, and Harry joined his friend.

Harry asked, "Tell me more about your mission?"

"I am going to the hills to render a pine ovelos. As you know, a pine ovelos makes the best tasting ovelias because it infuses the lamb with the flavor of resin. All Greeks know that. It is simple, no? The youngsters in camp tried to convince me that a metal spit would be better. I told them I would find a straight and true ovelos so we can prepare our feast in the traditional manner. Am I not right? The hills to the west are full of pine. I am going there. We will spy on the guards as we pass. Their camp is only four hundred yards to the south of the road," Dimitri explained.

"Ilias says that many of the guards have left, but the ones that remain are the worst. He worries about what they are planning. Tuesday night, more than a hundred men enlisted as deputies, and they are staging at the guards' camp. Ilias said that Linderfelt is back, and something is up," Harry offered.

"What a shame. I should have brought the Mannlicher. Alex would not object. If we spot him in camp, we could honor our pledge."

"In daylight, with a hundred of his supporters at hand? That, my friend, would be the last time you fired a weapon," Harry chided.

"True, but the deed would be done. Still, it would be better to wait. You are right."

Harry added, "You talk like Alex."

Both men chuckled.

As they walked past the guards' camp, they saw men in civilian clothing handing out Springfield rifles and wooden ammunition crates. It was not a comforting sight. The air filled with foreboding on an otherwise light and cheerful day.

In the pinyon-covered hills a mile down the wagon road, Dimitri found what he was looking for. Among a stand of tall, straight, young pines filling with sap in the warm spring sunlight, one rose supple and long enough for an ovelos. Dimitri went to work with his hatchet. In a few minutes, he had amputated a six-foot section of pine for the spit rod and an S-shaped section for the handle. Pleased with himself, he exclaimed, "Now we cook proper ovelias!"

Harry smiled and glanced from the hillside to the wagon road below. From their vantage point in the pines thirty yards above the roadway, Harry and Dimitri could see a mile in either direction. Approaching from the west, two military trucks pulled wheeled weaponry. Harry motioned Dimitri to duck and pointed to the vehicles. As the trucks came closer, the Greeks could see that they were towing machine guns. Harry and Dimitri could not tell the make or manufacturer. But they knew from the Balkan battles and the war in Epirus that the range of these weapons made Ludlow a target from the guards' camp. They estimated the firing distance between the guards and Ludlow to be six or seven hundred yards. The camp was in the line of fire.

Upon their return to Ludlow, Dimitri went to gloat about finding the perfect spit, and Harry went to report the weaponry to Tikas. As Dimitri wove through the tent colony, he came upon Charles Costa with a group of children circled around him. The kids loved Costa. He was their comedian. Costa broke his act and asked Dimitri, "What have you there, my Greek friend?"

Dimitri answered in a spooky voice, "I have here the spear I will use to kill the cyclops that lurks in this camp!"

The younger children looked convinced, and the older ones rolled their eyes. Dimitri laughed as he walked away.

Harry told Tikas about the machine guns, and the leader of Ludlow confided, "It is a time to rejoice. This I know, but my heart is heavy. The governor told the guards to leave. But now we have more than a hundred across the road. I'm afraid the worst could be on us."

Harry nodded and took his leave. On his way to find Dimitri, Harry thought about what to do next. Should they stay in Ludlow for Easter or return to Segundo? Alex and Marta would be back in Segundo after the holiday. Other than the nightly patrols of the Greek strikers, there would be little for him and Dimitri to do there.

Harry questioned how much longer he should stay in Colorado. He'd been away from Indianapolis for two months. The murderer of Eleni was dead. The debt of honor paid in part. Still, there was the matter of Linderfelt and his atonement. But Linderfelt would be hard to reach while surrounded by guards.

Then there was Marta. Harry found the woman fascinating, and his attraction was compelling. But Marta was obligated, too. Family bound her to help raise and care for her brother's children. Harry understood that. But he also realized that she was unlike any woman he knew.

Harry thought about his boxing career. It bothered him not to be training. Boxing, like any sport, soon forgot you if you weren't

145

winning and in the public spotlight. His agent, Leo P. Flynn, was concerned. He wanted the young Greek to tour with a rising heavyweight from Utah, Jack Dempsey, and Harry couldn't train in the hills of Colorado.

The hanging thread was Linderfelt. He was a loose end. Harry needed to talk with Alex, Dimitri, and Marta about how they would pursue the make-believe soldier and craven sadist when the strike was over. If they could arrive at a plan, Harry would return to Indianapolis.

Chapter 55

Christ is risen!

April 19, 1914, was Greek Orthodox Easter, the most revered day in Greek religious practice. The Catholics celebrated the Gregorian holiday a week earlier, and the Greeks would not be outdone. Barron Beshoar, son of the union's doctor, described Ludlow as a "riot of color," with strikers' native costumes accenting the weathered canvas city made vivid in the warm spring sunlight.[104] As Tikas walked among the jubilation proclaiming *"Christós Anésti!"* (Christ is risen!) he elicited the traditional response, *"Alithos Anesti!"* (Indeed, he has risen!). Yet foreboding instincts tempered his spirit.

It was more than instinct. Although never documented, well-placed people assumed the union tapped the phone lines. The union cultivated informers among the guards and the guards among the strikers. And there were rumors, rumors every day. Rumors that Linderfelt had returned, vowing to burn the colony to the ground. Rumors that machine guns were in position in the hills. Rumors that the guards were armed with poison gas. Rumors that Tikas was sleeping with an American woman. Rumors that Diamond was a traitor. Rumors that the UMWA was bankrupt. Something was in the air. Ambling through the celebration clothed in traditional Cretan *vrakas*, on the day before his death, Tikas spoke to confidants with troubled preoccupation.

The festivities captured the moment. The Greeks roasted a lamb on Dimitri's preferred pine spit and bought two barrels of beer. They presented the women with improbable gym bloomers, then posed them for photos. The women played a baseball game, and then the men and women played one together. The children ran everywhere playing tag and hide-and-seek.

It was all great fun, but during a baseball game, four guards on horseback with rifles approached the diamond, and the women jeered. It was common for the guards to watch the games but, before today, they had come unarmed.[105] The guards did not interfere. But the women chided them, yelling that if they had a BB gun, the guards would take flight. As the guards rode away, a militiaman named Patton shouted back, "Never mind, girlie, you have your big Sunday today, and tomorrow we'll get the roast."[106]

Dancing and drinking continued into the night. In the main tent, chords from squeezeboxes mixed with the staccato rhythm of folkloric stringed instruments. The Italians were musicians and loved their concertinas. The Greeks played too: lyre, bouzouki, and mandolin. All were dancers, but the boundless leaping and daring acrobatics of the young Greeks left a lasting image.

Some Greeks took the train to Denver or Pueblo to receive communion and make the sign of the cross. But with few Greek women in camp to reinforce tradition, each man dealt with his conscience. They may have fasted before Easter, but fasting was a way of life, no longer ceremony.

They were young male Greeks crammed into tents for eight months. They numbered about a hundred hardened fighters.[107] They lived alone in Ludlow, in their own block of tents apart from others. They listened to the lies, the stories, the boasting, and the rumors, and as Greek men deferred to no one, until time for battle. They loved their guns. Through all the camp searches, the militia never disarmed the Greeks. They had earned a reputation, long before the strike, of being quick to violence, fierce and defiant.[108] Young Barron Beshoar remembered, "Every time a battle was fought in this county, whenever the miners fought a battle, the Italians ran that way, and the Greeks ran at the militia. The Greeks were fighting men. Now there's no question about that. They'd been soldiers in Greece. They were good fighting men."[109]

The Greeks argued and plotted against Tikas as surely as they planned raids on the guards. Now, with spring teasing, their excuse for dancing and rejoicing was Easter.

Through the Greek tents, the light of coal oil lanterns cast shadows from the inside out as canvas apparitions pantomimed the liberation songs of 1821 and the Turkomachia. In pitch darkness, Tikas filled his mind with phantoms and the reality of catastrophe. Tikas rolled on his cot and muttered damnation.

Earlier in the evening, while the families were dancing in the big tent, Tikas got a call from Major Patrick Hamrock. Hamrock was a veteran of the Sioux Ghost Dance War and Wounded Knee who, when not on guard duty, ran a saloon in Denver.[110] Hamrock was new on the scene, only three days in command.

Hamrock insisted Tikas turn over a boy. Tikas told Hamrock the boy was not in the colony. Hamrock respected Tikas and took him at his word. But Hamrock's tone troubled Tikas. Martial law had been lifted, but he feared Hamrock would attempt a search, and the Greeks vowed never to allow another search.

The guards from the ball game returned, prowling the perimeter of Ludlow. At the train depot, two of those guards, Zimmer and Martin, itching for a fight, beat up two strikers.

Tikas phoned Lawson, and Lawson counseled him to sit tight. Sensing impending doom, weary Tikas earned the relief of a fitful sleep.

Chapter 56

"Shush. Quiet. Grab your bedroll and your Ruby. We must leave camp for a better location," Harry whispered to Dimitri. His friend was still groggy after the day's beer and lamb and dancing. He had only moments earlier fallen asleep. "Dimitri, do you have binoculars?"

Dimitri shook his head. Then he said, "Wait, wait, there is a pair on the foot chest. Why are we leaving camp?"

"If you were positioning a machine gun against the strikers, where would you put it?" Harry asked of his muzzy comrade.

"I . . . I would place it on the high ground south of the train platform. What they call Water Tank Hill. From there you have direct fire, and you're out of range of carbines and pistols. Do you think that is happening?" Dimitri quizzed.

"I'm sure of it. The signs are ominous, are they not? They have the weapons, and they have well-armed reinforcements a mile away.

"There is a railroad embankment eight hundred yards southeast. From there we can fire on the guards and retreat to the hills farther east if we must." Harry assured Dimitri.

"But we have only American carbines and two pistols. The guards on Water Tank Hill will be out of range, no?" estimated Dimitri.

"We can use the embankment to move closer, fire, then retreat. It might give the Greeks time to join us and time for others to evacuate the camp.

"My friend, there is no way to defend this camp. When the guards attack, everyone will be a target," Harry intoned, still speaking in a whisper. "The cellars might protect from bullets but not fire. Ludlow will be a death trap."

Dimitri asked, "Should we tell Tikas and wake other men?"

"Ilias knows. In his heart, he knows. The other men. . . ." Harry waved his arm over the six sleeping tentmates, "They're sleeping like horses after the ovelias and beer. Better just you and I stake a position. Bring your gear. We will move now in darkness, so the guards cannot see us."

Chapter 57

Major Hamrock is handed a note from Linderfelt on Monday morning at 7:30. Linderfelt is a mile southwest in command of his thirty-four yellow bands. Hamrock has twenty-two men with him on Water Tank Hill, less than a mile south of Ludlow.

Linderfelt reports that the wife of an Italian miner claims her husband is missing and being held against his will in Ludlow. Hamrock orders three armed troopers to ride to Ludlow and question Tikas. Tikas tells them his men have searched the camp and the woman's husband is not there.

The troops leave Ludlow without incident. But their bravado and arrogance riles the strikers, who pressure Tikas to never allow another search of camp. Tikas calls Lawson to report the ominous news. Tikas fears the worst, and Lawson counsels him to make no provocation.

The troops report back to Hamrock, who is now in the company of an older Italian woman who doesn't speak English. She is looking for her husband, Carindo Tuttoilmando. Hamrock phones Tikas to request a meeting at Hamrock's tent, but Tikas declines. Then, Hamrock phones Linderfelt, ordering him to bring up reinforcements and drill them on the edge of Water Tank Hill in full view of Ludlow.

Tikas calls Hamrock and suggests a meeting at the train depot, halfway between Ludlow and Water Tank Hill. Hamrock accepts, then calls Linderfelt, telling him to "Put the baby in the buggy and bring it along."[111] The baby is one of seven company-purchased Colt-Browning M1895/14 machine guns. The camp cook loads the weapon on a wagon and hitches two mules.[112]

With the sun just over the horizon on the day after Easter, the gambit awaits. The guards are in motion. The weaponry positioning. And the casus belli established. Harry and Dimitri guessed correctly. More Greeks would join them in the Colorado and Southeastern Railroad sand cut within minutes.

At 8:50, after counseling the Greeks to stand down and not act rashly, Tikas meets Hamrock. It is a short walk to the depot and a shorter meeting. As Tikas speaks, armed guards with full ammunition belts stand behind Hamrock. Tikas tells the woman and Hamrock that he ran her husband, Tuttoilmando, out of Ludlow on Saturday evening and that he is unwelcome among the strikers. Then, an excited young lieutenant on horseback rides up, kicking dust and interrupting the meeting. He points to a column of thirty-five armed Greeks running for cover. The Greeks see what Tikas would on his return to camp, what Harry and Dimitri anticipated the night before.

Starting back to Ludlow, Tikas's heart drains and fills with icy fear. The ridge of Water Tank Hill is dark with *melish*, what the strikers call the guards and militia. Tikas breaks into a fast walk, waving two white handkerchiefs, and then he sees the machine gun nest. The Greeks are racing to take out the nest before the melish reinforce it. They are not waiting for Tikas's orders.

If we freeze-frame Tikas, running to regain control of his Greeks and the history of the moment, consider a question that bedevils accounts of what happens next. We see Tikas, a nervous panic written in the lines of his twenty-eight-year-old face. He is wearing a dark wide-brimmed hat with red knee-high leggings and field glasses strapped around his neck. It's ten o'clock, and some in the camp are still asleep, some Greeks are still drunk. In this instant before the first shot, contemplate the question: who fired first?

If we ask the question plainly, it was probably a Greek. Probably a Cretan war veteran. Perhaps Dimitri. But was this instant on the morning of April 20, 1914, the historical beginning of the Ludlow Massacre?[113]

The origins of Ludlow arose from deep within capitalistic relations of production and US anti-union ideology. Rockefeller's single-minded obsession with his vaunted open shop principle was the reaction of an economic automaton. Instincts of class survival made Rockefeller twitch like a mindless mass of muscle at the long end of a neuron struck by history's sharp mallet. Rockefeller's insentient great principle framed Ludlow and the terrible tapestry bullets and flames would weave.

The synaptic discharge triggering the reflex that fired the first shot at Ludlow arose in a mind whose archetypes, perceptions, and expectations ignited history, regardless of judgment, regardless of philosophy. Perhaps there was no first shot, no single spark. Only the ebb and flow, the torrent of change that sweeps our vision from one fractional glimpse of reality to the next. Knowing who fired the first shot that fated morning is akin to asking how many stripes has the tiger poised to eat you. The tiger's the thing.

At 9:55, before Tikas reaches the tents, three bombs, each composed of eight sticks of dynamite, explode in quick succession. Linderfelt later says they were a "military precaution that any commander would take."[114] They are a signal to his reinforcements and the guards at other coal camps in the canyons. Upon hearing the bombs, the machine gunners on Water Tank Hill set their rear sights for fourteen hundred yards.

At 10:01, the guards fire on Ludlow, the two machine guns raking its one hundred and fifty frail tents in lethal crossfire. Cracking rifle rounds whistle while the dark mechanical cadence of the machine guns sings bass in a choir of hate. Tikas sees canvas shredding all around him. Women and children, some not yet dressed, first run out of tents then scurry back seeking safety in cellars or under beds. Bullets zing as they ricochet off heavy cast-iron stoves inside the tents. The Greeks in the railroad cut flanking Hamrock's troops open fire on Water Tank Hill. They hope to draw fire away from Ludlow and disrupt the frantic construction of breastworks around the machine guns.

Tikas races to the headquarters tent and phones Lawson in Trinidad. Tikas tells him the guards are going to wipe out the colony, and Lawson knows it's true. He tells Tikas to care for the women and children and he will come as soon as possible with reinforcements. Lawson straps on a pistol, issues orders to organize a relief squad, and then leaves for Ludlow in the Red Special.

At the strikers' forward position in the Colorado and Southeastern Railroad sand cut, disciplined Greeks snipe at machine gunners when presented with clear targets. Other defenders, mostly Greeks, scatter and hold positions along the north–south axis of the Colorado and Southern railroad tracks.[115]

North of Ludlow, women and children run down the shallow arroyo to a railroad pump station. There the pumpman hides seventy of them in a ninety-foot well before coming under fire. Some strikers and their families flee west to the nearby Bayes Ranch, and others cower in cellars. Hamrock later testifies it looked like a picnic party, with everyone carrying baskets and blankets and running to catch a train.

At the same time as Linderfelt orders the firing to begin, he sends a detachment to the right of Water Tank Hill to clear the railroad cut. The detachment advances a short distance, then retreats under withering fire from the Greeks. The battle's first casualty is the belligerent guard Martin, remembered for beating unarmed strikers at the depot the night before. Wounded in the neck, the Greeks intensify their assault on his squad, and his comrades abandon him. The militia won't recover his body until nine o'clock. They find him with his face caved in by the steel butt plate of a Mannlicher and both arms broken. He has powder stains on his mouth.[116] Such was war in Colorado, like war in Macedonia.

Chaos reigns as Tikas orders everyone to flee the camp. He searches tattered tents for women and children and tends the wounded with Pearl Jolly. Jolly, twenty-one years old and a nurse at Minnequa Hospital in Pueblo, pins Red Cross badges to her dress and apron but continues drawing fire.[117] Bullets tear her dress and blow away the heel of her shoe.

The men scatter to their rifle pits to draw fire from camp, away from the women and children. But the militia fire into the tents.[118] Tikas hears a six-shooter firing from somewhere among the tents and begins a maddening search for the idiot drawing the guards' fire toward camp. It is almost two hours before he realizes there is no shooter. The cracking sound is from military-issued explosive bullets striking all around.

At eleven o'clock, Linderfelt and a detachment advance to the railroad depot toward their objective, the pump station north on the Colorado and Southern mainline. Once at the pump station, Linderfelt will flank Ludlow and be able to fire on evacuees escaping in the arroyo north of camp. From his position at the depot, he trains fire to the east into the railroad cut and the forward Greeks. By 11:30 the fire on the Greeks, armed with American carbines and no match for machine guns, is overwhelming. Their position untenable, the fighters retreat to the east, taking to the Black Hills.

Around 11:50, Lawson makes his way to within a few hundred yards of Ludlow. Traveling by car from Trinidad, he continues on foot cross-country after the automobile draws machine-gun fire. Lawson crawls to a small group of strikers returning fire from the railroad embankment and asks for Tikas. When the Greek arrives, he clasps Lawson's hand.

Lawson tells Tikas to hold out until nightfall because it will take that long to organize reinforcements. Tikas reports the ammunition exhausted, but he will do everything possible to prevent the guards from charging camp. The two leaders embrace. Then Lawson departs for Trinidad around 1:30. By four o'clock., he has gathered five hundred volunteers. A sympathetic train crew agrees to move his men north.

All afternoon Tikas and Pearl Jolly dodge sniper fire. They run from tent to tent, prodding women and children to take to the arroyos and on to the Black Hills a mile and a half east. At 7:20, a Colorado and Southeastern southbound local freight train crew abandons an engine and a cut of thirty-six cars. The brave crew shields the camp from machine-gun fire, allowing hundreds of trapped colonists to escape.

Forty strikers, their ammunition low, meet with Tikas for orders. Tikas sends them to the Black Hills. There is no way to hold off the guards until night, and Tikas knows it.

Frank Snyder, eleven years old, tries to get his fainted mother a cup of water. As the boy crawls from the tent cellar with his battered tin cup, a guard's bullet rips through his brain. The youth dies instantly.

In the hills with the strikers, Charles Costa, Ludlow's comedian who the children follow around like the Pied Piper, peers over a rocky ledge searching for his wife and family.[119] As he raises his head, a bullet shatters his skull. When comrades scurry to his side, he asks they sing the union song. As they begin the chorus, he mouths the lyric and dies. By day's end, the entire Costa family would die: Charles; his pregnant wife, Cedilano; and their two children, Onafrio and Lucy.[120]

Between four and five o'clock, militia reinforcements arrive with a third machine gun they locate on Water Tank Hill. This puts the total militia force at 177 men. Orders go out to burn the colony before sundown. At seven o'clock, they torch the first tent. Guards dodge from tent to tent with flaming brooms soaked in coal oil to spread the inferno. Linderfelt follows the advancing guards, setting tents aflame and looting. He loads ammunition and plunder from the headquarters tent into an automobile.

Mary Petrucci crouches in Tent Number 1 with her three small children. As she raises the cellar door, flames sweep through the entrance. Mary grabs her children, lurching through the opening and into the tent behind hers, Tent Number 58. She pushes her children down into the cellar, their ersatz refuge. Other women and children huddle in the underground of Tent Number 58, cowering in fear. Mary alone will somehow escape the coming flames, but nine days pass before she grasps that her children are dead.[121]

The macabre scene goes on. Captain Carson, commander of the irregulars, and Linderfelt with his shock troops round up strikers, soak tents with coal oil, and burn them to the ground. A young boy grabs Carson's ammunition belt, crying about prickets in his foot, his tiny appendage shattered by an exploding bullet. Guards rip down three torn, bullet-shredded American flags, douse them with coal oil, ignite them, and drag them through the dust.[122] William Snyder carries his dead son to the depot, wrapped in a gunnysack, while guards prod him with the barrels of their rifles. The guards of Troop A cart away loot, one with a sewing machine, another an accordion, their pockets bulging with Easter candy the Greeks had given children the day before. A shaggy blond Saint Bernard, his skull creased by a bullet, trots through the camp with a flaming timber in his mouth.

Lawson arrives at Barnes four miles south of Ludlow at 8:15 p.m. He commands reinforcements traveling in five Denver and Rio Grande Railroad gondolas. They march toward Ludlow on the eastern flank. The melish now controls the primary access to Ludlow and flanking territory to the west.

At 9:30 just west of Ludlow across the Colorado and Southern mainline, Tikas marches through the pandemonium unarmed. He approaches guard-held territory and strides to a group of militia

156

officers to seek a truce. Surrounded by guards, they take him to Linderfelt.

Linderfelt curses the Greek, and as Tikas proposes a ceasefire, Linderfelt grabs a soldier's Springfield, whirls it over his head and batters Tikas. Tikas blocks the rifle, breaking his arm, but suffers a staggering blow to his skull. The stock of the Springfield splinters into two parts.

The final sequence is uncertain, but the end comes when three jacketed shells rip into Tikas's back and hip. There, on the dusty blood-soaked plains of Colorado, melish rifle his pockets and kick his lifeless body.

Melish also kill local union secretary James Flyer, there to retrieve his family. The bullet that enters the back of his head blows away his face. Tikas and Flyer lie for three days before guards permit anyone to attend the bodies. Flyer and Tikas number among the thirty-two who pay freedom's price that spring day in Colorado. Among them are thirteen women and children under Tent Number 58.[123]

Chapter 58

It was just before noon when Harry and Dimitri retreated from the railroad cut after Linderfelt's advance on the train depot. Outgunned and low on ammo, they weren't finished with Linderfelt.

Through Dimitri's field glasses, they spotted the leader of the guards advancing to the railroad depot and asked another Greek if the officer was Linderfelt. The Greek told them it was the devil, and Harry and Dimitri should pray they never draw near him. That was exactly what Harry and Dimitri planned to do.

As the other Greeks in the railroad cut fell back to the Black Hills, Harry and Dimitri joined in the maneuver. They gave covering fire and leapfrogged in reverse as the three squads retreated. When their comrades were out of range, the two Greeks crossed a thousand yards from the wagon road to the shallow arroyo north of Ludlow in a low run. When they reached the arroyo, they started west toward Ludlow as a huddled flow of refugees and strikers streamed past on their way to the Black Hills.

The Greeks' retreat from the railroad cut allowed the militia to increase their fire on the camp. Now, two machine guns swept Ludlow west to east, and their bullets carried to the edge of the arroyo. Harry and Dimitri ran crouched and low. They approached the pump station just as Charles Costa fell from his wound. There was nothing to do for Costa, and the two continued west. They left the arroyo and raced for the pumpman's home, a converted Colorado and Southern boxcar one hundred yards south.

Harry and Dimitri reasoned Linderfelt was moving north to flank the camp. The pump station and nearby iron bridge, held by outnumbered strikers, were his objectives. They planned not to engage the advancing troops but to stay in cover, waiting for Linderfelt to present a target. Then they would pick him off.

Their problem was that the Winchester carbines they carried, unlike the Mannlicher, were not long-range battlefield weapons. The Winchester 1894 .30-30 was a reliable gun and almost indestructible. But with uncalibrated open sights, its accuracy was limited beyond one hundred yards. Their guns were serviceable but not up to a three-hundred-yard shot, even in Dimitri's expert hands. Three hundred yards was the distance from the pumpman's boxcar to the crossing of the wagon road and the Colorado and Southern mainline, where they expected to spot Linderfelt. And there was no cover, nowhere to hide between the pumpman's boxcar and the target. This was as close as they were going to get and still have a retreat.

Dimitri cursed under his breath, "With the Mannlicher, we would have a shot. From here, I do not see how we make the shot. The sun will sink lower as we wait. Then we will shoot into the light. My friend, I don't think this will work."

Dimitri was right, but they waited anyway, then waited some more. Both men knew it was an opportunity to kill Linderfelt and settle the debt of honor, Eleni's requite.

At three o'clock, the gunfire on Ludlow intensified. Around four, militia reinforcements arrived from Trinidad with a third machine gun, a .30-40 Gatling gun and began advancing on the pump station. Still, there was no sign of Linderfelt.[124] Harry and Dimitri, about to be overrun, retreated to the arroyo, then on to the Black Hills. Killing Linderfelt would have to wait. This battle belonged to the melish.

Chapter 59

Remember Ludlow!

In the quiet morning of the next day, militia gunners fired on the Bayes Ranch where many colonists had found refuge. Their target was Frank Bayes perched atop his windmill, watching guards burn anything left standing in Ludlow.[125] Susan Hollearan saw the same thing from the Ludlow train depot. Hollearan, the local postmistress, found Mary Petrucci wandering in a daze, unable to tell where she'd left her children. She also found Alcarita Pedregon in shock and uncommunicative, and she put both women on the train to Trinidad.[126]

Harry, Dimitri, and hundreds of evacuees and armed reinforcements waited in the Black Hills, watching through field glasses. The strikers' capacious damnation of the melish contrasted with Harry and Dimitri's vain search for the precise soulless devil they wished hell bound.[127] Linderfelt was asleep in the train depot, out of range and untouchable.

Miners and their families straggled into Trinidad. The town became striker-occupied territory. Among them trudged a half-dressed, cold, chattering woman carrying her newborn, a child of the prairie night.[128]

Late afternoon, a railroad telephone lineman discovered the thirteen bodies under Tent Number 58. Lawson dispatched three dead wagons from Trinidad to recover the remains. The wagons made it to Cedar Hill, where they met a hail of machine-gun spray that killed a grazing calf and spooked their teams. The undertakers made a fast retreat to Trinidad. The next day, Wednesday, Lawson got a wire from the Colorado and Southern Trainmen and Engineers union in Rugby, saying:

> *Bodies of women and children exposed in tent colony . . . Death from suffocation the cause. Please do something with the bodies, for God's sake, for they are human souls and deserve a decent burial.*[129]

160

About that time, a representative of the Red Cross arriving from Denver requested Hamrock allow the recovery of the dead. It took five hours for Hamrock to grant the mission. Then, traveling under a flag of truce, John McLennan, twice arrested during his journey, accompanied the undertakers' wagons on their terrible task.

News of Tikas's murder and the militia attack spread through the Greek coffeehouse network even as Ludlow smoldered. Hundreds of Greeks and other workers left for Trinidad preempting the union's April 22 call to arms.

The same day, President Wilson ordered the US Navy to bombard Vera Cruz. The action resulted in the death of over a hundred people, mostly civilians, and overshadowed the news from Colorado.[130] As Wilson addressed Congress to ask for advanced authorization of military force, reports filtering out of Colorado played second fiddle to the likelihood of war with Mexico. Somewhere in the inky abyss of the day's coverage were the names: Patricia Valdez, mother; Elvira, three months; Eulala, eight; Mary, seven; and Rudolph, nine; Cedilano Costa, pregnant and mother of Onafrio, six and Lucy, four; two Pedregon children Gloria, four and Roderlo, six; and three Petrucci children, Frank, six months, Lucy, three, and Joe, four.[131]

The strikers regrouped. They organized mobilization camps in the Black Hills on April 21st, and on the 22nd, they counterattacked. At the scab-run Victor American mine in Delagua, 160 strikers attacked and burned the outbuildings. The strikers took the high ground from the guards. But militia reinforcements from Cedar Hill forced their retreat. The reinforcements arrived late, delayed by resistant train crews.[132]

While the strikers were in retreat at Delagua, flames consumed buildings at five other big mines. At the Empire Mine, west of Aguilar, the company president ordered thirty-five mine employees, their wives, and children to shelter in the tipple house. The strikers set the tipple afire. The occupants retreated into the mine shaft, and the strikers wrecked the ventilation fan with dynamite. The strikers released the women and children but swore to starve the men. Strikers pounded out the union song on a piano mounted on a buckboard pulled through the dusty streets of Aguilar to celebrate their victory.[133]

Thirty armed Greeks marched through the Raton Pass from New Mexico to Trinidad. Two hundred men quit the mines in El Paso County north of Pueblo, where seventeen Greeks shouldered rifles and boarded a train to Trinidad. More Greeks from Fremont County west of Pueblo joined the Union army.

William Hickey, Secretary of the Colorado Federation of Labor, became the unions' military coordinator. The UMWA, the Denver Printing Press Assistant's Union, Denver Trades and Labor Assembly, and the Western Federation of Miners signed a call to arms. It read in part:

> *Organize the men in your community in companies of volunteers to protect the workers of Colorado against the murder and cremation of men, women and children by the armed assassins in the employ of coal corporations, serving under the guise of state militiamen. . . Hold all companies subject to order.*[134]

Cash donations of over $20,000 reached the UMWA office in Denver before the end of the day as calls pledging armed help streamed in from across the country. Denver Italians organized a company of one hundred armed men and placed them under UMWA command. New York unions sped a train of nurses to Colorado while sisters in the Denver Garment Workers Union organized four hundred attendants.[135]

Miners in the northern fields organized two hundred men into four companies. Missouri unions offered armed assistance, as did a group of five hundred in Thurber, Texas. The Denver Machinists drilled in the city's baseball park before supportive crowds. Their brothers in Cigar Makers Union No. 129 pledged five hundred men and held an emergency meeting where they passed a special assessment to purchase weapons. The Cigar Makers also called for Ammons's impeachment and a general strike. Thousands of Denver residents responded to the UMWA's appeal for citizens to write or wire President Wilson.

More than a thousand miners, many led by Balkan veterans, attacked coal company properties along a forty-mile front. Miners stormed the Rouse, Primrose, Brodhead and Royal mines, destroying over $300,000 worth of property.[136] The cry "Remember Ludlow!" raised mortal fear among guards and militia. Meanwhile, at Ludlow, Major Hamrock watched strikers digging trenches through his field glasses and feared being surrounded.

In the state capital, Lieutenant Governor Fitzgarrald ordered General Chase to muster a force of six hundred. He signed the decree only after business stalwarts promised to support a call for a special session of the legislature. The state was broke.

Chase couldn't fulfill his charge. Entire companies of troops refused to serve or fabricated excuses. Eighty-two soldiers mutinied and detrained in front of the general, disobeying direct orders.[137] Of the authorized force of six hundred, Chase could muster only two hundred fifty.[138] A special troop train rolled out of Denver with riflemen at the windows, cannon in the hold, and machine guns positioned fore and aft. Chase's predicament worsened when railroad workers refused to move his men from Trinidad to Ludlow.[139]

On April 25, the miners buried the women and children from Tent Number 58. The two black caskets of the mothers and the eleven small white ones of the children traveled the streets of Trinidad on hay wagons adorned with flowers. The bells of Holy Trinity Catholic Church peeled over the solemn ceremony as Tikas's casket led the procession, then returned to its bier to await a Greek priest. Two days later, they buried Ilias.

Chapter 60

Alex learned of the union caravan in the Pueblo kafeneion. The small shop was abuzz early Tuesday morning when word began filtering in of trouble at Ludlow. Now, Thursday morning, Alex itched to go south and join the fight.

He and Marta talked, and Alex convinced the strong-willed woman that only he should go for now and that she should stay with the children. She agreed when Alex told her he needed her to be with Stavros for his own peace of mind. His openness and conviction touched Marta. Sitting in Peter and Domna's living room, Alex at the end of the sofa and Marta in a wing chair beside him, they spoke in earnest tones. In his earnest words, Marta glimpsed the man's heart. She had grown to like and respect Alex. That afternoon, the young couple forged a bond that would find full career in the years to come.

Marta recoiled from Alex's sentiment no matter how heartfelt. She, too, wanted to join the fight. She finally agreed it was for the best, but for only a few days. She relented and busied herself working with a Catholic church relief group, collecting clothing, and making wound compresses for the strikers and their families.

In Denver, William Hickey headed a four-car supply caravan. Union volunteers overloaded the automobiles with weapons, ammunition, and medical supplies, then began a race with General Chase's troop reinforcement train. The unionists were on rutted, unpaved, sleet-pelted roads and the general on steel rails.

The general headed south with about half of the six hundred promised recruits. His current troops hadn't been paid for three months and his potential recruits didn't think getting shot at by angry strikers was worth doing for free. The seventy-six men of Troop C, the current assignment of Chase's two sons and three other relatives, mutinied and refused his order to board.

The train crews weren't helping either. The railroad called seven crews before they found one that would operate southbound.[140] The special train, engine 628, rolled out of Denver Union Station just after noon on April 23rd. The double-header pulled nine coaches and three baggage cars loaded with machine guns and ammo. Two three-inch fieldpieces and 220 shrapnel shells were blocked on separate flatcars. Sharpshooters rode in the engine cabs, and the locomotives shoved two flat cars ahead of them as an early warning for explosives or blocked tracks. The leading flatcar buoyed a .30-40 Gatling gun.[141] But, for all its intimidating efforts, speed was not one of them. The train took over twelve hours to reach Walsenburg, 160 miles south. UMWA organizer Ed Doyle telegrammed the train's departure down the line, alerting union forces along the way.

Meanwhile, Hickey got a jump on Chase. His caravan left Denver an hour before the general, but the weather was rough south of Pueblo where Alex volunteered for the caravan. Alex, now considering himself an experience driver, was a valuable addition to the entourage. Fortunately, he was not at the wheel when the first car in line slid sideways off the sleet-covered road into a swollen creek south of Pueblo. After gathering what they could from the sunken vehicle, the remaining three cars continued south. They ran low on fuel, requiring a four-mile hike to a friendly farmer for cans of gas. Still, with all the distractions, Hickey's caravan beat Chase's train to Walsenburg, arriving before midnight.[142]

Alex stayed with the convoy to Aguilar, eighteen miles farther south, where he ran into fellow strikers from Segundo. They told him of the mobilization camps in the Black Hills, the de facto center of the counterattack and probable location of Harry and Dimitri. In the early hours of the morning, Alex bunked down in the Aguilar town hall with other weary strikers. They fell asleep to the repurposed melody of "The Battle Cry of Freedom." A tinny piano accompanied the union anthem's haunting lyrics.

Chapter 61

Alex made his way to the Black Hills with a group of strikers returning from the raid on the Empire Mine west of Aguilar. General Chase sent reinforcements from Ludlow, but the miners' retreat left a burning relic, a smoldering monument to their dispossession and grievance. In the Black Hills, Alex learned that the center of the counterattack was in Trinidad. The city, now in the hands of strikers, had no melish and no local law enforcement, save the organized miners and their supporters. All was peaceful there. The melish encamped at Ludlow, honoring a truce negotiated between Lawson and Chase prohibiting troops from moving south of the burned camp. Chase abided by the agreement because he feared being overrun and sensed that the morale of his men was poor. The strikers honored nothing. They scorned the whims of a general responsible for the deaths of women and children whose burial was on this very day.

Alex joined the funeral procession for the victims of Tent Number 58 on Saturday morning at Trinidad's Holy Trinity Catholic Church. It was there he reconnected with Harry and Dimitri. As the church bells tolled their solemn dirge, the horse-drawn drays clomped to the cemetery, the first with the two black caskets of the women, followed by the eleven smaller white coffins of the children. The cortege traveled first on Commercial, then on Main for the journey to the Catholic cemetery. Thousands of mourners lined the streets. All were peaceful; all were reverent. After the procession passed, the three friends went to the nearby Trinidad Hotel to sit and talk in the lobby.

They chose three wingback chairs to the side of the entranceway, apart from prying eyes and curious ears. Harry asked, "How are Marta and the children?"

Alex heard a melancholy in Harry's voice. Alex assured Harry and Dimitri, "Everyone in Pueblo is fine. I insisted to Marta that I come alone and that she should stay with the children. The news of Ludlow is all over Pueblo. Her nephew and niece are terrified that troops may come for them. It is a pity. But they feel safe with Marta. Stavros, he knows nothing. He is happy to eat and sleep and crawl and play when it suits him. A child lives in bliss when he finds all he

166

needs. The Georgallas family are Godsent. How will I ever repay them?"

Dimitri interjected, "You are fortunate, Alex. Repay them with caution and stay alive to raise your son."

Alex nodded, "But there is still the matter of Linderfelt."

Harry looked around to make certain no one could overhear. "The strikers are raiding mines north of here. They are burning buildings and destroying mine property for revenge. There is no strategy for taking and holding territory except Trinidad. The strike leadership is confused. There is much bravado but also much hatred. These actions are unplanned. There is talk of United States Army troops coming. If that happens, there will be no fighting against such a force.

"The militia is at Ludlow. We can't get near enough to spot Linderfelt. We don't know that he is there. If he is, it will be almost impossible to get to him. There are three hundred troops at Ludlow. They dispatch details from Ludlow to stop the strikers' raids.

"For now, it is best we stay in Trinidad. We have rooms at the boardinghouse, and you can stay with us. From here, we can help the strikers and try to locate Linderfelt. Then we will honor our promise."

Alex asked, "How can we track Linderfelt? Do we have anyone among the guards who will help us?"

Dimitri shook his head, "Ilias was our eyes and ears. Now he is gone. And the Greek who has taken his place is not so good. It hurts me to say, but the new man brags and boasts. He is not someone to trust."

The three men were quiet, thinking about their predicament. Then Dimitri said, "There may be a way to spy on Ludlow. But we need to talk to Gustav first. Meanwhile, Alex, you go to Segundo and retrieve your Mannlicher."

Chapter 62

Alex went to Segundo for the Mannlicher after the funeral on Saturday. He met Harry and Dimitri at the boardinghouse in Trinidad later in the day. While Alex was away, Harry went with Dimitri to the Colorado and Southern Railroad freight yard north of the passenger depot. It was late afternoon, and in the crew shanty, Dimitri found his friend Gustav. He and his crew were engaged in an animated discussion about the murder of Tikas.

The two Greeks entered the wooden structure, passing the crew call board. Drawing near the break room, they heard Gustav's resolute voice. "I do not care how much you hate a man. It is disrespectful and unchristian to leave a body unattended for three days in plain view. Every passenger train that traveled that block saw the Greek and the union man lying there . . . like . . . dead meat. That is all they were to those guards . . . dead meat. Hell, that is all these miners are to Rockefeller . . . dead meat. Rockefeller cares more for the mules than he does for the miners. Mules are harder to replace!" From the half-dozen railroaders in the shanty, there were only nods of agreements.

When Gustav finished his speech, he looked up at the entrance and saw Dimitri standing just beyond, with Harry behind him. Gustav got up from the table where the railroaders were playing cards and working bills and joined the Greeks in the hallway.

Dimitri said, "You speak the truth, Gustav? Did they leave the bodies unattended?"

"It is the truth as I live and breathe. I saw the bodies every time we dispatched north. They left them only forty feet from the mainline, lying there face down in the dirt. No blankets, nothing. The railroad called CF&I and told them, and they did nothing. No respect."

"No honor," added Dimitri.

"Gustav, you have been a good friend. We have a favor to ask. You are a union man and a man of conviction. Harry and I need to know about the guards at Ludlow. We need to get close enough to can watch them. Since you and your train crew travel that way, we are here to ask for your suggestions and, perhaps, your help."

Gustav looked away. He returned his gaze first to Dimitri, then to Harry, "The guards have moved their camp to catty-corner from

168

Ludlow. They are on the southwest corner of the railroad and wagon trail. The guards are always in the Ludlow depot and always looking for strikers. They are armed and nervous. They should be. Hell, they even brought artillery—two cannons, if you can believe that. They have about three hundred troops. But some are away at mines to the north. They use the railroad to deploy. I don't know how many remain. Maybe two hundred are still in camp."

Dimitri asked, "Is there a way to get close and watch them? Do they guard the pump station north of Ludlow?" Dimitri and Harry were familiar with that location from the day Ludlow burned.

Gustav thought, "No, they do not have guards there. Not that I remember. There is no one there but the pump station attendant, M.G. Low. Passenger trains do not stop there. But we do."

Gustav was referring to the fact that he was the conductor on a local freight working Trinidad to Walsenburg, a round trip of eighty miles. Gustav's crew switched out local industries along the way and returned each evening to Trinidad.

"If you want to watch the guards, the pump station is as close as you can get without being shot on the spot. We can drop you there in the morning and pick you up on our way back to Trinidad. I won't know how long our job will take until I see our bills. Each day is different. If we do not meet for the return trip, you will be on your own. It is a long walk back to Trinidad. Go cross-country to avoid the guards while you are north of Ludlow.

"We won't be able to stop at the pump station northbound unless we have orders. But we can slow down so you can dismount and run for cover while the cut blocks the guard's view. Be here tomorrow morning at six. We will get you onboard. Bring lunch and something to drink. Bring enough in case you have to walk back to Trinidad. Oh, and come armed," Gustav ventured.

Dimitri nodded, "Can three men come?"

"Two is best. It will be easier to get on and off. Less chance the guards will spot you," Gustav replied.

Dimitri and Harry nodded.

The men shook hands, and Dimitri and Harry left for the boarding house. That evening, when they rejoined Alex, they sat in Harry's room and talked about their next move.

Alex wanted to go with Harry and Dimitri. But Alex did not know what Linderfelt looked like, so he'd be of no use spotting the man. Harry told Alex it would be better for him to return to Trinidad and help the strikers, but to be careful in the hills. Rumors circulated that a dozen or more strikers had died in the raids. Alex worried he might miss the funeral of Tikas on Monday. Harry and Dimitri assured him they would pay his respects if he did. The three agreed that bringing justice to Linderfelt is what Tikas would have wanted. Few knew at the time how correct they were.

An independent, comprehensive, credible account of the last moments of Ilias Tikas is lost to history. What came out, what became public record weeks later, resulted from a Colorado National Guard court-martial of ten officers and two dozen men. It was an exercise in deflecting blame. The tribunal heard sixty-two charges of murder, arson, manslaughter, looting, and larceny arising from Ludlow. On these, they convicted not a single guardsman.

Of the murder of Tikas and local union secretary, James Flyer, this much is sworn. Tikas approached the guards under a white flag seeking a truce. Linderfelt beat Tikas with a Springfield rifle, breaking its stock into two pieces. Flyer was trying to rejoin his family when captured. Both prisoners were threatened with hanging, surrounded by guardsmen, and then shot from behind.

The tribunal found Linderfelt guilty of assault on Tikas with a Springfield rifle, but concluded:

> *The court finds the accused, Karl E. Linderfelt, first lieutenant, second infantry, National Guard of Colorado, guilty of the facts as charged, that is to say that part of specification 1, charge 6, reading as follows:*
>
> *Having then and there a deadly weapon, to-wit: A United States Springfield rifle, did then and there with said weapon, commit an assault upon and against one Louis Tikas, but by reason of the justification as shown in the evidence adduced before the court attaches no criminality thereto.* [143]

Linderfelt would come to realize that not everyone honored his pardon.

Chapter 63

Harry and Dimitri arrived at the railroad yard at six the next morning. After working his bills and switching together their cut of cars, Gustav's crew coupled into their waiting caboose. With the train made, Gustav received orders from the trainmaster and waved the engineer an ahead signal. The Walsenburg Local cleared the yard limit sign at 7:43.

Fourteen miles north of Trinidad, the train pulled through the Ludlow depot at five miles per hour, and Harry and Dimitri saw Gustav was right. The depot was full of armed guardsmen. Gustav pointed out the mounted field cannons in one of the siding tracks.

Half a mile north and just five hundred yards from the guards' camp, the train slowed. As Harry and Dimitri made ready to dismount, Gustav said, "Remember, 1208. That is our engine number. If it is dark when we return, that will be the only way to identify us for your ride home.

"With these bills, we should not be late. Maybe six this evening. But you never know when railroading. Anything can happen. We will slow down at the pump station, and if you get aboard, then everything is fine. If you do not get aboard, we will keep moving and assume they have captured you or you are on your way back to Trinidad."

Harry and Dimitri nodded and shouldered their rifles, Harry the Winchester and Dimitri the Mannlicher. They grabbed their packs and moved to the forward right side steps of the caboose. When they were on the steps, Gustav yelled, "Face the cab! Step off with your left foot first! Always use your trailing foot when you dismount!"

Both men nodded, then stepped off onto the rugged ballast of the track bed. They ran to the nearby pump house before troops could spot them.

Pumpman M.G. Low was working on his boiler repairing damage from militia bullets fired during the siege of Ludlow. The Greeks introduced themselves and said Gustav told them Low was a friend.

Low was a soft-spoken man in his late fifties. He disliked the guards, but things hadn't started out that way. In September, when the strike began, he had been neutral. He did his job and allowed the nearby tent colony to use an old railroad well for their water supply. He told Harry and Dimitri that in the early days, everyone got along, the strikers, the guards, and himself. But the situation soured after Linderfelt took charge.

Low said in late December, a cavalryman's horse tripped over barbed wire in the road. Linderfelt ordered his men to cut down all the barbed-wire fencing surrounding the camp. Then the militia threw the rusty barbed wire down the well that Ludlow used for their water. Low said he watched troopers cut up the fencing and throw it into the well. After they left, Low walked to the well and saw the wire below. He said the union men came later and pulled the trash from the well.[144]

That night, still angry and embarrassed, Linderfelt beat a Greek boy in the train depot, gashing his skull and cursing him. A young schoolteacher from Missouri and her companion were at the nearby post office and witnessed the beating. When they confronted Linderfelt, he cursed the couple. He bellowed, "I am Jesus Christ, and my men on horses are Jesus Christs, and we have got to be obeyed!"[145]

Low said he was in the pump station, working on his boiler around 8:30 on the day Ludlow burned. The pumpman told Harry and Dimitri that his wife had gone to Trinidad that morning on the Colorado and Southern, and his five-year-old daughter was with him. She was playing outside. Then she ran into the station crying, "Take me, Daddy, there is going to be a fight."

Low picked up his daughter and said, "I guess you just saw some militia riding around that has kind of scared you."

But the terrified little girl said, "No, there is going to be a fight."

Then a bomb exploded.

Harry asked, "You must have been worried about being this close to the militia and Ludlow?"

M.G. Low nodded and continued with his story, relieved at being able to tell it. He explained that when he heard the explosion; he stepped to the door of the boiler house, looked west, and saw dust in the air. He thought nothing of it because he thought maybe they were exploding some confiscated dynamite. The little girl was still in his arms pleading, "Take me out of here, Daddy, there is going to be a fight."

Low told her to, "Keep quiet; you are scared."

They reentered the pump house, and minutes later, a second bomb exploded. When Low opened the door, he saw women, some carrying children and others leading children by the hand, running from the tent colony in all directions. They were running toward the pump station and toward the arroyo, scattering out. Then, he heard a rifle discharge and a minute later, a general volley from along Water Tank Hill.

The shots from Water Tank Hill struck the top of the pump station. They hit high. One hundred and nine bullets hit the boiler house and his home. Seven rounds hit the head of the boiler, and two penetrated.

It was about a 10:15 when he took his little girl in his arms and went outside to help the fleeing women and children. They were standing around the old well, which was almost dry. The well was a hundred feet deep, and its steps were rotten. The pumpman told the refugees, "Be careful going down those steps, you might as well be shot as drown."

Then Low took his little girl and ran to the big arroyo and later to the Bayes Ranch. As he passed the boiler house, a bullet fanned his ear. With tears in his eyes, Low told Harry and Dimitri, "If I had had my little girl in my right arm, she would have been killed, but she was in my left arm."[146]

Dimitri asked if Low saw Tikas's body when he returned to the pump station. Low pointed south of the station, "Down there, east of the railroad, about two hundred yards. They left Louis the Greek and another man. They left them for three days."

Dimitri looked at Harry with restrained fury and gripped his Mannlicher even tighter.

The pumping station was railroad property just north of Ludlow. It replenished locomotive tenders with water. The pumpman's house was a converted Colorado and Southern boxcar with two framed additions. A water tank tower with a swinging spigot arm, a pumping building, and two deep-pit dug wells completed the property. The wells were

174

one hundred feet deep. One was almost dry and unusable. Low had shepherded seventy-five Ludlow refugees, mostly women and children, into the dry well the day Ludlow burned.

Low showed the Greeks the best place for a lookout. He told them to stay down and remember that the guards watched the pump house only five hundred yards away. He pointed the Greeks to the pumping building and a window facing the militia camp. The Greeks could watch the camp unless trains blocked their view. Low explained that if a northbound train has orders for a water stop, its cut of cars will block their line of sight. Watering takes fifteen minutes, then the train would continue.

Harry and Dimitri thanked Low and told him they would stay out of sight. They didn't mention to the kind man that they intended to shoot and kill Linderfelt if they spotted him. That would put the onus on the pumpman and draw him into danger. For this, he was unprepared and unaccountable. Harry would weigh these matters only if they spotted their target.

Low impressed the Greeks as a well-intentioned, peaceable man, a family man. But he cursed the troops. They attacked his station with disregard for the lives of the women and children. In Low's mind, there was no redemption.

As the two Greeks settled in, Dimitri said, "It is unfortunate that we cannot climb to the top of the water tower. From there we could see farther and have a better shot at Linderfelt."

"You are right, my friend. But we are lucky to have what we have, no? Yesterday we had no way of finding Linderfelt and today here we are, five hundred yards away with a sharpshooter and a Mannlicher.

"Let me ask you. Should we spot Linderfelt, and he presents a target, our only retreat is through the arroyo, as before. Then to the hills. We will only have a five-hundred-yard head start. But what of Low? If the shot comes from his building, the guards will come for him, and likely he will die. Which obligation is greater, the death of Linderfelt or the life of Low?"

Dimitri scratched his head, "I am your humble enlisted soldier, Kapetánios. You give the order, and I will comply. Enlisted men like me have no philosophy; we have only ears. We hear, we obey."

175

The morning and afternoon faded. As the hours dragged on, Linderfelt went unseen, but the guards' camp was active. They watched men moving in organized units from the bivouac to the Ludlow train depot. Armed troops boarded passenger cars in a station siding. These were reinforcements for beleaguered mine guards struggling to hold off armed and angry strikers. This deployment was bound for the Chandler Mine near Canon City, far to the north and forty miles west of Pueblo. General Chase left Ludlow at six thirty and arrived with two hundred men at nine that Sunday night. Harry and Dimitri passed Chase's outbound train aboard the southbound Walsenburg Local on their return to Trinidad.

As the day wore on, the two Greeks took turns with the field glasses. They scoured the guards' camp and noted officers but failed to spot Linderfelt. Dimitri remarked they might substitute any of the officers for Linderfelt because they were all guilty of something. Harry chuckled. But the life of just any officer was not worth the danger it would bring to Low. By shooting any officer instead of Linderfelt, they would exact retribution, but at what price? The life of a good man? No, the honorable course was to wait for Linderfelt, no matter how long. Then give justice.

Engine 1208 approached the pump station, prepared to stop. Gustav had a water order. This made the Greek's remount easier. The locomotive came to a clattering halt with its tender alongside the water tank. The Greeks started up the track bed on the east side of the cut toward the caboose. They saluted Low on the water tower, swinging the spigot into position as they jogged by. He nodded. They heard the locomotive fireman jerk the chain on the spigot, and the sound of rushing water followed as the tender car filled.

Aboard the caboose, the Greeks greeted Gustav. He asked, "Mission accomplished?"

Harry replied, "We did not see who we hoped to see. Still, we know more than we did. We must thank you and the train crew for your help. Without you, we could never know what we know now. We are in your debt."

"Do not give it a thought," replied Gustav. "We are happy we can be of service in this fight. All working men must stand together and demand respect from their bosses. This is a fight we started with the railroads many years ago. We know the struggle is long. But the reward is dignity."

The Greeks nodded, then settled back into their caboose seats for the return to Trinidad.

Gustav looked up from working his bills and asked, "Would you like some stew?"

Chapter 64

Miners stood silent honor guard for Tikas on his bier. Two other
Orthodox strikers, Loupiakes and Tommich, reposed alongside.
Mourners shuffled by in the hushed viewing room at MacMahon's
Mortuary. They knelt and prayed, some wept, and some touched the
corpse for a farewell remembrance. Father Paschopoulos arrived from
Denver. Minutes before the white-robed priest began the service, four
Greeks with the hard eyes of veterans marched into the mortuary. They
slammed the butts of their rifles on the wooden floor four times and
swore an oath of revenge for the fallen leader.

Solemnity cut through the celebration that was Trinidad. With
armed strikers in control, a sense of liberation swelled in the property-
less army. Young Barron Beshoar remembered the town.

> *After the massacre at Ludlow, the miners took*
> *Trinidad. And my sight, the thing I see, is my father,*
> *who was a very young man. He took my mother and me*
> *in his car, open car, and he drove proudly around*
> *Trinidad. And on each corner there stood a stalwart*
> *miner, with his red bandanna and his rifle.* [147]

Now, as volunteers patrolled the peaceful town, saluting
victorious brethren, all were somber. Today belonged to the martyrs.

In the musty incense and dim light of burning tapers, the
bearded priest sprinkled dust on the cheeks of the dead as Pete
Katsulis, Tikas's successor, intoned the Mass. It was a Greek funeral,
orderly, reverent, and stoic. Katsulis swung the brass censer in a wide
arc, miming the pendulum of a hypnotic timepiece for the timeless
invocation.

The funeral procession advanced with Tikas's white, horse-
drawn hearse followed by five hundred Greeks marching in two
columns. There were no guns and no bands. Two thousand mourners
filed behind the Greeks, first up Main Street, then Commercial, and
finally up the long hill to the Knights of Pythias Cemetery. After
lowering the caskets, the priest trickled a fist of red earth. They filled

the graves, hymns intoned, and the ceremony concluded. It was then a familiar face approached Harry, Dimitri, and Alex.

Yiorgos Vedros walked up behind the three Greeks. Dimitri was the first to notice him. Yiorgos looked unlike the man Dimitri remembered. Instead of a fine suit and starched shirt, Yiorgos wore common clothing. He looked like one of the thousands of mourners he walked among. A faint smile crossed his face at Dimitri's recognition. Yiorgos said, "Perhaps you remember me, no? From Pueblo?"

Harry turned in his direction and after a second glance said, "Yiorgos, good to see you. This is Alex, and you have met Dimitri."

The two men nodded and shook Yiorgos's hand.

Yiorgos looked around, then again over his shoulder. The other three noted his nervousness. "It would be good to talk, but we need to meet in private. Here, it is too public. There are too many eyes and people unknown to me."

"We have rooms at the Purgatoire Boardinghouse on West First Street. Do you know the place? It is one block south of Main, off Beech Street," answered Harry.

"Is it possible we can meet there in two hours?" suggested Yiorgos.

The three Greeks nodded, and Yiorgos melted into the milling mourners.

Alex asked, "Who was that?"

Harry said, "Yiorgos is one of Ilias's spies. He is a friend. He works at CF&I headquarters in Pueblo. Yiorgos told us of the Greek spy and Linderfelt. But Yiorgos knew neither name. He identified Linderfelt later. He saw the wound to Linderfelt's neck from your brave wife. *Eonia I mnimi.*"

Alex was stunned by this information. He knew nothing of Yiorgos. He reasoned Harry and Dimitri had kept this from him to protect their source of information.

Dimitri wondered aloud, "What do you think he can tell us?"

Harry shook his head. "We will find out in two hours."

Yiorgos arrived at the boardinghouse, and Harry, who had been watching the street, walked to the entrance to greet him. The two men climbed the stairs to Harry's room, where Dimitri and Alex waited. The day was sunny. Alex suggested they walk to Cimino Park near the

179

river. Yiorgos shook his head and told the young man it was better to not be seen together. This made Alex curious. He asked, "Harry and Dimitri told me you helped find my wife's killer. For this, I am forever grateful. With God's help, we will finish the obligation. But why are you here today?"

"I am here as a spy. A spy for CF&I. But please, I will explain."

Harry understood and nodded to Yiorgos to continue.

"CF&I sent me because they want a report on Trinidad, the Greeks, the strikers, and anything else I might learn. They told me to travel here and pretend to be a mourner.

"The irony is, even had they not ordered me here, I would have come. Ilias was a dear friend. I knew him before the union. We met at the University of Athens many years ago.[148] His death is tragic. But he was a brave man, and fate calls brave men to tragedy. Does it not?

"I will return to Pueblo, report that all is what CF&I expects it to be. And I will go about my work like nothing ever happened. CF&I will never know that I paid my respects with a heavy heart or that I have spoken with you," Yiorgos confided.

Harry asked, "We have redressed half of our obligation, Yiorgos. The Greek spy was Nick Michaels."

Yiorgos knew from the past tense, Michaels was dead.

Harry continued, "Our remaining obligation is Linderfelt. He is hard to track and hard to get close to. Since the day he burned Ludlow, we do not know where he is. Yesterday, all day, we looked for him in the militia camp but never saw him. Do you have any idea where he is?"

"No, no. I do not know. They may have ordered him north after the burning. They say at headquarters he will stand before a court-martial for his actions. They say he killed Tikas. This is the talk at headquarters. I am sorry I cannot say where he is. If I could, I would kill him myself."

The declaration surprised Harry and Dimitri, but Alex nodded.

Yiorgos told the three comrades what he knew about the events since Ludlow burned. He told them about the attack on the Delagua and the Empire mines. He said strikers held the town of Aguilar for a day. There were casualties on both sides, but the mine guards took

180

worse. He said the aim of the strikers seemed to be to destroy buildings, mines, and property, and that has CF&I more worried than the loss of life.

He said there are rumors of five thousand armed miners in Wyoming waiting for orders to come to Colorado. He noted with glee that a thousand women trapped Governor Ammons in his office demanding he request federal troops, which he did. He said on Saturday, strikers infiltrated Walsenburg staging to attack the Chandler Mine. On Sunday, while Harry and Dimitri watched for Linderfelt at the pumphouse, over five thousand people protested at the state capital in Denver.

Yiorgos concluded by reporting the mood at CF&I headquarters was defiant but worried. Losing property alarmed them. But Rockefeller would never recognize the union. The company would demand the state recruit more militia as soon as the legislature returned to session and voted for more money. But Colorado was bankrupt.

He mentioned the truce that Lawson and Chase negotiated. For that reason, General Chase would not send troops south of Ludlow. Yiorgos said General Chase feared being overrun by the strikers in Trinidad who grew stronger by the day.

According to Yiorgos, CF&I was ambivalent about the call for federal troops. They didn't like the idea because they couldn't control federal men, unlike the Colorado guard. But the company wanted to secure their mines, and the federal forces would see to that.

Yiorgos said he wanted to help. He said the best way to reach him was to call the kafeneion in Pueblo, ask for Manolis from Milos and leave a phone where he could call back. Yiorgos promised to relay information on Linderfelt as soon as he got it, but he didn't know how to get in touch. Dimitri told him to contact the Georgallas family, and they would know.

Yiorgos left the boardinghouse after shaking hands all around. After he left, Dimitri said, "We now have eyes and ears in Pueblo. This is good, no?"

Chapter 65

General Chase was worried. Word had reached him that five thousand miners under WFM command were massed in Wyoming awaiting the UMWA's call to entrain for Colorado. WFM had a keen memory and held historic grievances against Colorado capitalists. Chase worried with good reason.

Meanwhile, dozens of sorties against coal company property exploded without a coordinated strategy or command. The leadership of the counterattack often fell to the Greek war veterans.

The fighting spread. In the northern fields, a battle raged near Louisville, and Chase split his small force to cover the attack. As his men arrived in the north, attacks began in Walsenburg, then Forbes.

At Forbes, Greeks commanded a disciplined force that advanced on the guards with tactics proven against the Turks.[149] Instead of charging en masse, a squad of Greeks sprinted toward the enemy, screaming at the top of their lungs. They knelt and laid down cover fire for comrades who rushed beyond, knelt, and fired.

The Balkan tactics and the strikers' fierce resolve devastated the guards. Their slow retreat became a humiliating rout as they scattered, leaving their dead behind, like the Turks at Monastir. Chase's troops at Ludlow, only six miles from Forbes, declined to engage.

Governor Ammons, away in Washington, DC, returned to Denver to reclaim charge of the embattled state. He phoned Lawson in Trinidad and gave him one hour to stop all the shooting. Ammons blustered to Lawson, "The men have got to lay down their arms and go to their homes."

Lawson responded, "Their homes were in Ludlow and Forbes colonies destroyed by your militia. Now the only homes they have are in the rifle pits."

Politics bedeviled Ammons. The Women's Peace Association, a middle-class alliance founded following the massacre, nipped at his heals. These comfortable women of Denver demanded the governor recall all troops from the strike zone, arrest Hamrock and Linderfelt, request federal troops, and decommission the National Guard.

On Saturday, April 25th, Ammons requested President Wilson send federal forces. Wilson, preoccupied with the Mexican crisis, delayed his decision until the end of the month. Colorado roiled, with Linderfelt at large.

Chapter 66

Marta longed to travel south to rejoin her brother and the Greeks, but she couldn't bring the children. She heard the reports of battles at the Delagua and Empire mines. Rumors of armed incursions circulated like dust devils, spinning myth with truth. Nothing seemed real, and everything seemed possible. She wanted to go south to see for herself. She wanted to reconnect with her brother and Alex and Dimitri, and especially Harry. She wondered what they were up to. Were they safe? Were they tracking Linderfelt? Were they planning an attack? What were they doing? She had not talked to Alex since Alex left with the arms caravan the past Thursday. It was now Tuesday, and she was beside herself.

She sat with Domna, a calm and intelligent woman fifteen years older than Marta, and let her feelings flow. She told Domna that she could help in Trinidad—or wherever the men might be. She was strong, healthy, and unafraid. She could handle a gun, and she could keep up on a march.

Domna bounced Stavros on her right knee and listened like a saint. Marta calmed, drained of emotional charge. Then she wept and Domna handed her a handkerchief. She was well-stocked for Stavros. As Marta wiped her eyes, she said, "There is too much death. My brother's wife is dead. Eleni is dead. The women and children under the tent are dead. God has forsaken Colorado." Then she crossed herself. "When my business here is over, I will leave here on the fastest train and never return."

Domna asked, "What is your business, Marta? You must help with your brother's children. But you are a young woman. You will have a life of your own. Your brother will remarry, will he not? After this strike and this horrible winter and the guns and fighting, he will not stay in the mines. There is no future there for the children nor him nor you.

"Why not go back to St. Louis and help in your parents' business? St. Louis has many Italians, and it is a proper city to raise children. Your nephew will be ready for school in a year and your niece a year after. And, for you, a proper place to find a husband, no?"

"Antonio came to Colorado to save his money and buy land. He wants to farm and to raise animals and crops. He is a dreamer," Marta answered. "I am here because of his misfortune. I care not for sheep and goats and crops. But he is my brother, and I must help.

"We have talked. Antonio knows that the pay of the mines is not enough to buy land. They don't even pay in American dollars. How can you expect to buy land with company script? But he holds to his idea and his dream."

"Then why not take the children back to St. Louis with you? Raise them there. There you will be with your family and not alone, not so. . . ." Domna trailed off.

Marta nodded and dabbed her eyes. She yearned for her friends in the southern field. But she would sit tight for a few more days. For her to leave would not be fair to Domna or the children. She couldn't leave Domna with all the work. She hoped to hear something, some news that would settle her mind. Something from Antonio, Alex, Dimitri, or Harry—someone who could help her understand her world. Someone to tell her what might happen next, in the strike and in her life.

Chapter 67

A strikers' colony arose outside of Trinidad. Camp Beshoar swelled on San Raphael Heights, the abandoned encampment of the militia reserves. In the early hours of Wednesday, April 30, 138 strikers left Beshoar and marched seven miles to Forbes mine. In the hills above the mine, strikers joined them from surrounding camps and numbered three hundred by five in the morning. Antonio, Marta's brother, joined from Segundo.

Forbes mine was lightly defended. A defective Gatling gun covered the narrow canyon approach to the south. The mine presented a tempting target for the unforgiving strikers. "Remember Ludlow!" echoed off the canyon walls ahead of the first wave of attackers. The mine was vulnerable, but that didn't save three strikers in the second wave charging down the eastern slope. The rickety Gatling gun had yet to fail and took all three. Antonio's lifeless body bowled down the hillside and wedged into a pinyon stump. Alex, with the strikers since Beshoar, saw it all.[150]

The strikers wrecked the mine, killed nine guards and scabs, and burned the stables with thirty-seven mules. They set fire to the tipple, the scales, the post office, and the boiler house.[151] The attack was over by ten o'clock, and the strikers retreated.

Two hours before, the first federal troops had detrained in Trinidad.

186

Chapter 68

Alex helped recover Antonio's body and rode with it and two other dead strikers back to Trinidad in a commandeered Rocky Mountain Fuel mine truck. He delivered the body to MacMahon's Mortuary, then walked stunned to the boardinghouse. It was late afternoon when Harry and Dimitri returned. They found Alex sitting alone in the hallway outside of Harry's room, dejected and dirty. Harry saw bloodstains on his jacket.

Dimitri spoke first. "Alex, have you heard? Federal troops are here in Trinidad, at the depot. They have ordered all to disarm, including the militia and mine guards."[152]

Alex nodded, then looked up from the floor at both Greeks. He spoke so low that neither Harry nor Dimitri could hear, "Antonio is dead."

"Who?" Dimitri asked, cocking his head.

"Antonio, Marta's brother."

Harry asked, "How, Alex? How did it happen?"

"This morning at Forbes. A Gatling gun. He was advancing down the canyon to the mine. I saw it all. He died the instant they hit him. He took bullets in his chest and legs. There was no chance to save him," reported Alex.

"May his soul be blessed," offered Dimitri. "He died a brave man doing a brave thing."

Alex nodded. Then he spoke as if unaware anyone else could hear, "He died for nothing. He was brave. This is true. But he died for hatred and anger and retribution and honor and all the things we tell ourselves make death seem good. Now his children are orphans. What of them?"

Dimitri looked at Harry, who shook his head. Then Dimitri said, "You are worn and tired, my friend. Sleep here tonight, use my room. You were up early, and you marched and fought.

"But Alex, where is Antonio now?"

"He is at the mortuary where they brought Tikas. I brought him there this afternoon. I thought that is what Marta would want."

"Yes, yes. Well done, my friend. You did the right thing," said Dimitri. "Now we must tell Marta without delay."

Dimitri looked at Harry, and Harry knew the task would fall to him. He said, "I will go to Pueblo on the early train tomorrow. Dimitri, you go to Segundo and gather his things. Make sure we account for everything. That is something we should not burden Marta with, no? Alex, stay here and rest and check at the mortuary tomorrow. Tell them Marta will return on the late train to make plans."

Alex and Dimitri nodded, relieved that they did not have to tell Marta.

Harry concluded, "Let us forget about all this burning and killing mine guards. We have our pledge to fulfill. But for now, only Marta and her family matter. With federal troops here, we will not be playing at war any longer."

The rain pounded the dusty plains, and the rivers rose outside of the boardinghouse. The weather arrived with the federal troops, and flooding in the southern fields brought fighting to a standstill. Thousands of battered souls prayed that the torrent careering through the rivers and arroyos would wash away fire and death, cleanse the living, and carry in its flow hope anew.

Chapter 69

Harry wished his train ride to Pueblo were a waypoint on a journey home to Indianapolis. But his debt was yet unpaid. Linderfelt was still alive, and his friends needed help.

At Trinidad Station, he watched the federal troops muster and fraternize with the strikers and travelers. Kitted and disciplined, their carriage was one of confidence and training. He admired them, and he knew that the days of cowboy warfare were over.

The train stopped at Ludlow Station. Harry saw thirty or forty militia troops, all unarmed, waiting to board. No Linderfelt among them. In fact, he saw no officers among them. He assumed these men were inactive because they dressed sloppily and were unconcerned about their surroundings. The troops entered the car ahead of Harry's. Then two men crossed the connected walkway into Harry's car and sat behind him. As they passed, he saw they were unarmed. Harry paid them little attention.

The train pulled away from Ludlow Station. Harry sat on the right side of the passenger coach with a view of the burned camp and pump station. He thought of the lives lost that day, the day Ludlow burned. He was there, armed and fighting. Still, he couldn't fathom the terror visited on the luckless men and women and children.

Harry supported the strikers and his countrymen. But his support didn't stop him from weighing good and evil, hope and desperation. The striking miners were untethered from society, but not history. History was on their side. They fought for dignity, a struggle universal. Harry understood this. But, against the state, the rich, the corporations, their climb from tattered canyons and dank mines to honorable, productive lives was steep and faraway. Perhaps unreachable.

His mind returned to the battle in Epirus the day the Evzone saved him. That day had brought him to Colorado. He saw the bullet holes stitched across the Evzone's chest. The valiant Evzone had saved his life and given his own. Now Harry must repay the debt only half retired. His confusion vaporized like the mist melting on the mountain peaks. All was clear. The debt was his life.

North of Walsenburg, Harry overheard the men behind him talking about a military tribunal to convene on May 11. That was all that Harry could discern, the date of the court-martial and the fact that officers would answer questions about Ludlow. One man asked the other if he would testify. The second man said he thought they would only question officers.

Harry's thoughts turned to Marta. Antonio's death would overwhelm her. She was so full of life and spirit, yet destined for the depths of despair. He must help her see she had friends, and she could count on Harry.

She would be the only one to parent Antonio's children. He knew she would have to move. She would have to go somewhere. She couldn't go on living in a tent in Segundo. Even if the strike ended tomorrow, and the miners got all they demanded, Marta would have no support there, no way to make a living. Those were decisions for the smart, independent woman. He was no one to point her in any direction.

As the train entered Pueblo, it pulled north past the CF&I Steel and Iron Works at Bessemer on the south side of the city. The belching complex looked like Harry imagined Hades. Towering stacks of flames and portals of rusty brown emissions blocked the horizon. It stretched for over two miles, smelled of acrid coal and coke fumes over which a metallic tinge floated, insulting the senses. The facility made Kingan look like a resort. Pulling farther north into the heart of the city, the train crossed the Arkansas River, arriving at Union Depot a half mile later.

Harry took a taxi from the station to Peter and Domna's house near St. John's church. Along the way, his stomach roiled. It felt empty and nervous. But he needed to be strong for Marta. It was just after ten in the morning when he arrived.

Domna was the first to the door. She smiled at Harry, knowing that it would please Marta to see him. But Harry didn't smile back. Her expression paled. It was sad news. She asked, "What is it, Harry?"

Harry breathed, "Antonio, Domna. He died on a raid."

Domna crossed herself twice and muttered a blessing.

Harry said, "I need to tell Marta."

"Come in, come in. I will get her. Sit here in the living room," she offered.

Harry remained standing.

Before Domna could walk to the kitchen, Marta entered the living room. She was wearing an apron and wiping her hands on a kitchen towel. When she saw Harry, she said, "Well, look what the cat dragged in." A smile beamed across her lively face.

Then she saw Harry's demeanor and Domna's downturned eyes. She let the towel drop to the floor. She looked at Harry. "Who is it?"

Harry said, "Antonio."

"Oh, God!" she cried and buckled into a chair, her gaze far away. "Oh, God," she repeated.

Domna moved to her side and put her hand on Marta's shoulder. Then Marta wept and muttered again, "Oh, God."

Harry moved closer to Marta, holding his hat in both hands. He lowered his head, "I'm sorry, Marta. Antonio was a good man. *Eonia i mnimi.*"

The three were silent for a moment. Then Marta filled her lungs, "What of it? How did he die?"

Harry spoke. "Alex saw everything. Your brother died in battle. They were attacking the mine at Forbes yesterday morning. Antonio was leading a charge when. . . ." Harry didn't finish when Marta sobbed. Details were unnecessary.

Harry went on, "Alex brought his body to the mortuary in Trinidad. That's where he lies now. Dimitri is going to the camp to tend to his belongings. I will go with you to Trinidad and Segundo if that is your wish."

Marta looked up at the tall Greek through flushed eyes and nodded.

Domna knelt next to Marta, "Marta, should I gather the children? They will need to know?"

Marta said, "Not now. In a moment. Now, I just need to. . . ." She sobbed again. After a silence, she continued, "I will need to wire my mother and father in St. Louis. It will destroy them. Antonio was their hope and future. He was the oldest son, a god in his own right. They will be lost and so sad . . . so sad."

Harry said, "We can wire from the station in Pueblo, Marta.

"Domna, can you continue to look after the children while Marta and I tend to matters?"

Domna nodded.

Marta, now stronger, sniffled. "I will tell the children. Then we will go to Antonio. Is there a late train today?"

Harry nodded, "It leaves Pueblo at one fifteen this afternoon. We should be in Trinidad around four."

They returned to Trinidad in silence. Marta dressed in black and wore a black scarf. They sat together in the passenger coach, and Harry put his arm around the wounded woman. For all the tragedy and pain, he felt he would never know Marta better than at this moment.

Chapter 70

Smoldering ruins seared a forty-five-mile arc across an indifferent Colorado landscape. The charred trail of the dispossessed ran through McNally, Primrose, Green Canon, Royal, Empire, and Forbes. These storied battles and countless unnamed skirmishes claimed dozens of lives, sometimes innocent, paralyzing communications and commerce. The tenants of private property vanished in the smoke of tipples and toolsheds. Strikers and supporters, their numbers growing by the hour, occupied and governed the capital city of the southern fields, Trinidad. Ten days following Ludlow, Colorado authorities no longer controlled a substantial part of the state, one of its major towns, and a key industrial sector.

The first federal troops reached Denver in the early morning of April 29, then moved on to Trinidad the next day. By May 8, the federal deployment totaled 1,590 enlisted men and sixty-one officers.[153] Following meetings with union representatives and coal company lawyers, Major Holbrook, commander of the federal troops, issued orders. Soldiers would remain neutral and allow strikers to rebuild Ludlow and Forbes. Strikers' constitutional liberties would stand, including picketing. He ordered the disarming of the Colorado National Guard by force.

The federal troops promised neutrality. Lawson knew armed actions against the United States Government would be suicidal and ordered the strikers to disarm and obey President Wilson's troops. The elated strikers thought victory was at hand. They were wrong. There would be no union victory until 1928.

Behind the scenes, in the nation's capital, President Wilson tried to persuade Rockefeller Jr. to begin discussions to end the strike. His secretary of labor appointed Hymel Davis and W.R. Fairley as special mediators. Secretary of State William Jennings Bryan added urgency by announcing that foreign governments were protesting the murder of nationals in the coalfields of Colorado.[154]

Rockefeller remained unmoved.

Chapter 71

Dimitri and Alex loaded the pine casket into the baggage car of the northbound Colorado and Southern passenger train. Harry stayed with Marta and waited in the Trinidad Station for the call to board. She wore black with a black scarf gathering her dark hair. She sat erect, her posture proper, staring straight ahead. Harry waited in silence and felt he was fortunate to be in her presence.

The stationmaster called the train to board, and the young couple walked to the platform. Alex and Dimitri stood waiting with their shoulders slumped, holding their hats in front of them. This was the goodbye Marta dreaded. This and one other. Marta went to each and hugged them without saying a word. They, too, were silent. She said, "I love you both. I command you stay safe and visit me in St. Louis. When you come, I will have for you espresso and sweets that will make you forget your barbarian tastes."

Both Greeks smiled and fought back tears.

Harry smiled at Marta, then spoke to Alex and Dimitri, "I will return tomorrow, and we can make plans." Both men nodded. Then Harry and Marta turned to board the train.

It was a brief ride to Ludlow Station, the first stop on the trip north. After boarding passengers, the train pulled away and again passed the rubble of the colony. The federal commander had decreed that the union could rebuild the camp. But Harry wondered what good that would bring. He knew tents meant shelter for strikers and their families. But the impermanence of canvas reminded Harry that the strikers' lives were as transitory as their flimsy shelters.

Marta said, "It is too sad to think about. The people, on that terrible day, with their children. I cannot imagine. It is just too sad."

She looked away from the desolation beyond her window. She locked eyes with Harry. "I wish you were coming with me to St. Louis. And I wish you would stay in St. Louis with me. At least for a while. Does that surprise you, Harry Hantzis?"

Harry stammered, "Yes . . . yes . . . surprised."

"I know it is but a dream and a childish desire, but there it is. This is what I want. I speak to you the truth. Let it be known and honored." Then she turned and looked out the window.

Harry regained his composure. "I will see you when I return to Indianapolis. I will entertain your efforts to refine my primitive ways. But for now, Marta, you know of my obligation. That will keep me in Colorado. I hope not for long.

"I will talk with our friend Yiorgos in Pueblo after you gather your niece and nephew. He may have some information so we can form a plan.

"You and the children will be fine. You will have a sleeping berth from Denver to St. Louis. That will make the trip more comfortable, sad though it will be. I will wire you at your parents' house when we have news from Colorado. This is the way things must be. But I too wish I were coming with you to St. Louis."

Marta looked back at Harry, pursed her lips, and nodded. Then her gaze returned to the rugged arroyos and canyons. She looked upon the haggard pinyons and scrub bushes, and the bleak and lackluster landscape she was leaving behind. She thought none of it was worth the lives of her brother, his wife, or Eleni. It was a desolate nightmare.

She turned again to Harry and commanded, "You stay safe. You and the other two avengers. Stay safe because the obligation you have, the honor you must keep, is only a hair more valuable than your life. And, at this moment, on this train, to me you are more valuable than your honor."

Harry understood, but offered no response. His pledge remained. Marta's plea, honest as it was, stood apart, irreconcilable from Harry's obligation.

He said, "Yes, I will be safe. You should only worry about your niece and nephew and your family. Do not worry about me. I will keep the others safe, too. As safe as I can."

Harry reached over and took Marta's hand in his. It was soft and warm and felt as natural as life.

Domna waited with the children at Union Depot in Pueblo. Marta detrained just long enough to gather them and their bags. On the platform, she rose on her tiptoes and kissed Harry on the lips. Her closeness left him glowing. Then Marta turned to shepherd her charges up the steps and into the passenger car. She waved from inside as she situated the children and took her seat. Harry waved back, then felt

195

empty. He looked at Domna, tears in her eyes, "She'll be better off in St. Louis. With time, the sadness will pass."

Domna nodded and whispered, "Bless them all." Then she crossed herself.

Harry and Domna turned and left the platform as the steam vented from the locomotive's drivers. The train inched from the depot. To Harry, the inches became feet, and the feet became miles. No matter the measure, it was separation from Marta. His heart sank.

Inside the station, Harry saw Yiorgos waiting in an unpopulated corner of the building. He nodded to the Greek, then told Domna he would see her and Peter later, and they would go out for dinner. But Domna shook her head and insisted, "No, no. I am cooking our dinner. It will be no other way. You are my guest. I insist."

Harry chuckled, surrendered, and nodded. Then he took his leave and walked toward Yiorgos. About fifty feet away, Yiorgos looked up from the newspaper he was pretending to read and nodded toward the main entrance on B Street. Harry followed at a discreet distance.

On B Street, Yiorgos turned right and kept walking for three blocks. Then he entered a small, unmarked, brick building across the tracks from the Colorado and Southern's massive locomotive turnstile and roundhouse. Harry followed him and entered a minute later.

The establishment served beer and simple food, Hungarian goulash and sausages. It buzzed with working railroaders. Yiorgos was sitting at a table to the rear of the dingy room, facing the door. When Harry joined him, Yiorgos shook his hand, "I hope you don't mind the humble surroundings. The owner is Greek, but he serves Hungarian food, excellent food. I came here all the time when I worked for the railroad. I cleaned the pits in the locomotive roundhouse just across the main tracks. They have forty-nine bays, each with a pit, all dirty, oily, and slippery, as you can imagine.

"When I arrived in America, Greeks were the new workers. We got the worst jobs. They sent us into the pits with a shovel and a bucket. The other workers looked down at me. I didn't like them lording over me.

"Now, I have grown soft. I would not last one day in the pits. Still, I like to come to this place to eat. Do you know what they call it?"

Harry shook his head.

"The Spot. That is its name. There is no sign, no carving, no engraving, no menus, but that is what all the railroaders call it. I like to come to The Spot to remind myself that hard work is the noblest work, is it not?"

Harry nodded, not in agreement but to be polite.

"Then again, perhaps the noblest work is the work before us?"

Harry cocked his head and gave Yiorgos a questioning glance.

"The work of honor, my friend. That is the most noble, no? Please, I hope not to offend if I include myself in this task. Ilias was a dear friend. I hope I can help redress his cruel death," Yiorgos intoned in a low tenor.

Harry said, "Yiorgos, you have already helped. Alex sleeps much better knowing one of Eleni's killers has paid. Linderfelt deserves no better. He deserved no better even before he killed Ilias, no?"

"Yes, yes. You are on the mark, my friend. That is why we must talk. But first, we should order something and keep this old Greek in business. He is a Cypriot. Somehow, he married a Hungarian. So now he only knows how to cook goulash! A bowl for you?"

Harry nodded.

Yiorgos went to the counter and ordered the goulash and two beers. He walked the beers back to the table and returned for the steaming bowls of stewed beef seasoned with paprika.

Yiorgos placed the unmatched bowls on the table, "Today is a good day. We have a cut of beef instead of hamburger! No matter. It always costs the same. Enjoy."

Yiorgos raised his beer bottle to Harry, and as the men tapped the necks. They both said, "*Yassou.*"

After a spoonful of the hearty stew, Harry looked at Yiorgos. "Do you know the best way to attack Linderfelt?"

Yiorgos sipped his beer. Then leaning over the table, he confided, "He will be hard to isolate. He is with the militia all the time. His wife is in Colorado Springs, but from what I can tell, Linderfelt seldom goes there. His life is in uniform. He loves being a soldier. But he is odd. He served in the Philippines and Mexico. He was a mine guard at Cripple Creek before he talked his way into the Colorado National Guard. He went to Berwind mine near Trinidad as a deputy sheriff in charge of an outfit of thugs. Then he was commissioned into the militia. He is a creature of violence. Everywhere he goes, death follows him. He enjoys it.

"CF&I has a file on him," Yiorgos whispered, pulling a piece of paper from his jacket pocket. "I have read it. I could not make a copy, but I have notes.

"He is thirty-eight, born in Janesville, Wisconsin, in 1876. His father came to America from Sweden. He has two brothers also in the Colorado National Guard, but they are ordinary men, not bloodthirsty like him.

"Here is a bit of background I found intriguing, although I know not how it influences his behavior. His father was an educated man. In 1891 he was elected President of the American Library Association. A year later, he was arrested and locked up for embezzling funds from the Milwaukee Public Library as far back as 1883.[155] His father advocated for a made-up universal language called Volapük and authored papers praising it. Better they learn Greek, no?

"At his trial, Linderfelt's father told the judge he stole the money because his modest public salary did not meet the financial demands of his prestigious position.[156] The judge handed down a suspended sentence. This outraged the public. Then his father fled to England and on to Paris before Wisconsin prosecutors could arrest him for resentencing. I thought that was a strange bit of background.

"A year later, his son Karl, our prey who answers to Monty, dropped out of Beloit College south of Janesville, Wisconsin, and went to live with his uncles in Cripple Creek.

"Monty went to the Philippines around 1900. There, they discharged him as a favor. I do not know why. He came back to Cripple Creek to enlist in the National Guard. Then he went to Mexico as a mercenary. There is a note in his file that says Linderfelt started a firefight in Juarez where Americans died. He was drunk.[157]

"In 1905, he married Ora Smith from Silver City, New Mexico. He was working as a machine man at the Portland mine in Cripple Creek.[158]

"Now, get this. This may explain a good part of why the man is out to get unionists and foreigners. In 1906, Molly Maguires beat him to the doorsteps of death."

Harry didn't know the name and shrugged his shoulders. Yiorgos picked up on his question. "The Molly Maguires were a secret society of Irish coal miners. They got their start in Ireland in the 1840s. When the Irish came to America during the Great Famine, the Maguires organized here. They circulated among all kinds of miners, some in the metalliferous mines, the hard rock mines in the Rockies.

"In 1877, authorities hanged ten of their leaders in Pennsylvania. But they are still around. At least they were in 1906 in Bingham, Utah. The newspaper clipping said that Linderfelt was working in a mill. But the Maguires held a grudge from his service in Troop A at Telluride, where he helped break a strike. Linderfelt went to Bingham to work in a mill after the strike, wore a beard and mustache, but kept his name. When the Maguires found out, they sent a pack after him, beat him senseless, and he spent weeks in the hospital. They almost killed him.[159]

"In 1911, he signed on with Mexican rebels and commanded an artillery unit for General Madero. They reported him dead in May of that year.[160] A mistake? Perhaps. Perhaps misdirection, no?

"In 1912, someone poisoned him and his wife at a dinner in Iron City. At first, I thought someone tried to kill him. But that does not seem likely. I read further, and six miners died from ptomaine after eating the boardinghouse food. Many others got sick. In January of this year, he and his wife sued the Mary Murphy Boarding House for $45,000. But, in February, the jury could not agree on a verdict, and the case is unresolved.[161]

"Poisoning may be a theme in this man's life. Back in 1909, someone poisoned his dog, Carlo, and he offered a ten-dollar reward for information.[162]

"Then, he is back in Colorado working as a mine guard at Cripple Creek before they deputized him in Trinidad last October. In November, they commissioned him in the National Guard but

199

decommissioned him just before the attack on Ludlow. He has been trouble from the day he arrived in the southern fields. From what I can tell, he has been trouble his whole life.

"I believe the Guard has relieved him of duties. He is awaiting court-martial. They will convene May 11, a little more than a week away. I'm sure it will take many days because they have charged ten officers and a dozen enlisted men. That is the word at CF&I headquarters.

"I do not know where he is now or how to find him. We know he will be at the court-martial, but what day and what time, nobody knows. They will convene at the Officers' Club on the State Rifle Range in Golden, just west of Denver. This is the headquarters of the Colorado National Guard. This is where they stage all their deployments and store arms and ammunition. Security will be heavy."

Harry nodded. "You have an excellent memory."

"Thank you. It is a professional requirement."

Harry's thoughts revolved around the fact that they knew where Linderfelt would be on what days. But it was a secure location.

Yiorgos asked, "Do you think there might be a way to get him at the court-martial?"

"It is the best opportunity we have. But it will not be easy. There will be security. I should scout the location to know if it would give a line of sight and a retreat. Better, Dimitri should scout the location. He is the trained marksman."

For the next few minutes, the two men ate their stew in silence. Then Yiorgos asked, "Should we go look?"

Harry countered, "Dimitri and I should look. If we fashion an attack, it will only require two men. Dimitri is the marksman, so he must go. I should go as his lookout. If more go to scout the location, we might be obvious. I will call Dimitri and have him come north tomorrow. Then he and I can travel to the rifle range. That would be best. Meanwhile, you keep your eyes and ears open at CF&I. We might get lucky with more information. Is that agreeable, Yiorgos?"

Yiorgos nodded and the men again tapped the necks of their beer bottles.

Chapter 72

"The militia has a weapon, a .30-06 M1903 Springfield rifle with a Warner and Swasey optical sight. It is odd looking. The monocular is mounted on the receiver. The target is sighted through the monocular and it magnifies the image six times. It is clumsy and awkward to handle. It is the only gun that might work for such a distance.

"Captain Van Cise, a good man, a fair man, and Linderfelt's superior, showed me this weapon in the Ludlow guards' camp. These were the days before the bitterness. He knew I trained in Greece with the long-range marksmen. Van Cise said they could adjust the gun sight to three thousand yards. But he said in battle that distance was of no practical use. Maybe with the wind and sun in your favor and a standing, stationary target, you might make a one-thousand-yard shot. Maybe. But here, we would never be so lucky. And we don't have such a weapon.

"In Greece, we shot the Mannlicher using the tangent sight. We shot special ammunition. They honed all the rifles to perfection and sighted them. But we never used a monocular. A thousand-yard shot with Alex's Mannlicher would be impossible. The target will be moving. No, not that this distance. And I see no way to get closer.

"I am sorry, my friend." Dimitri concluded his assessment of targeting Linderfelt at his court-martial with a shake of his head.

Dimitri and Alex came to Pueblo when Harry called the day before. Then, Harry and Dimitri traveled first to Denver and on to Golden on the city's western outskirts. They wore clothing that Harry found uncomfortable but drew no unwanted attention. Peter went with them to raid the St. John's charity offerings in Pueblo. Gone were their red handkerchiefs, ammo bandoliers, and tall boots. Now, the two Greeks looked like cowboy drifters or out-of-work stable hands, perhaps even prospectors. They both wore wide-brimmed hats and ponchos.

They arrived at the State Rifle Range around two in the afternoon and sashayed north on Kilmer Street past the well-guarded main entrance of the camp. The Officers' Club, farther north, was constructed of unworked native stone from a nearby creek. The Club's bungalow style carried over to the other buildings on the property. Its low-pitched, gabled roof with overhanging eaves and exposed rafters covered a full porch under the roof gable supported by battered stone piers.[163] The Club sat on the eastern edge of a military campus of about one hundred acres.

Harry and Dimitri continued north past the camp's perimeter and walked up a foot trail to the heights of South Table Mountain. This was the nearest elevation offering a retreat from where they presumed Linderfelt would enter the Officers' Club. From their vantage point above the camp, Dimitri estimated they were one thousand yards from their target.

The mountain gave the Greeks an elevation of one hundred yards relative to their target. From this height, they surveyed the camp's acreage laid out before them. The rifle and artillery practice range were to the far right, to the west. In the middle of the expanse stood more buildings and forty white tents with uniformed militia moving about. A dozen artillery pieces and ammo carts covered with tarpaulins rested a hundred yards east of the tents. Eighty horses tethered farther east. The Guard parked a dozen automobiles and trucks near a quartermaster's building, north of the horses.

The two men stood in full view of the camp, arms folded, looking into the distance. Neither wanted to say what the other was thinking. Reluctantly, Harry said, "This won't do. The distance is too great, even for your eagle eyes, Dimitri."

Dimitri shrugged. "Some things are not meant to be, my friend."

For another moment, they scanned the horizon as if they might have missed another perch from which to execute their plan. They hadn't. This was the only elevation that fit the bill, and it wouldn't do.

Harry was the first to turn away and start back down the mountain trail. They traveled light. Neither man was armed except for their knives. Dimitri carried a pouch over his shoulder with some water, cheese, and a pair of binoculars. They intended to go back to Pueblo before sundown.

From behind him, Harry heard his friend editorializing on their future. "Perhaps we should apply for work at the beer brewery in Golden. I know Greeks who work there. It is owned by a German named Coors. The business is growing. Anything to get away from coal, no?"

Harry chided, "They would assign you to shovel coal for a furnace on your first day. Then where would you be?"

"Ah yes. But I would be a foreman when they saw how I performed my work. I have much practice, no?" offered Dimitri.

Harry shook his head and continued down the trail. A few paces farther, he asked Dimitri, "What is it you plan to do next? This strike, I fear it will not make things better, not soon. Living in a tent is no better than being in the Greek Army. Have you thought about where you might go from here?

"My brother and I can help you find work in Indianapolis. You would have to start in a low job if you worked in the packing industry. Also, in Indianapolis, there are many railroad jobs. And, to your relief, no coal mining anywhere.

"Nick and I are saving for a business. So, I need to return to Indianapolis to work and contribute. We have a small amount saved. We hope we can be in business in five years. Nick has a girlfriend, Pearl, an English woman. He may marry soon. I have no such burden."

"You ask good questions, my friend. But I have no answers for you. I should think about where to go because they will not want strikers working in the mines or the ovens. And they won't trust Greeks, either. Greeks have given the mine superintendents and Rockefeller too many headaches. We burned their mines and bloodied their militia guards. No, they will want nothing to do with the Greeks after this. Better to change my name to Smith or Jones, I think. I'll go by John Jones. How does that suit me?" asked Dimitri.

"In your poncho, you look more like José," answered Harry. And both men laughed.

It was a little more than a mile walk to the Denver and Rio Grande station in Golden. Golden was a frontier town, situated where the Great Plains give way to the Southern Rocky Mountains. South Table Mountain, where Harry and Dimitri reconnoitered the Officers' Club, rose to six thousand feet. Only thirty miles farther west, the Rockies soared to twice that.

Golden was home to transient hard rock miners, prospectors, homesteaders, brewery workers, and railroaders, and its social accommodations reflected this clientele. Its days as a genuine Wild West entanglement had come and gone. A more refined gentry now ruled the roost. But Golden still wore a bit of a rough edge.

It was in a human form that Golden's rough edge appeared to Harry and Dimitri just before they arrived at the station platform. Two men, armed with pistols intent on relieving the two "Mexicans" of their belongings. They were big men, rough men. They held their guns low and stood in untrained stances. These were not soldiers.

The lead man and biggest man told them to drop their packs and empty their pockets. But the mistake he and his partner made was waiting too long before emerging from behind a wooden equipment shed. Now, they stood too close to the Greeks. Dimitri glanced at Harry just before he swung his pack containing the sturdy pair of binoculars at the big man's pistol, knocking it from his hand. When the Greeks saw how unbalanced his response was, they knew both men were drunk. The second thief raised his weapon but couldn't bring it to bear because his partner stumbled into his shooting lane. Harry charged the big man, and he collapsed in a heap, knocking the second thief farther away. He, too, stumbled, falling backward. They fell like dominos.

Dimitri jumped at the second thief and kicked his pistol out of his hand out of reach. Now, with both thieves disarmed, combat was hand-to-hand. Harry and Dimitri positioned themselves between the thieves and their guns.

The big man was the first to charge. He came at Harry like a rushing bull and, just like a bull, he was all mass and little agility. Harry rocked as he shifted his weight to the balls of his feet. He assumed a boxer's opening position, left foot forward, right foot back at a forty-five-degree angle to his center line. He bent his knees. He held his left arm in defense with his right arm cocked and loaded. His stance, formed from muscle memory and hours in the ring, came without thinking.

As the big man charged, Harry dodged to the left and connected with a right jab to the bull's temple. His dusty, tattered Stetson flew off. He fell to his knees, shaking his head, stunned. Dimitri ran at the second thief and before he could stand, kicked him high in the ribs on his right side. Then he kicked him again. Dimitri

204

felt the bone and cartilage give way and the second thief cried out in pain. He tried to stand, and Dimitri swung his pack once around his head and smashed it into the second thief's skull. The man went flat like a calf in a slaughter chute.

Dimitri turned to see if Harry needed help. Foolishly, the big man rose and wobbled into a tottering stance, but only for a second. Harry's left cross, a punch that gets its power from a full body rotation, the shoulder, chest, and bicep muscles, landed on the big man's jaw. The big man staggered for an instant, then fell like bricks to the mat for the count. Today the mat was a dirt road, and the count was long.

Dimitri caught his breath. "Well, that was exciting. More so than I expected. What now?"

Harry said, "We should take their weapons and drag them behind the shed. They'll be out for a while. The train should be here soon. I doubt they will awake before then."

Dimitri said, "Should we cut their throats for good measure?"

Harry shook his head, "They probably deserve it. But we are done. No reason to return to Golden. Unless you want a job at the brewery?"

"I will find something else to do with my young life. I don't like beer. It is a barbarian drink. I prefer the tsipouro."

The Denver and Rio Grande southbound passenger number 31 arrived on time five minutes later.

Chapter 73

The kafeneion was empty save for its Pontic owner and four Greeks seated at a corner table. The bells of St. Johns chimed twice on the hour as Harry, Alex, Dimitri, and Yiorgos received their second round of coffee and otía. During the first round, Dimitri told of the would-be-robbery in Golden and the unsuitability of the rifle range to target Linderfelt. The foursome quieted while the owner cleared their table and removed the dirty cups and plates. The men trusted the owner, but there was no need to share their comings and goings with the man. As the owner set the new round on the table, Yiorgos thanked him in the heavy Pontic dialect and praised the pastry, so crispy and sweet. Alex and Dimitri couldn't understand a word Yiorgos said. Harry understood some of it.

The mood was light after Dimitri's colorful rendition of the ambushers' downfall. His declaration that the trip to Golden was profitable since he returned with two used pistols as spoils brought laughter. Dimitri's proclamation that he was a born businessman again drew chuckles. Alex suggested Dimitri open a gun shop. This was a follow-on to an earlier discussion of their futures after the southern fields. They treated the somber subject with humor, but weighty decisions loomed.

Yiorgos entered the conversation as an inquisitor. "What should be done about Linderfelt? We all must make a living, and no one will pay us to track this man, no matter how evil he may be. Please, do not misunderstand. I am only being practical.

"Alex, you and Dimitri will need to find work somewhere. It won't be in the southern fields. Greeks will not be welcome. Harry needs to return to Indianapolis. He is obligated to his brother and their plans for a business together, and he would like to pursue his boxing career."

Dimitri chimed in, "He started training yesterday. But he went only one round!" This drew chuckles, even from Harry.

Yiorgos continued, "There is philosophy in this discussion, no? If a man is bound by honor and bound to a task, then what is the balance between honor and practicality? Between honor and living the life he has before him? None of us are wealthy men. We cannot pursue an honorable course without concern for earning a living. Alex and Harry both have obligations that rest on making a living. For Harry, you and your brother are saving for your venture. And Alex, your plump little son, Stavros, needs a provider. These are obligations, too, no? Does one obligation weigh more than the other? Honor versus family?

"And Dimitri, too, you are no less obligated. You are less entangled than Harry and Alex. Still, you must seek a good life, perhaps even happiness. Can a man be content without honor? Or with honor deferred? Can a man delay his pursuit of honor until his obligations are in balance? Can he then strike the blow that restores *eiréné*, our wholeness? Or perhaps that delay is part of the act of honor? In a perfect world, honor would bestow without delay. But we live in the temporal realm, no? Is one minute of delayed honor different from one day, or one year? These are all delays, deferrals, no?

"I am sorry to make what seems simple, complicated. Blame the university or my perplexing nature. But answers to these questions, or a dialogue about them, may inform our decisions. I offer this as a friend and a man committed to honor Ilias and the Linderfelt obligation. So please, let us speak our hearts and minds."

Alex said in a subdued but insistent tone, "Linderfelt should die now. This very minute." Then, after a thoughtful pause, "No, he should have died on the day of his crime, or better still, the day before his crime. Every day he lives, he steals from the memory of Eleni, and now Ilias and all the other souls he has tormented. He is a criminal and a murderer. But more than that, he is a thief of time."

"As a practical matter," offered Dimitri, "we cannot kill him today because we know not where he is. But I agree with Alex, sooner is better than later. Still, as a matter of tactics, we should not rush to action until the opportunity is ripe. We must kill him, not allow ourselves to be killed. This will require time and knowledge. Of this, we have no choice. Among the Titans, Chronos was king, was he not?"

Yiorgos smiled at Dimitri's reference. "Time is king, in the days of the Titans as it is today. All our plans and efforts take place within its boundaries and limitations. We may wish that time mattered not, yet it does. We could not have had this dialogue without time. Every word we speak is in order. One word follows another, as every second follows another. Just as our plans and efforts must be ordered."

Harry said, "In the village, these matters are simple. Chómori is a small world where everyone knows everyone else. There are few secrets. Strangers are questioned. When my father judges someone or settles a dispute, he does it in days, not weeks. Here, people toss about. Their world is a restless ocean. They drift untethered, unmoored. It takes time to know the truth, then it takes time to act. The bigger the sea, the more time to complete the obligation. But the obligation stays and does not diminish or fade with time. That is the challenge of honor, to stay resolute in the face of time . . . to do what is right. Even when acts are distant, and memories faded.

"Let us not forget that we have fulfilled part of our obligation. We know the truth, and justice is half done. That is an accomplishment, is it not? Yet, we have the same weight of obligation ahead of us. This has not diminished.

"All stories have a beginning, a middle, and an end. I think we are in the middle of our story."

As Harry finished his thought, Father Mardikes entered the kafeneion with an envelope in his right hand. The priest nodded to the owner, then walked to Alex and presented the letter, "Son, I believe this is for you." Then the priest nodded to the men at the table and turned to leave the kafeneion.

Yiorgos took a quick survey of the faces of his friends and then called to the priest, "Father, would you like to join us for a coffee? We can make room at the table and in our dialogue."

Father Mardikes was an older, well-respected member of the Greek community. He was of medium stature, dressed in the traditional black cassock. Wisdom, rectitude, and erudition shown in his eyes. He was always ready with a knowledgeable and thoughtful opinion. As the priest of St. Johns for fifteen years, he knew well the struggle of his flock. His hard-working parishioners toiled and sacrificed to make peace, set down roots, and come to grips with their new land.

He looked over the table to see if anyone objected to his joining, since it was apparent the dialogue was confidential. He said,

"For just a moment, maybe one cup of coffee. I am meeting a young couple at three. They are to be married. And life goes on, no?"

With that unconscious contribution to the dialogue, Father Mardikes pulled a chair from a nearby table as Dimitri and Harry made room. The priest held up his index finger to the owner, who nodded.

Yiorgos, seated across from the priest, put his hands together at the base of his chin. He placed his elbows on the table and looked like a schoolboy saying his bedtime prayers. Yiorgos, however, was not praying when he asked Father Mardikes, "Our dialogue is concerning honor and time. If I might summarize, when a man has an obligation of honor, is that obligation diminished by time. Does the time between the act and the restoration of honor, the retribution, the requite, does that time define honor? Can a man maintain his honor and defer action?"

The owner arrived carrying a tray. He set a saucer, cup, and spoon in front of the priest. Then he poured the thick, steaming Greek mud from the briki into the small cup, leaving a perfect *kaimaki* on the surface. He placed a small dish with sugar cubes to the side, bowed to the priest, and returned to the counter. The other four Greeks noted the special service afforded the priest.

Father Mardikes stirred in one cube of sugar and held the little cup with both hands, sipping the smooth crema from the steamy surface. He returned the cup to the saucer before speaking. "It perplexes you how to proceed with your obligation. You worry that if you delay until you are ready and capable, you will give up your honor. Is that correct?"

After a moment, all the heads nodded.

The priest stroked his long gray beard and seemed lost in thought before he continued, "As a priest, you know I must ask, how would God view this obligation? Is it worthy in his eyes? Is it something worth pursuing at all?"

The wise priest knew of the obligation. There was little in the Greek community that he didn't know. He was the father confessor. He knew that both Alex and Dimitri—and he presumed Harry—had fought with the strikers in the southern fields. He knew of Alex's loss and Eleni's death, and he knew of Yiorgos's deep friendship with the leader of the strikers. And, like the honorable man he was, he kept everything to himself. He presumed the weighty dialogue of these proud men involved retribution and elimination, the death of someone who had wronged them or their loved ones. His biggest concern was not for their obligation, but for their safety and the sanctity of their souls. He knew there were men who should die for their sins. He was grounded. He was a part of his countrymen and their community. Still, he lived by a code of spiritual discipline. His vows were his obligation to promulgate. All civilized people need guidance and moral certainty, and Father Mardikes provided that. It was his job, his craft, and his calling. Just as any community requires a baker, a farmer, or even coal miners, his job was part of the whole. His had been a calling since the days of Paul.

The priest began, "Let me say this. I will speak plainly. Please forgive my directness. If honor requires you to take the life of another, it is not honor. It is sin living by another name. It is an obligation to transcend, not pursue."

Hearing no rebuttal or denial from the men confirmed the priest's assessment of their intention. Father Mardikes continued, "The blood on your hands from committing such an act will never wash away. You may ask for salvation, and if your heart is true, this you will receive. But your life here on earth will forever be stained and imperfect.

"My sons, you have asked for my thoughts and these I have given. Now, let me ask you, is there another way for you to honor this obligation? We are civilized, are we not? We have laws to protect us from transgressions. Is it possible the authorities can right the wrong you seek to redress?"

The priest knew his proposition was weak. He was addressing men who had lived in lawlessness and terror for years before the strike began and the ensuing months since. Father Mardikes had buried miners killed in fights with mine guards and militia, deaths he knew that would never be redressed.

Yiorgos said, "The laws will not help us, Father. They will block the path to justice."

"I fear you are right, my son. I cannot speak of justice within the law. There are many judgments in the Bible, but 'Thou shalt not kill' is a commandment. These you cannot skirt. Commandments are inviolate. If we break them, we harden our hearts against love of God. It is a sin to kill. If you can live with this sin, and I fear this you must do so to complete your obligation, then your actions are of the temporal world. They are of the mortal coil, not of the divine transcendent."

Then, with a smile, he sipped the remaining dregs of his coffee, "My sons, it sounds like you may want to talk to a lawyer, not a humble priest." Then, he excused himself, and all the others at the table rose as he left.

Alex was the first to talk when the men returned to their seats. As he opened the envelope, he said, "Father Mardikes is a good man, a man of God. But God has forsaken us, and the will of men must prevail in the coming days. I do not believe that God sent the devil Linderfelt to kill Eleni or Ilias."

The other three watched as Alex unfolded the one-page letter and remove two ten-dollar bills. Then he reported, "It's from Eydokia Pendagioti, Eleni's sister." The young Greek read in silence as the others looked on. When he finished, he said, "Eydokia is responding to my letter, the one I sent after we finished the Nicholas matter. I think you may want to hear it, no?"

There were nods all around, and Alex read,

Dear Alex,

Thank you for writing to let me know that one of my sister's tormentors has received justice. And please, when you see Harry Hantzis, tell him that the gratitude of our family to him is without bounds. We still mourn for Eleni and Vasilios, but their spirits are at rest. Perhaps they have moved on and are now at peace.

My dear brother-in-law, I want you to know that the family in Greece worries about your safety and your duties as a father. The child, Stavros, is our first thought in the morning, and our last prayer at night. If you feel you cannot raise the child, then perhaps my husband and I could care for him on Crete. We would have to arrange for his travel, and maybe it would please you to make a trip to your home to bring him. But, whatever your decision, please be safe. We know you are brave, but now you must be brave for two people, yourself and Stavros. If the family were to lose you or Stavros, we would plunge back into the darkness that has thankfully lifted.

Please thank the Georgallas family for their charity and kindness. They are saints on earth. We are sending a little money for you to give them and I wish we could send more. Love and kisses to you and Stavros.

In the bond of Christ,
Eydokia Pendagioti

When Alex finished reading, the table was again quiet. Alex refolded the letter and returned it to its envelope, then slipped the letter and the cash into his jacket pocket. Questions hung in the air.

Alex broke the silence. "It is good that the family is at peace. They are kind souls who work hard to make their living, and it is good that they are more settled, more whole. Perhaps eiréné has returned.

"I will raise my son. And they are right. I should be careful and make Stavros the center of my life. He is small today, but in a few years, he will be a man. He will be my partner and son, a man I can be proud of and a man of honor."

Yiorgos said, "Here, here!"

Dimitri and Harry looked at each other. Their eyes questioned how Alex could raise Stavros and make a living. They knew it would be an impossible thing to do on his own. But they said nothing. Alex had made his commitment in public, and it was not their place to question. The path ahead for Alex would be harder than fighting mine guards in the canyons of Trinidad.

Yiorgos asked, "Should we continue our dialogue, or have we traveled that road far enough to see the end?"

"I do not know if we can see the end, my friend," said Dimitri, "but we can smell the ocean. Harry is right, our task is floating on an endless sea, and time will be necessary to bring it to a conclusion.

"We learned in the Greek Army that retreat is not dishonorable if done intending to regroup, battle again, and win the war. This is how I see our situation, brothers."

212

Everyone knew that retreat meant to reenter their working lives and complete their obligation as time allowed As each man fell into reflective silence burdened with his thoughts and decisions, the bells of St. John's tolled three times.

Chapter 74

Purgatoire swelled. The river of lost souls rushed with a burden its banks fought to contain.

The three Greeks stood on the Commercial Street Bridge, leaning on the railing above the torrent. They faced southwest as the sun set beyond the hills. Alex said, "I know that peak." He pointed into the sunset. "There, the one where the sun is setting."

Dimitri said, "Of course you do. You are part mountain sheep. You have stalked these hills like a ram searching for his lost harem."

Alex continued unfazed, "There is an old cemetery on the top of that hill, Jansen Cemetery. There are forty graves, most marked with wood.

"There is a wooden entranceway to the cemetery with a beam across the top. It is ready to fall. On that beam are the words LET THE PERPETUAL LIGHT SHINE UPON THEM. The names on the crosses have faded, and the wood rotted. They are only scratches. Soon even those will vanish, and their names and memories will turn to earth. Their inscriptions will mix in the rain and snow and disappear. Now the sun deserts them all."

"Only in *this* world, my friend. Only in *this* world," offered Dimitri.

Harry said nothing and watched the last rays of sunlight bend around the curvature of the mountaintop. When it was over, he said, "Our train awaits."

Each man shouldered a pack, the contents of their lives in the southern fields. Harry's was the lightest. Alex and Dimitri carried more; clothing, photographs, odds and ends. And Alex concealed his disassembled Mannlicher wrapped in a blanket. He hoped the federal troops at the depot wouldn't notice. They balanced their burdens and began the short walk to Trinidad Station, each with a known destination but an uncharted fate.

Harry and Dimitri were going to Indianapolis. Harry telegrammed Nick and told him he was coming home. He told Nick that Dimitri would stay with them for a few weeks until he could find work and rent a place of his own. The two Greeks planned to spend a night in St. Louis to check on Marta.

Alex was traveling to Pueblo, where he hoped Yiorgos could help him find a job in the CF&I works or on the railroad. There, he could help with Stavros and support the Georgallas family until better times.

They boarded the train, and it left Trinidad Station on time. As always, the first stop was Ludlow, where a few passengers climbed onboard. Again underway, the train pulled past the camp's remains and the Greeks saw that most of the wreckage and burned tents were gone. In the corner nearest the pump station, a new tent with UMWA stenciled on the end facing the railroad stood fresh and unmarked. The construction material stacked next to the tent presaged a hollow victory. The Greeks wondered in silence what rebuilding Ludlow meant for the thousands of souls whose lives depended on the strike's outcome.

To the three of them, the testament of Ludlow was no longer tents and strikers, guards and Greeks, but of lives reentered and futures unknown.

Chapter 75

The weather warmed, and the demand for coal slackened. This lessened pressure on the operators to settle or use scabs. But the strike dragged on.

The union rebuilt Forbes and Ludlow, and by summer, the camps teamed with strikers and their families. Wide-ranging gun violence stopped after federal troops arrived, but not the slow ruin of poverty and despair. Strikers drifted away from the camps. Some, with no place to turn, lived in the tents for the next two-and-a-half years.[164]

President Wilson endorsed a settlement plan that the miners voted to accept in mid-September. The owners rejected it. But owners felt the heat of public pressure as Wilson's plan gained broad approval. Pressure or not, Rockefeller refused union recognition.

Meanwhile, coal barons launched a judicial offensive in Colorado. Raids on union offices saw the arrest of scores of local unionists. Handpicked grand juries of company sympathizers indicted 124 union leaders. They charged John Lawson with nineteen counts, fourteen for murder.[165]

On the political stage, the Democratic nominee for governor, Thomas Patterson, made industrial relations his primary campaign issue. He lost by forty thousand votes to Republican George Carlson, who won by importing Evangelist Billy Sunday, the temperance movement's point man. The pyretic Sunday hammered on the evils of liquor, but never a word on the plight of thousands of sober citizens abiding in the state's tent cities.

In November 1914, the UMWA International Board voted to quit the strike. Four hundred thousand dues-paying UMWA members were no financial match for the Rockefeller family. The UMWA faced a critical and expensive campaign in the mines of Ohio. The union had borrowed $875,000 to maintain the struggle in Colorado. It was time to cut losses.[166]

With a public statement by the president of the United States, the strike ended on December 1, 1914. Wilson's statement condemned mine owners for intransigence and announced a special mediation commission. The president tasked the commission to "create the instrumentality by which, like troubles and disputes, may be amicably and honorably settled in the future."[167] Thus, the bloody struggle that stained Colorado for fifteen months had ended.

What did it mean? Sixty-six lives lost. Hundreds wounded emotionally, financially, and physically. The turmoil and deprivation. The burned property, the wrecked mines. The political crisis. What did it all mean?

To the striking miners, it meant gaining the self-respect that comes with honorable struggle but losing the economic base from which the struggle had arisen. The years following the strike were a nightmare of blacklists and exile. Families were uprooted, friendships were frayed, and resentment soared. The hardest hit were strike leaders. Those not in jail packed up and left.

By 1917, the Victor American mines had come under UMWA contract, but three years later, the pact was not renewed.[168] In 1927, the second largest operator in Colorado, the Rocky Mountain Fuel Company, fought a militant strike by the IWW. The company's way out was to sign a contract with the safer UMWA.[169] The big prize fell in 1933, when CF&I and Rockefeller capitulated to a different United Mine Workers of America.[170]

Between April 1, 1910, and June 1, 1915, the union spent $3,695,514 on strikes in the northern and southern fields, a respectable campaign chest even by today's standards.[171] Although the Great Colorado Coal Strike of 1913–14 was a defeat, the union's total membership had grown by 150,000.[172]

What of the Greeks?

They suffered the same fate as the other strikers, with twice the intensity. Their blood was too hot, and the union distrusted them. They roamed the southern fields. Some got work on the railroads, and a few even returned to the mines. They changed their names, bribed their way into jobs, and survived. More than anything, against all odds, they worked like hell.

A mass of humanity swept into the spiral of US industrial development in the early years of the twentieth century. The investment capital wrought from the sweat and broken bodies of millions of immigrant workers launched an economic takeoff in mass-production industries. Greeks toiled among the lowest paid and most exploited at the base of this multitude.

Today, Greeks in America are well-educated and well-off. In a land where the American Dream is often more myth than reality, Greeks lived the myth.

Chapter 76

Harry and Dimitri stopped twice on their way to Indianapolis. Harry retrieved his Midwestern clothes in Denver, and they visited Marta and her family in St. Louis.

Marta and her family lived in The Hill neighborhood with hundreds of other northern Italians. The community had deep roots. Marta's mother and father ran a successful business selling fruits and vegetables to local restaurants and groceries. They awoke early six days a week for the trip to Soulard Market, a place bustling by five o'clock, to haggle with farmers and vendors over prices and quality.

They sold the produce to cafés and restaurants on The Hill and in Irish and German neighborhoods along their four-mile route. Their produce was high quality, and customers appreciated their reliability.

Harry wired ahead to let Marta know they were coming. She greeted the Greeks at the door of the family's apartment on a warm afternoon in a long black skirt and a white blouse with a ruffled neck. Her black hair tumbled over the ruffles. She wore a simple necklace with a silver cross. Harry thought she looked dressier than she had in the southern fields. But he, too, was better dressed. Dimitri wore a borrowed suit jacket from the charity pile at Transfiguration of Christ Church over his old baggy pants and tall boots.

Marta had been in St. Louis for two weeks. They had buried Antonio two days after her arrival, and the family was still in mourning. Speaking Italian, she introduced the Greeks to her parents, calling them friends and guardians. The Greeks bowed to the parents and said they were sorry for the death of their son. The parents excused themselves and went back to their work. Marta, Harry, and Dimitri sat and talked.

Marta said, "So, you two are off to Indianapolis. Let us hope the city is more peaceful than what you leave behind. I've only been in St. Louis for a few days, and already I feel like Colorado was a fiction, a bad dream. Here there is routine, and people are not afraid the militia will come and burn their homes. I miss Antonio, but his idea for Colorado was fantasy. And it got him killed.

"Tell me, what are your plans in Indianapolis?"

Harry said, "We are sorry about Antonio. He was brave.

"My brother Nick said that I can return to my job at Kingan. I will work and save for our business together. When I get back, I will telegram Flynn in New York, my boxing agent, and see if he still wants to represent me. If he does, I will train and put together a card. Then we will see what happens.

"Nick thinks Kingan will hire Dimitri. He will find work. If not at Kingan, perhaps on the railroad or somewhere else. He is smart and strong. Someone will hire him."

Dimitri said, "I too plan to open a business."

Harry cocked his head. This was the first he heard of such plans.

Dimitri continued, "I will be a florist."

Harry and Marta couldn't help laughing.

Dimitri was undeterred. "I have talked to Peter about this business. He said I can do well if I save for investment. He said the profit on flowers in a rich neighborhood is remarkable. They wilt, they die, and people need more. They need them for funerals—my apologies, Marta—and they need them for weddings and dances and—"

Marta interrupted, "You? Dimitri? A flower man?"

"Yes, Marta. I am a born businessman. Just ask Harry. When we needed pistols, did I not arrange it? When we needed an automobile, did I not negotiate the lease? I recently sold two handguns for one hundred percent profit! Ask Harry."

Harry just shook his head.

Dimitri continued, "I will work hard, save my money, then ask Peter for advice. Then I will enter the business. There are many Greeks in the business. I speak their language, no?"

The threesome sat with their spirits floating on the levity. Then Marta asked, "What of the other matter? Our pledge?"

Harry spoke first. "The pledge remains. The commitment will go forward. But for now, we need to reenter our lives and work for our futures. Alex received a letter from Eydokia. He wrote to her after the Nicholas matter. How did she put it, Dimitri?"

"She said the darkness had lifted," he answered.

"Yes, that is what she wrote," Harry confirmed. "She offered to raise Stavros in Greece. But Alex is determined to raise him here. He plans to stay with Peter and Domna, find work in Pueblo, and support his son.

"Yiorgos will stay in touch and learn what he can at CF&I. He will tell us when an opportunity arises to complete our obligation.

"And what of you, Marta? What are your plans?"

Marta hesitated, "For now, I have the children. They are not so much of a burden with my mother and father's help. They love their *nipoti*, sometimes too much. I fear my parents are spoiling them.

"The children will be in school soon. That will give me time to help with the business. My father tells me of opportunities he hears about from his customers. They own restaurants and cafés and always need help. I have not asked him more than that. But I will work someday, at something, this I know. I will go crazy if I stay in this apartment and bake cookies all day.

"Oh . . . where are my manners? I must have left them in Colorado. Would you gentlemen visitors like some coffee and sweets?"

Both men nodded.

While Marta was away, Dimitri asked Harry, "Would you like me to leave so you and Marta can be alone?"

This puzzled Harry. He furrowed his brough, "Why?"

"I thought you two might want to spend some time together . . . alone," Dimitri said, drawing out the last word.

Harry said, "That time has passed. Marta is a lovely woman. She will always be close to my heart. We are friends. No more. Good friends, I hope."

Dimitri nodded. Marta reentered the room a smiling, radiant hostess. She carried a tray of sweets and coffee. Proper Italian coffee.

Chapter 77

The train pulled to a stop at Pueblo's Union Depot, and Alex said goodbye to Harry and Dimitri. The three Greeks stood on the station platform engulfed in steam rising from a valve in the coach's heating lines. It was a manly affair. Alex wished his friends the best of luck, and they returned the sentiment. There were promises to stay in touch and handclasps. The bond the men shared was unbreakable and their pledge intact. Alex gathered his pack and the blanketed Mannlicher. Before he turned to leave, Dimitri said, "Stavros will soon be big enough to shoot. Call me on that day, and I will teach him to be a marksman." Everyone smiled.

Dimitri was prescient. Twenty-nine years later, in 1943, Stavros would train as a marksman at Camp Carson near Colorado Springs with the 122nd Infantry Battalion, the Greek Battalion.[173]

Alex found a job as a trackman on the Colorado and Southern Railroad with Yiorgos's help. It was demanding, back-breaking work, but it was a union job with fair pay and benefits. Railroaders had been at the union game since the 1860s. Alex earned enough to rent an apartment, and with Domna's support, he raised Stavros. Then Domna put two and two together. Or, more precisely, two and three together.

Domna and Marta stayed in touch. Over the next year, Domna wrote on a sensitive subject, inquiring of Marta, "Would you consider marrying Alex?"

The thought never crossed Marta's mind. She liked and respected Alex, but he was a Greek, a barbarian. Worse than that, he was from Crete. His temperament was like that of the wild beasts living in the island's mountains and canyons. Or so she thought. He was an attractive man when he shaved and dressed, and with Alex, honor would always be maintained. His word was his bond. But no, it was a ridiculous notion.

Or was it?

Domna wrote to Marta that Alex took raising Stavros seriously. He was a good father. Domna thought the man had grown and matured. As a gentle creek wears away the stones it washes over, Domna wore down Marta's resistance. Marta's two children and Alex's Stavros would make a beautiful family. And Marta's father told her of cafés and restaurants where owners needed help. Those jobs wouldn't pay like the railroad. But if Alex came to live in St. Louis, her father could find him work. Then, with her mother's help, Marta could work. Domna's formula began to make sense.

Marta surrendered and Domna began prodding Alex. She started with, "Marta asked about you the other day in a letter I received." She snared Alex before he knew it.

A few weeks later, with Domna caring for Stavros, Alex made a trip to St. Louis. There, the young couple talked about marriage in practical terms, their affection for each other well-rooted in the hills of Colorado. Three months later, the couple married in St. Ambrose Catholic Church and took an apartment near Marta's family.

Marta's father found Alex his first job in a respectable but poorly managed restaurant in the Chase Park Plaza Hotel. It was the smallest of three places to eat on the property, and the owner leased the space from the hotel. Alex learned every job and became a manager. Marta took a job as a greeter at the newly opened St. Louis Municipal Opera Theatre, the Muny. Alex had savings from the railroad. His savings, along with his current earnings and Marta's income, qualified the young couple for a loan to buy the restaurant. A year later, they sold a lucrative, well-managed enterprise to an eager buyer and made their first profit. Alex continued to purchase and resell restaurants in St. Louis and throughout the Eastern states, doing very well. Neither he nor Marta ever returned to Colorado.

Chapter 78

Yiorgos was lucky and smart. He burrowed into the CF&I bureaucracy and weathered the administrative fallout after Ludlow. The Sociology Department, already waning during the strike, saw its funding slashed by Chairman Lamont Bowers. His was a relentless search for a Rockefeller-pleasing bottom line.

Bowers and his iron-fisted administration were out by 1915. In his place, the Colorado Industrial Plan took root. This forward-thinking labor relations strategy was the brainchild of the future three-time Prime Minister of Canada, Mackenzie King. Dubbed the Rockefeller Plan, it set up an in-house system of worker representation, promised decent working conditions, and foresaw upright company towns. It didn't last. But if it had, the plan would have been outlawed in 1935 under the National Labor Relations Act as a "company union."[174]

Eighteen months after the Ludlow Massacre, as King urged, Rockefeller Jr. put on store-new, creased overalls. He descended into a Colorado mine to hack at a seam of coal for ten minutes. Upon ascent, he shared lunch with dubious workers and declared, "These beans are bully!" He implored the men to speak their minds and speak honestly, for they were partners in his "square deal" enterprise. As mine bosses scanned the boardinghouse for security threats, and underlings choreographed photo opportunities, the workers stared in disbelief and silence, insulted beyond words.

Yiorgos rose in CF&I management during the 1918 influenza pandemic. In the fall of that year, CF&I physicians, nurses, and volunteer staff treated 4,600 cases in the southern Colorado mining camps, and at the Steelworks Dispensary in Pueblo.[175] The disease killed fifty million worldwide. Yiorgos designed an effective tracking system so that CF&I could quarantine and isolate patients at coal camp facilities. They cared for sick workers and their families in local medical dispensaries and YMCA clubhouses. Previously, the sick had been moved to Minnequa Hospital in Pueblo.

Yiorgos retired from CF&I in 1944 and returned to Greece in 1950, following the country's vicious Civil War. By then, Greece had been at war for ten years. The small country suffered 450,000 dead during the Italian, German, and Bulgarian occupation. Then another fifty thousand dead at the hands of their countrymen.[176] Hundreds of thousands of Greeks were displaced and uprooted in these years.

Yiorgos applied himself without reservation to the country's reconstruction. He worked more hours in Greece than he had in Colorado. From his post in the Greek Ministry of Education, Research and Religious Affairs, Yiorgos authored a modernized national sociology curriculum. He died in 1962 at his family's village near Paros. He left behind an unfinished manuscript of his years in Colorado. It working title was *Mountains of Blood.*

Chapter 79

Dimitri found work on the New York Central Railroad in Indianapolis at the massive Beech Grove Shops. He started as a trackman and worked his way to a car inspector's job, thanks to Harry's soon-to-be father-in-law. By January 29, 1919, at the start of Prohibition, Dimitri had considerable savings for a working man. He lived in the town of Beech Grove, walked to work, and saved like a Scotsman.

It's unclear whose idea it was or who had the contact, but Dimitri and Harry knew a guy. The Greeks made this fellow a business loan. Repayment was generous. They made another loan and were again well-compensated. By 1933 and the end of Prohibition, their liquid investments and day jobs allowed them to finance conventional businesses.

Dimitri, true to his word, talked with Peter Georgallas and bought into a flower shop in the Astoria neighborhood of New York City's Queens Borough. He owned the business outright in three years and began wholesaling and retailing. He was right; he was a born businessman.

Dimitri married a lovely young Greek woman he met at Harry's wedding in December 1918. Eleni was the love of his life, and he treated her like royalty. Dimitri found his happiness.

Harry returned to Kingan, where he worked with Nick until 1926. That year, they opened the Hantzis Brothers Restaurant in the Lorraine Hotel next door to Indianapolis Union Station. When the Great Depression struck in October 1929, most people stopped eating out. Some people just stopped eating. The brothers closed their business a year later, went back to work where they could find it, and opened another restaurant when the economy improved during the war years. In the 1950s, Harry owned a small lunch counter on Indiana Avenue near downtown. The neighborhood wasn't great. When it was time to go to work, he slid his long barrel .38 revolver into his belt, pull his apron on over it, and off he'd go.

Harry reconnected with Leo P. Flynn, his boxing manager. He began training and sparring with local up-and-comers. Flynn got Harry a tour with rising star Jack Dempsey, "The Manassa Mauler." Dempsey won the world heavyweight title in 1919 and held it until

1926. Harry boxed super middleweight, and he was good, always quick on his feet, agile, and accurate. But the paying customers wanted to see the big brawlers.

Harry's first child, James, my father, was born in 1920. Harry and his German wife, Margaret, had four more children, all girls, and took up residence on the Near Eastside of Indianapolis.

Following World War II and my father's service in the 721st Railway Operating Battalion, he returned to the New York Central Beech Grove Shops as a journeyman machinist. This was where his German grandfather had repaired cabooses and Dimitri, before moving to Astoria, had inspected rolling stock. My father worked there until 1950, a year after I was born.

My father and Mary Lou, his Hoosier farm bride, ditched the big city for a forty-acre farm twenty-five miles west of Indianapolis. This humble tract of crops, pastures, livestock, wildlife, and bucolic creek lay between the rustic towns of Lizton and North Salem. Dad switched jobs. He went to work as an experimental machinist for General Motors Detroit Diesel Allison Division and somehow still found time to farm.

My mother tended to my brother and me, and she tended to local first aid emergencies. Mary Lou was a registered nurse, and the news spread in our underserved community. She'd get a call on our ringer phone, two longs and a short. The emergency was typically someone kicked by a bull or gashed by a farm implement. She'd grab her brown medical bag, and off we'd go in the family Plymouth. Day or night.

Behind an old barn rose a circular concrete foundation, the base of a long-gone silo. Harry liked to sit there with his grandson. He dismembered pears from our orchard with his always honed pocketknife and revealed the shapes in the clouds. He walked with a cane then. He'd point the tip skyward and say in his broken English, "See that cloud, Stevie? It looks like Italy. Or that one looks like a horse. Or see the clouds on the horizon, they look like mountains."

227

Chapter 80

Stavros excelled at St. Ambrose Catholic School, a short walk from Alex and Marta's apartment on The Hill. He was a smart, good-looking boy and trilingual by the time he was twelve. He worked hard for his grandparents, sorting and boxing fruits and vegetables and making deliveries. A few months after he graduated with honors in 1929, the Great Depression struck, and Stavros stayed in St. Louis to help with the family business.

In the summer of 1933, Stavros attended *The Desert Song* at the St. Louis Municipal Opera Theatre. Marta was now an administrative assistant at the Muny, and Stavros attended for free. Sitting on a folding chair in an exit wing, he watched and listened, enthralled. The operetta drew inspiration from the 1925 uprising of Moroccan freedom fighters. Music by Sigmund Romberg and lyrics by Oscar Hammerstein artfully portrayed the guerrilla struggle against French colonial rule. The narrative drew upon sensational exploits of Lawrence of Arabia. Stavros, mesmerized and open as a book, was called. He would study history.

In 1934, Stavros enrolled in Park College in Parkville, north of Kansas City on the Missouri River. He worked nights at the bustling Kansas City Stockyards in West Bottoms, driving cattle from railcars to holding pens and attended classes during the day. He graduated with honors and went straight into the master's program. Stavros was teaching Western History at the college and planning a PhD program in December 1941 when the Japanese attacked Pearl Harbor. He stayed at Park until early 1943 when he relinquished his draft deferment and enlisted in the US Army's 122nd Infantry Battalion, the Greek Battalion.

The 122nd, named for 122 years of Greek independence from the Ottomans, trained for unconventional warfare against the Germans and Axis troops occupying the Old Country. Greece was a potential point of invasion for the Allies' reentry to Europe. Camp Carson, near Colorado Springs in the foothills of Cheyenne Mountain, was a suitable surrogate for the massifs of Greece.

Major Peter D. Clainos, the first Greek American West Point graduate, drove his troops. To survive in the wilds of Greece, his men would have to be as hard as the oak tables they pounded to toughen the edge of their hands.[177] Clainos ordered thirty-five-mile hikes up and down Cheyenne Mountain with full packs and arms. Recruits climbed the mountain, carrying only their water. There they spent the night and hiked back to camp. The next trip, they packed only their food. The next, no water or food.[178] Then, the men were ordered onto the mountain for two weeks without food or water. They drank from streams and ate rabbits, lots of rabbits.[179]

Stavros excelled and enjoyed the company of the other Greeks. He was an outstanding recruit, an ideal candidate, fit, educated, multilingual, and motivated. He drew a G2 assignment working intelligence on the commander's staff.

The 122nd drew the attention of the freshly minted Office of Strategic Services (OSS), America's first intelligence agency. The OSS looked to the British Special Operations Executive (SOE) for training, organization, and inspiration. America needed commandos.

After seven months at Camp Carson, the political winds shifted, and the US Army's 122nd Greek Battalion disbanded. There was shock and disbelief in the ranks at this news. Then the OSS asked for volunteers. Before calling for a show of hands, the OSS warned volunteers would operate behind enemy lines in Greece. They must speak Greek. Top physical condition was imperative for commando and parachute training. The OSS recruiters said the assignment was perilous and could result in 90 percent casualties.[180] Hands went up for six hundred men, not a man's unraised. Most were disappointed and reassigned into regular US Army combat forces.[181]

Stavros was one of 181 men selected and began rigorous training under British tutelage.[182] The OSS designated eight Greek American Operational Groups (OGs). Stavros was commissioned a first lieutenant and given command of an OG.

Stavros reported to OSS HQ in Washington, DC, then trained for three weeks at Area F, the repurposed Congressional Country Club in Bethesda. In Maryland, they learned how to handle C-1 and C-2 explosives. They learned demolition techniques and the operation and maintenance of American, British, German, and Japanese firearms. They learned how to kill without weapons.[183] They spent hours studying tactics and staging. They wore no rank or insignia. Then, the

OGs moved to a remote location west of Hagerstown, Maryland, bivouacking near Shangri-La, now known as Camp David. There, they maneuvered in rugged terrain and dense woods and practiced demolition. They received their first briefing on Greece. They grew confident and capable, but the Secret Service curtailed their rabbit hunting near President Roosevelt.

The outfit looked sharp when they left Hagerstown for the Charleston, South Carolina, Port of Embarkation. They wore paratroop boots with their trousers tucked in and sported brand-new, not-yet-issued Eisenhower jackets. They wore insignia of their rank and the crossed rifles of infantry, and they might have been mistaken for British Royal Marines. They were cocky and young.

They shipped out from Hampton, Virginia, on Christmas Eve 1943. Their battered Liberty ship, the *Pierre L'Enfant*, rendezvoused with a convoy to cross the Atlantic. They arrived in Suez, Egypt, thirty-one days later, completing their voyage with a gauntlet run through Bomb Alley, the perilous seas between Crete and Libya.

An outbreak of bubonic plague in Suez hastened their transport to Cairo,[184] where the OGs pretended to be truck drivers at Camp Huckstep. As they settled in at Huckstep, the OSS informed them the British would train two OGs as paratroopers. They drew straws, and Stavros and his group left on a train for Palestine the next day.

At the British paratrooper school in Palestine, the Americans rushed through the course. They arrived on Sunday, trained on Monday, and jumped twice on Tuesday and Wednesday. On Thursday, they jumped at night. With five jumps to their credit, all without reserve chutes, they were qualified in less than a week. American training took ninety days.[185]

They left Egypt for Italy aboard an Indian luxury liner from Port Said on February 1, 1944. They landed in Taranto seven days later and moved on to Mola di Bari.[186]

On the night of April 21, 1944, under a waxing crescent moon, Stavros and his OG of twenty-three men shoved off from Monopoli on the East Coast of Italy. They arrived in Western Greece two nights and 210 miles later at Aphrodite's Cave, near Parga.[187] The last forty miles were tense as the landing craft killed its noisy Detroit Diesel engines to dodge German patrol boats. While they were dead in the water, the unyielding northern currents of the Eastern Adriatic carried them off course. After the deadly game of cat-and-mouse, they fired the engines and sought to reestablish navigation. The captain proved his mettle at dead reckoning, and the flicker of a small signal fire on the mainland's rocky shore beckoned. The one hundred and sixty-foot-long ship snaked through the tricky narrow straights between the islands of Paxos and Antipaxos to Parga.

When Stavros's boots touched Greek soil, he knelt, steadying his pack and Thompson, and dug his right hand into the wet sandy gravel. He rose from his crouch, letting the cold, hard mix dribble through his fingers. A grizzled *andarte* stood before him, shouldering an ancient Mannlicher carbine. He said, "*Pístis i patrída*." (Faith and fatherland.)

They joined a detachment of ELAS andartes, the local Greek Resistance.[188] The Americans arrived with their arms, ammunition, explosives, and rations for forty-five days, dehydrated mutton.[189] They expected limited resupply, no reinforcements, no medical aid, and no tactical support. They had no route of retreat. They wore American flags on US Army uniforms, but these wouldn't save them from Hitler's execution order. They were on their own in Greece for the duration.

That night and four more, the train of fighters and mules moved east to their base in the Nafpaktian Mountains, the Monastery of Panagia Kavadiotissa. From there, they supported Operation Noah's Ark, the Allied campaign to harass German troops withdrawing from Greece.

When they left Greece on September 5, 1944, the OG and their andarte allies had blown up bridges, disrupted strategic communications, ambushed convoys, and sunk a ferry. They punished the Germans as ordered. Stavros's group was lucky and suffered only incidental injuries. Of the eight Greek Operational Groups, 181 men, eleven suffered wounds and one man died.[190] The Americans were skin and bones, sunbaked and bearded by the time they returned to Italy.

Stavros shipped to China from Italy. There he led a team that worked with the Loyal Patriotic Army, LPA. The Americans set up a weather station and trained guerrillas to rescue downed Allied pilots.

After the war, he returned to Missouri to teach at Park and work on his PhD, In 1947, remnants of the OSS made up the Central Intelligence Agency. Stavros reentered the secret world in 1949 and returned to Greece in 1951. After a successful tour, he received a promotion to a CIA headquarters position in September 1952. In 1957, Stavros met a friendly agency researcher for lunch and asked for a favor. He said, "I need to find someone."

Two weeks later he entered the room of an assisted living facility in San Diego, California, where a man lay in a hospital bed, gaunt of frame and milky-eyed. Stavros approached. When the man focused, he asked, "Monty, do you remember me?"

The man didn't speak, but his vulnerability cast an air of confusion and fear in the room.

Stavros reached into his coat pocket, and pulled from it a single 6.5×54mm Mannlicher-Schönauer cartridge, and set it upright on the bedside table.

The dying man rolled his head to look at the bullet. He puzzled. Then his expression changed to fear when Stavros said, "Segundo, 1913."

The man's eyes widened, and he gasped. He croaked his first and final word, "Greek."

Epilogue

Harry Hantzis, my grandfather, came to America in 1904 with his brother, Nick, from Chómori, Greece. Harry returned to fight in the Balkan Wars, then came back to America in 1913 to work as a butcher in Indianapolis. He was a middleweight boxer who toured with Jack Dempsey. Harry was the son of a Nafpaktian assassin, my great-grandfather, Demitris Konstantinos Hantzis. But so far as I know, Harry never set foot in Colorado.

The events of the strike are true. I took care to weave Harry's narrative into and around the hard, factual boulders of the Great Colorado Coal Field War 1913–14. Should the reader want to learn more about the deadliest conflict in American labor history, start with a good map. With the map spread before you, proceed to the 3,100 pages of Volumes VII, VIII, and IX of the *Industrial Relations Final Report and Testimony.* Congress received these accounts from the Commission on Industrial Relations in 1916. All eleven volumes, a broad inquiry into American labor relations, are a lot of reading but open a fascinating porthole into a turbulent era. These reports are online at the National Archives website.

Now, here's an example of my version of creative nonfiction. I have Dimitri, a character based on an actual person but fictional in this context, discuss buying pistols. He says that he can't buy them from the Greek baker at Ludlow depot because they raided the baker in November. The baker and the raid are real, but Dimitri less so.

The murder of Eleni is fictional. Eleni is fictional. There were many unsolved murders before and during the strike, and her death is a convenient construct, a gathering of unsung souls.

The Greek Battalion and the OSS Greek American Operational Groups are real. But you could not have proven they were real until 1986, when the CIA declassified these records. The records appeared at the National Archives only recently. Stavros's story in the battalion and the OSS OG is a composite of flesh-and-blood Greek American heroes. You will learn more about their remarkable exploits in *American Andarte.*

K.E. Linderfelt was real, as were his transgressions, except for Eleni. She is fictional. He died on June 3, 1957, in Southern California.

The Greek Stories: A Four-Book Series

A journey begins with *The Greek Boxer*. A babe left forlorn in a defiled tent on an indifferent Colorado hillside, grows to adulthood. In *American Andarte*, Stavros joins other Greeks to battle Nazis in the Old Country as an OSS commando. As he leads his operational group in the mountains of Greece, a mythical kapetánios, Dimitra, captures his heart. *Wolf Pelt* unfolds in 1951 Greece, at the peak of American influence. Stavros, now CIA, orchestrates an influence campaign in Athens while covertly aiding the attempted overthrow of Albania's Hoxha regime. The treachery of romance and espionage play side by side. *Fifty-Seven* caps the series, with Stavros returning to Greece. America is shaking in Sputnik's shadow. Stavros must ferret Soviet agents in a vital NATO shipyard while Enosis, the Cyprus independence movement, intensifies. Threats loom over Stavros and friends, the stakes are high, and love endures.

The Greek Boxer Maps

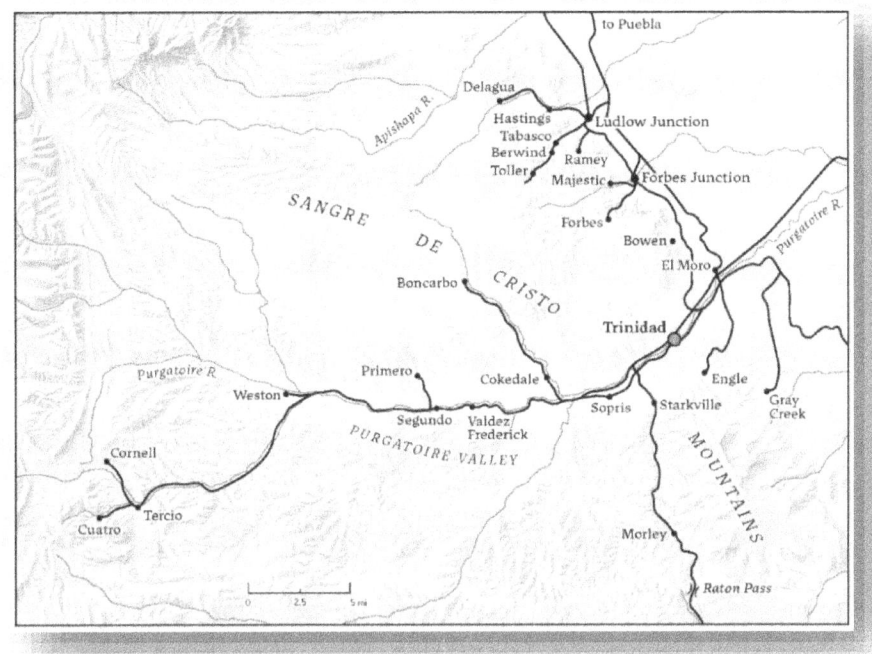

Map 1 *Coal Mines of the Southern Fields (Erin Greb Cartography). Note: Trinidad is 200 miles south of Denver.*

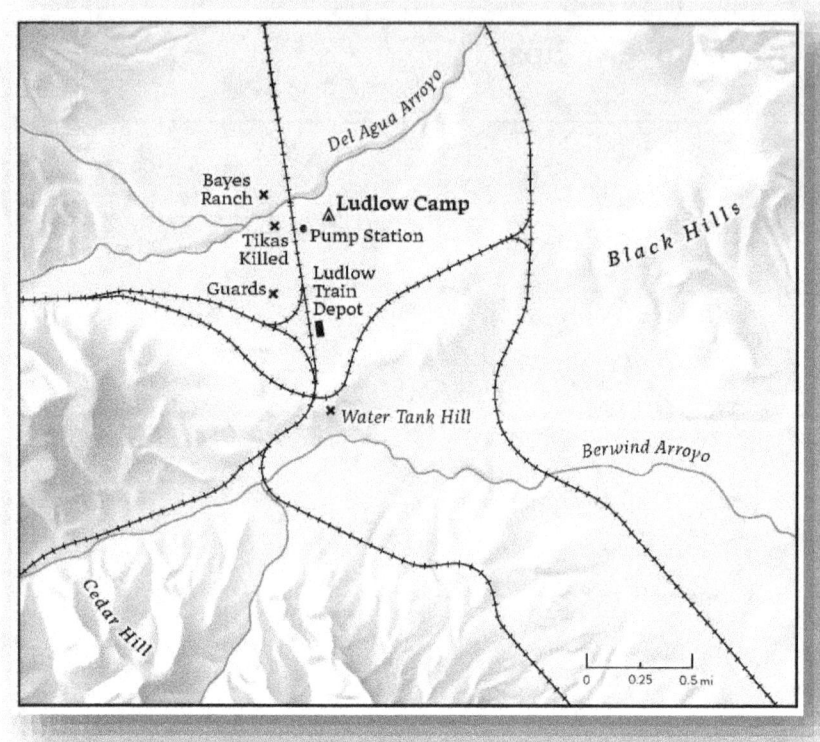

Map 2 Siege of Ludlow (Erin Greb Cartography)

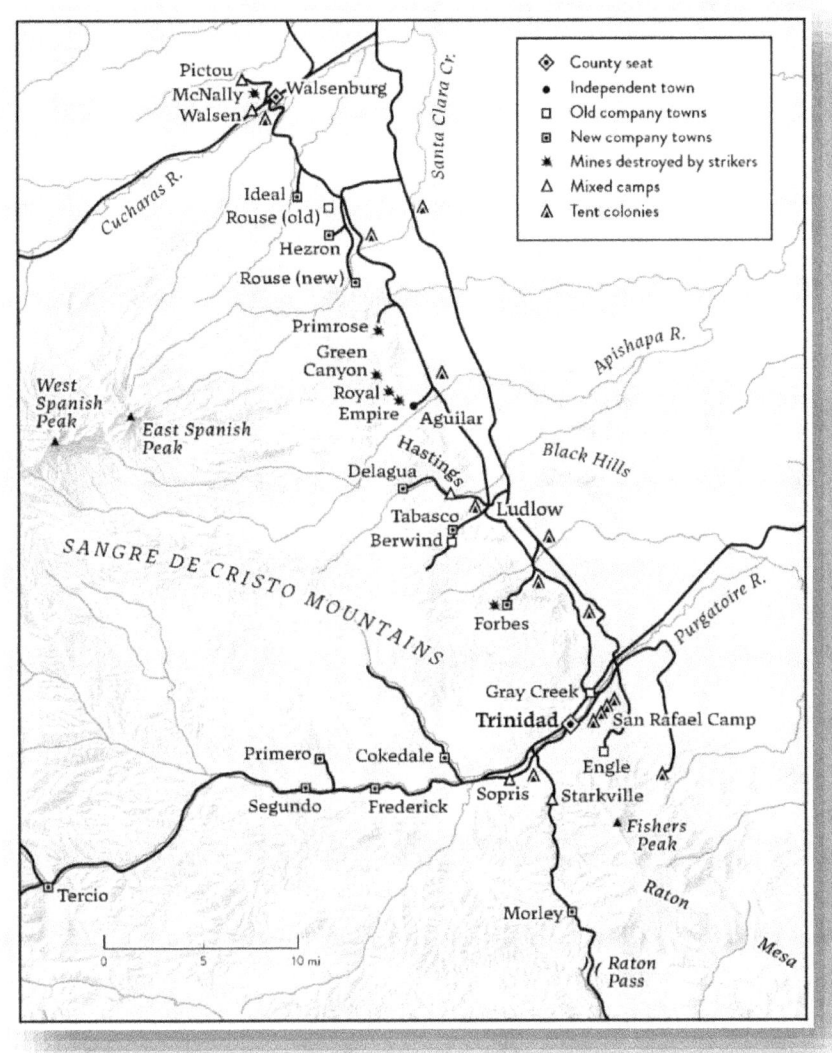

Map 3 *Ten-Day War Following Siege of Ludlow (Erin Greb Cartography)*

The Greek Boxer Photographs

HOME FROM THE BALKAN WAR.

Wil Meet Any Middleweight Boxer.

Harry Hantzis, the Greek boxer of this city, who left in 1912 to go to

fight in the Balkin war, is home again and willing to meet any local middle-weight boxer.

HARRY HANTZIS,
The Greek Boxer.

Epaminondas Demetrins Hantzis,
(Harry Hantzis the Greek Boxer).
Clipping from November 7, 1914,
Indianapolis Recorder.

Harry Hantzis, Hellenic Army, 1912

Greece

Steven and Kathy Hantzis on road to
Chómori, 2003

Chómori Plateia

Hantzis Family Home Chómori, Greece

Demitris Konstantinnos Hantzis (Jimmy the Assassin)

Courtyard of Hantzis Home

Chómori, Greece, (Church top right)

Chómori Plateia

Colorado

CF&I Iron and Steel Works, Pueblo, Colorado. El Pueblo History Museum.

Coke Ovens at Cokedale. Trinidad Collection, Scan #20004889, History Colorado, Denver, Colo.

Women's March to Support Mother Jones, 1913. Denver Public Library Special Collections, call number X-60490.

Armed Strikers 1914. Denver Public Library Special Collections, call number X-60411.

Baldwin-Felts Detectives in Death Special. Denver Public Library Special Collections, call number X-60380.

Ludlow Colony 1914. Denver Public Library Special Collections, call number Z-193.

Ludlow Colonists 1914. Denver Public Library Special Collections, call number X-60474.

Inscription on back of photograph by Stuart Mace: "Lieutenant Karl Linderfelt (right) and other members of the Colorado National Guard trotting down the dusty street of Forbes, 8 miles south of Ludlow. The photo captures Linderfelt as he imagined himself: 'Jesus Christ of Horseback' (Beshoar, 1942:125). This was the force of former mine guards who were inducted into the Colorado National Guard to confront the immigrant miners and their families who dared to defy the power of the coal operators." Denver Public Library Special Collections, call number X-60538.

244

Machine gun on Water Tower Hill at Ludlow. Denver Public Library Special Collections, call number X-60560.

Near view of ruins Ludlow Tent Colony. Denver Public Library Special Collections, call number Z-199.

245

Hole where bodies of 11 children and 2 women were recovered from after fire at Ludlow Tent Colony. Denver Public Library Special Collections, call number X-60481.

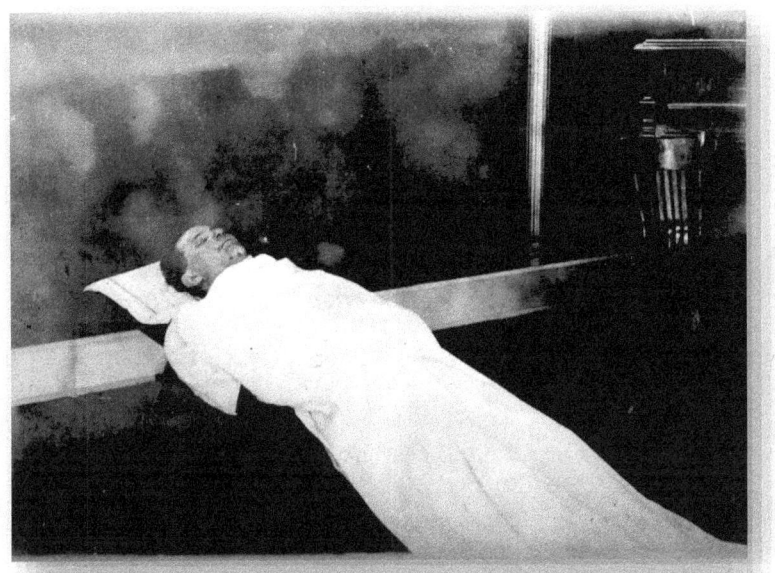

Louis Tikas, Ludlow Victim. Denver Public Library Special
Collections, call number X-60502

Funeral of Ilias Tikas, Trinidad, Colorado. Denver Public Library
Special Collections, call number X-60442.

Camp Beshoar, U.M.W. of A. military headquarters, Trinidad, Colo. Denver Public Library Special Collections, call number X-60421.

Ludlow Memorial on 110th anniversary of massacre. Photo: United Mineworkers of America

The Greek Boxer Bibliography

Books

Army History Directorate of the Hellenic Army General Staff. (1998). *A Concise History of the Balkan Wars 1912–1913*. Athens, Greece: Army History Directorate Publications.

Beshoar, B. B. (1970). *Out of the Depths*. Denver, CO: Golden Bell Press.

Clyne, R. J. (1999). *Coal People: Life in Southern Colorado's Company Towns 1890–1930*. Denver, CO: Colorado Historical Society.

Fink, G. M. (1977). *The Greenwood Encyclopedia of American Institutions: Labor Unions*. Westport, CT: Greenwood Press, Inc.

Foner, P. S. (1965). *History of the Labor Movement in the United States Vol. 4* (Vol. 4). New York, NY: International Publishers.

Foner, P. S. (1980). *History of the Labor Movement in the United States Vol. 5* (Vol. 5). New York, NY: International Publishers.

Giannaris, J. (1988). *Yannis*. Tarrytown, New York: Pilgrimage Publishing Inc.

Kousoulas, D. G. (1974). *Modern Greece Profile of a Nation*. New York, NY: Charles Scribner's Sons.

McGovern, G. S., and Guttridge, L. F. (1972). *The Great Coalfield War*. Boston, MA: Houghton Mifflin Company.

Papanikolas, Z. (1982). *Buried Unsung Louis Tikas and the Ludlow Massacre*. Salt Lake City, Utah: University of Utah Press.

Rees, J. (1966). *Representation and Rebellion: The Rockefeller Plan at the Colorado Fuel and Iron Company, 1914–1942*. Boulder, CO: University Press of Colorado.

Robertson, D. (2010). *Hard As The Rock Itself: Place and Identity in the American Mining Town*. Boulder, CO: University Press of Colorado.

Schurman, J. G. (1914). *The Balkan Wars 1912–1913*. Princeton, NJ: Princeton University Press.

Steel, E. M. (1985). *The Correspondence of Mother Jones*. Pittsburgh, PA: University of Pittsburgh Press.

Trotsky, L. (1980). *The Balkan Wars 1912–13*. New York, NY: Pathfinder Press.

Zinn, H. (1980). *A People's History of the United States*. New York, NY: Harper Colophon Books.

Government Documents

Commission on Industrial Relations (1916). *Industrial Relations Final Report and Testimony Vol. IX*. Washington, DC: Government Printing Office

Commission on Industrial Relations (1916). *Industrial Relations Final Report and Testimony Vol. VII*. Washington, DC: Government Printing Office

Commission on Industrial Relations (1916). *Industrial Relations Final Report and Testimony Vol. VIII*. Washington, DC: Government Printing Office

Simmons, R. L., and Simmons, T. (1992). *Multiple Property Documentation Form Historic Resources of Camp George West, Golden, Colorado*. Washington, DC: Government Printing Office Retrieved from https://www.historycolorado.org/sites/default/files/media/document/2017/621.pdf

Interviews

Beshoar, B. (1976) *Interview of Barron Beshoar/Interviewer: E. Margolis and R. L. McMahan*. University of Colorado Boulder Archives, Boulder, CO.

Kraras, G. C. (2011) *Tales of World War II/Interviewer: S. W. W. C. Dialectos*. Berks Community Television (BCTV), Pennsylvania, Veterans History Project, American Folklife Center, Library of Congress.

Online Multimedia

American Hellenic Institute. (Producer). (2013, September 26, 2020). The Greek American Operational Groups - Secret US Forces in WWII Greece. [Online Video Documentary] Retrieved from https://www.youtube.com/watch?v=_ADAplXTwXk

Journal Articles

Blanchard, R. (1925). The Exchange of Populations between Greece and Turkey. *Geographical Review, 15*(3), 449-456. Retrieved from https://www.jstor.org/stable/208566?seq=1#page_scan_tab_contents

Long, P. (1989). The Voice of the Gun. *Labor's Heritage, 1*(4).

Margolis, E. (1985). Western Coal Mining as a Way of Life: An Oral History of the Colorado Coal Miners of 1914. *Journal of the West, XXIV*(3).

Wiegand, W. A. (1977). The Wayward Bookman: The Decline, Fall, and Historical Obliteration of an ALA President. *American Libraries, 8*(3), 134–137. Retrieved from https://www.jstor.org/stable/25620999?seq=1#page_scan_tab_contents

Newspaper Articles

Linderfelt in a Cell. (1892, Apr. 29). *The San Francisco Examiner*. Retrieved from https://www.newspapers.com/image/458010163/?terms=Linderfelt%2Bin%2Ba%2BCell

Monty Linderfelt Marries. (1905, May 18). *Daily Journal (Telluride)*. Retrieved from https://www.coloradohistoricnewspapers.org/cgi-bin/colorado?a=d&d=DJT19050518.2.7&srpos=2&e=-------en-20--1--txt-txIN-Linderfelt-------0-

Molly Maguires Assault Linderfelt. (1906, Dec. 6). *Daily Journal (Telluride),* p. 1. Retrieved from https://www.coloradohistoricnewspapers.org/cgi-

bin/colorado?a=d&d=DJT19071206.2.6&srpos=3&dliv=
none&e=-------en-20--1--txt-txIN-Linderfelt-------0-

$10 Reward. (1909, Apr. 5). *Daily Journal (Telluride).*
Retrieved from
https://www.coloradohistoricnewspapers.org/cgi-
bin/colorado?a=d&d=DJT19090405.2.35&srpos=14&dli
v=none&e=-------en-20--1--txt-txIN-Linderfelt-------0-

Monte Linderfelt Reported Killed. (1911, May 18). *Telluride
Journal.* Retrieved from
https://www.coloradohistoricnewspapers.org/cgi-
bin/colorado?a=d&d=TTJ19110518.2.2&srpos=6&dliv=n
one&e=-------en-20--1--txt-txIN-Linderfelt-------0-

Gunmen Flocking Into Trinidad. (1914, Sep. 17). *The Voice of the
People.* Retrieved from
https://www.newspapers.com/image/61358051/?terms=
Gunmen%2BFlocking

Jury Fail to Agree Linderfelt Case. (1914, Feb. 10). *Salida Mail.*
Retrieved from
https://www.coloradohistoricnewspapers.org/?a=d&d=S
DM19140210-01.1.4&e=-------en-20--21--txt-txIN-
Linderfelt-------0-

More Regulation of Labor Disputes Urged. (1914, Feb. 4). *The
Indianapolis News.* Retrieved from
https://www.newspapers.com/clippings/download/?id=
22302172&name=Colorado%20coal%20Strike&print=1

Hail, M. (1940, May 31). Shadow of Revolt has Fallen on Border
Port Nine Times; Twice Named Provincial Capital. *El
Paso Herald-Post.* Retrieved from
https://www.newspapers.com/image/10631327/?terms=
Shadow%2Bof%2BRevolt%2Bhas%2BFallen%2Bon%2BB
order%2BPort%2BNine%2BTimes%3B%2BTwice%2BNa
med%2BProvincial%2BCapital

Thesis

Andrews, T. G. (2003). *The Road to Ludlow: Work,
Environment, and Industrialization, 1870–1915.*

University of Wisconsin--Madison, Retrieved from
//catalog.hathitrust.org/Record/005802999
http://hdl.handle.net/2027/wu.89079546917 (iv, 646 p.)

Web Pages

Cokedale, Colorado. Retrieved from
https://westernmininghistory.com/towns/colorado/coke
dale/
The Ludlow Massacre. *The American Experience*. Retrieved
from
https://www.pbs.org/wgbh/americanexperience/feature
s/rockefellers-ludlow/
Trinidad's History. Retrieved from
http://takearoadtrip.com/trinidad-history.html
The Battle of Sarantaporos. (2006). Retrieved from
http://wiki.phantis.com/index.php/Battle_of_Sarantapo
ro
Beech Marten Martes foina. (2013). Retrieved from
http://www.nhmc.uoc.gr/en/museum/photo-
archive/selection/images/nhmc.image.93988
The Strike Song. (2013). *Ludlow Centennial Commemoration*.
Retrieved from
https://www.facebook.com/Ludlow100/posts/the-
%22colorado-strike-song%22-
played/220324548143685/
Cokedale. (2014). Retrieved from
https://huerfanoworldjournal.com/cokedale/
The 1918 Influenza Epidemic. (2016). Retrieved from
http://scalar.usc.edu/works/the-colorado-fuel-and-iron-
company/the-1918-influenza-epidemic?path=short-
stories
6.5×54mm Mannlicher–Schönauer. (2018). Retrieved from
https://en.wikipedia.org/wiki/6.5%C3%9754mm_Mannl
icher%E2%80%93Sch%C3%B6nauer
Cathedral of the Sacred Heart (Pueblo, Colorado). (2018).
Retrieved from

https://en.wikipedia.org/wiki/Cathedral_of_the_Sacred_Heart_(Pueblo,_Colorado)

The Great Population Exchange between Turkey and Greece. (2018). Retrieved from https://www.aljazeera.com/programmes/aljazeeraworld/2018/02/great-population-exchange-turkey-greece-180220111122516.html

Union Stock Yards. (2018). Retrieved from https://en.wikipedia.org/wiki/Union_Stock_Yards

Pontic Greeks. (2019). Retrieved from https://en.wikipedia.org/wiki/Pontic_Greeks

World War II Casualties. (2019). Retrieved from https://en.wikipedia.org/wiki/World_War_II_casualties

Bartels, B. (2011). The Irony of Industrial Welfare and Progressive Education: The CF&I Sociological Department's Educational Programs in Southern Colorado1901–1915. Retrieved from https://scholar.colorado.edu/concern/parent/z316q177j/file_sets/3t945q91w

Boucher, D. (2010). Coke Ovens of Cokedale, Colorado. Retrieved from https://activerain.com/blogsview/1568833/se-colorado-part-2---coke-ovens-of-cokedale--colorado

Bowley, N. (2017). Cokedale Historic District. Retrieved from https://coloradoencyclopedia.org/article/cokedale-historic-district

Britannica, The Editors of Encyclopaedia Britannica. (2018). Greek Civil War. Retrieved from https://www.britannica.com/event/Greek-Civil-War

Chrysopoulos, P. (2018). Greek American Labor Hero Louis Tikas Statue to be Unveiled in Colorado. Retrieved from https://usa.greekreporter.com/2018/05/04/greek-american-labor-hero-louis-tikas-statue-to-be-unveiled-in-colorado-video/

Clogg, R. R. M., and Bowman, J. S. (2019). Greece. *The Balkan Wars*. Retrieved from https://www.britannica.com/place/Greece/Building-the-nation-1832–1913#ref297996

Fenton, D. (2014). Weapons of the Ottoman Army. *The Ottoman Empire*. Retrieved from https://nzhistory.govt.nz/war/ottoman-empire/weapons-of-the-ottoman-empire

Hirst, L. The Ludlow Massacre. Retrieved from http://www.dmm.org.uk/pitwork/html/lhirst2.htm

Keighin, C. W., Rice, D. D., and Finn, T. M. (2001). National Assessment of Oil and Gas Project - Raton Basin-Sierra Grande Uplift Province (041) Boundary. Retrieved from https://certmapper.cr.usgs.gov/data/noga95/prov41/text/prov41.pdf

Margolis, E. (2000). Life is Life: A Mining Family in The West. Retrieved from http://margolis.faculty.asu.edu/life/homepageexp.htm

Mousalimas, A. S. (2004). Greek-American Operational Group Office of Strategic Services (OSS) Memoirs of World War II. Retrieved from http://www.pahh.com/oss/toc.html

Schreck, C. J. (2015). Colorado Fuel and Iron. Retrieved from http://scalar.usc.edu/works/the-colorado-fuel-and-iron-company/company-history

Schreck, C. J. (2017). CF&I Employee Relations Company Publications. Retrieved from http://scalar.usc.edu/works/the-colorado-fuel-and-iron-company/company-publications?path=labor-relations

Spyro. (2017). Thousands of Greek Immigrants in US Go Back to Fight Balkan War – 1912. Retrieved from https://ourodysseys.wordpress.com/2017/11/26/thousands-of-greek-immigrants-in-u-s-go-back-to-fight-baltic-war-1912/

Ze'evi, D., and Morris, B. (2020). When Turkey Destroyed Its Christians. Retrieved from https://www.wsj.com/articles/when-turkey-destroyed-its-christians-11558109896

The Greek Boxer Endnotes

[1] 2006. "The Battle of Sarantaporos." accessed Jan. 8. http://wiki.phantis.com/index.php/Battle_of_Sarantaporo.

[2] Clogg, Richard Ralph Mowbray, and John S. Bowman. 2019. "Greece." Encyclopædia Britannica, inc., accessed Jan. 7. https://www.britannica.com/place/Greece/Building-the-nation-1832–1913#ref297996.

[3] Spyro. 2017. "Thousands of Greek Immigrants in US Go Back to Fight Balkan War – 1912." accessed Jan. 7. https://ourodysseys.wordpress.com/2017/11/26/thousands-of-greek-immigrants-in-u-s-go-back-to-fight-baltic-war-1912/.

[4] Army History Directorate of the Hellenic Army General Staff. 1998. *A Concise History of the Balkan Wars 1912–1913*. Athens, Greece: Army History Directorate Publications.

[5] Fenton, Damien. 2014. "Weapons of the Ottoman Army." New Zealand Ministry for Culture and Heritage, accessed Jan. 7. https://nzhistory.govt.nz/war/ottoman-empire/weapons-of-the-ottoman-empire.

[6] 1914. "More Regulation of Labor Disputes Urged." *The Indianapolis News*, Feb. 4. Accessed Jan. 7, 2019. https://www.newspapers.com/clippings/download/?id=22302172&name=Colorado%20coal%20Strike&print=1.

[7] Papanikolas, Zeese. 1982. *Buried Unsung Louis Tikas and the Ludlow Massacre*. Salt Lake City, Utah: University of Utah Press, 6.

[8] Papanikolas, Zeese. 1982. *Buried Unsung Louis Tikas and the Ludlow Massacre*. Salt Lake City, Utah: University of Utah Press, 288.

[9] Papanikolas, Zeese. 1982. *Buried Unsung Louis Tikas and the Ludlow Massacre*. Salt Lake City, Utah: University of Utah Press, 185.

[10] Papanikolas, Zeese. 1982. *Buried Unsung Louis Tikas and the Ludlow Massacre*. Salt Lake City, Utah: University of Utah Press, 275. According to Greek Historian Saloutos, repatriation was as high as 40 percent by 1931.

[11] Margolis, Eric. 1985. "Western Coal Mining as a Way of Life: An Oral History of the Colorado Coal Miners of 1914. "Journal of *the West* XXIV (3), 26.

[12] Margolis, Eric. 1985. "Western Coal Mining as a Way of Life: An Oral History of the Colorado Coal Miners of 1914. "Journal of *the West* XXIV (3), 27.

[13] Margolis, Eric. 1985. "Western Coal Mining as a Way of Life: An Oral History of the Colorado Coal Miners of 1914. "Journal of *the West* XXIV (3), 42.

[14] Spyro. 2017. "Thousands of Greek Immigrants in US Go Back to Fight Balkan War – 1912." accessed Jan. 7. https://ourodysseys.wordpress.com/2017/11/26/thousands-of-greek-immigrants-in-u-s-go-back-to-fight-baltic-war-1912/.

[15] McGovern, George S., and Leonard F. Guttridge. 1972. *The Great Coalfield War*. Boston, MA: Houghton Mifflin Company, 77.

[16] Beshoar, Barron B. 1970. *Out of the Depths*. Denver, CO: Golden Bell Press, 4. The population of Walsenburg was roughly 4,000.

[17] Papanikolas, Zeese. 1982. *Buried Unsung Louis Tikas and the Ludlow Massacre*. Salt Lake City, Utah: University of Utah Press, 68.

[18] Long, Priscilla. 1989. "The Voice of the Gun." *Labor's Heritage* 1 (4), 6.

[19] Beshoar, Barron B. 1970. *Out of the Depths*. Denver, CO: Golden Bell Press, 43. Lawson reported to the Executive Board that he had spent $791,418 to organize the northern fields and that it would require many times this amount to organize the south.

[20] McGovern, George S., and Leonard F. Guttridge. 1972. *The Great Coalfield War*. Boston, MA: Houghton Mifflin Company, 79.

[21] Margolis, Eric. 1985. "Western Coal Mining as a Way of Life: An Oral History of the Colorado Coal Miners of 1914. "Journal of *the West* XXIV (3), 46.

[22] Margolis, Eric. 1985. "Western Coal Mining as a Way of Life: An Oral History of the Colorado Coal Miners of 1914. "Journal of *the West* XXIV (3), 57, 61.

[23] Margolis, Eric. 1985. "Western Coal Mining as a Way of Life: An Oral History of the Colorado Coal Miners of 1914. "Journal of *the West* XXIV (3), 61.

[24] McGovern, George S., and Leonard F. Guttridge. 1972. *The Great Coalfield War*. Boston, MA: Houghton Mifflin Company, 25.

[25] Papanikolas, Zeese. 1982. *Buried Unsung Louis Tikas and the Ludlow Massacre*. Salt Lake City, Utah: University of Utah Press, 28.

[26] Foner, Philip S. 1980. *History of the Labor Movement in the United States Vol. 5.* Vol. 5. New York, NY: International Publishers, 198.

[27] McGovern, George S., and Leonard F. Guttridge. 1972. *The Great Coalfield War*. Boston, MA: Houghton Mifflin Company, 22. Margolis, Eric. 1985. "Western Coal Mining as a Way of Life: An Oral History of the Colorado Coal Miners of 1914. "Journal of *the West* XXIV (3), 67.

[28] Margolis, Eric. 1985. "Western Coal Mining as a Way of Life: An Oral History of the Colorado Coal Miners of 1914. "Journal of *the West* XXIV (3), 18.

[29] Margolis, Eric. 1985. "Western Coal Mining as a Way of Life: An Oral History of the Colorado Coal Miners of 1914. "Journal of *the West* XXIV (3), 18.

[30] Margolis, Eric. 1985. "Western Coal Mining as a Way of Life: An Oral History of the Colorado Coal Miners of 1914. "Journal of *the West* XXIV (3), 17.

[31] Margolis, Eric. 1985. "Western Coal Mining as a Way of Life: An Oral History of the Colorado Coal Miners of 1914. "Journal of *the West* XXIV (3), 25.

[32] Margolis, Eric. 1985. "Western Coal Mining as a Way of Life: An Oral History of the Colorado Coal Miners of 1914. "Journal of *the West* XXIV (3), 25.

[33] Margolis, Eric. 1985. "Western Coal Mining as a Way of Life: An Oral History of the Colorado Coal Miners of 1914. "Journal of *the West* XXIV (3), 25.

[34] Papanikolas, Zeese. 1982. *Buried Unsung Louis Tikas and the Ludlow Massacre*. Salt Lake City, Utah: University of Utah Press, 73. The date of the letter to Doyle was August 28, 1913.

[35] McGovern, George S., and Leonard F. Guttridge. 1972. *The Great Coalfield War*. Boston, MA: Houghton Mifflin Company, 82.

[36] Long, Priscilla. 1989. "The Voice of the Gun." *Labor's Heritage* 1 (4), 8.

[37] Zinn, Howard. 1980. *A People's History of the United States*. New York, NY: Harper Colophon Books, 347.
Papanikolas, Zeese. 1982. *Buried Unsung Louis Tikas and the Ludlow Massacre*. Salt Lake City, Utah: University of Utah Press, 83.
Margolis, Eric. 1985. "Western Coal Mining as a Way of Life: An Oral History of the Colorado Coal Miners of 1914. "Journal of *the West* XXIV (3), 75.

[38] Long, Priscilla. 1989. "The Voice of the Gun." *Labor's Heritage* 1 (4), 13. Baseball was the principal sporting event but some reported seeing the Croatians playing bolo.

[39] Beshoar, Barron B. 1970. *Out of the Depths*. Denver, CO: Golden Bell Press, 64.

[40] Long, Priscilla. 1989. "The Voice of the Gun." *Labor's Heritage* 1 (4), 14.

[41] Margolis, Eric. 1985. "Western Coal Mining as a Way of Life: An Oral History of the Colorado Coal Miners of 1914. "Journal of *the West* XXIV (3), 77.

[42] Beshoar, Barron B. 1970. *Out of the Depths*. Denver, CO: Golden Bell Press, 81. Billy Diamond was a controversial UMWA official who played a doubtful role in the arms deal.
Papanikolas, Zeese. 1982. *Buried Unsung Louis Tikas and the Ludlow Massacre*. Salt Lake City, Utah: University of Utah Press, 308. Doyle and Lawson privately thought Diamond was a traitor.

[43] Beshoar, Barron B. 1970. *Out of the Depths*. Denver, CO: Golden Bell Press, 81. A normal payday saw approximately $2,000 distributed.

[44] McGovern, George S., and Leonard F. Guttridge. 1972. *The Great Coalfield War*. Boston, MA: Houghton Mifflin Company, 121.

[45] Papanikolas, Zeese. 1982. *Buried Unsung Louis Tikas and the Ludlow Massacre*. Salt Lake City, Utah: University of Utah Press, 108.

[46] Foner, Philip S. 1980. *History of the Labor Movement in the United States Vol. 5*. Vol. 5. New York, NY: International Publishers, 202.
McGovern, George S., and Leonard F. Guttridge. 1972. *The Great Coalfield War*. Boston, MA: Houghton Mifflin Company, 158.

[47] "Trinidad's History." accessed Jan. 8. http://takearoadtrip.com/trinidad-history.html.

[48] Keighin, C. William, Dudley D. Rice, and Thomas M. Finn. 2001. "National Assessment of Oil and Gas Project - Raton Basin-Sierra Grande Uplift Province (041) Boundary." United States Geological Survey, accessed Jan. 7. https://certmapper.cr.usgs.gov/data/noga95/prov41/text/prov41.pdf.

[49] McGovern, George S., and Leonard F. Guttridge. 1972. *The Great Coalfield War*. Boston, MA: Houghton Mifflin Company, 158.

[50] Papanikolas, Zeese. 1982. *Buried Unsung Louis Tikas and the Ludlow Massacre*. Salt Lake City, Utah: University of Utah Press, 161.

[51] Long, Priscilla. 1989. "The Voice of the Gun." *Labor's Heritage* 1 (4), 7.

[52] McGovern, George S., and Leonard F. Guttridge. 1972. *The Great Coalfield War*. Boston, MA: Houghton Mifflin Company, 162.

[53] McGovern, George S., and Leonard F. Guttridge. 1972. *The Great Coalfield War*. Boston, MA: Houghton Mifflin Company, 159.

[54] McGovern, George S., and Leonard F. Guttridge. 1972. *The Great Coalfield War*. Boston, MA: Houghton Mifflin Company, 191. Some authors believe that Mother Jones's age was inflated for emotional appeal and count her, at the time of the strike, only in her seventies.

[55] Papanikolas, Zeese. 1982. *Buried Unsung Louis Tikas and the Ludlow Massacre*. Salt Lake City, Utah: University of Utah Press, 171.

[56] Papanikolas, Zeese. 1982. *Buried Unsung Louis Tikas and the Ludlow Massacre*. Salt Lake City, Utah: University of Utah Press, 172.

[57] Beshoar, Barron B. 1970. *Out of the Depths*. Denver, CO: Golden Bell Press, 138.

[58] 2013. "The Strike Song." Facebook, accessed Jan. 8. https://www.facebook.com/Ludlow100/posts/the-%22colorado-strike-song%22-played/220324548143685/.

[59] Papanikolas, Zeese. 1982. *Buried Unsung Louis Tikas and the Ludlow Massacre*. Salt Lake City, Utah: University of Utah Press, 142.

[60] Margolis, Eric. 1985. "Western Coal Mining as a Way of Life: An Oral History of the Colorado Coal Miners of 1914. "*Journal of the West* XXIV (3), 72. Lippiatt was shot on August 18, 1913.

[61] Hirst, Leigh. "The Ludlow Massacre." Durham Mining Museum, accessed Jan. 7. http://www.dmm.org.uk/pitwork/html/lhirst2.htm.

[62] Beshoar, Barron. 1976. Interview of Barron Beshoar. edited by Eric Margolis and Ronald L. McMahan. Boulder, CO: University of Colorado Boulder Archives, Cassette #D, p16 (Page 58 overall).

[63] Papanikolas, Zeese. 1982. *Buried Unsung Louis Tikas and the Ludlow Massacre*. Salt Lake City, Utah: University of Utah Press, 150.

[64] Relations, Commission on Industrial. 1916. Industrial Relations Final Report and Testimony. Washington, DC: Government Printing Office, Vol. 7, Brewster testimony (search: 6645).

[65] Beshoar, Barron B. 1970. *Out of the Depths*. Denver, CO: Golden Bell Press, 140.

[66] Beshoar, Barron B. 1970. *Out of the Depths*. Denver, CO: Golden Bell Press, 152.

[67] McGovern, George S., and Leonard F. Guttridge. 1972. *The Great Coalfield War*. Boston, MA: Houghton Mifflin Company, 193.

[68] Relations, Commission on Industrial. 1916. Industrial Relations Final Report and Testimony. Washington, DC: Government Printing Office, Vol. 7, Brewster testimony (search: 6526).

[69] Relations, Commission on Industrial. 1916. Industrial Relations Final Report and Testimony. Washington, DC: Government Printing Office, Vol. 7, Boughton testimony (search: 6375).

70 Papanikolas, Zeese. 1982. *Buried Unsung Louis Tikas and the Ludlow Massacre*. Salt Lake City, Utah: University of Utah Press, 308. Doyle and Lawson privately considered Diamond to be a traitor-on the company's take.

71 Papanikolas, Zeese. 1982. *Buried Unsung Louis Tikas and the Ludlow Massacre*. Salt Lake City, Utah: University of Utah Press, 177.

72 Chrysopoulos, Philip. 2018. "Greek American Labor Hero Louis Tikas Statue to be Unveiled in Colorado." Greek Reporter, accessed Jan. 7. https://usa.greekreporter.com/2018/05/04/greek-american-labor-hero-louis-tikas-statue-to-be-unveiled-in-colorado-video/.

73 Schreck, Christopher J. 2015. "Colorado Fuel and Iron." Steelworks Center of the West, accessed Jan. 7. http://scalar.usc.edu/works/the-colorado-fuel-and-iron-company/company-history.

74 Schreck, Christopher J. 2017. "CF&I Employee Relations Company Publications." Steelworks Center of the West, accessed Jan. 7. http://scalar.usc.edu/works/the-colorado-fuel-and-iron-company/company-publications?path=labor-relations.

75 2019. "Pontic Greeks." Wikipedia, accessed Jan. 7. https://en.wikipedia.org/wiki/Pontic_Greeks.

76 2019. "Pontic Greeks." Wikipedia, accessed Jan. 7. https://en.wikipedia.org/wiki/Pontic_Greeks.

77 2018. "The Great Population Exchange between Turkey and Greece." Al Jazeera, accessed Jan. 7. https://www.aljazeera.com/programmes/aljazeeraworld/2018/02/great-population-exchange-turkey-greece-180220111122516.html.
Blanchard, Raoul. 1925. "The Exchange of Populations between Greece and Turkey." *Geographical Review* 15 (3): 449-456.

78 Bartels, Bradley. 2011. "The Irony of Industrial Welfare and Progressive Education: The CF&I Sociological Department's Educational Programs In Southern Colorado 1901–1915." CU Scholar School of Education Graduate Theses and Dissertations, accessed Jan. 7. https://scholar.colorado.edu/cgi/viewcontent.cgi?referer=https://www.google.com/&httpsredir=1&article=1018&context=educ_gradetds.

79 Long, Priscilla. 1989. "The Voice of the Gun." *Labor's Heritage* 1 (4), 14.

80 2018. "6.5×54mm Mannlicher–Schönauer." Wikipedia, accessed Jan. 7. https://en.wikipedia.org/wiki/6.5%C3%9754mm_Mannlicher%E2%80%93Sch%C3%B6nauer.

81 Long, Priscilla. 1989. "The Voice of the Gun." *Labor's Heritage* 1 (4), 18.

82 Long, Priscilla. 1989. "The Voice of the Gun." *Labor's Heritage* 1 (4), 18.

83 Beshoar, Barron B. 1970. *Out of the Depths*. Denver, CO: Golden Bell Press, 165.

84 Beshoar, Barron B. 1970. *Out of the Depths*. Denver, CO: Golden Bell Press, 231.

85 Margolis, Eric. 1985. "Western Coal Mining as a Way of Life: An Oral History of the Colorado Coal Miners of 1914. "Journal of *the West* XXIV (3), 77.

86 Andrews, Thomas G. 2001. "The Colorado Coal Strike of 1913-14 and Its Context in the History of Work, Environment, and Industrialization in Southern Colorado." *Research Reports from the Rockefeller Archives Center* Fall/Winter 2001, 3.

87 Beshoar, Barron B. 1970. *Out of the Depths*. Denver, CO: Golden Bell Press, 81. Billy Diamond was a controversial UMWA official who played a doubtful role in the arms deal.
Papanikolas, Zeese. 1982. *Buried Unsung Louis Tikas and the Ludlow Massacre*. Salt Lake City, Utah: University of Utah Press, 308. Doyle and Lawson privately thought Diamond was a traitor.

88 Andrews, Thomas G. 2001. "The Colorado Coal Strike of 1913-14 and Its Context in the History of Work, Environment, and Industrialization in Southern Colorado." *Research Reports from the Rockefeller Archives Center* Fall/Winter 2001, 6.

89 Relations, Commission on Industrial. 1916. Industrial Relations Final Report and Testimony Vol. VII. Washington, DC: Government Printing Office, (search: 6807).

90 Beshoar, Barron B. 1970. *Out of the Depths*. Denver, CO: Golden Bell Press, 231.

[91] Papanikolas, Zeese. 1982. *Buried Unsung Louis Tikas and the Ludlow Massacre*. Salt Lake City, Utah: University of Utah Press, 213.

[92] 2018. "Cathedral of the Sacred Heart (Pueblo, Colorado)." Wikipedia, accessed Jan. 7. https://en.wikipedia.org/wiki/Cathedral_of_the_Sacred_Heart_(Pueblo,_Colorado).

[93] Acts 9:1–22

[94] 2013. "Beech Marten Martes foina." Natural History Museum of Crete, accessed Jan. 7. http://www.nhmc.uoc.gr/en/museum/photo-archive/selection/images/nhmc.image.93988.

[95] "Cokedale, Colorado." Western Mining History, accessed Jan. 7. https://westernmininghistory.com/towns/colorado/cokedale/.
Boucher, Debi. 2010. "Coke Ovens of Cokedale, Colorado." DBoucher Photography Nature and Wildlife, accessed Jan. 8. https://activerain.com/blogsview/1568833/se-colorado-part-2---coke-ovens-of-cokedale--colorado.

[96] 2018. "Union Stock Yards." Wikipedia, accessed Jan. 7. https://en.wikipedia.org/wiki/Union_Stock_Yards.

[97] Bowley, Nicoli. 2017. "Cokedale Historic District." Colorado Encyclopedia, accessed Jan. 7. https://coloradoencyclopedia.org/article/cokedale-historic-district.

[98] 2014. "Cokedale." World Journal, accessed Jan. 7. https://huerfanoworldjournal.com/cokedale/.

[99] Bowley, Nicoli. 2017. "Cokedale Historic District." Colorado Encyclopedia, accessed Jan. 7. https://coloradoencyclopedia.org/article/cokedale-historic-district.

[100] 2014. "Cokedale." World Journal, accessed Jan. 7. https://huerfanoworldjournal.com/cokedale/.

[101] McGovern, George S., and Leonard F. Guttridge. 1972. *The Great Coalfield War*. Boston, MA: Houghton Mifflin Company, 204.

[102] "The Ludlow Massacre." WGBH PBS, accessed Jan. 7. https://www.pbs.org/wgbh/americanexperience/features/rockefellers-ludlow/.

[103] McGovern, George S., and Leonard F. Guttridge. 1972. *The Great Coalfield War*. Boston, MA: Houghton Mifflin Company, 205.

[104] Beshoar, Barron B. 1970. *Out of the Depths*. Denver, CO: Golden Bell Press, 166.

[105] Papanikolas, Zeese. 1982. *Buried Unsung Louis Tikas and the Ludlow Massacre*. Salt Lake City, Utah: University of Utah Press, 213.

[106] Papanikolas, Zeese. 1982. *Buried Unsung Louis Tikas and the Ludlow Massacre*. Salt Lake City, Utah: University of Utah Press, 213.

[107] McGovern, George S., and Leonard F. Guttridge. 1972. *The Great Coalfield War*. Boston, MA: Houghton Mifflin Company, 213.

[108] Margolis, Eric. 1985. "Western Coal Mining as a Way of Life: An Oral History of the Colorado Coal Miners of 1914. "Journal of *the West* XXIV (3), 45.

[109] Beshoar, Barron. 1976. Interview of Barron Beshoar. edited by Eric Margolis and Ronald L. McMahan. Boulder, CO: University of Colorado Boulder Archives, Cassette #2C, page 42.

[110] McGovern, George S., and Leonard F. Guttridge. 1972. *The Great Coalfield War*. Boston, MA: Houghton Mifflin Company, 213.

[111] McGovern, George S., and Leonard F. Guttridge. 1972. *The Great Coalfield War*. Boston, MA: Houghton Mifflin Company, 214.

[112] McGovern, George S., and Leonard F. Guttridge. 1972. *The Great Coalfield War*. Boston, MA: Houghton Mifflin Company, 221.
Relations, Commission on Industrial. 1916. Industrial Relations Final Report and Testimony Vol. VII. Washington, DC: Government Printing Office, (search: 6449).

[113] Papanikolas, Zeese. 1982. *Buried Unsung Louis Tikas and the Ludlow Massacre*. Salt Lake City, Utah: University of Utah Press, 218.

[114] McGovern, George S., and Leonard F. Guttridge. 1972. *The Great Coalfield War*. Boston, MA: Houghton Mifflin Company, 216.

[115] Margolis, Eric. 1985. "Western Coal Mining as a Way of Life: An Oral History of the Colorado Coal Miners of 1914. "Journal of *the West* XXIV (3), 91.

[116] Relations, Commission on Industrial. 1916. Industrial Relations Final Report and Testimony Vol. VII. Washington, DC: Government Printing Office, (search: 6891). From Linderfelt testimony.

[117] Relations, Commission on Industrial. 1916. Industrial Relations Final Report and Testimony Vol. VII. Washington, DC: Government Printing Office, (search: 6348). From the testimony of Pearl Jolly.

[118] Long, Priscilla. 1989. "The Voice of the Gun." *Labor's Heritage* 1 (4), 18.

[119] Long, Priscilla. 1989. "The Voice of the Gun." *Labor's Heritage* 1 (4). 13.

[120] Margolis, Eric. 1985. "Western Coal Mining as a Way of Life: An Oral History of the Colorado Coal Miners of 1914. "Journal of *the West* XXIV (3), 94.

[121] Long, Priscilla. 1989. "The Voice of the Gun." *Labor's Heritage* 1 (4), 19.

[122] Long, Priscilla. 1989. "The Voice of the Gun." *Labor's Heritage* 1 (4), 6.

[123] Foner, Philip S. 1980. *History of the Labor Movement in the United States Vol. 5*. Vol. 5. New York, NY: International Publishers, 207.

[124] Relations, Commission on Industrial. 1916. Industrial Relations Final Report and Testimony Vol. VII. Washington, DC: Government Printing Office, (search: 6893).

[125] McGovern, George S., and Leonard F. Guttridge. 1972. *The Great Coalfield War*. Boston, MA: Houghton Mifflin Company, 234.

[126] McGovern, George S., and Leonard F. Guttridge. 1972. *The Great Coalfield War*. Boston, MA: Houghton Mifflin Company, 234.

[127] McGovern, George S., and Leonard F. Guttridge. 1972. *The Great Coalfield War*. Boston, MA: Houghton Mifflin Company, 239.

[128] Long, Priscilla. 1989. "The Voice of the Gun." *Labor's Heritage* 1 (4), 20.

[129] McGovern, George S., and Leonard F. Guttridge. 1972. *The Great Coalfield War*. Boston, MA: Houghton Mifflin Company, 236.

[130] Zinn, Howard. 1980. *A People's History of the United States*. New York, NY: Harper Colophon Books, 349.

[131] McGovern, George S., and Leonard F. Guttridge. 1972. *The Great Coalfield War*. Boston, MA: Houghton Mifflin Company, 235.

[132] McGovern, George S., and Leonard F. Guttridge. 1972. *The Great Coalfield War*. Boston, MA: Houghton Mifflin Company, 240.

[133] Margolis, Eric. 1985. "Western Coal Mining as a Way of Life: An Oral History of the Colorado Coal Miners of 1914. "Journal of *the West* XXIV (3), 98.

[134] Beshoar, Barron B. 1970. *Out of the Depths*. Denver, CO: Golden Bell Press, 183.

[135] Zinn, Howard. 1980. *A People's History of the United States*. New York, NY: Harper Colophon Books, 348.

[136] Beshoar, Barron B. 1970. *Out of the Depths*. Denver, CO: Golden Bell Press, 190.

[137] Zinn, Howard. 1980. *A People's History of the United States*. New York, NY: Harper Colophon Books, 348.

[138] Beshoar, Barron B. 1970. *Out of the Depths*. Denver, CO: Golden Bell Press, 193.

[139] Zinn, Howard. 1980. *A People's History of the United States*. New York, NY: Harper Colophon Books, 348.

[140] McGovern, George S., and Leonard F. Guttridge. 1972. *The Great Coalfield War*. Boston, MA: Houghton Mifflin Company, 247.

[141] Relations, Commission on Industrial. 1916. Industrial Relations Final Report and Testimony Vol. VII. Washington, DC: Government Printing Office, (search: 6377) Testimony of Maj. Boughton.

[142] McGovern, George S., and Leonard F. Guttridge. 1972. *The Great Coalfield War*. Boston, MA: Houghton Mifflin Company, 249.

[143] 1914. "Gunmen Flocking Into Trinidad." *The Voice of the People*, Sep. 17. Accessed Nov. 27, 2018, 3.

McGovern, George S., and Leonard F. Guttridge. 1972. *The Great Coalfield War*. Boston, MA: Houghton Mifflin Company, 287.

[144] Relations, Commission on Industrial. 1916. Industrial Relations Final Report and Testimony Vol. VII. Washington, DC: Government Printing Office, (search: 6850) From the testimony of M.G. Low before the Commission edited for readability and narrative context.

[145] Relations, Commission on Industrial. 1916. Industrial Relations Final Report and Testimony Vol. VII. Washington, DC: Government Printing Office, (search: 6646) From testimony of Professor Brewster

[146] Relations, Commission on Industrial. 1916. Industrial Relations Final Report and Testimony Vol. VII. Washington, DC: Government Printing Office, (search: 6850) From the testimony of M.G. Low before the Commission edited for readability and narrative context.

[147] Margolis, Eric. 1985. "Western Coal Mining as a Way of Life: An Oral History of the Colorado Coal Miners of 1914. "Journal of *the West* XXIV (3), 96.

[148] Relations, Commission on Industrial. 1916. Industrial Relations Final Report and Testimony Vol. VII. Washington, DC: Government Printing Office, (search: 6645) Testimony of Prof. Brewster.

Relations, Commission on Industrial. 1916. Industrial Relations Final Report and Testimony Vol. IX. Washington, DC: Government Printing Office, (search: 8121) Testimony of Edward P. Costigan.

[149] Margolis, Eric. 1985. "Western Coal Mining as a Way of Life: An Oral History of the Colorado Coal Miners of 1914. "Journal of *the West* XXIV (3), 99.

[150] McGovern, George S., and Leonard F. Guttridge. 1972. *The Great Coalfield War*. Boston, MA: Houghton Mifflin Company, 263.

[151] Relations, Commission on Industrial. 1916. Industrial Relations Final Report and Testimony Vol. VII. Washington, DC: Government Printing Office, (search: 6373). Testimony of Maj. Boughton.

[152] McGovern, George S., and Leonard F. Guttridge. 1972. *The Great Coalfield War*. Boston, MA: Houghton Mifflin Company, 267.

[153] McGovern, George S., and Leonard F. Guttridge. 1972. *The Great Coalfield War*. Boston, MA: Houghton Mifflin Company, 267.

[154] Beshoar, Barron B. 1970. *Out of the Depths*. Denver, CO: Golden Bell Press, 228.

[155] 1892. "Linderfelt in a Cell." *The San Francisco Examiner*, Apr. 29. Accessed Nov. 27, 2018, Page 1.

[156] Wiegand, Wayne A. 1977. "The Wayward Bookman: The Decline, Fall, and Historical Obliteration of an ALA President." *American Libraries* 8 (3):134-137.

[157] Hail, Marshall. 1940. "Shadow of Revolt has Fallen on Border Port Nine Times; Twice Named Provincial Capital." *El Paso Herald-Post*, May 31. Accessed Nov. 27, 2018, Page 37.

[158] 1905. "Monty Linderfelt Marries." *Daily Journal (Telluride)*, May 18. Accessed Jan. 8, 2019. https://www.coloradohistoricnewspapers.org/cgi-bin/colorado?a=d&d=DJT19050518.2.7&srpos=2&e=-------en-20--1--txt-txIN-Linderfelt-------0-.

[159] 1906. "Molly Maguires Assault Linderfelt." *Daily Journal (Telluride)*, Dec. 6, 1. Accessed Jan. 8, 2019. https://www.coloradohistoricnewspapers.org/cgi-bin/colorado?a=d&d=DJT19071206.2.6&srpos=3&dliv=none&e=-------en-20--1--txt-txIN-Linderfelt-------0-.

[160] 1911. "Monte Linderfelt Reported Killed." *Telluride Journal*, May 18. Accessed Jan. 8, 2019. https://www.coloradohistoricnewspapers.org/cgi-bin/colorado?a=d&d=TTJ19110518.2.2&srpos=6&dliv=none&e=-------en-20--1--txt-txIN-Linderfelt-------0-.

[161] 1914. "Jury Fail to Agree Linderfelt Case." *Salida Mail*, Feb. 10. Accessed Jan. 8, 2019. https://www.coloradohistoricnewspapers.org/?a=d&d=SDM19140210-01.1.4&e=-------en-20--21--txt-txIN-Linderfelt-------0-.

[162] 1909. "$10 Reward." *Daily Journal (Telluride)*, Apr. 5. Accessed Jan. 8, 2019. https://www.coloradohistoricnewspapers.org/cgi-bin/colorado?a=d&d=DJT19090405.2.35&srpos=14&dliv=none&e=-------en-20--1--txt-txIN-Linderfelt-------0-.

[163] Simmons, R. Laurie, and Thomas Simmons. 1992. Multiple Property Documentation Form Historic Resources of Camp George West, Golden, Colorado. edited by National Park Service. Washington, DC: Government Printing Office, Section Number E Page 8.

[164] Margolis, Eric. 1985. "Western Coal Mining as a Way of Life: An Oral History of the Colorado Coal Miners of 1914."*Journal of the West* XXIV (3), 102.

[165] Beshoar, Barron B. 1970. *Out of the Depths*. Denver, CO: Golden Bell Press, 240.

[166] McGovern, George S., and Leonard F. Guttridge. 1972. *The Great Coalfield War*. Boston, MA: Houghton Mifflin Company, 301.

[167] McGovern, George S., and Leonard F. Guttridge. 1972. *The Great Coalfield War*. Boston, MA: Houghton Mifflin Company, 309. President Wilson named Seth Low, President of the National Civic Foundation, Charles W. Mills, a manufacturer and Patrick Gilday, UMWA Pennsylvania District 2 President to serve of the special mediation commission.

[168] Margolis, Eric. 1985. "Western Coal Mining as a Way of Life: An Oral History of the Colorado Coal Miners of 1914."*Journal of the West* XXIV (3), 106.

[169] Margolis, Eric. 1985. "Western Coal Mining as a Way of Life: An Oral History of the Colorado Coal Miners of 1914. ”*Journal of the West* XXIV (3), 108.

[170] Margolis, Eric. 1985. "Western Coal Mining as a Way of Life: An Oral History of the Colorado Coal Miners of 1914. ”*Journal of the West* XXIV (3), 104.

[171] Papanikolas, Zeese. 1982. *Buried Unsung Louis Tikas and the Ludlow Massacre*. Salt Lake City, Utah: University of Utah Press, 317.

[172] Foner, Philip S. 1980. *History of the Labor Movement in the United States Vol. 5*. Vol. 5. New York, NY: International Publishers, 211.

[173] Mousalimas, Andrew S. 2004. "Greek-American Operational Group Office of Strategic Services (OSS) Memoirs of World War II." Preservation of American Hellenic History, accessed Jan. 8. http://www.pahh.com/oss/toc.html.

[174] Rees, Jonathan. 1966. *Representation and Rebellion: The Rockefeller Plan at the Colorado Fuel and Iron Company, 1914–1942*. Boulder, CO: University Press of Colorado.

[175] 2016. "The 1918 Influenza Epidemic." Steelworks Center of the West, accessed Jan. 7. http://scalar.usc.edu/works/the-colorado-fuel-and-iron-company/the-1918-influenza-epidemic?path=short-stories.

[176] 2019. "World War II Casualties." Wikipedia, accessed Jan. 7. https://en.wikipedia.org/wiki/World_War_II_casualties.
Britannica, The Editors of Encyclopaedia. 2018. "Greek Civil War." Encyclopædia Britannica, Inc., accessed Jan. 7. https://www.britannica.com/event/Greek-Civil-War.

[177] Giannaris, John. *Yannis*. Tarrytown, New York: Pilgrimage Publishing Inc., 1988, 42

[178] Kraras, Gust C. 2011. Gust C. Kraras Collection (AFC/2001/001/64311), Veterans History Project, American Folklife Center, Library of Congress. In Tales of World War II, edited by Sharon Wells Wagner Christine Dialectos. Berks Community Television (BCTV), Pennsylvania.

[179] Giannaris, John. *Yannis*. Tarrytown, New York: Pilgrimage Publishing Inc., 1988, 41

[180] Mousalimas, Andrew S. "Greek-American Operational Group Office of Strategic Services (Oss) Memoirs of World War II." Preservation of American Hellenic History, http://www.pahh.com/oss/toc.html. Part 2.

[181] Kraras, Gust C. 2011. Gust C. Kraras Collection (AFC/2001/001/64311), Veterans History Project, American Folklife Center, Library of Congress. In Tales of World War II, edited by Sharon Wells Wagner Christine Dialectos. Berks Community Television (BCTV), Pennsylvania.

[182] Mousalimas, Andrew S. 2004. "Greek-American Operational Group Office of Strategic Services (OSS) Memoirs of World War II." Preservation of American Hellenic History, accessed Jan. 8. http://www.pahh.com/oss/toc.html.

[183] Giannaris, John. *Yannis*. Tarrytown, New York: Pilgrimage Publishing Inc., 1988, 46

[184] Kraras, Gust C. 2011. Gust C. Kraras Collection (AFC/2001/001/64311), Veterans History Project, American Folklife Center, Library of Congress. In Tales of World War II, edited by Sharon Wells Wagner Christine Dialectos. Berks Community Television (BCTV), Pennsylvania.

[185] Kraras, Gust C. 2011. Gust C. Kraras Collection (AFC/2001/001/64311), Veterans History Project, American Folklife Center, Library of Congress. In Tales of World War II, edited by Sharon Wells Wagner Christine Dialectos. Berks Community Television (BCTV), Pennsylvania.

[186] Giannaris, John. *Yannis*. Tarrytown, New York: Pilgrimage Publishing Inc., 1988, 73

[187] Giannaris, John. *Yannis*. Tarrytown, New York: Pilgrimage Publishing Inc., 1988, 5

[188] Institute, American Hellenic. 2013. The Greek American Operational Groups - Secret US Forces in WWII Greece. edited by Patty Stern.

[189] Kraras, Gust C. 2011. Gust C. Kraras Collection (AFC/2001/001/64311), Veterans History Project, American Folklife Center, Library of Congress. In Tales of World War II, edited by Sharon Wells Wagner Christine Dialectos. Berks Community Television (BCTV), Pennsylvania.

[190] Institute, American Hellenic. 2013. The Greek American Operational Groups - Secret US Forces in WWII Greece. edited by Patty Stern.

There are discrepancies in the number of OSS commandos who served in Greece and the number of killed and wounded. Mousalimas, a corporal in OG IV, cites the following in his fascinating memoir but the citation is not specific. Mousalimas, A.S. Co C 2671 Special Reconnaissance Battalion, Office of Strategic Services (Oss), Greek US Operational Group, World War 2: Memoirs. North-Eastern Federal University Publishing House, 2018. National Archives, Greek US Operational Groups, Operations in Greece 1944, p. 11

Report filed at OSS Headquarters, 24 December 1944
No. of operations in Greece: 76
Results of Operations
Trains Attacked: 14
Locomotives Destroyed: 11
Train Cars Destroyed: 32
Armored Cars Destroyed: 2
Convoys Attacked: 5
Trucks Destroyed: 61
Bridges Destroyed: 15
Roads Mined: 5
Yards of Rail Blown: 9920
Garrisons and Pillboxes Attacked: 6
Enemy Killed, Wounded, Prisoners, est.: 2000
OGs Wounded: 23
OGs Killed: 3

The OSS Operational Group Organization at http://oss-og.org/greek.html lists a total of eight groups and 181 men. They show one killed in action and eleven wounded. They cite the following sources: This summary of these Operational Groups was extracted from records of the National Archives provided through the courtesy of Lt. Col. Ian D. W. Sutherland. Attorney Sutherland is the compiler of the encyclopedic "Special Forces of the United States Army, 1952–1982"

www.ingramcontent.com/pod-product-compliance
Lightning Source LLC
Chambersburg PA
CBHW071553110726
47908CB00007B/2080